TEFUGA

BY THE SAME AUTHOR

NOVELS

Skin Deep
*The Old English Peep Show**
The Seals
Sleep and His Brother
The Lizard in the Cup
The Green Gene
*The Poison Oracle**
*The Lively Dead**
*King and Joker**
*Walking Dead**
One Foot in the Grave
A Summer in the Twenties
*The Last Houseparty**
*Hindsight**
*Death of a Unicorn**

CHILDREN'S BOOKS

The Weathermonger
Heartsease
The Devil's Children
(Trilogy republished as *The Changes*)
Emma Tupper's Diary
The Dancing Bear
The Gift
The Iron Lion
Chance, Luck and Destiny
The Blue Hawk
Annerton Pit
Hepzibah
The Flight of Dragons
Tulku
City of Gold
The Seventh Raven
A Box of Nothing

*AVAILABLE FROM PANTHEON

TEFUGA

PETER DICKINSON

PANTHEON BOOKS, NEW YORK

Library of Congress
Cataloging-in-Publication Data

Dickinson, Peter, 1927-
Tefuga.

I. Title.
PR6054.I35T4   1986   823'.914   85-43458
ISBN 0-394-55180-X
ISBN 0-394-75181-7 (pbk.)

The naked fisherman flung his net, and posed, one arm aloft. His blackness, silhouetted against the light reflected from the silky river surface, seemed featureless, flat, incomprehensible. But the net floated in the three dimensions of air, transparent as a jellyfish in its wave, then fell. As it made its rippling pattern across the water Jackland began to speak.

'This, literally, is where I began,' he said. 'A cell dividing in a womb. An unwelcome surprise to all concerned.'

As he spoke the camera swung from the fisherman, lingered for a moment on Jackland's well-known profile—weathered but still just short of haggard—and then on to allow the eventual audience to share in the scene Jackland himself was looking at, a broad mound of reddish earth in a clearing ringed by drab trees. The earth was mostly bare, but mottled with patches of a coarse tufted grass, and down one flank of the mound was a cultivated patch, its well-hoed rows of strong green growth contrasting oddly with the dereliction of the building on top of the mound. This was a complex structure, patched and botched over the years, its walls part mud, part breeze-block and its roof an uneven assemblage of corrugated iron and cane thatch. Black pullets scratched around. A goat with a bald rump was tethered to a stake. An African with a thin grey beard posed in the doorway, wearing an embroidered brown and yellow robe, a loose turban of the same colours, and blue track shoes.

'This is the remains of The Warren,' said Jackland. 'My father had it built for my mother when he was District Officer at Kiti in Northern Nigeria and she came out to join him late in 1923. They had met and married on his last leave. The gentleman you see by the door was their houseboy, Elongo. He is now Sarkin Kiti, spiritual leader of the Kitawa and a major figure in Nigerian politics. He does not, of course, live here, but at his palace in Kiti town, three miles up stream.

'The programme you are about to watch is presented as fiction, with actors in the roles of my parents, the young Elongo,

5

and other characters such as the then Sarkin Kiti, one Kama Boi. But it is as close to the truth as I have been able to get, or guess, being based on my mother's private diary, supported by the records of the British administration at Kaduna. It is not an attack on that administration, still less a defence of it. The British tribe who ruled Nigeria for some sixty years practised rituals and revered fetishes as bizarre to me as those of any of the peoples they governed. It is impossible for me to avoid reflecting on the nature of colonial rule, but I would submit that the story you are about to watch illustrates aspects of our inward nature far more enduring, far more profound in their effects for both good and ill, than any empire that ever ruled.

'I make no claims for the story because it is of relevance to myself. It is not. Though in those days it was sometimes possible for the wives of colonial officers to join their husbands on station in Nigeria, it was wholly forbidden for them to indulge in what the *Book of Common Prayer* had, at their marriage ceremony, described as the chief object of their union. My mother's pregnancy was a decree of banishment, a ukase as unappealable as that of a despot. She never saw my father again. I never saw him at all.'

Jackland turned from the camera and looked downstream. In front of him the scene was empty, with only the broad, smooth river curving away as it had done for centuries. The modern human clutter was all behind him, the camera crews and production team, and then a rough arc of spectators, local Nigerians, the men wearing shirts and trousers or shorts and the women gaudier blouses with long wrap-around skirts. While Jackland had been speaking they had managed to remain quiet, influenced probably less by the shushings of production assistants than by Jackland himself, the harshly ringing tone, the elaborate roll of sentences, the hard and furrowed features, deep eyes under bony brows, voice and face moulded for the denunciation of vices in this or any other age. The crowd were presumably mostly Muslims, but even the few remaining animists would have recognized the authority of the hieratic mode.

'Cut,' said Burn. 'Christ, you'd think it might be starting to cool off a wee bit. Who told us it would be like Bournemouth this time of year?'

Jackland relaxed. A touch of flabbiness softened the many-folded skin. The crowd saw that the ceremony was over and started to chatter, argue, tease the fisherman who was coming up the slope, fully clothed and grinning with self-deprecation because lack of recent practice at his craft had caused him to make half a dozen bosh shots before producing a net-throw worth photographing. Burn, a chubby and fretful figure made clownlike by the combination of peeling pink skin, large sun-glasses, ginger moustache and broad-brimmed bushwhacker's hat, turned to Jackland.

'Two mins forty,' he said. 'We are really going to have to lose some of that, Nigel.'

Jackland took his own sun-glasses from his shirt pocket, polished them and put them on.

'Let's wait and see, old man,' he said.

Burn nodded, turned, and began to give orders.

'Clear those laddies right up the slope now, Brian. Sally, get on to Trevor and tell him to start the canoes off in five minutes. You, er, Jalo, get those extras stripped off. No clothes, only grass belts. No wristwatches, right? Get cracking, everyone. The light isn't going to last. Fred . . .'

Jackland turned away and strolled up towards the hut, taking a cigarette out as he went and offering one to Sarkin Elongo when he reached him. The Sarkin took the whole pack and held it into the doorway. Immediately, like the feelers of a sea anemone closing round an edible scrap, hands—dark-skinned, pale-palmed—came out of the shadows and plucked at the pack. The Sarkin took a cigarette for himself and handed the pack back to Jackland, almost empty. Jackland flicked a lighter and lit for the pair of them.

'What happens now, Mr Jackland?' said the Sarkin. 'May I put my sun-glasses on?'

His voice was deep and soft, his speech slow, with hardly a trace of Nigerian usage. Even quite trivial remarks, such as this, seemed to vibrate with Biblical undertones. Close up he appeared at least a decade younger than he had from a distance, or than Jackland's account of his past declared him to be. Some of the apparent wrinklings on the dark brown skin turned out to be tribal scars, a triple row above the outer corners of the eyes which gave the whole countenance a look of mild bewilderment. Until very recently all male Kitawa bore these marks.

That, and the tribe's primitive lifestyle, had often deceived strangers into thinking them simple.

'Of course, Sarkin,' said Jackland. 'And your chaps can come out from there if they want. Hell of a lot of waiting around always, but we've got a bit of a rush on now to catch the sunset. When they're set up I'm going to go and watch the river with the camera looking over my shoulder. Later we'll fool around with the film a bit so that as the canoes come up I fade away. Just a gimmick for taking the audience back in time. The canoes come in to the jetty, the actors playing my parents land, the lad playing you greets them. That'll be about it for today. Tomorrow morning we'll do my mother's departure while the mist's still on the river, and then we'll come along to Kiti to do the shots of the Old Palace and the ferry. Couple of days of that and if we don't make the standard balls-up of something we should be able to clear off and trouble you no more.'

'You are not going out to Tefuga?'

'Wish we could. I wish we could have done the whole thing here, because that's my natural instinct.'

'I do not understand how you can come all this way and film so little. When you first came to consult me you said . . .'

'I know I did, Sarkin, and I wish we'd been able to do it that way, but the cost accountants ruled it out. It is axiomatic in this trade that the fake is cheaper than the real. You have studios which you are paying for in any case so you use them if you can. Then there is the paradox that although the centres of what passes for civilization are where the cost of living is highest, the further you get from them the more things cost. We're only up here at all because Miss Tressider refused to spend Christmas in England, which under the terms of her contract we could have insisted on, and I was able to resolve the dilemma by suggesting we bring a unit up to Kiti and spend the festive season filming her doing my mother's entrance to the Old Palace. And now, while we are here, we might as well lend a spurious authenticity to the whole enterprise by filming my mother's arrival and departure on the veritable site and letting the audience see what has become of the veritable Warren, and so on. Such is the suggestive power of the camera that everything else will seem to be taking place between those two points in time, though actually they have already been shot, most of them, in London and down south in Ilorin. For my sins I have been a professional journalist all my life, and I have the journalist's obsession with authenticity. Now it turns out that the only authentic parts of my film are in it as the by-product of a woman's whim.'

'It would have pleased me greatly if my grandson could have played my part. He is almost the right age.'

'Too late, Sarkin. We'd already shot most of his scenes before you mentioned the possibility. Matter of fact, I'm not too keen on Piers Smith playing my father, but we were stuck with him for reasons beyond my control. We are all, don't you think, animalcules in the digestion of some great mindless beast which is not even aware of our existence, but pumps us around its organs regardless of our wishes or feelings and eventually with a sigh of relief excretes us into the grave.'

It was a characteristic of Jackland's conversation that it flickered between his public and private style. Without apparent gear-change, slapdash mumblings would transmute to the shaped and orotund, most likely a far-fetched metaphor concerning one of the great themes of philosophy. Sometimes this would be a scrap of an old script—he was not the man to waste a good thing by saying it only once—but just as likely he had thought it up as he spoke.

The Sarkin smiled. 'Into Independence, in the case of Nigeria, he said. 'You describe your colonial administration very well.

'It was never mine. I take no responsibility.'

'A big stomach and a small brain. Fewer than five hundred officers ruling all our millions.'

'After a fashion. Oh, looks as if we're ready for the next bit. Sorry about your grandson. But I'll remember him in case anything comes up. You never know.'

The Sarkin smiled with unreadable charm. Jackland nodded to him and loped down towards the bank. The old man was highly intelligent and must have known his grandson was impossible for the part, too young and a sulky-looking slob, quite incapable of portraying the youth described so enthusiastically in the diary. In the Sarkin's mind, perhaps, the spoiling of the whole enterprise by his inclusion would have been secondary to the increase of prestige and cash to the family.

As the canoes came up the river the watchers chattered and

argued. The production team made no effort to quiet them. The sound-track for this sequence was to be dubbed on later, bird-calls and river noises, snatches of chants and drumming, and Mary Tressider's voice reading from Betty Jackland's letters describing her journey to join her new husband. The five canoes, despite keeping out of the main current, made slow progress. The river, shrunken since the rains but still immense by European standards, ran from the west and curved away south, with the remains of The Warren standing on the inside of the curve and looking across the water to the monotonous dingy trees of the far bank. When the canoes were still a couple of hundred yards away the slow-moving scene was startled by a cry. It came from Malcolm Burn.

'Cut!' he yelled. 'Oh, Jesus bloody Christ, what's Trevor up to not stopping that boat!'

From where the curve of the bank had concealed the starting-point of the canoes a launch came creaming into sight. The mutter of the crowd changed note. Some of them started to walk away. Jalo, the interpreter, was arguing with one of the naked extras who wanted to dress and join the defectors. Though the river, as if resting after the turbulence of the rapids at Kiti, seemed from the shore to be moving all of a piece in glassy calm, the canoes had been keeping close to the bank to avoid what was in fact the much stronger current at the centre. The launch, despite its fairly powerful engine, chose the same path and drove past only twenty yards to their right, rocking them vigorously with its wake.

'Sods,' said Burn. 'Brian, take one of the trucks and bomb up and meet them when they land. Find out who they are. Sally, get on to Trevor and . . .'

'They're coming here,' said Jackland.

The launch had curved out but was swinging back towards the landing-stage. By now it could be seen that four of the occupants, Africans, wore khaki. The fifth was a white man in a mauve shirt and a floppy straw hat.

'Forget about Trevor,' called Burn. 'They've brought him along. I might have known the bloody police . . .'

'Army, I think,' said Jackland.

'They're going to make a balls of it, whoever,' said Burn. 'Christ, look at that. Serve the buggers right.'

The driver of the launch had evidently not realized that the landing-stage had been built for the purposes of the film on a projecting shelf just below water level. In a fortnight's time it would be high and dry, and already it would barely take the shallow draught of the canoes. He had intended a snappy manoeuvre and so approached much too fast and rammed his keel well into the mud, the launch stopping with uncanny abruptness a few yards short of the bank. He then tried to force his way in, thus grounding himself so firmly that he was unable to reverse out. The man beside him stood up, gripping the windscreen. Thus seen he was clearly an army officer, with a very black lean face under the smart cap. He studied the gap between himself and the shore, then spoke to the driver; the uselessly churning propeller stopped at last. The officer turned and gave orders to one of the men in the back, who rose with obvious reluctance, scrambled to the prow, lowered himself into the river and paddled ashore, holding his automatic rifle well above his head as though wading neck-deep; in fact the water barely covered his boots. More of the onlookers began to drift away.

The soldier squelched up the bank, studied the half-dozen naked extras and prodded his gun-barrel against the chest of one of them. Without word or gesture the man walked down into the water, stood with his buttocks against the side of the launch to let the officer climb on to his shoulders and ferried him ashore. The officer slid to the ground and flicked long thin fingers at his uniform where he had made contact with his bearer. He turned, unsmiling, as Burn went strutting down to confront him.

'What the hell do you think you're up to?' said Burn. 'Can't you see we're trying to shoot a film? We'll miss the sunset thanks to your assing around. And coming so close to the canoes—you did that on purpose.'

'You in charge of this outfit, Mr . . . ?'

'Burn. Malcolm Burn. And I want to know your name because I'm going to report your behaviour to your superiors. It was criminally dangerous passing so close to the canoes. I've got plenty of witnesses.'

'My name is Major Kadu. I am sure my superiors will be interested by what you have to say. Now to business. The civilian in my launch tells me that he is one of this your team.'

'Trevor Fish. Yes.'

'He is under arrest.'

'What the hell for?'

'Impeding a detachment of the Nigerian Army in the course of its duties.'

Burn twitched his head towards the launch where the man in the mauve shirt, less cramped now that one of his guards had left, was lolling on the back bench and talking to the other guard, who was responding with white-toothed laughter.

'Better get him out of there PDQ, Malc,' called one of the cameramen, Fred Pittapoulos. 'They'll be doing him for seducing a soldier on active service.'

Several of the team laughed—it was a new variant on a standing joke. Burn puffed out scarlet cheeks and bristled his moustache.

'Let me tell you,' he said, spacing the words out but failing to eliminate a squeak, 'that we do not merely have permission from the Ministry of Information to make this film, we have documents instructing all local officials to give us every assistance, and that includes not barging into the picture when we're shooting.'

Major Kadu gave different anger signals, widening nostrils and eyes and tightening his shoulders to military rigidity.

'And let me tell you, Mr Burn,' he said, 'that when you bought your so-called documents from the Minister you did not buy the Nigerian Army.'

Burn was one of those men who, despite superficial dither and ineffectiveness, have great resources of will and actually thrive on conflict. They are like tennis rabbits who, while not ceasing to scoop and scuttle, manage to do so in a way that can baffle technically better players. Major Kadu, on the other hand, gave some impression that within the military carapace lurked a nervous and uncertain creature, so the two would have been quite evenly matched had each had equal resources outside his own will to call upon. This was not the case. A more experienced hand than Burn (he was an assistant director, told off to be victim of Miss Tressider's whim while the director flew home to his family for an English Christmas) would have seen the danger of attempting to outface in public an officer of the army of a Third World country. Jackland was moving to intervene—too late, for Major Kadu had already drawn breath for his next command—when the catastrophe was prevented. The Major clamped his lips shut and stared up the slope with narrowed eyes.

Sarkin Kiti was processing down from the hut, escorted by the small entourage who had been concealed in its entrance—two guards with tasselled spears, a brolly-man carrying not the usual immense and gaudy parasol but a leaf-shaped wicker fan with which to shade his master, and an official whose main duties seemed to be those of opponent in the local variant of ludo. All these wore bright-coloured robes, several layers thick, and looked as old as the Sarkin himself. The spearmen came in front, levering a path through the remains of the crowd with their spear-butts.

Major Kadu let the indrawn breath out in a long snort, stood to attention and snapped into a spruce salute. The Sarkin made that loose-wristed gesture of greeting which seems common to royalty of whatever race.

'Major Kadu,' he said. 'You have not visited us for much too long. Allow me to introduce my friend Mr Nigel Jackland. His father was D.O. here at the time of our Tefuga Incident—before you were born, of course. Mrs Jackland began to teach me English.'

Jackland and the Major shook hands. It was clearly a moment for maximum formality.

'Mr Jackland is a famous television reporter,' said the Sarkin. 'This is Mr Malcolm Burn, who is assisting him. Do I understand that you have had to arrest one of Mr Jackland's servants?'

'Detained, only,' said the Major.

He turned and shouted in Hausa to the launch. Another spectator was press-ganged into ferrying the prisoner ashore. By this time the crowd had become aware of Trevor Fish's reputation, not by any mysterious empathy but because many of them would have known enough English to get the point of Pittapoulos's joke. So the man who carried him had to put up with a good deal of jeering, its general meaning perfectly obvious, even in an unknown language. The Sarkin enjoyed the episode, chatting to his official while he watched.

'We're going to miss Fred's bloody sunset,' muttered Burn. 'It only lasts about ten mins. Not a hope of getting the launch off in time.'

Jackland moved to where he could see the landing-stage.

'Oh, I don't know,' he said. 'If Fred sets up right in the water it'll be out of shot and the other camera can stay in close-up.'

'We'll have to bloody hurry.'

'Right, you get on with it. I'll endeavour to distract your military friend.'

'You do that,' said Burn, and bustled down to the shore. Jackland moved smiling over to Major Kadu. Just as he had been able to switch on quasi-Biblical authority for his piece to the camera, so now, as if from some psychic dispensing machine, he poured out for the Major's benefit another flavour of his personality—not exactly charm, or if charm more at an intellectual than a social level, an apparently sincere absorption in the ideas of the person to whom he was talking. For somebody who had seen so much and met such various strangers, this seeming simplicity of interest was a valuable gift.

'Sorry about that, Major,' he said. 'We're all a bit on edge. It's rather like a military operation, I suppose, everything timed and needing to dove-tail.'

The Major nodded, clearly not prepared to relax immediately from his indignation. Jackland seemed not to notice.

'You in charge of this district?' he said. 'Birnin Soko's your base, I suppose.'

'Colonel Goondo is O.C. I do not think he would have been impressed by what Mr Burn had to tell him, and he would certainly not have been pleased by public mockery of the morals of one of his men.'

'Cameramen are like that, for some reason. Fred especially. So wrapped up in visual effects that their other sensibilities seem to have atrophied. It sometimes seems to me that cameramen only come to this continent to film the more primitive of its people performing some stone-age labour silhouetted against a dying sun. Let me assure you that I am aware there is more than that to Nigeria.'

'Very much more.'

'Incredible diversity, to coin a phrase, not to be encapsulated in picturesque images. A marvellous country, in spite of everything.'

'In spite of what, Mr Jackland?'

'This last election, to take a prime example. Tell me, if it's not a tactless question, what the feeling is about that in military circles.'

It was, of course, a profoundly tactless question, but part of Jackland's general style. He had the TV interviewer's professional interest in the awkward point combined with something like the gambler's compulsion to take unnecessary risks in potentially embarrassing situations. The fact that this was clearly a bad moment perhaps only enhanced the stimulus.

'The Army would much prefer not to meddle in political matters,' said the Major.

'There must be limits to its abstinence. There were in 'sixty-six.'

'What happened in 'sixty-six was little more than a series of accidents.'

'Only superficially, I'd have thought. The pressure was there. Something had to burst. And to the outside observer it certainly looks that way again.'

'I would prefer not to discuss it.'

Jackland smiled, unrebuffed. Sarkin Kiti was after all only a few feet away, a senior political figure who had introduced Jackland as his friend. Indeed perhaps he was able to hear, or at least sense what was being said, for he turned at this moment and spoke.

'May we go down closer, Mr Jackland? I would like to see them land.'

'Oh, I should think so. Come and meet Mary Tressider, Major. I want the Sarkin to tell me how close he thinks she's got to my mother.'

They walked together down the slope, the spearmen again clearing a path with their spear-butts. The Africans did not seem to resent this—indeed, they may have regarded it as a natural part of their relationship with the Sarkin. On the other hand they seemed in little awe of him, judging by the way they jostled in close as soon as he had reached a point from which he could watch the landing.

The sunset, dull and fuzzy after the long heat of day, gleamed off the water, lighting the muscled arms of the naked paddlers. There were three of these in the front of the leading canoe, then

Mary Tressider in white cotton shirt, jodhpurs and sun-helmet, then Piers Smith in white shirt, khaki trousers, tennis shoes and helmet, and then three more paddlers. The canoe (there had been several rehearsals) slid cleanly in to the landing-stage. Paddlers at front and rear grabbed the staging so that Smith could stand and step up. He bent to take Miss Tressider's hand. She rose, balanced against an unrehearsed lurch of the canoe, stepped up on to the landing-stage and straightened, still holding Smith's hand but gazing now up the hill as though film-crew and crowd were invisible. She was freckled, with a flattish, earnest face, pale eyes set wide, something hesitant about the line of the full-lipped mouth. The sunset light rippled up her cheek under the brim of her helmet. The Sarkin was muttering to himself, not in English.

'Well?' whispered Jackland. 'Pretty good to judge by the photos, anyway.'

'It is not the same woman. It is the same spirit. Mrs Jackland carried her head so. Exactly so. Yes, she is there.'

The Sarkin too had whispered, but his tone implied more than the need to keep quiet for the sake of the shot. It was as if he was in the presence of something before which he would naturally have lowered his voice.

Still paying no attention to anyone, Miss Tressider stared up the slope. At last she turned to Smith with a quivering smile.

'But, Ted,' she said, 'it's beautiful. Why wouldn't you tell me? I can't think what you were worried about.'

Thurs Dec 13, 1923

Our house. It's called The Warren. Ted chose that 'cos he calls me Rabbit when he's being fond—not terribly tactful, but *very* Teddish. I'll do some sketches, of course, but it's too hot to paint just now. Too hot to do anything! Will I *ever* get used to this heat? There's always a sort of haze in the air so the sun doesn't look nearly as glaring as I'd expected, but the moment you walk out it presses down on you like an enormous load. I'll do a sketch this evening. The light's more interesting then, anyway. That's when I first saw The Warren too.

Ted utterly refused to tell me anything before but I guessed he was worried—it'd be his fault if I didn't like it, you see. Usually, when you're posted you find there's a house there already and you just move in and lump it, but when Mr Hardinge and then Mr Prout died one after the other, Kaduna (that's what we call the Govt) ordered a new compound to be built further from Kiti Town, so Ted could do what he liked. He actually spent some of his own money, making it nice for me, which Mr Wallace-Hodge, the D.O. at Fajujo, said was silly as we're sure to be posted somewhere else soon, but I think is rather darling. Ted wouldn't have dreamed of doing it for himself.

Anyway, he wouldn't even tell me what it *wasn't* like. I asked him at Fajujo where he came to meet me if it was like Mr Wallace-Hodge's horrid tin bungalow, but he did his trick of being too busy lighting his pipe to answer. He didn't even point it out when we came round the last bend, and I thought the compound was just another native village till I noticed the flagpole. Apart from that, The Warren's completely native-looking—all roof, made of cane-stalks and needing a haircut round the edges. There are proper walls but the brim sticks out so far you don't see them—just that great silvery-gold raggedy roof. Rather a shock, first time. The idea of this being home!

I daresay we could've had a tin bungalow if Ted had wanted but I suspect . . . oh, isn't it extraordinary how little I know

17

about my dear man! Just the tennis club, and walks along the beach, and tea-rooms, and then our week in Torquay (don't like to think about that). He does so hate talking about himself, so I have to guess. Lots to find out. All rather interesting! Where was I . . . Yes, I suspect he actually prefers doing things the African way if he can. Mr Wallace-Hodge gave me a hint about this. We were sitting in his mosquito-cage after dinner, but Ted had gone back to the house to fill his baccy-pouch and Mr W.-H. took the chance to try and pat my knee. He had had six big whiskies—I'd counted—just habit from watching Daddy—tho' Ted says it's not the same as it would be back home 'cos you sweat it out so quick. I'm jumpy about things like that—knee-patting, I mean —I know they can't help it but I wish they wouldn't—and I slapped his hand rather hard instead of just pushing it away. Then he leaned back in his chair and said, 'I'm glad old Ted's marrying. Steady him up. He's always been a bit too keen on things African. That's why he's not got his step, though he's senior enough in all conscience. They don't like it in Kaduna, so you keep an eye on him, my dear, and we'll see him a Resident before he retires.'

Quite a nasty little speech if you think about it, rubbing in that Ted's twenty-three years older than me, and hinting about African women. I don't think that's true—in fact I'm almost sure. Not just because Ted is so decent, but really he didn't know any more than I did when we first tried!

Goodness, I shall have to tear this page out and burn it—I never meant to be writing things like this! Surprising how much I want to. Not having anyone to talk to, I suppose. Better get back to The Warren.

Inside it's not quite so native, apart from the mud floor, which *is* rather a drawback. European boots scuff it up, so there's always a fine layer of dust settling all over everything. The walls are mud too, which helps you keep cool in the day-time but by night they've sucked in the heat so you do rather roast in bed.

The front room, which we call the dining-room tho' we spend most of our time here, is really rather nice. It's more like an enormous deep veranda than a room, with mosquito-wire instead of the outside walls, and just the poles that carry the roof-beams interrupting the view. I can sit and look right up and down the river. Sometimes there are fishermen throwing their nets from their boats, or just paddling by or a big trading canoe going up to Kiti, or cranes coming in to drink, and so on. I thought when I first looked at it the river wouldn't be very interesting if nothing like that was happening, but now I don't know. The light keeps changing in tiny subtle ways—not like English light at all—I expect I'll spend quite a lot of time trying to paint the river. Quite a challenge. The dining-room has a cloth stretched across the top to make a pretend ceiling, and some proper furniture, and the gramophone (*very* important). Not many books.

That's the front half of the house, almost. If Ted'd just left it to the Govt to pay for, all there'd have been behind is one more room, but we've got four! Our bedroom, a tiny room of my own (for me to have tantrums in, I told Ted!) a bathroom and Ted's dressing-room which we can use for a spare bedroom if we have to put someone up. Mosquito-wire over all the windows (more of Ted's own money!) and we still have to Flit every two hours and carry our Flit-guns to the B.G. (that's the latrine—horrid!), and sleep under a net, in case. I'll get malaria anyway, Ted says, and there's tsetse too, but not all the year round 'cos we're just on the fringe and so the bad season for that is over. Ted says malaria isn't any worse than flu. He usually works on through when he has a go.

Idea! When I've done writing this I'll draw a cartoon for Ted—a line of bearers going through the bush with loads on their heads, only the bearers will be *white* and the loads will be labelled MALARIA and BLACK-WATER and TYPHUS and so on. Some natives standing by laughing. I'll call it THE WHITE MAN'S BURDEN.

Behind our house there's the compound. It's a big clearing and the huts are at the back of it, all nice and new, not tumbledown like I saw down-river. They're just round native huts, one room each. Kimjiri, our cook, has two, 'cos of his wives, then there's one for Elongo, the houseboy, one each for the grooms, Mafote and Ibrahim, and one for the horses, one for the gardener, who's called Joe 'cos his real name is too difficult, two for the police-men tho' there's only one policeman at the mo, two for messen-gers (the head messenger lives at Kiti) and one for Mr Yo, Ted's clerk. Last of all, over at the side, Ted's office, which *is* made of corrugated iron, perfectly horrid, but it's harder to break into and white ants can't eat it.

All these natives make an incredible lot of noise, and on top of ours there's always at least half a dozen waiting outside the office to see Ted. About once a week, Ted says, he calls everyone together and makes a little speech, in Hausa and pidgin, telling them they don't *have* to talk as tho' the person they were having the conversation with was on the other side of the river. They think this is a marvellous joke, and *roar* with laughter, and remember for about half a day and then start yelling again!

Kimjiri's wives are the worst. He is fat and pale brown, about forty, I should think, only it's hard to tell. He came with Ted from Yola. He belongs to a small tribe over that side, but when he was a boy he was caught in a slave raid and sold in Bornu market. That was just before the English came. He was sent to work on a farm belonging to the Emir's cousin, but he wasn't very obedient so they decided to have him made into a eunuch! They sent him off to a special place where they were going to give him a drug and when he woke up he'd find out what had happened to him, but luckily he'd heard about this place and managed to run away on the journey and after a bit he stumbled into the camp of a touring A.D.O. (the English had got here by then) who took him on as a cook and passed him on to someone else later and eventually he came to Ted. He's got four wives and masses of children, and whenever Ted sees one of them he makes a joke about the eunuch-making place not being very good at its job, and everyone in earshot laughs as tho' it was the first time they'd heard it.

(Interesting. Ted's terribly shy about talking about s * *. He simply refused to when we were finding things so awkward the first few goes—we just had to learn in deaf-and-dumb, in the dark! But 'cos Kimjiri's a native Ted can make public jokes about it—and explain them to me, too!)

K. is *not* a good cook, but Ted says that doesn't matter compared with us being quite certain he's cooked everything right through. A lot of white men, he says, explain carefully to their boys about bilharzia and cholera bacilli and so on, and the boys smile and say they understand and then fill the water-cans straight from the river or forget to wash the filters or something. Ted told K. there was a very dreadful fetish over all that, so now

20

K. is quite certain that if the water isn't boiled and filtered and if the food isn't properly cooked ghastly things will happen, not just to Ted but to K. and his wives and children! (Joke about fetishes. Ted says our sun-helmets are one! We have to wear them whenever we go out, you see. It's a rule. If you've got a skylight in your bathroom which the sun might come through, you wear your helmet in your bath! Natives say when the White Man stops wearing his sun-helmet he'll lose his juju-power which makes everyone obey him, and then he'll go away!)

Elongo is quite different. He isn't married, for a start, 'cos he's only about sixteen. He was the one I really noticed when they all came down to meet us on the landing-stage. He is a proper Bakiti. (Difficult—the town and the district are called Kiti, and so is the language. The tribe are the Kitawa, but if there's only one of them he's a Bakiti.) Tall and lithe but strong-looking. His skin is a beautiful soft dark brown with a sort of light inside it like you get on polished wood. If he were white he'd have a marvellous complexion, like a girl's. His eyes are large and wide apart. He's got a snub nose but not the fat sort of lips I saw down-river. There are three little scar-lines on the corners of his forehead which give him a funny sort of frown as tho' he spent the whole time trying to remember something he's forgotten. All the Kitawa boys are marked that way when they're fourteen —rather a pity but not nearly as horrid as some of the scar-marks you see. He wears a white cotton robe and a little white skull-cap. He wasn't used to wearing *anything* till a few weeks ago except a grass belt! He came and asked Ted for a job when the hut was building, and Ted took to him and asked him to stay on and be houseboy 'cos perhaps he won't try and cheat me as much as an experienced houseboy might. Ted sacked his last one for stealing tinned pilchards. It was clever of Ted to choose Elongo. He's exactly right for me. He moves with such grace, and cleans everything with slow proud movements and stands so still when he's waiting at meals, almost as tho' he's left his body and gone somewhere else. But he's very quick if you want anything. Another nice thing is that his Hausa is even worse than mine. He hardly knows any. I'm truly grateful to Ted for making me start learning before I came out, and I've got on far better than he'd guessed—but I always liked French best at school, after art. Hausa is rather easy. Ted says Kiti is absolute h ⋆ ⋆ ⋆ ! It's what's

21

called tonal, which means singy. You have to say the syllables on the right note or they mean something else. It's never been worth white men learning it 'cos sure as eggs, soon as they'd got anywhere they'd get posted. Anyway the Govt at Kaduna don't like D.O.s knowing too much about the real Africans in case it upsets the emirs.

After lunch. I wrote all that this morning and I've just read it through. Goodness, what a lot. You know, I think I won't tear out the private bits and burn them. I think I need something like this. There are all sorts of things I can't say to Ted and I've got to say to someone. I'll find somewhere to hide it. I know, with my thingy. Ted would never dream of poking around there—he's terribly squeamish about that side of things.

Ted laughed like billy-oh at my cartoon and got out a pencil and started to add things. He can't really draw at all, just stick-men. He drew black ones on top of all the loads and another white man labelled ME with the bearers, carrying a much bigger load than anyone else with a big black man and a little white man sitting on top. The load was supposed to be office files but they didn't look anything like. The men on top were labelled K B and de L. I guessed that meant Kama Boi and de Lancey. Kama Boi is the Emir. We're going over to visit him on Monday. Mr de Lancey is the Resident at Birnin Soko about eighty miles away on the other side of the river, and he's Ted's boss. 'Don't you like Mr de Lancey?' I said, but Ted just laughed and lit the paper at the corner and watched it burn. I can't imagine what Elongo thought of all this!

Tired of writing now. Nothing to say. Still too hot to paint. I shall slop in a chair and listen to the gramophone and try and read *Henry Esmond*. (Qy: Why are good books so *boring*?)

Mon Dec 17
Started off for Kiti soon as it was light (no breakfast till we got back, either. Hope I'm going to get used to these funny meal-times, breakfast not till 9.30, lunch not till 2.30 so's Ted can get all his office work over and have the rest of the day for other things). I rode Ted's best pony, Salaki, almost pure Arab. He's only just got his horses back after the tsetse season—he sends them up north with Mafote for that. He's looking for one for me

but he says it may take a bit of time to find the right one. In fact, I rather think he's a bit strapped for cash at the mo 'cos of spending more than he meant on The Warren! He's terribly proud of Salaki—talks about her as tho' he was trying to make me jealous (he wouldn't know how to, actually, dear man!). She's beautifully easy to ride without being boring and makes me feel quite the horsewoman, but Ted had to wrestle along with Tan-Tan, a rough old roan with an iron jaw (you couldn't call it a mouth, Ted says) and a pig of a temper.

The track leads out through the trees and almost at once you're in thick scrub. When I was coming up river it felt as tho' we were paddling along through jungle most of the way, but really except in the south the trees are a bit like stage scenery, just a thin line along the river banks and emptiness behind them. Only here in Kiti, between the trees and the emptiness, there's a belt of rather nasty scrub, a bit like elder but with little cactusy leaves and thorns. It's terribly difficult to clear 'cos every bit of root grows, so nobody lives in it. The real Kitawa live out beyond, in the hinterland. The track wound through this stuff, usually only wide enough for one, but where possible Ted came up alongside and gave me a history lesson before I met the Emir. I'm going to write it down to get it clear in my head, 'cos it's important I shouldn't put my foot in it by saying the wrong thing.

Kiti is at the bottom edge of Northern Nigeria, and in Northern Nigeria the Law and the Prophets and the Laws of Cricket is something called Indirect Rule. That's how we British govern the natives. Thing is, when we got here first we didn't find just a lot of jungly tribes, like down south, but a sort of tottery empire with its own laws and its own princes, called emirs, ruling the different bits. They were all Mohammedans, tho' some of the people they ruled over weren't. So we said, 'Alright, you go on ruling, and we'll just put in a District Officer or a Resident to advise you how to do it better, and stop you slave-raiding and things like that, and show you how to collect your taxes more fairly. And we'll pretend you are still the real rulers and we're just advisers, only you'd jolly well better do what we advise!' So that was alright.

We got to Kiti almost last of all—it's always been a complete backwater—and we found Kama Boi calling himself Sarkin Kiti, which means King of Kiti so we thought we'd do the same thing here. We made him Emir and gave him an adviser and told him to carry on. Only things were a bit different here, which we didn't realize. You see, there are three sorts of people in Kiti. There are the Emir and his lot at Kiti Town. There are the river people, who are the usual mixed bag of fishermen and farmers and traders and so on. And there are the Kitawa, who are a quite big tribe who live inland and don't wear any clothes and keep themselves to themselves as far as they can. What we didn't realize when we told Kama Boi he was Emir now and had to collect taxes from everyone was that he wasn't really ruler of anything except Kiti Town. The Kitawa simply weren't used to paying taxes to anyone.

About a hundred years ago, you see, there was a terrific war in the north, and one lot called the Fulani beat another lot called the Hausa and made themselves emirs. Then one of the beaten Hausa who was Kama Boi's great-grandfather came south with his men and crossed the river and said to the Kitawa, 'Look, if you let me build a fort at Kiti Rapids, which is the only good crossing-place for miles, and give me some land to farm, I'll stop the soldiers from Soko slave-raiding you across the river.'

The Kitawa must have thought this was a good idea, 'cos there'd been a lot of slave-raiding (it was the emirs' favourite sport, like fox-hunting in England). So they made a treaty with Kama Boi's great-grandfather and to show how sacred it was they held a juju ceremony (human sacrifice, Ted says!) at the holiest place in Kiti, and they did the same for his successors, including Kama Boi. Nothing's written down, of course, but Ted says it's just as binding as a treaty between France and England, and still matters tremendously. He's had a lot of trouble with it 'cos Kama Boi is *not* a good ruler and Kaduna are always trying to send for him to tell him to pull his socks up, only he refuses point blank to cross the river. He says part of the juju is that he must never leave Kiti, and that's that!

Well, Kiti's such a backwater that at first Kaduna only grumbled a bit about the taxes not getting paid, and Kama Boi grumbled back at them about not being allowed to slave-raid into Soko so how were he and his people going to run their farms, but nothing happened till a man called Harry Bestermann was sent here as D.O. He was a real goer, Ted says. (Ted's got a little song—'Harry was a goer. Harry's been and gone. Tick fever.' Rather horrid—Ted isn't a goer, you see. More of a stayer, really. That's rather good—better not tell him, tho'—he's sensitive about things sometimes.)

Well, Mr Bestermann bullied Kama Boi into taking his spearmen and his *dogarai*—they're the Native Authority police, fearful ruffians, Ted says—out into the bush and going from village to village and *making* the Kitawa pay up, and next thing the quiet, peaceful Kitawa were in revolt! Their women got hold of five *dogarai* and gave them drugged beer and did frightful things to them and then put them in a hut and set fire to it, and before you could say Jack Robinson all KB's men had to come scuttling out of the bush and shut themselves up in Kiti Town.

Then of course KB came to Mr Bestermann and said, 'Now look what's happened,' and Mr Bestermann persuaded Kaduna to let him have something called Bestermann's Patrol, which meant marching to and fro with forty soldiers and a machine gun showing the Kitawa that if they didn't let themselves be counted and start paying taxes nasty things would happen to them. We didn't hear about any of this in England 'cos it was 1916 and we were too busy with the war. Anyway it was all very fair. The patrol only shot people when they tried to fight, and cleared them out of the huts before they burnt them, and when they caught someone they thought might be a ringleader they didn't hang them straight off but sent them to Lagos to be tried and hanged there. So in the end the Kitawa gave in.

It's still all very difficult, Ted says. The taxes are tiny and Kama Boi's a lot poorer than he used to be and so are his nobles, and Kaduna can't make up their minds what to do next. After the patrol they allowed Kama Boi to go on being Emir but to show everyone the revolt was really his fault (!) they sort of demoted him by putting Kiti under Soko, which was an absolutely terrible idea, Ted says. The Emir of Soko is a Fulani and so he's Kama Boi's hereditary enemy, and his ancestors used to slave-raid the Kitawa so they hate him too, and Kama Boi used to slave-raid the Sokowa. (Suppose I have to make allowances, because if Kaduna hadn't done it that way Ted would be a Resident instead of just D.O., so naturally he feels a bit sore! Remember the way he laughed about Mr de Lancey when he scribbled on my cartoon?)

Then we got to Kiti. That was quite exciting. First off you hear the rapids, then you see the river-trees, but before you reach them you come out of the bush into neat Hausa fields and straight ahead there's one great mud wall, towering up. You think, 'Golly! How could natives have built anything so big?' Then you see it's on a cliff. Actually there's a ridge of rock running all the way across the river, and that's what makes the rapids where the river's smashed it down, but this side it's a proper cliff. Still, the wall's pretty impressive even allowing for that, thirty feet high and ten feet thick, Ted says. It's a bit ruined in places 'cos Kama Boi doesn't bother to keep it mended now he knows we British will stop the Fulani attacking him. I shall come and do a picture. The most exciting bit is where the track bends and you're going along almost under the wall and you see the yellow rapids tumbling down beyond.

That's where we found Ted's Messenger, Lukar, waiting for us on his donkey. He's the head messenger, so he has a capital M—the others are just errand boys, but Lukar's quite important 'cos he can speak Kiti tho' he's a Hausa and he's been Messenger for years, since before Mr Bestermann's time. We come and go but they stay on. He's a very black little man, thin-faced and hooky-nosed. He wears a white robe and a pill-box hat. He led the way. A scrambly track slanting up the cliff. Quite a good road between the river and the town ditch, with the wall beyond it. Ditch full of fearsome thorn scrub. Islands in the river. Extraordinary tangles of wood between some of them and a fisherman scrambling around like a shiny black spider 'cos of the spray, getting at his fish-traps. Beyond the town what Ted calls New Kiti, another of his jokes 'cos it's only a jumble of tin shacks and mud huts, higgledy-piggledy round the market. More about that in a mo.

But first, something that happened inside me. While we were riding between the river and the wall I suddenly had the most extraordinary feeling. Here we were, in the middle of Africa, just the two of us, and I hardly count 'cos of being a woman. The nearest white man was probably Mr de Lancey at Birnin Soko, eighty miles away. If you look at a map you see all this enormous country coloured pink. Kiti mayn't look like much on the map, but it's big as an English county. And it's pink because of Ted being here. Just one man. The natives talk about *the* White Man.

The White Man orders this. The White Man forbids that. As far as they can see there is only one White Man—Ted, with his sun-helmet and his pipe and his red face and his red knees showing under his shorts!

Well, the road goes on a bit further than you'd think, to join with the ferry-crossing and then turns back to the main gate. I expect you could find a way through by the wall, but we were going to meet the Emir so of course we had to go round by the grand way. The only sensible thing Mr Bestermann ever succeeded in getting Kama Boi to do was to make a wide avenue leading to the gateway so there could be a proper place for the market, with shade-trees. The trees are quite decent now. The market is terribly exciting—lots of pictures later, but no time for that for the mo. All that bustle and colour after the sameness of things out on the river. Smells, too, I'm afraid, and such flies! Everyone stopped and stared at us as Lukar led our little procession through. I got the feeling they were just curious, but not specially respectful. I'd have thought the natives would have liked Ted, and been grateful to him, 'cos he's doing his best for them, but I'm afraid they didn't show it. Of course these were practically all river people, not the real Kitawa.

The town has a grand gate, two good towers and an arch. A bit of a space in front. An official was waiting for us. He has a perfectly lovely title—he's the Bangwa Wangwa. That isn't Hausa, it's a sort of Hausa-ized Kiti, 'cos his main job is interpreting for the Emir to the Kitawa. It's hereditary. He was taught Kiti by his father, and he's teaching it to his sons. Lukar is some kind of relation of his, which is why he can talk Kiti too, which of course the D.O.'s messenger has to, tho' Ted says some of the Kitawa men talk a bit of Hausa.

Anyway he led us through the gate and there was the Emir and his courtiers and his bodyguard, all drawn up ready to meet us. The Emir was sitting on a special stool with a lovely leaf-shaped wicker fan held over him to keep the sun off. Stools and parasols for Ted and me. The Emir wears a funny loose sort of turban, brown and yellow, and an embroidered robe, same colours, with a loose cotton thing like a tea-gown over. When you get closer you see that none of it is at all clean! The courtiers, eight or nine of them, dress the same. The bodyguards are the best, on horses, with tasselled spears and quilted 'armour'—terribly hot—only two of them but *very* impressive.

The Emir shook hands with Ted but not with me, 'cos he's supposed to be a Mohammedan. (Ted says the Prophet must be turning in his grave! KB's hardly Mohammedan at all, he says, and hardly Hausa at all either, 'cos of his father and grandfather marrying women from other tribes. He's really a jungly savage inside, but the funny thing is his children have started going the other way. They've spotted we like the Hausa best, so they think it's a good idea to be as Mohammedan and as Hausa as they can, and then the other emirs will respect them. By the by, about shaking hands, Ted says he's got a circular from Kaduna saying he mustn't do it with anyone below the rank of emir in case they start getting cheeky—so we're just as peculiar in our own way!) The Emir is an old man, about seventy, very fat, with dark wrinkled skin, smelly as a goat. I forgot almost all my Hausa but managed to tell him I thought the sun was hot. He laughed like billy-oh. Beastly.

Then I sat on my stool while Ted talked to the Emir. It wasn't a business meeting, just us calling and leaving our cards, sort of. Flies everywhere. Luckily I'd come with a veil on my sun-helmet 'cos of KB being a Mohammedan, but poor Ted had to swish away with a whisk. KB just let the flies crawl over him as tho' they weren't there. I couldn't bear to look at him, but luckily there were lots of other things.

Kiti's a great surprise, 'cos it isn't a town at all! I mean, there aren't enough houses to count as a town. Mostly inside the walls it's little patches of 'garden', rather like the allotments you see out of railway windows but more higgledy-piggledy. Natives hoeing between the rows. There are houses, tho' some of them are empty, Ted says, 'cos of only the proper Hausa who came with KB's great-grandfather being allowed inside the walls, and now we've stopped the slave-raiding and the slave-farms some of them have given up and gone away. The grand houses are made of mud, thick walls, only a few tiny windows near the top, buttresses like a church, flat roofs and funny little pinnacles (Ted says I ought to approve of them 'cos they're called 'rabbit's ears'!) along the parapets. Some ordinary native huts, with thatch. Ted says proper Hausa towns are *huge*, miles of wall and thousands of people, but still mostly open space so's people could go on farming when there was a siege. Kiti's tiny, compared, not much more than a fort, really. The gate towers are the best bit. KB's own palace was down at the far end, so I couldn't see much of it. Ted says it's nothing special.

He'd cunningly arranged for Lukar to bring some of our own ginger pop so we'd know where what we were drinking came from. We sucked it out of the bottles. It was warm as blood and fizzed up my nose and made me sneeze. The Emir loved that. He kept looking at me sideways while he was talking to Ted and I knew exactly what he was thinking about! I didn't like him one bit. He seemed more like an animal than a person, black and piggy, with the flies coming to drink his sweat.

On the way back Ted asked me what I thought of KB. I had a bit of a headache by now, what with the sun and the smells and the foul warm ginger pop.

'I thought he was perfectly horrible,' I said.

'He has the reputation for being a bit of a charmer, you know,' said Ted.

Of course he didn't mean it like that, but because of the way KB had been looking at me that's how I couldn't help taking it.

'Well, he didn't charm me,' I said, snappish as I could make it.

Ted didn't notice.

'He has his good points, you know,' he said.

If it hadn't been for the headache I might have been more careful, but I really let go and started saying just how disgusting I thought KB was. Ted laughed at first, then he turned serious and pulled me up.

'Now listen, Rabbit,' he said. 'You're going to have to start thinking differently about things. There's a lot about Africa which'll send you off your rocker if you keep trying to judge it by English standards. You're not going to change it, so the only thing is to learn to like it, or at least put up with it.'

'There's lots of things I like,' I said. 'Really. I love our house and I like most of the natives I've met. I don't mean just the ones who're special, like Elongo, but f'rinstance I do like Kimjiri, spite of his cooking and the racket his wives make. But I don't like it being so hot and I don't like smelly old men with flies crawling about on them.'

I *just* stopped myself saying anything about the way KB had kept looking at me.

'If it weren't for that smelly old man you wouldn't be here,' said Ted.

'What do you mean?'

'You're here because I'm here. Kaduna owe me a bigger post on a better station, with other white people around. There wouldn't be much fuss about you coming out to join me somewhere like that. But they're not normally happy about white women coming to places as cut off as Kiti. You don't strike bargains with Kaduna, but there was a sort of understanding that if I took this posting you could come too. They want me here, you see, because they've got de Lancey at Birnin Soko. He's dug himself in there very successfully. It's one of their show places, roads, hospitals, schools, Emir due for an O.B.E. soon. De Lancey's a goer, you see. Like Harry Bestermann but a sight more intelligent. He thinks you can do something about Africa, make it into a kind of black Europe one day. I don't. I think you have to do things the African way or Africa will break you. That's the difference between us, and it's a difference that runs right through the service, to the very top. If you know the ropes you can usually find someone up there to take your side, specially when it comes to something like getting rid of an emir. Point is, de Lancey has pretty well got Soko the way he wants it and now he's turning his attention to Kiti. It's a delicate situation all round. One small thing could tip it. Technically de Lancey's my superior, but Kiti is a separate emirate, so though I report to him I also report direct to Kaduna. De Lancey wants to come in here and start building roads and so on. In particular he's got plans all drawn up for a bridge at Kiti, so he can open up the interior. Open it up for what, for god's sake? There's nothing there. But he's bright enough to see he's never going to get anywhere while Kama Boi's Emir, so his first step is to try and get him out. My main business is to see he doesn't get given a reason.'

'But Kaduna are on your side?'

'Kaduna are never on anybody's side, at least no longer than the interval between one memo and the next. No, Kaduna can't make up their mind. They don't want to think about it. They're terrified since Bestermann's Patrol it might mean trouble and

30

they wouldn't find it so easy to hush things up the way they did in 'sixteen. But they want to keep de Lancey happy, because he's made Soko into a show piece, so they aren't going to tell him he can't get his hands on Kiti and do the same here. Not till Kama Boi's dead, at least, and they hate deposing chiefs. Bad advertisement for Indirect Rule. Their answer is to put a D.O. in here who's on the other side and is senior enough to stand up to de Lancey.'

'And then they've got to keep the D.O. happy by letting him have his own little wife with him.'

'That's about it.'

The track got too narrow for two for a bit, so I rode ahead, not really thinking about what Ted had been telling me—really just brooding on my headache and the heat, tho' it was only just after nine, and worrying about the poor horses. Soon as the track widened Ted trotted up beside me. He *had* been thinking.

'I say, Rabbit,' he said. 'I suppose it's a bit rough on you. You'd have had much more fun on a bigger station, with other white women around, and tennis and all that.'

'Oh, no, darling,' I said. 'I was a bit frightened, I've got to admit. But now I'm here I'm glad. Just us two, alone.'

'Me too,' he said. A funny little grunt. Hardly words at all, but I understood. Nicer than roses.

Something strange. I don't know what to do.

After lunch, when Ted had gone back to his office, Elongo came in. I was lying in the long chair listening to the gramophone and reading what I'd written. It's an awful lot but it just seems to come out of the end of the pencil without me having to think about it. Anyway I didn't notice E. was there till I got up to wind the gramophone. He was standing against the back wall. I could hardly see his skin, just his robe and cap, like a ghost. I jumped a mile!

'What is it?' I managed to say. In Hausa of course.

'Madam go to Kiti this morning?'

'Yes.'

'Madam speak with Kama Boi?'

(I'd better explain something. It doesn't look fair, me making myself talk proper English and E. a sort of pidgin when we were both talking in Hausa and mine isn't that hot either, but it was

31

like that. The only Hausa he knows, almost, is about things like cleaning Ted's boots and bringing our meals and so on, and even then he muddles in Kiti words. I made Kimjiri laugh yesterday when I used the Kiti word for 'knife' which I'd picked up from Elongo—it was the best joke for years, a white woman talking bush African!)

'I spoke to the Emir,' I said. I knew I ought to show him I thought it was cheek him not giving KB his proper title, but he was too serious to notice.

'Madam see the women?'

'I saw no women,' I said. There'd been quite a few in the market, actually, but I didn't suppose he was talking about them. He stood still. I felt he was unhappy or frightened or something. I tried to help.

'Why do you ask?' I said.

'My sister is in the house of Kama Boi,' he said.

'We did not go close to the house of the Emir,' I said.

He was still terribly worried, I was sure.

'What is the matter?' I said. 'Is your sister unhappy?'

'I do not know. I do not hear my sister speak. Kama Boi takes her.'

'Takes her? Do you say he stole her?'

Of course they taught us the words for stealing almost first thing, but I don't think Elongo understood. Ted says Africans are naturally honest until we let them into our houses. Anyway, poor Elongo just gave a deep unhappy sigh and bowed and glided away, leaving me wondering what to do.

The obvious thing is to consult Ted, but I don't think I shall—not yet, anyway. From what he told me this morning Ted doesn't like hearing accusations about KB, and I really don't want him to take against Elongo, who I think is absolutely perfect, so I'm going to keep quiet till at least I know a bit more. But I *would* like to do something . . .

Idea! I'm going to go and paint Kiti—I've simply got to. Terribly exciting. There's something about Africa. I mean I don't really like it, it's so uncomfy in such a lot of ways, but my eye and my hand love it! I don't think I've ever painted so well as I've started doing now, and there's lots and lots of subjects at Kiti. So when I go I'll take Elongo with me to carry things and help, and I'll get Ted to ask KB for permish for me to paint his palace, and then I might be able to get him to send some of his women out to pose in front or something. Can't think of a way of making sure E.'s sister is one of them. I really need to find out more.

Second idea! I'm going to get Elongo to teach me Kiti! I'll teach him English in exchange. Give me something to do all these long hours when Ted's working, and it's too hot to paint. Yes, that's rather a good idea. The other one I'm not sure about, but I think I'll give it a try.

THREE

'The same spirit,' said Miss Tressider. 'That's really nice. Things like holding my head right are easy once you've got that. I hope there'll be time for me to have a chat with the old billy-goat when we've finished.'

She lolled naked on the bed of her small portable cabin—the 'wholly separate accommodation' written into her contract. It and the three larger ones used by the unit formed a small encampment a few hundred yards downstream from the clearing in which the remains of The Warren stood. The hotel accommodation in New Kiti town had been judged for a number of reasons unsatisfactory.

The air conditioner muttered away beneath the closed window. The glass was grey with river-mist and the light of dawn. Jackland, wearing a thin green cotton bath-robe, sat in an upright chair which he had tilted and was rocking with a push of his toe against the corner of the bed. His bed-roll lay in hummocks on the floor. Though their affair had begun abruptly only a few days earlier and was still fresh—still, for him, perhaps, astonishing—he had insisted that his age excused him from having to share a single bed all night. Indeed he did look older at the moment than he had when speaking to the camera, but this was mainly the effect not of his sleeping arrangements but of heavy reading spectacles, which somehow enhanced the hollows below his cheek-bones, edging the mildly haggard a year or two further towards the cadaverous.

Miss Tressider had aged too, but more deliberately. On set she had contrived to seem barely into her twenties. Now she had relaxed to her own age, some ten years more. She had changed in other ways. It would have been difficult, of course, to imagine the woman who had stepped from the canoe lying in a pose of such feline languor, but there was more to it than that. Her off-stage face, though not so pretty as her press photographs, was much less run-of-the-mill than the one she had invented for her portrayal of Betty Jackland, mouth firm and with a hint of the

34

archaic smile seen on early Greek statues, the chin somehow less bulky, the eyes sleeping and sly.

'I keep saying you should have,' said Jackland.

'And I keep saying not till it's all over. Imagination's more important than truth, Nigel. You can't see it because you're a journalist, really. Betty didn't know the truth, did she? She didn't have much clue what was going on, and none at all what would happen next. I don't want to either. Knowing what's next in the script is knowing too much—I have to imagine it away. All Betty knew was that Ted was her ticket of escape from that fucking awful father and she'd chosen fucking awful Africa instead, so now here she was in the stink and heat trying to find out how to love her funny old husband.'

'Do you think she did?'

'Oh, yes. Not the way she thought, though.'

'I suppose he provided her with a more admirable and adequate father-figure than the one issued to her by the heavenly quartermaster.'

'A bit of that. Oh, I don't go for that sort of explanation much. It's all too coggy. We aren't made of separate bits and pieces. We've grown. Branches and roots and leaves aren't the tree. The tree's the pattern they make. When I get a part right it means I've managed to copy the pattern. I do it by imagination. I just need one or two things to go on. But it's no use you telling me how Betty held her riding-crop unless I've grown into someone who'd hold it like that without thinking.'

'My mother would not have lain around like a starlet attempting to catch the eye of the *Playboy* centrefold editor.'

'Do you want me to be Betty all the time, Nigel?'

'No thanks.'

'Are you sure? Come here, then.'

'I'm trying to read.'

'Come here.'

Jackland put his *Economist* down, removed his spectacles, rose and stood gazing down at her. She raised her left arm in succulent invitation while her right slipped languorously over the edge of the bed. He was shrugging himself out of his robe when with that lolling hand she caught the edge of the sheet and flipped it across her body, leaving only her head, arm and naked shoulder visible. She put the hand to her face and with the gesture of an uncle amusing small children by a variety of grimaces slid it downwards, wiping out Mary Tressider and replacing her with the woman who had landed from the canoe. Jackland looked for a moment at the young, tremulous, earnestly bewildered features, then nodded and pulled his robe back round him.

'Am I to take it,' he said as he sat down, 'that your current amiability towards me is an aid to you in your portrayal of a woman sexually involved with a much older man?'

The harsh public tone was marked. He might have been in front of the cameras, pinning down the slitherings of some industrial spokesman. Miss Tressider twitched the sheet away and re-odalisqued, but answered as though also involved in an interview, cool and serious.

'Oh no. I don't need that. It's in the imagination. Reality would get in the way.'

Jackland put on his spectacles and started to read, or to pretend to. Miss Tressider stared at the ceiling.

'Has it been bothering you, Nigel?' she said.

'Not greatly, but it seems an obvious question to ask. One point that emerges strongly from the diary is the way in which two presumably inhibited and, so to speak, uneducated people should have contrived to get so much out of the sex act. One is bound to wonder what it might have been like for them.'

'But we aren't like that, are we? Besides, they were in love.'

'I have the grace to pretend on suitable occasions.'

'And sometimes I have the honesty not to act. You're very self-centred, aren't you, Nigel? Have you actually loved anyone, ever?'

'Not to my knowledge.'

'Betty?'

'Oedipally, you mean? Again, not . . .

'I don't mean. Anyway I shouldn't have asked. When it's over you can tell me all about her. I'd like that. I rather go for old Ted, you know. I don't think he was anything like the stick dear Piers is making him out. I can see quite a bit of him in you, Nigel.'

'I find it hard to imagine anyone more totally different. He was a steady, decent, unimaginative elderly schoolboy who'd come to Nigeria because he could think of nothing better to do with

36

his limited talents, and then proceeded to take the job too seriously for his own good. The only similarity I can perceive is that the old boy could express himself on paper. I've read his reports at Kaduna. He could put a case over and he had a spare, accurate, natural turn of phrase. You get the impression from the diary that de Lancey could run rings round him, but they were more evenly matched than you might imagine. Bugger! Where did *he* come from? That's not supposed to happen in here.'

Jackland had slapped at his shin while speaking and now brushed the flattened corpse of the mosquito away.

'She, not he,' said Miss Tressider. 'The blokes are vegetarians.'

'Why me, anyway? There you are, laid out like a banquet for the Mayor and Corporation of Mosquito City and they home in on my sapless shanks.'

'Female solidarity, I expect. Keep taking the pills and you'll be all right.'

'For malaria. There are plenty of other things. When I was doing the research for this job I read about an A.D.O. who ate some inadequately cooked river fish and contracted a parasite which burrowed into his brain and drove him mad. His servants sent for a doctor who rode thirty miles and arrived to find the man dying. As he bent over the bed to try the pulse the A.D.O. pulled a revolver from under his pillow and shot the doctor dead.'

'Charming. Keep off fish, Nigel. Or go and sleep with the others. Anything else?'

'Sleeping sickness, cholera, typhoid, black-water, tetanus, hepatitis—various parasites—there's a guinea worm in the diary—tick fever—that's in the diary too, Bestermann died of it—I believe there's a specially nasty variant round here—river blindness—lot of that because of the spray from the rapids, in fact there's a W.H.O. project on it at Kiti . . . You know, the insurance premiums alone on this trip would pay for an hour of screen time shot in the Home Counties . . .'

'How did you get it off the ground, Nigel? I mean, I think it's a terrific script—wild horses wouldn't have got me here for anything less—and even then if I hadn't been breaking up with Alphonse—but how did you sell it to them? It isn't the Raj, is it? No howdahs or durbars or tiger shoots, just three or four people sweating their lives away in a stinking jungle slum. By no means mass audience. How did you get them to spend the money?'

'The rest of the series is dirt cheap. Me going to places where I've done programmes over the years and seeing what they look like now. Old film, talking heads, location shots. Finance department's dream. I sold them that, then conned them into this as a spin-off. We're doing this on the cheap too, all things considered.'

'I'm not cheap.'

'But you're going to sell the series round the world, they think. My guess is very few networks will buy the whole package, just this and the episode that concerns them, if any.'

'So it's going to make a loss.'

'Probably. It doesn't bother me. I've been wanting to do this for over twenty years—effectively since I found the diary among my father's kit.'

'And I've been wanting to play Bernhardt playing Hamlet with a wooden leg. Can I get anyone to see . . . Among *Ted's* kit, Nigel?'

'That's right.'

'But she says . . .'

'She must have changed her mind.'

'I suppose she could have put it there when the kit came back from Africa. It would be a way of getting rid of it. A bit like telling Elongo to bury it in the bush.'

'No. It came with his stuff.'

'He'd read it?'

'One presumes so.'

Miss Tressider closed her eyes. The archaic smile vanished. Her face became blank and then, without any apparent movement of muscle, underwent faint shifts, hints and suggestions of an underlying personality trying to emerge. She sighed and opened her eyes.

'Thank God you didn't tell me before,' she said. 'It changes everything, doesn't it? If he was going to read every word . . .'

'She didn't know that while she was writing it.'

'Are you sure?'

'There's no way of knowing. Assuming the diary to be veridical within the limits of my mother's perceptions, we know what happened up to and including the Tefuga Incident. At that point

38

she says she is going to give it to Elongo to bury in the bush, and we know that that did not happen. That is all we know until my father's death. You might almost say I brought us all here in an attempt to fill that gap. If so, I am none the wiser. Did Elongo give it to him after she'd gone? Did she leave it for my father to find? Did he purloin it from her cases as a keepsake?'

'Why don't you ask the Sarkin?'

'I've tried more than once. He changes the subject.'

'You don't say anything about it in the script, Nigel.'

'Failure of nerve. As you say, it changes everything. Suppose she left it behind as a way of telling him . . .'

'I'm not going to think about it. I'm going to forget you told me. I don't want to know any of that till we've got this thing finished. It's not in the script, that's all that matters. Talk about something else, Nigel.'

'I was reading, if you remember.'

'Be like that.'

But as Jackland searched for his place there was a rattle of the door-knob. Miss Tressider flipped a sheet over her body. Jackland rose and tied the belt of his robe before crossing to unbolt the door. These were perfunctory proprieties. The rest of the unit were of course aware of the affair, perhaps rather more interested in it than usual because of the gossip value of anything to do with Miss Tressider, slightly inquisitive too because of the disparity in ages, while those in the men's quarters welcomed the extra sleeping space. The sheet enhanced, if anything, the Baudelarian lassitude of Miss Tressider's pose.

The visitor was Trevor Fish. Though the door, in its brief opening and closing, had revealed a dawn well short of the full mid-morning swelter, he leaned his back against it and gasped exaggeratedly. Part of his stock-in-trade was such pantomime gestures.

'Sorry to intrude,' he said. 'Malc says could you come and reason with your military pal, Nigel.'

'What's up?'

'It's Fred's fault. He slipped the guards on the launch a bottle of vodka. He thought if he got them insensible he and the boys could shift the launch in the small hours and we could shoot the departure as planned. Nice try, except that they found they couldn't shift the launch. Now Major Kadu's rolled up and found his men tiddly. He's a follower of the dear old Koran, himself, of course, so his reaction is not one of pleasure. He's refusing to let anyone near the landing-stage and he wants to commandeer a truck to take him in to Kiti. Malc thought he could smooth it all over with the naira treatment.'

'Dear God in heaven!' said Jackland.

'Bribed him?' said Miss Tressider.

'The one obvious sea-green incorruptible in the landscape,' said Jackland. 'Typical Malcolm. What happened?'

Fish put a hand to his forehead, closed his eyes and shuddered. The shudder prolonged itself beyond the needs of drama.

'Are you all right, Trevor?' said Miss Tressider.

'Death scene just coming up. May I die in your arms, Mary? I've got a lovely aria ready.'

Jackland, who had been moving towards the chair on which his clothes lay, turned and came back. He laid a hand on Fish's forehead.

'Come and sit down,' he said.

'It's just something I've eaten.'

'Let's hope not. That could be a sight worse. Come and sit down.'

Fish was obviously about to refuse when his body decided otherwise. Jackland helped him to the chair, took a clinical thermometer from a shelf, dipped it into a bottle and slid it into Fish's mouth. Fish grimaced at the taste of disinfectant. Jackland started to dress, talking as he did so.

'There's always at least one who thinks he can skip the chloroquin,' he said. 'It seems to be a law of nature. It's in all their contracts.'

Fish mumbled round the thermometer. Jackland ignored him.

'There's some point if you're a cameraman and the pills give you teleopsia, I suppose, but then you shouldn't take on jobs like this. Feeling sick isn't enough. Let's have a look . . . A hundred and two. Straight malaria, I should think.'

He fetched a glass of water and counted pills into his palm.

'Knock them back,' he said. 'Lie on my roll while I go and talk to the Major. Do you mind, Mary? Then, far as you can when we're shooting, try and stay in the shade.'

'He can't possibly work today,' said Miss Tressider.

'Yes he can. In my father's time at any given moment one fifth of the political officers had malaria, a tenth had something else and another tenth were drunk or going insane. Forty per cent at a rough estimate. You just stuffed yourself with quinine and carried on. If Trevor doesn't show up and Malcolm learns why he'll insist on fining him. That'll mean a fight with the unions. I've got a whole eight-part series to put together when this lot's over, remember.'

'I don't think I feel like doing the departure today,' said Miss Tressider.

'What on earth do you mean?'

'I want to do it last of all. I've just realized. Don't let's have a row, Nigel. I would like to do that scene last, really. It's just a feeling I have. But if you force me I'll show just why I'm going to make such a terrific Bernhardt one day. Go and tell Malcolm I'm being unreasonable. I've been as sweet as pie so far, haven't I? That's because I rather fancied you. But has anyone ever told you what I did when they were shooting *Jade Lilies*? Remind Malcolm about that. Oh, I know what. Tell him I don't feel I can do the departure scene till I've been and seen Tefuga. I do want to go. That's honest. You can think of a reason for him to leave Trevor behind. Malcolm will have a lovely time switching his schedules round.'

'He'll want Trevor for that.'

'I need Trevor to play piquet with. Don't be obstinate, Nigel. I'm going to get my way, can't you see? Malcolm will love it, really. You aren't a real director till you've got your very own Tressider story to tell people.'

'You would seriously prefer to shoot the departure scene last of all?'

'I insist on shooting the departure scene last of all because I shall do it best. That's true, Nigel. And it's true it would help to have gone to Tefuga. Give my love to Major Kadu.'

'I forgot,' muttered Fish. 'He wants to nick one of the trucks.'

Miss Tressider raised her eyebrows.

'The card-play is going to be of less than Olympic standard,' said Jackland. 'I'll tell Malcolm he's got a touch of sunstroke, whatever that may mean.'

Miss Tressider lifted her hand towards him. He touched it with his fingertips as he went past the bed. When he had gone she lay for a while, relaxed beyond languor. Only her face occasionally changed, as if in response to attitudes she was experimenting with in front of some inward mirror. At length she reached to the shelf beside the bed and took from a shallow metal case a volume like a school exercise book, but thicker and better bound. It was composed of sheets of sketch-paper interleaved with ruled pages. Both kinds were covered with large, slanting handwriting in pencil. Miss Tressider closed her eyes and slid a finger at random between two pages. The action was clearly a deliberate ritual. Keeping her finger in the place she put on a pair of large-lensed spectacles, then opened the book and began to read.

FOUR

Thurs Jan 3, 1924

I've had my first fever. Only six days but it seemed weeks. I missed Christmas completely! You get hot and then you get cold and that feels like a day and a night, you see. And the room's dark, of course. It wasn't too bad, actually, rather like flu, only now I'm quivering all through like a gong someone's just finished hitting—that's the quinine, Ted says.

He was terribly worried, poor man. He can't help thinking women are feebler than men but he didn't really want to get the doctor all the way from Birnin Soko, 'cos that would let Mr de Lancey tell Kaduna I was being a nuisance. I told him he was better than a doctor—not just to please him—I really don't want another white man here. Ted slept in his dressing-room and Elongo had a mattress in the dining-room in case I needed anything. They were both marvellous. Too tired to write any more.

Oh, before I stop. KB must have heard somehow. He sent me a present. It was a fever fetish! A thin bone—part of a monkey, Ted thinks—with green feathers tied round one end and stained with something, blood, I think. Rather horrible. Ted says he's going to keep it in his office for next time he has to work through a fever.

Fri Jan 11

We've started our language lessons. Ted says it's a rotten idea me learning Kiti. He thinks I'd do much better learning Arabic, which a few educated people can speak all over the north, but no one talks Kiti except here. I don't care. I'm a terribly ordinary person, I told Ted, but if I become the only woman in the world who speaks Kiti—the only *white* woman, I mean!—then that'll be something a bit extraordinary about me. Ted just said I was the only woman in the world who'd thought fit to get married to him and that was quite enough extraordinariness to be getting on with. That's his idea of a compliment! Isn't he funny!

I'm not surprised no one else talks Kiti—it's a pig! To begin with, you have to sing it, almost, 'cos the same word means different things according to how you pitch it, tiny changes I could hardly hear at first, high to low or low to high, or with a dip in the middle, and so on. And most of the words have strong and weak forms, and you say things quite differently if you're talking to a friend or a stranger—oh, lots more than just words and grammar to learn. Hausa's child's play compared.

For instance, counting. First you go to twenty on your fingers and toes. They all have different names, no pattern at all. The first twenty are man numbers, and the next twenty are baboon numbers, and then fox numbers, then spider numbers, then snake numbers—tho' spiders have eight legs and no fingers or toes and snakes don't have anything at all! But at least you've got to a hundred, so you put a stick on the ground and stand on it to remind yourself and start again! Even Elongo agrees it's funny.

He's a dear. So intelligent and thoughtful. He quite understands that if I teach him English he mustn't put on side about it, specially in front of Ted. If there's one thing Ted hates it's the educated native coming up from Lagos in a suit and a loud tie and talking law-court English and pretending he knows anything about how the real Africans think and feel! I'm teaching Elongo A1 English. No slang. I read ten pages of *Esmond* before lessons to get me in the mood. (Good for me, too!)

Been up a week now, but hardly done any painting. Something called the harmattan started while I was ill—you look out in the morning and you think 'Oh, fog!' but it isn't. It's dust, blowing all the way down from the desert. Cold like fog, tho', specially after malaria. Couple of days back there was a fishing family down on our bank so I went down to do a picture and got them to pose for me. They were v. nice and smiling about it but after they'd been standing still twenty minutes their poor teeth were chattering and they were pale grey all down one side! It made them look like photographic negatives! N.g. for painting. Anyway I'm taking things easy 'cos I've got to get myself properly well 'cos next week we're going on tour!

It's a bit tricky—me going, I mean. There's absolutely no reason why I shouldn't, Ted says, but he ought to inform Mr de Lancey at Birnin Soko only he doesn't want to. You see, 'cos of de L. and Ted being on opposite sides about KB and things he's bound to try and do Ted down over anything Ted wants. He did his d—est to stop me coming at all, for a start, and now he just might try and think of some reason why I shouldn't go on tour. Ted can't go straight to Kaduna over de L.'s head, either. He has to be terribly careful about that. Even if it was something important, they'd come down on him like a ton of bricks. He told me an awful story about an A.D.O. over in Gombe who discovered there was trouble coming and told his D.O. but the D.O. was lazy and didn't do anything so the A.D.O. wrote to the Resident. The Resident agreed with the A.D.O. and when he reported to Kaduna all they were interested in was the A.D.O. breaking the rules. They reprimanded the Resident and they posted the A.D.O. to the worst station they could think of, and then when the trouble broke out and quite a lot of people were murdered and it became obvious the D.O. hadn't been doing his job properly they stuck by him because otherwise it would have shown the Resident and the A.D.O. had been in the right!

I'm glad I'm going. I don't want to stay here alone. It would be horribly easy to work myself into the dumps. Just now, while I was writing, a shower of fine fawn dust floated down onto the page. It came through a place where the ceiling-cloth doesn't quite fit. Some kind of borer is up there, chewing its way through Ted's lovely new timber. Africa's like that. Terribly soon there'll be dust dribbling down everywhere. If I sit very still I think I can hear them, wriggling and munching into our thatch and beams, like the little nasties wriggling around inside me when I had the malaria. We can't give the poor house quinine!

Cheer up, Bets! No use brooding. If only the harmattan would let up—it does, some days—I could ride over to Kiti and do a few pictures. Start outside then ask if I can come in—just getting KB used to the idea. I'm not going to do anything about Elongo's sister for the mo. (It's funny, he doesn't want to talk about her now. Almost as tho' he wishes he'd never said anything. Perhaps when I know a bit more Kiti.) Ted says he doesn't think KB will mind me sketching inside the walls, 'cos he's not a thorough-going Mohammedan. When the Fulani emirs further north pay visits to their Residents the Residents' wives and dogs have to be put somewhere out of sight. The dogs are unclean and the women almost as bad!

Goodness, what a day! Yesterday, I mean. Absolute, absolute luck, everything happening just how I could have prayed for, without me having to do anything to deserve it. And on top of that the three best sketches I'll ever do in my life!

Moment I woke up I felt the harmattan had stopped. Ran to the dining-room and looked down the river. Dawn. River mist. Pale, pearly sky. I could *feel*, tho' it was nice and cool still, there was a scorcher coming! So I rang for Elongo and told him to stop everything and tell Mafote to get Salaki saddled and be ready himself to come with me. Twenty minutes later we were off. My idea was to get two good hours in and be back for breakfast.

Soon as I'd set up outside the main gate of Kiti one of KB's people came out to see what I was up to and I told him in my best Hausa and asked him to send a message to KB saying could I come and do some sketches inside the walls. (Of course I could, without asking, but I wanted to get the horrid old man used to the idea.) Then I started dabbing away. It was only eight o'clock but getting hot already. Fascinating trying to paint that light, so heavy and strong but somehow *thick*. If you get it right you find you've painted the heat as well.

I'd almost finished the first sketch—quite nice—and Elongo was doing his best to keep the flies off me—and the little native children who were almost as bad!—when a squawky trumpet blew and KB and all his 'court'—far more than last time—came out to see how I was getting on!

KB was tickled pink by what I'd done so far but immediately said I'd got to paint him and his court. I did three quick brush sketches, Chinese style, one of the group, one of KB with his waziri, and one of a spearman on his horse. Terribly quick, like a pavement artist, but my hand seemed simply to be longing to paint after the gap and they came out all right. I managed to put enough Hausa together to tell KB they were a present for him, and he immediately sent a servant (a slave, I expect, but we aren't supposed to know that) off to bring me a present in return. It was a live turkey!

Then I pulled my Hausa together and asked KB if I could go and do another picture inside the walls. In fact, I took the bull by the horns and said I'd like to paint his house. He jumped at the idea (thinking about it now I think perhaps he'd already thought

46

of it for himself). I wanted Elongo to come too but everyone was frightfully shocked, including E. Apparently Kitawa don't go inside the walls. Another juju, I suppose, like KB never crossing the river. So I left him outside to look after Salaki and my poor turkey. One of KB's people took my brolly and stool and another insisted on carrying my paints and off we traipsed. KB must be about seventy but he does a good steady waddle. The natives working in the 'gardens' got down on their elbows and knees and put their heads on the ground as we passed.

I was a bit disappointed as we got nearer the palace, 'cos I could see it was going to be a tricky subject. I know I wasn't really there for that, but one doesn't like to waste one's efforts, specially on a day when one feels one's on form, and really there wasn't anything. It was only a wall, you see, cutting off the bottom corner of the space inside the main wall. No windows. Buttresses and a central gate with two towers. In front of the gate, looking quite out of place, a sort of big thatched porch. I could see the tops of buildings inside the wall, rabbit's ears poking up and bits of parapet, and I realized they'd be gone if we got too close, so when we were still a sensible distance away I tried to stop, but KB, soon as he realized, turned round and waved quite angrily at me to come on. My heart jumped. He wanted me to paint the *inside* of his palace!

Some of the courtiers left us at the entrance but four or five followed us in. The rooms were better than I'd expected, almost no furniture, flaky whitewash with coloured patterns round the doors, one or two rugs on the walls sometimes, but airy and cool—by African standards, anyway. KB didn't give me much chance to look. We went out into the sun again. This was better—a sort of courtyard, with two shade-trees only one was half dead, some men under the other one watching a sort of nursery game they play here, moving pebbles around on a pattern in the dust—Ted says they'll play it for hours, and gamble on it like billy-oh. Dark low doorways in the walls and tiny square windows. People going around doing things. KB was in a tearing hurry but I got a bit of a chance to look 'cos a man—some kind of court official, I think—came up to him and grovelled and started to tell him something in a wheedling voice but he'd hardly started when KB put his great foot on the poor man's shoulder and pushed him right over! He roared with laughter, peering at me between his blubbery eyelids to make sure I was enjoying the fun, then waddled on to one of the dark little doors.

All the courtiers stood aside. I hesitated but KB waved at me to follow. Inside I got a terrible shock, 'cos straight in front of me was an enormous fat man with a naked sword, grinning at me with cruel thick lips. There was a vile sour smell in the room. I think it came from him. KB said something to him and waddled straight on through to the next room, which was smaller still —not much bigger than our bathroom at The Warren and quite empty except for the man with the sword. The doors were crooked to each other. KB slipped through like an owl popping into its hole and I followed. The next room was tiny too, and almost dark—just the light from its two doors—crooked to each other again—and beyond that another one, lighter tho', 'cos it was leading out into the open. *Two* guards with swords here. The same smell. As I bent to go through the outside door—they really were tiny, I'm only five foot one!—I saw two black bare feet on the sunlit earth in front of me. The legs the feet belonged to were kneeling. There was a silver bracelet round one ankle, and the hem of a dark blue skirt.

All in a blink I understood. KB was taking me into his harem! The men with the swords were eunuchs, and the funny crooked entrance rooms were like that so you couldn't see right through from the outside. I remembered how KB had looked at me when we first met and a mad horrible idea crossed my mind and I'm afraid I actually turned half round to run away. It was no use. The other door was blocked by one of the eunuchs coming through. It was like the worst possible nightmare for a mo, but then I saw he was carrying my parasol and paints and stool, and—I don't know why—that told me I was just being silly. Nobody would dare. They know what would happen if they did. I think the eunuchs guessed, tho', from the way they grinned.

A hammering noise had begun outside and when I got through the door I found KB banging away with a sort of cudgel at an old bit of carved black plank which was hanging by the doorway. There were about a dozen women, the two or three nearest grovelling to KB and the ones further off just sitting. Soon as I showed up they started to stare. I thought that was all his wives but almost at once more of them came. More and more. They *oozed* from tiny doors which must have had little dark rooms behind them—hardly a window anywhere. I began counting but lost track almost at once 'cos of the way they kept appearing, around sixty in the end, I should think, all sorts milling around and staring at me in a vague, scared way, pale cattle Fulani and black Hausa and dark brown little women with terrific face-scars, and glossy Kitawa and three who I think must have been half-castes—half-*Chinese*, one of them—and a tall purply-black girl with huge bones like a horse and her hair knotted into yellow beads, and others too—Africa's extraordinary like that, how *many* there are! They were all dressed in long, loose, wrap-around cotton, worn like a plaid, with a different coloured skirt, mostly rather dirty. Some of them didn't look more than about thirteen, and none of them very old, though KB's seventy. Only half a dozen children that I could see, clinging to their mothers like babies tho' they were much too big for that.

I've made it sound rather picturesque, but really I felt absolutely sick to look at them. It was *disgusting.* Like being in a farmyard—not 'cos it was dirty which it wasn't specially, but 'cos the women weren't people. They were cattle. They stared at me with dark stupid cow-eyes. They didn't know anything, they didn't do anything, they were just herded into this place and kept here for that filthy, fat, leering old brute to—I *will* write it—to copulate with. It was so shocking I almost fainted, not 'cos of the heat or the smells, but the absolute horror of it. But I clenched my teeth and told myself this was what I'd chosen and I'd got to go through with it. I tried to smile at them but they didn't smile back.

There was a shade-tree here too so I turned away and started to set up my easel while KB went strolling among his women picking out the prize ones for me to paint. Some of the others rolled huge clay pots out from inside and dragged out special clothes, grander and brighter than what they were wearing. KB chose who should be dressed in what for her picture. I was ready ages before he was so I started a quick practice sketch of the courtyard with KB pushing his wives around—my hand was absolutely aching to paint. The flies were a nuisance so I called out in Hausa for a whisk and KB turned and pushed one of the women towards me—only a girl, really, about fourteen. She hadn't understood what she was supposed to do but soon as I

49

showed her she whisked away. I wasn't really paying attention to her 'cos my sketch was going so well. It was only a cartoon, really, but I think it was 'cos I was so furious with KB and couldn't say so that it came alive, the way they sometimes do.

By now a few of the other women had drifted over to watch what I was doing and got interested. Soon I had a real audience. At least it meant there were more people for the flies to land on and someone kneeling on the other side fanning away and someone fanning behind for the privilege of standing near the Great Artist! They began to chatter and comment. I only had to run a block of shadow down a wall and they'd all sigh with appreciation, and when I took a fresh sheet of paper and started to do a serious sketch of the courtyard—straight off with the brush, risking absolutely everything, dashing it in—and at first they couldn't make out what the blobs and lines were meant to be and then someone realized and a brown arm would come over my shoulder and point and explain and point at the right bit of a building—oh, the chatter and laughter! I simply had to carry on. I wanted to, anyway, but this was probably the most exciting thing that had happened to those poor girls for months!

I hadn't really finished that one when KB was ready at last and paraded his prize cattle in front of me. He wanted them as a group but by now my blood was really up and I refused to let that fat devil tell me what to paint, as if he owned me and my brushes as well as those unlucky women! I jumped off my stool and chose the ones I wanted and smiled at them as I posed them and then rushed back and slapped and dabbed them onto the paper, fast as my hand would move, never a hair wrong. I just knew my hand would do it without me having to think, tho' it was a great help having had a bit of practice with the skin colours on the way up river. I don't know. Even if I'd never tried to paint a black skin before I think I'd have got it right. That's how I felt yesterday—quite, quite certain that my hand would do what my eye was seeing, as tho' there was nothing else of me between them. Oh, if only it was always . . . no, I suppose not. Mustn't be greedy, Bets.

I did a group of three, one of them carrying a dark red jar on her head. They stood like queens, and so still in that blazing sun. And those beautiful bright robes. Then I did the big woman with the horse-bones and the yellow beads—not at all beautiful, but interesting. I wonder why KB chose her—so much I'll never know. I did her standing beside a pale thin Fulani woman—a complete contrast except for the lovely native dignity. The Fulani was wearing earth green and ochre stripes and the horse-face the most marvellous royal blue edged with gold, which set off the blue-shot lights in her skin to perfection. I wonder if KB chose it on purpose for her. If so he's really got an eye, in spite of being so horrible every way else! Then I did four sitting in a pose like a Victorian photo. That came out just right too. And then, snap, it was over. I was exhausted. Drained. I only just had strength to clean my brushes and put them away. When the women understood they sighed, all together, slow and soft.

Something interesting. Oh, what a futile way to say it! *Something really important!* While I was painting the women my audience behaved quite differently from before. Perfect decorum. Silence. Stillness. We might have been in church. Yes, awe. I know what that funny word means now. Perhaps they're better at feeling it than we are in spoilt Europe. I don't mean awe at me or what I was doing. There was something there, working through me—not just me, all of us—a force, a spirit, something to do with us all being women. They gathered it, standing behind and around me, and then it came funnelling through me into the pictures I was painting, making them special. I don't believe, however much practice I have, I'll ever do anything as good as those three sketches in my whole life.

Of course the only one who didn't understand was the Emir. He'd been sitting over to one side having a snack (goodness, I was hungry!) which some other women had brought him, so he didn't notice at once that it was all over. I'd put my paints and brushes away and turned to say thank you to the child who was still kneeling beside me, whisking the flies off. Then I saw that she was a Bakiti. Do you know, from the moment I'd had my fright just before I came into the courtyard, right through till now, I hadn't even tried to look for Elongo's sister. There'd been too much else—that scare, and then the horror of finding what it must be like for them in the harem, and then of course the painting. Anyway, I do know how to say thank you in Kiti, so I said it. She looked surprised for a moment, and then she smiled. Such a smile! I told her my name and she was starting to wish me a strong spirit before she told me hers (it's all terrifically formal among the Kitawa when strangers meet) but just then horrible KB came barging up and interrupted. He stared pop-eyed at the girl as tho' he was going to eat her and she lost her smile and got down on the ground and grovelled. I showed him the pictures and he was pleased—tho' of course he thought I'd been painting for him—but I wouldn't let him keep them. I told him, *very* firmly, that I'd got more work to do on them and he could have them when I'd finished. Now I suppose I'll have to do copies for him. I'm certainly not going to let him have the real ones, those women as they were made to be in their beauty and their pride. He doesn't own them like that!

I was almost dropping with exhaustion and hunger but KB insisted on dragging me off to show me his bed. It is huge. Brass knobs. From Birmingham, I should think. On the way out I was stupid enough to look properly at the black board he'd banged to call the women out. I thought the carvings might be interesting. Such a fool. Revolting, of course. The usual thing. KB pretended to be shocked that I'd looked but he was amused, really. And inquisitive. And then so rude all of a sudden. He just took me to the first of the entrance rooms and told one of the eunuchs to see me out and went scurrying back to his women. Or his meal, I suppose. I hope so. Poor things.

Lukar was waiting for me in the palace courtyard. Ted had sent him to find out where I'd got to. Believe it or not I'd been four and a quarter hours in the harem! When I looked at my watch and saw I suddenly felt so done in that I could hardly walk as far as the Town gate. Elongo was there, patient as ever, looking after Salaki and my turkey. He had to lift me into the saddle—Lukar didn't think of helping—but E.'s stronger than you'd think. Then he took the reins and led me home. Poor Ted was furious with me for overdoing things in the heat of the day, just after a fever, and I was too tired to explain. We were having our first proper quarrel—at least he was—when I fell asleep in the middle of it! He picked me up and put me to bed and I didn't wake up till supper.

He was being terribly apologetic about losing his rag and I was saying it was all my fault and he was quite right except that it just happened, and then I noticed he was eating with only his left hand. Poor man, something frightful has happened to his right arm, and he hadn't even told me! He's a saint about things like that. It's called a guinea worm. He wouldn't think of sending for a doctor all the way from Soko, so we dealt with it after supper. I was v. nearly sick several times. It's just a swelling like a boil, but you have to lance it and then there's this thready thing inside and you get hold of the end and you take a match-stick (really!) and wrap the end round and begin to wind it out. You wind a little each day and then strap the match down again. It's absolutely vital not to break the worm 'cos then it dies and goes bad inside you. Poor Ted. The only good thing was he couldn't have done it without me, using only his left hand. He really did need me. That was nice. There are so many ways Africa can be horrible, but men like Ted still love it!

Wed Jan 16
I wrote all that yesterday morning when I still felt that doing the pictures in the harem was the most important thing I'd ever have happen to me. Well, almost. Like saying 'Yes' to Ted. 'Cos of the guinea worm I'd been too busy to try and tell Ted—and, you know, it's funny but I don't think I quite understood how important it was myself till I'd written it down. Anyway, yesterday lunch-time I showed him the pictures and tried to tell him. He pretended to understand how good they were (dear man), but he couldn't help showing that he was only pretending to be interested because my painting is something that stops me being bored, so it doesn't matter whether what I do is any good or not. I might just as well be playing patience! So I gave up after a bit and just chatted, but I was rather disappointed. Silly of me. I can't expect him to understand.

Then he rode down river in the afternoon to try and settle some kind of dispute about fishing rights which KB was supposed to have dealt with months ago, so I sent for Elongo for a Kiti lesson. I told him I thought I might have seen his sister in the harem and I tried to describe the girl and told her she'd smiled when I'd talked to her and so on, but do you know he wasn't very interested either! After all that! I could have wept. The trouble is we don't both know enough of any of our languages to have a proper conversation. We can say, 'The monkey is in the tree,' or 'Bring me fresh tea,' but nothing like 'I'm feeling a bit low because I had a terribly important and exciting experience two days ago and now it's beginning to fade away as tho' it was only a dream.' Real talk doesn't start till you can say things like that. E. *did* say, 'My sister is happy,' but I don't know whether he meant someone else had told him or that he was just guessing 'cos I'd seen her smiling (if it was her).

By supper I was in a proper dump. I'd made it worse by starting to copy my pictures for horrible KB, and even the real ones started looking like just coloured water on paper—nothing *in* them. Ted thought I must have another fever coming on 'cos I do my best in the evenings to be cheerful and chatty and interested 'cos that's what I'm here for. I couldn't stop thinking about those women. And me. I mean, how different *am* I? Really different? In the end I thought I'd do best to get it off my chest—not about me, of course—that'd be hopeless with Ted —but them.

Ted wasn't very sympathetic.

'You're looking at it with white eyes,' he said. 'If you could get inside their minds you'd probably find they thought of themselves as extremely fortunate. They are fed and clothed and protected and they have a minimum of work to do. That's the African's idea of paradise.'

'They're hardly *alive*, darling. The women I saw on the market stalls down river were having a better time selling a couple of yams. Twenty times better!'

'That's another white illusion, judging Africa by the river life. You'll see when we go on tour how most Africans live.'

'But these ones aren't even living, darling. That's what I'm trying to tell you!'

'Well, accepting that, which I don't, but for the sake of argument. What are you going to do about it? Or rather, what do you propose I and Kaduna and Lagos and London should do about it? It's a central element in a whole way of life.'

'Oh, nonsense, darling. What earthly difference would it make if Kama Boi had one wife and treated her like a human being?'

'It would make all the difference in the world. Everything here depends on authority. Who gives orders, who accepts them, and why. Why is the most important. The native has to recognize your right to rule. You have to keep showing him your reasons. You can't show him the real reasons, of course. We can't send out the soldiers and shoot someone once a week, so we keep a

54

flag in front of the house and run it up and down. It is a juju—a way of saying without doing.'

'I don't see what that's got to do with Kama Boi keeping women like cattle.'

'Being able to send for the soldiers isn't the only source of power. In Africa if you are believed to have magical powers that can be just as important. Down south you got kings who only appeared to their people once a year. They shut themselves away and ruled by mystery. I often think we owe a bit to that, you know. The white man is incomprehensible, therefore mysterious, therefore magical. In the pagan tribes it's mostly a matter of tradition. Up in the north, it's . . . let's call it greatness. You have to keep showing the people you are a great man. You have robes, and processions, and you get given presents and dish out titles and so on. And you have more possessions than anyone else. More slaves in the old days. More wives.'

'More cows, you mean!'

'That's the cattle Fulani . . . Oh, I see what you're getting at. It's something everyone understands, Rabbit.'

'I don't believe that was all Kama Boi was thinking about when he insisted on showing me his collection.'

'It was certainly one of the things he was thinking about. He was boasting.'

'Why wives? Why's it got to be those wretched women? Why not horses or . . . or *stamps*? Our king collects stamps. Why shouldn't he?'

'Because people wouldn't understand. This is a semi-paganized area. Kama Boi himself is only dubiously a Muslim. People here have a very primitive view of power. When I was over south of Gombe in 'twenty-one the local chief, a nominal Muslim like Kama Boi, took a cracking fall out hunting. He was stunned, out cold for twenty minutes, and groggy for the rest of the day. Spite of that, the first thing his followers did when they saw he wasn't going to die was round up a local corvée—it was a pagan area—and set them to building a hut. Then they sent a couple of chaps to the nearest village to choose a suitable girl. The chief married her on the spot—I doubt if he had much notion what was happening, tell you the truth—and took her to the hut that night. Divorced her first thing next morning and sent her home with five shillings. She was as pleased as Punch and so I bet were the village. But the thing that mattered was that all the people had been shown their chief was still fit to rule over them.'

Ted always talks slowly. He doesn't like saying anything he hasn't thought about, but you know he *has* thought. I'm just the opposite, quick and silly! During that last bit he'd been talking extra slow 'cos he was trying to get his pipe going. The shadows sort of came and went as he sucked at the flame. It was almost like looking at two people, dear old Ted and then, suddenly, sharp black shadows like a painted mask, a devil-mask. Then Ted again. I could see he was a bit excited by the story—excited about telling it to *me*.

'Well, I think it's perfectly disgusting,' I said. 'And if I had my way I'd stop it, whatever you say about power and things. I think people should only give orders when they know what's best, and other people should only take orders when they can see it's a good idea. I always thought that was why we're here, 'cos we're doing the Africans good.'

'That may be our justification to ourselves,' said Ted, 'but I think you'd find it hard to get more than a handful of natives, rulers or ruled, to accept it. They might tell you they accepted it, but that's just another aspect of the same thing. Rulers get told what they wish to hear.'

'That still doesn't stop it being disgusting.'

'Shall we change the subject? What about a dancing lesson?'

'All right. You needn't put your pipe out.'

It's really extraordinary, this business of s * *. I don't understand myself at all. I didn't really feel like dancing but I felt guilty about arguing with the poor man and sounding snappy and cross when I'm supposed to be jolly, especially with his poor arm hurting, so I felt I had to. I don't like myself when I'm snappy, either. Ted's a rotten dancer but I'm doing my best with him. I tell him I'm going to make him a real lady-killer by the time we go on leave next spring. (Next spring!) So we turned the lamps down and cleared the chairs aside and wound up the gramophone and fox-trotted round on the smoothest patch of floor with the moon yellow along the river and Ted sucking at his pipe over my shoulder. 'Cos of his sling he had to hold me closer than's really right—for a lesson, anyway—and then by the time we'd wound the gramophone up once or twice Ted had put his pipe down so that we could have some baccy-ey kisses and I could feel the hardness growing under his trousers which made me remember KB's horrible plank but it didn't seem to matter—in fact 'cos of the shadows from the lamps or something I could see how Ted's dear face and the devil-mask really were the same thing and that was rather exciting—very exciting, so that I stopped dancing while the gramophone still had plenty of wind in it and told Ted to count slowly to fifty (just time to put my thingy in) and scampered off to the bedroom.

And then you change again. I'm not saying it 'cos of doing it—in fact, that was lovely—we really *are* getting cleverer, both of us!—but I woke up in the middle of the night and found I was thinking about KB and his plank and his wives, and how Daddy treated Mummy, and Ted—not my dear own Ted but someone else in the same body, breathing thickly beside me—one of *them*. They've made the whole world the shape they want it and we've got to fit in the corners they've left, and I'm simply not going to stand for it! I'm going to do something about it. I'm going to start by doing something about KB and his wives. I don't know what, yet, but I really am. And then I went to sleep.

The funny thing is that usually that kind of night idea turns out complete nonsense in the morning, but this one didn't. I still feel like that, or at least part of me does. It's real. You've made yourself a promise, Bets, and you're going to keep it.

FIVE

The road to Kiti was appalling. Though in the fairly recent past it had been surfaced with tarmac, this had apparently been done with no other preparation than a levelling of the old earth surface, and the quality of the tarmac itself may well have been dubious. At one point the truck passed, rusting in a small clearing, one of the machines which had been imported to do the work and then had never been reclaimed, it being in no one's interest to do so. Indeed it could be said that since this section of road led almost nowhere the real function of the machine had been completed before it had ever crossed the river. K.H.P., the Kiti Highway Project, of which the machine and this road were only a minuscule fragment, had allowed a large number of people in London, Lagos, Birnin Soko and elsewhere to make a great deal of money for themselves. The actual laying of the tarmac on the ground had been little more than a concluding ritual, gone through to propitiate the eventual Commission of Enquiry. A sepulchre for the whitewash to adhere to. Rain, heat, and the upthrust of suckers from the roots of inadequately cleared scrub had broken the road surface up, but not yet down. A pot-hole was usually feet, not inches, deep and surrounded by the boulders churned from it. The best patches were now those where the worst tarmac had been used, and had soon crumbled into soft dark gravel. Elsewhere it was seldom safe to exceed a walking pace.

Jackland was steering his way up out of a road-wide crater when the roar of the Landrover's engine was drowned for the moment by a clatter from the rear seat as the soldier lounging there loosed off a burst of automatic fire at a heron passing overhead. Jackland finished the climb and stopped with the engine idling.

'Please tell him not to do that,' he said. 'I'm only used to London traffic.'

Major Kadu had apparently been going to ignore the incident —had not in fact blinked or moved a muscle, as though actually deaf to the racket—but now turned and spoke briskly to the man in Hausa. Two minutes later the same thing happened, again at a point where driving demanded extra care, though this time there seemed to be not even the excuse of a target. Jackland braked, switched the engine off and twisted round. The soldier —one of the pair to whom Pittapoulos was said to have supplied the vodka—laughed in his face.

'Get out,' said Jackland.

'You scared from just bit noise?' said the soldier.

'Get out,' said Jackland.

There was not exactly a clash of wills, though Jackland gazed at the soldier with firm and focused authority. The soldier gazed back but somehow seemed not to meet the stare. He did not accept Jackland's command, but nor did he challenge it directly. He appeared to be in that stage of post-inebriation where sporadic efforts are made to return to the high spirits of drunkenness, followed by relapses into the sullenness of the coming hangover. The confrontation was like a charge of crack cavalry into a bog. At last Major Kadu, who would clearly have preferred to ignore the whole episode, turned stiff-faced and gave orders. For a moment it looked as though they might not be obeyed, but then the man scrambled out, scowling. Jackland drove on, leaving him standing in the middle of the road and making tentative motions with his gun, like a beaten batsman rehearsing the stroke he might have played.

'Thank you, Major,' said Jackland. 'The walk ought to sweat it out of him, with luck. As it happens we may be better off without him.'

Major Kadu did not answer but sat erect in his seat, staring forward. He may simply have been trying to dissociate himself from the display of indiscipline, but he gave the impression of being engaged in some spiritual exercise, contemplation perhaps of the pure Military Idea, purged of all material content. His behaviour from the first had been enigmatic. Having arrived on the scene apparently by accident, on his way to Kiti, he had immediately begun to behave, though with absolute correctness, as though his whole purpose in being there was to obstruct shooting. As soon as the Sarkin had driven off he had asserted himself, refusing to let Burn organize the assembled extras and spectators to shift the launch on the grounds that they were likely to damage military property. He had then put guards on it, and himself bivouacked alongside their camp-site, a couple of hundred yards down stream. This morning he had used Pitta-poulos's attempt to shift the launch by stealth as an excuse to seal the whole landing-stage area off.

The film-team's natural assumption had been that they were dealing with a bureaucratic technique they were now well used to, the erection of an obstructive maze which the official in question could then demand payment for guiding them through. Burn's attempt to act on this after the incident with the vodka had met with a reaction which seemed to make it clear that the problem was not that the bribe had been inadequate. This raised the more alarming possibility that the Major, discovering the film-team on his patch, was preventing their doing anything until he received orders from his superiors. Even after sixty years the Tefuga Incident might be thought a sensitive one. It had required careful manipulation of political factions as well as a number of cash gifts to get permission to shoot any of the film in Nigeria; in fact but for the intervention of Sarkin Elongo this might never have been given. If the Army chose to reopen the question at this point it would mean at the very least a costly delay. It was in the hope of exploring this possibility that Jackland had been so amenable to Major Kadu's demand to be driven to Kiti, and had chosen to do the job himself. So far, despite several efforts, he had elicited only a few monosyllables. Now, though, the Major suddenly spoke.

'And how better off, Mr Jackland?'

'We've been having a minor problem. You'll see when we get there. But I don't think it's the sort of thing you want a gun for. Hold on a mo.'

Conversation became impossible again as Jackland changed down for a detour round a burnt-out truck that entirely blocked the road. To judge by the subsidiary track which had been beaten round it the obstacle had been there for some months. Beyond it the surface suddenly improved. The road they had been using was in fact no more than an improvised spur from the official road to the K.H.P. fish-factory, whose mammoth but never-used sheds lay invisible behind the tree-line to their right. Ahead now, as the truck buzzed along through the scrub, rose the dusky red line of the wall of Old Kiti.

Once again, surprisingly, it was the Major who picked up the thread of conversation.

'In the end, Mr Jackland, is nothing else.'

'Than what, old man?'

'Than the gun. Even when the British were here this was so. They gave us new laws, which we obeyed. Why? Not out of admiration for these laws. Everybody could see that the British appointed rulers who were stupid or corrupt and who ignored the laws while the British looked the other way. So why? Because behind these their laws was the gun. First the Native Police and the Native Courts. Then the British police and the British courts. Then the soldiers with their guns. In the end, the gun.'

'The trouble with that, Major, is that the gun has limited usefulness. You can point it at a chap and say "Do this" and he probably will, but it's different when you try saying "Be this". In particular things like "Be public-spirited" or "Be efficient". Bumming around the globe in the course of earning my pittance I've seen a whole range of political systems, and I promise you that for all the inefficiencies of democracy, which I admit can be ghastly enough, the inefficiencies of force outweigh them every time.'

The brief flow of conversation had been accompanied by easier driving. The road curved in towards the tree belt and joined, immediately below the cliff and wall of Old Kiti, a splendid six-lane highway. To the left it ran in a straight line through the scrub belt as far as the eye could see. To the right, just before it reached the river, it turned up a cutting hacked from the cliff. Though presumably the same age as the spur road it seemed to have been built to first-class standards. Not a pot-hole marred its surface. There was no traffic on it at all. At the northern end of the town wall a rubbish-tip had begun to encroach on the southbound lane. This was the spine of the K.H.P. network, and represented a major outpouring of funds from the Federal Government in the effort to open up this remote province. Jackland swung the truck on to the highway.

'I do not argue to this point,' said the Major. 'Agreed, in only the sports field the gun can say "Go!" All other places it must say "Stop!" Soon I show you one instance.'

Talk again became impossible as Jackland changed down to take the abrupt curve and drive up the steep slope between the booming rock walls of the cutting. They emerged on the upper level with the highway ahead of them running between the Old Town wall and the river. The moat had been filled in to take the inner lane, but this had been narrowed again by an erratic line of shanty-houses built along it, using the wall for stability.

'Stop here, please,' said the Major. 'Now, consider this.'

He nodded towards the river, churning in yellow hummocks and cream foam over the upper boulders of the rapids and then roaring down the slope. Spray floated in the breezeless air, dank but welcome. The huge weight of water produced the usual if inexplicable effect of deep, almost tragic satisfaction in the spectator, but it did not wholly dominate the scene. It was partnered in the unintentional aesthetic effort by something man-made. From the further bank projected in the clean curves of modern engineering the first five arches of a bridge, its huge piers based on the bed-rock of the rapids. The final span was missing, but though this gave the bridge the attractive melancholy of a great ruin, the West African equivalent of Wordsworth's Tintern Abbey, it was not literally one. The bridge had never been completed. A swaying rope footbridge was all that spanned the final gap.

This morning the already visually thrilling effect was enhanced by the presence of three human beings, as minute in the large-scaled scene as figures in a Poussin landscape. In the channel of the second arch a fisherman had constructed a spillikin-like network of timber to which to attach his fish-traps. He was attending to them at this moment, a grizzled old figure, his naked body shining with spray as he hoisted himself through his web. A ten-year-old child followed him, copying every move. On the stub of roadway above them a cherry-red Datsun had been parked. A young woman wearing jeans and a violet blouse was in the process of locking its doors. These two pricks of unnatural colour, the paint of the car and the silk of the blouse, focused the whole scene. Jackland evidently felt so, for he held his hands up with index-fingers and thumbs squared against each other, making a screen-shaped frame for him to look through.

'Do you know why the bridge is never finished?' said the Major.

'Money ran out, I gather. Some kind of jiggery pokery.'

'The Sarkin diverted major part of the funds to build himself one new palace.'

'Not our friend Sarkin Elongo, I imagine.'

'His predecessor. The present Sarkin gave evidence to the Commission. This is not my point. These people only do these things because they are operating in system where is nobody to stop them. No sanction of custom, of tolerable dealing. You destroy all that. You leave us only the sanction of the gun.'

'You don't think something of the sort would have happened if we'd never come? No colonial powers, I mean. No slave trade, even. It seems to me that the current mode for blaming everything on us—or rather, if I may say so, our predecessors, for we do enough breast-beating ourselves now, in all conscience— this seems to me a classic example of trying to write history as it might have been. Europe would still have been there, you know. Some kind of infection would have taken place. Whether it would have been better or worse, who's to tell?'

Once again as he spoke Jackland raised his hands to frame the bridge and river. The young woman was now walking away from the car towards the footbridge, dissolving with every step the satisfying focus of the original scene. The Major, though no doubt familiar with the commonplaces of the colonial argument, had paused before replying. Jackland took the chance, and the excuse of his own gesture, to move the discussion, not too wrenchingly, nearer the subject of his own real interest.

'I could have used that if I'd spotted it sooner,' he said. 'Oh, I don't know. There's so much you can't fit in without raising extraneous questions. It would have done for a straight documentary, though.'

'You are making this your film about the Tefuga Incident?' said the Major, so readily that it was apparent that he too had been waiting his chance.

'Not exactly. We're making a film about my mother's experiences as the young wife of a colonial official. The deposition of Kama Boi and the Tefuga Incident happened while she was here. We couldn't have avoided them. The whole thing's practically finished—we're just here to do a spot of tidying up. We hadn't planned to go out to Tefuga at all, but now it looks as though we're going to have a free afternoon so some of us might make the trip.'

'The project is almost complete, you say?'

'Pretty well. We've seen the first rushes. The rest of it should be waiting for us in London when we get back.'

'I see.'

Having made all the points he wished, with complete truth if some disingenuousness, Jackland reached forward to switch the ignition on. As he did so he took a last glance towards the scene on the bridge. Seeing his head turn the young woman raised an arm in a waving gesture, a quite clear signal that she wished to make contact. Jackland took his hand from the switch and sat back, watching her come.

'You know this woman?' said the Major.

'Not yet,' said Jackland.

Despite her high heels the woman negotiated the swaying planks of the footbridge with complete confidence, and once on dry land came forward with long, elastic steps. The heels and her skin-tight jeans gave her the stilt-legged look of those Nubian dancers shown in Egyptian friezes and still, amazingly, performing (at least for touring TV crews) in their desert settlements. The insect-like effect was enhanced by enormous opaque sunglasses. Her skin was mid-brown, the wiry black hair cropped close on the small round skull. She looked in her early twenties.

'Mr Jackland?' she said, holding out a card. 'I am Annie Boyaba, A.N.B.C.'

The card confirmed the information, adding that A.N.B.C. was 'The Voice of the West'.

'I am hoping that you will grant me the honour of an interview,' she said.

Her voice was crisply English, almost absurdly so. Shut your eyes and you might have been listening to minor royalty.

Jackland smiled, not apparently at her but at some sudden private thought.

'This is Major Kadu of the Nigerian Army,' he said. 'We'll give you a lift into town and talk about it there. Let Miss Boyaba up, Major. She will provide excellent camouflage. By the same token, I wonder if you would mind removing your cap.'

'What is this for?' said the Major.

Jackland smiled yet more broadly. His pale blue eyes sparkled beneath the jutting brows.

'Please,' he said. 'I want it to be a surprise.'

With obvious doubt the Major moved to the centre of the bench seat and took off his cap, revealing short iron-grey hair. Miss Boyaba climbed up and Jackland drove on. The highway, though built mainly to link with the unfinished bridge, continued along the line of the old road as far as the ferry, skirting New Kiti, a sprawl of buildings ranging from two-storey breeze-block houses to iron-roofed huts, none at all pleasing. It was still barely a town, having expanded far less than most Nigerian conurbations. The hinterland of Kiti was too thinly populated to swell it greatly, and most of those with the initiative to leave their villages had also perceived its hopelessness as a place of opportunity and moved on, at least as far as Birnin Soko. Its only truly town-like feature was the fine tree-lined avenue that cut through the architectural mess and ended at the twin towers of the Old Town Gate. Beneath the trees spread Kiti Market, a drifting crowd of men and women between rows of stalls selling the usual hotchpotch—ingredients for traditional dyes, cassette players and radios, plastic kitchenware, magical drugs, brass trinkets, cheap imported cotton, cans of oil, the locally abundant fish already reeking with the heat under a maze of flies. The only variation from the standard African market was a queue of patients waiting at the W.H.O. clinic for treatment for river-blindness contracted in the spray of the rapids; also, perhaps, the absence of tourist-ware. It was the apparently least successful traders who gave the market its sense of being a timeless custom rather than a transitory commercial convenience—an old woman sitting beside a basket of dark orange beans, a child from the hinterland with nothing but a single kid to sell.

At the entrance to the avenue the police had set up a road-block, partly to extract unofficial tolls on the excuse of inspecting permits, and partly for the pleasure of browbeating, and occasionally just beating, those who came. Two policemen manned the block. Both carried guns, though one wore jeans instead of his uniform trousers. Another four drank beer with their friends under an awning commandeered from a nearby stall. The men on the block waved the Landrover to a halt. The one on Jackland's side rested the muzzle of his gun on the door.

'Where you steal this truck, now,' he shouted.

He was fairly drunk, the road-block being a self-financing binge that ran from Christmas through the New Year. Miss Boyaba's presence may have stimulated an extra show of aggressiveness, but he seemed not to have noticed Major Kadu.

'This was the problem I was talking about, Major,' said Jackland, completely ignoring the soldier. 'I wonder if you could make, ah, representations.'

The Major hesitated. This was another example of Jackland's characteristic behaviour, too deliberate to be described merely as tactlessness, the streak of the gambler that led him to take risks over personal relationships and to play what were almost practical jokes on the moral level, though he would have been far more cautious about, and less amused by, purely physical dangers and pratfalls. The policeman rattled his gun-barrel on the metal of the door. The Major put his cap on and stood up.

It was an odd movement, but sandwiched as he was between Jackland and Miss Boyaba he may have felt it was the only means by which he could assert his presence. Certainly it achieved that effect. The arrival of a car driven by a European and the bellowing of the policeman at it had already attracted mild interest along the nearer stalls. The sudden emergence of an Army officer, standing aloft and holding the top of the windscreen with one hand as if he were the central figure on some grand parade, produced an actual gasp, silence, a few murmurs, and then a single hoarse shout, clearly of welcome, from somewhere at the back of the crowd. The shout was taken up in several places and became a general bay, attracting attention from further and further down the avenue. Standing as he was, the Major could be seen from the furthest end. The shouting grew. Even the river-blind turned inquisitive milky eyes to try and stare, as though their saviour had come who would heal them at a touch. The crowd began to move in, but those nearest the truck stood their ground, not knowing any more than the Major what was expected of them.

Meanwhile in this, say, twenty seconds, the policeman had fallen back a pace allowing Jackland to open the door and get out, and the men under the awning had jumped up, gathering equipment and uniform and at the same time trying to shoo their cronies out of sight. Their corporal lined them up and came

66

over with a straight-spined marching step. He snapped up a salute, disciplined but not deferential, one power waiting formal confrontation with another. The effect was partly spoilt by his having put on a cap belonging to a colleague with a quite different skull-shape. Its brim only touched in two places, so that it teetered at every move.

The Major glanced down at him, but before descending to his level raised his right arm palm-forward to the crowd, a gesture which clearly showed that he too recognized and accepted his role as the expected saviour. A cheer rose, criss-crossed as it died away with shouts of anger. The crowd began to move again as the Major climbed down. As soon as he was clear Jackland slipped into the driving-seat and nudged the truck forward through the mob. This was only in fact a few hundred people and the road was wide enough to allow some movement, so that after the first twenty yards he was almost clear, though one or two late-comers to the crush insisted on leaning into the car and shaking his hand to congratulate him on the part he had played in the epiphany.

'God,' he said. 'I didn't mean to start anything like that. I must apologize for dragging you in.'

'But it was marvellous, wonderful,' said Miss Boyaba. 'Everything in this country has been so . . . You know, Mr Jackland, often I have felt positively sick to be Nigerian.'

She pushed her spectacles up on to her forehead and stared at him with large and earnest eyes. She was younger than she had seemed at first approach, very appealing in her naïve vehemence. Before Jackland could answer, the hubbub at the top of the avenue was pierced by two shots. It died away, then rose on a sharper note.

'Quick,' said Miss Boyaba. 'They will shut the gates.'

Indeed as Jackland drove towards the Old Town entrance two men in loose white cotton robes were dragging one leaf of the main gate across the archway. Jackland sounded his horn. They did not look up. Miss Boyaba rose and shouted in Hausa. The word 'Sarkin' was part of the phrase. The men stopped and waved the truck urgently through, but now apparently recognizing Miss Boyaba called a greeting to her as she passed. Jackland braked in the clear arena inside the gateway and looked back at the closing door.

'I suppose the Major's all right,' he said. 'I feel a bit responsible . . .'

'Oh, they won't hurt *him!* He's what they've been waiting for. We've all been longing for something like this to happen.'

'You're a local, then?'

'I meant everyone in Nigeria, but actually I am sort of quarter-local. We used to come up often for holidays. The Sarkin is my great-uncle, you see.'

'Is he indeed? These things have their uses. Um, I take it your selection to do this interview is not an entire coincidence?'

Miss Boyaba had pulled her spectacles down, but now, despite the hazy but powerful glare of mid-morning she pushed them up again and looked at Jackland with deliberately widened eyes.

'I'm afraid I haven't been quite straight with you, Mr Jackland,' she said. 'I'm only a trainee, really. Our head reporter wanted to do an interview with Mary Tressider but your publicity people turned her down. This was when you were at Ilorin. But when I heard you were up in Kiti I went to my boss and said because of the Sarkin being my great-uncle I might be able to wangle an interview here. It's how things work in Nigeria, you see.'

'And elsewhere.'

'But really it was you I was longing to meet.'

'Speaking as an old hand to a trainee I'd say you'd started off on the right foot but now you're overdoing it slightly.'

'Oh, no. I promise. Ever since I first saw your name—it was on a programme you did about President Marcos, actually—I've been hoping one day you'd come to Nigeria. That's true. That's why I was desperate to wangle the job. If you can spare me ten minutes I'll tell you.'

'Sounds as though we may have more than that,' said Jackland, jerking his head towards the continuing clamour from beyond the gateway. 'I want to go and check what's happening down at the Old Palace. Apart from that I have no pressing engagements. On the other hand, it's a bit hot here.'

'Let's go to Uncle Elongo's. That's what we call him, you know.'

'Is that all right?'

'Of course.'

From immediately inside the gate the Old Town seemed hardly to have altered since Betty Jackland had described it in her diary. Two or three cars and an ancient truck were parked in the gateway arena; a radio wailed Cairo-style rock from an upper floor; but otherwise there were the same thick-walled mud buildings and the same allotment-like strips of cultivated ground, where labourers still smote rhythmically between the rows with long-handled mattocks. But as Jackland drove out from between the flanking houses a new and dominant feature came into view. The whole southern segment of the Old Town, almost a third of the space between the walls, had been completely cleared. Down its centre stretched a long single-storey building, red-tiled and white-walled, with a deep colonnade running from end to end. In the shade beneath its arches groups of Africans waited, some probably for audience with the Sarkin, others to see minor officials, and yet others on no business at all but simply allowing time to flow by, enlivened by argument and gossip. Some of these had moved out into the open, evidently to listen to and discuss the new noises arising from the market. Behind them a dozen old men sat unperturbed in facing pairs, playing the ludo game. Down at the further end a dozen boys sat round their *mallam*, learning the lines of the Koran by chanting them aloud. There were no women visible.

The cleared spaces surrounding the palace had been landscaped into a formal garden, lawns, flights of white steps, cannas, yuccas, clipped low hedges of Jesus-thorn surrounding beds of scarlet pelargoniums. A stream diverted from the river separated the area from the rest of Old Kiti. The effect of both garden and building was international. One might have been looking at a palace, or more likely a hotel, in almost any hot, dry country—Jordan, Mexico, anywhere. Only the people made it African.

Miss Boyaba directed Jackland across the stream and round to the left of the palace. The building was H-shaped, with the Sarkin's private quarters, including those of the women, running in a mirror-image block parallel to the official wing in front. A shorter range joined the two, thus forming a pair of open-ended courtyards. Round the one into which Jackland now drove the colonnade was widened to make a series of parking-bays for the cars belonging to the Sarkin and his household.

Jackland chose an empty one, swung the Landrover round and reversed into the shade.

'OK?' he said.

'Perfect. I promise I won't keep you long, but I do want to explain why it's so important to me to meet you.'

'If you like, but before we start, though it's none of my business, thank God, don't you think that as a rising young reporter your first duty isn't to go and find out what's happening out there and file a story on it?'

Miss Boyaba sounded surprised.

'A little market riot?' she said. 'Not a hope. They're always happening. This isn't Yola, Mr Jackland. Anyway, I want to tell you about my granny.'

Despite being out of the glare she had not removed her sun-glasses, and had now twisted herself half-sideways into the furthest corner of the bench. The effect was of shyness and sudden uncertainty, of having discarded the easy pushiness she thought appropriate for her job and returned to an earlier style.

'Your grandmother?' said Jackland.

'Yes. You see, when I was a little girl I spent most of my time with her. She was Dad's mother, which meant she was a real Bakiti, so we used to talk Kiti together. She'd spent most of her life in Ibadan, so she knew Yoruba, but she wanted to make sure I knew Kiti too. It's sad. I've forgotten it all, almost. I can still say a few things like "Hello".'

'A strong spirit in Annie Boyaba.'

'That's right. Only it isn't quite "spirit". It's . . . I don't think there's a word for it. Where was I?'

'Ibadan.'

'Oh, yes. That's where my grandfather had been exiled to. He was dead ages before of course. He was sixty years older than she was.'

'A somewhat unusual disparity, even in Africa.'

'Not really. Or it didn't used to be, not with the big men going on taking wives all their lives. You'd have thought it was ghastly for Granny but I don't know. She used to take me to help look after his grave every Sunday. She put little fetishes there. That was for him, you see. The Kitawa don't do that but she said it was what he wanted. Daddy and Mummy were Christians and

70

Granny used to come to church with us, but I don't know what she really believed.'

'Your grandfather, I take it, was Kama Boi.'

'Didn't I tell you?'

'Not in so many words. And your grandmother was the sister young Elongo had come to look for when he asked for work building my parents' house?'

'I didn't know about that.'

'Apparently Kama Boi had stolen the girl.'

'Oh, no. I mean I don't think it was quite like that. Her uncles sent her away—she wasn't the only one—to work in strangers' fields. That wasn't too bad. But then she was sent away from there again to a big, big hut full of women. That was my grandfather's harem, of course, but she didn't understand that. She didn't know what she was supposed to do or where she fitted in. That's absolutely terrible for a someone who's spent all her life in a village. There were some Kitawa women there but they didn't talk to her much. She was miserable. She used to say her spirit-thing kept crying to go home.

'Then one day a white woman came to make pictures of my grandfather's wives and she was told to go and keep the flies off her. She was terribly afraid of the white woman. In her village they were full of stories about how dangerous white people could be. But the white woman didn't look at her or speak to her.'

'You are aware it was my mother?'

'Yes, but how did you know?'

'She kept a diary. I'll show you.'

'Oh, please!'

'Go on.'

'Well, when the painting was over the white woman turned and looked at Granny and spoke to her, just a few words, in Kiti. She spoke like a friend. She told Granny to keep her spirit-thing in her. I expect she was only saying "Hello", but that made Granny terribly happy. Just then my grandfather came up to talk to the white woman. I know this sounds funny but Granny and my grandfather had hardly noticed each other before. Of course he hadn't paid any attention to her, creeping about being miserable, but she hadn't either. It was the women who'd filled her view. But suddenly he saw her looking happy and young, and I expect having the white woman so close made him feel a bit randy anyway. Anyway, he took Granny to his bed that afternoon and made her pregnant. He was pretty bucked about that because he hadn't had any children for a year or two, and then nine months later when the baby came and it was a boy that was terrific. The last few had all been girls. It's sort of symbolic, you see. That didn't happen till after he'd been deposed. Daddy was actually born on the journey to Ibadan. My grandfather was allowed to take a few wives into exile and of course he'd chosen Granny to be one of them because she was carrying his child. Her being a Bakiti was important, too. Everybody took it as a sign that my grandfather was still really King of Kiti—that's what Sarkin means. The White Man could take the emirship away because they'd given it to him in the first place, but they couldn't stop him being King. That wasn't anything to do with them.'

'I don't imagine they grasped that point.'

'Course not.'

'My father may have. It's hard to tell. Go on.'

'Well, it meant that Granny was my grandfather's favourite. She looked after him when he was dying. And of course he adored the little boy, so though the English didn't let him have much of a pension he arranged things all right for her. She got a hut and a garden and a little money, and Daddy went to a mission school and got educated and became a dentist and built himself a proper house and Granny went to live with him.'

'Fascinating. I wish I'd known some of this earlier.'

'I haven't finished yet. I've got to tell you why it was so important to me to meet you. I was the first grandchild, you see. Everyone was terribly disappointed I wasn't a boy. I mean Mummy and Daddy, though they wore suits and cocktail dresses and talked English at home, they minded dreadfully. It was only my funny old peasant Granny who didn't.'

'Kitawa women appear to have considerable status.'

'That's right. So Granny sort of adopted me. Mummy's very social. She didn't mind. But from the very first Granny said, "I want this girl to be like the white woman who came and made pictures in the house of Kama Boi." She told my father to stop being a dentist and get rich. Mummy backed her up about that, of course. Just after I was born Uncle Elongo managed to get himself made Sarkin Kiti, and that was a help. And Mummy started to tolerate Granny a bit. I mean, after all, she wasn't a stupid old peasant woman any longer, she was the sister of a big man up north. Mummy's south—you couldn't be souther—but that doesn't stop her liking to tell her friends about the kids spending their hols in the palace at Kiti. *We'd* much rather have been in Switzerland, of course. So it all worked out wonderfully for me, just the way Granny planned. I went to school in England, and everything else happened. You see, Mr Jackland? Your mother is terribly important to me. I am what I am because of her. Meeting you is almost like meeting a brother I have never seen.'

After a few initial hesitations Miss Boyaba had been speaking with some vehemence, using a lot of body language, tilting her head on her long neck and gesticulating with sinuous pale fingers. Her speech did not quite match these movements. It was as though English had been dubbed with technical perfection on to an African original. The oddity might have been less apparent if the school chosen for her had not been, even by English standards, out of key with its age—evidently one of those mainly devoted to equipping its pupils to appear on the first page of *Country Life*. Jackland was clearly amused, both in ways she did and did not intend.

'I hope you don't mind my saying that,' she said.

'Of course not. Is your grandmother still alive?'

'She died when I was in England. That's why I've forgotten my Kiti. Mummy wouldn't let Daddy talk it with me. I suppose . . .'

She stopped, too late for tact. Jackland did not seem to mind.

'My mother died somewhat earlier,' he said. 'She preferred not to think about Africa in her later life, so I can't tell you whether she would have been pleased. I am, though.'

'I'm so glad.'

'Do you know your uncle well?'

'Oh, yes! That's to say . . . I mean . . .'

'Insofar as it's possible to know an elderly and distinguished relative?'

'He isn't easy. Why?'

'He's been very friendly and helpful about the film. We wouldn't have got it off the ground without him. On the other hand he has consistently managed to avoid telling me anything

73

serious about the time when he worked for my parents. There's one thing in particular I want to know.'

'I'll ask him, if you like. I'm a bit of a favourite.'

'No, that won't do. I wondered whether you'd ever heard him talking about those days.'

'I don't think so. He talks about growing up in the bush sometimes, and the old Kiti legends. Perhaps he doesn't like thinking about when he was a servant. He can be very proud. Have you got the diary here?'

'I'll show it you when you come out to our camp to talk to Mary.'

'Do you think she'll really see me?'

'I'll put in a word for you.'

'My boss wants me to ask about her love life.'

'I can't advise you on that.'

'You don't think I ought to? As a journalist, I mean?'

'I have asked more impertinent questions in my time. Mary is a totally serious artist who defends that area by behaving as a totally frivolous person. If you want truly startling revelations for your listeners, ask her for her opinions on Africa . . . It sounds as if my riot has calmed down. What do you want to do? The chaps who are supposed to be patching the Old Palace up for us are nothing like ready. Builders are the same all over the world. I've got to go and negotiate with them about becoming extras, so that we can film tomorrow while they're still working. The son speaks good English but I'm never sure how much the old boy in charge gets told. You wouldn't care to come and interpret for me?'

'I absolutely must pay my respects to Uncle Elongo first. That's terribly important. After that.'

'Right. I'll drive down and see if I can get over the idea of clearing the modern gear out of sight. You go and find the Sarkin and then come down there and see how I've got on. Then I'll take you out to the camp. This afternoon some of us are driving out to Tefuga.'

'Oh! Can I come too? I haven't been for yonks. There's nothing to see, of course, but it's still sort of special.'

'If there's room. The trucks have been playing up, so I don't know how many will be going. My mother went there, of course. Twice.'

Sun March 9

Nothing in here for eight weeks—I just haven't felt like it. Partly it was being too tired of writing 'cos of having to do all Ted's reports and things for him, but underneath that I really didn't want to. It was all my fault, boasting in here about how clever Ted and me were getting. Stupid, but I've honestly been feeling just like that. You see, two nights after I wrote that last bit we were doing it and it was lovely and we forgot about the beastly guinea worm and broke it. Poor Ted. He's had an absolutely terrible time.

First his arm swelled up like a balloon, end to end, and hurt like blazes, and then it burst into horrible sores. For a whole week he was in agony, living on whisky and aspirin, which meant he couldn't make much sense of his work, poor angel, tho' I did my best to sort the muddles out. Of course he wouldn't have a doctor. The sores grew and grew. They smelt of cream cheese gone sour and when I washed them out bits just flaked off like pieces of old mushroom. Ghastly. I tweezed out anything I could see which might be worm and bathed it several times a day with weak carbolic and slowly, slowly it got better. The last bit of worm I got out was five inches long. Dead. (Ted swears that was the whisky. I think it was the carbolic.) It still took three weeks to heal after that.

It's an ill wind, as usual. Not just feeling closer to Ted and being needed, like I said last time. Helping with his work means I understand so much more. Mr Yo, the clerk, is perfectly useless, ever so smiling and willing but Ted can't trust him to get the simplest thing right. Ted puts up with him 'cos he wears a robe and a little skull-cap, not shirt and trousers, like practically all the clerks do now, and anyway Ted says one of them would probably be just as hopeless. So it means Ted has to do practically all the paper-work himself. I'd no idea! All those words and figures going to and fro. Tiny little troubles up and down the province. Such stupid suggestions from Kaduna, such patient answers from Ted. Such tricky, trappy memos from Mr de Lancey at Birnin Soko. I've begun to *hate* that man, even tho' his whole object is to get rid of K B, which I think would be an excellent idea! The old devil is only just hanging on, 'cos of Ted sticking by him and Kaduna not wanting to make up its mind. Ted's only got one trump card which is that KB's son who'd succeed to the emirship—it doesn't have to be a son, but this time he's the obvious man—he'd be just as hopeless as KB. His name's Zarafio. He's going on tour with us, so I'll get a chance to see. We had to postpone the tour 'cos of Ted's arm. Come to that in a mo.

Another useful thing is I've really been able to get on with my Kiti lessons. So's E. with his English—and he's been marvellous about not showing off in front of Ted—honestly you wouldn't know he understood a word we were saying. I hope I'll be able to practise with real Kitawa when we're on tour. I'm good enough now for the lessons to be quite fun. We tell each other fairy-tales. I do Rumpelstiltskin and Goldilocks and he does Thundersnake and The First People. That's a funny one! The Kitawa are the only *real* people. There were nine of them to start with, and every Bakiti still has a bit of one of those nine in him. Or her. That's what they are talking about when they wish each other a strong spirit. Anyway, when some of the animal-spirits saw how clever the new people were they were jealous, so they turned themselves into pretend people. Different animals turned themselves into different tribes. So the Hausa are really only horses and the Fulani are cattle and the Yoruba are foxes and so on. I asked about white people. E. didn't want to tell me but I made him. We are really termites! I think that's rather clever, specially when you remember they've never seen London, but Ted says it's only because some termites are white too. Spoilsport!

Talking of ill winds, the harmattan seems to be over. In fact it wasn't that bad, and days when there was only just a bit of it it made you feel pretty well. Now the weather's starting to get really hot and we're off on tour in the worst of it. If we put it off till the hot weather's over it means the rains will have started, and that means tsetse, and that means we can't take the horses. So there's a terrific rush on and I oughtn't to be writing this at all. I'm supposed to be spending all my sitting-down time mugging up my First Aid and *Handbook of Tropical Medicine* so I can be some use to everyone. Only I was sorting through my boxes deciding what I'd need when I found my diary and suddenly I felt the itch to start again. I've been punished enough for my boasting.

Ted *still* hasn't told Mr de Lancey I'm going, and now I've seen so much of the Govt papers I think I can see this isn't really anything to do with Mr de Lancey, who wouldn't give a hoot (except for wanting to put a spoke in Ted's wheel, 'cos of Ted being his enemy). Mr de Lancey's v. contemptuous about what natives feel, it's Ted who minds, and KB's son who's coming with us, Zarafio, is a bit of a stickler about being a strict Mohammedan, so he might try and make a fuss. But Ted could easily say Pooh to him and that would be that. What I think is deep inside him Ted really wants to keep me as separate as he can, not part of anything else at all, like KB's wives in his harem. He wants to have me on tour with him (and I'm longing to go) but—oh, this is difficult, trying to explain what somebody else thinks when they don't even know they're thinking it!— suppose this was all part of a silly Shakespeare play where girls dress up as boys, he'd *love* that. Then I'd be his own special secret all day, and at night . . . The nights are important to me too, *very*, but I don't think about them all day long. Ted does, I'm fairly sure—suppose 'cos he began so late. Oh, I'd like to scribble and scribble about this—*terribly* interesting—but there isn't time. Must get on, shutting the house up. Dear Elongo's staying to keep an eye on it. I wish he could come too.

Mon March 10
Time now, masses of it. I'm lying on my tum in our little tent with the flaps up and a mosquito net over me. Just getting dark. Proper stars, not fogged like down by the river. Millions of insects fizzing away in the bush all round. The bearers' firelight away by the village—one of them playing a waily clay flute-thing. Night-smells from the bush, so all the same with its flat-topped trees and spiky tussocks and dust-patches. That's what you see by daylight, of course—now you just feel it, huge dark Africa spreading away out there, full of nightmares if I wanted to let them come. If I reach over the edge of my palliasse I can touch the whole continent with my fingertips. But in here,

under the Army and Navy lamp and the Army and Navy canvas, this is Europe! There's a rest house we were supposed to sleep in and some of the boys had been ahead to clean it out, but it still stank of bats and the boys had killed a rat the size of a dachshund so I'm sure there were others and I absolutely put my foot down. Snakes! (I didn't see any, but it's obvious.) All that's Africa. Europe for me, when it comes to that sort of thing!

Ted's down at the village, trying to smooth things over with Zarafio, who seems absolutely determined to make things as difficult as possible. Z. is a nasty twisty little specimen, *I* think. If he's the best we can do by way of a successor to KB, heaven help us! *And* heaven help the Kitawa!! He's not a proper Hausa, any more than KB, but he's got it into his head that if he behaves like one, all stiff and grand and never showing his feelings, people are going to respect him. Ted admits he's going to be just as bad as KB, only differently bad, but we've got to put up with him 'cos he's the one the other Hausa want.

Well, off we set this morning at 3 a.m. Ted, me, Kimjiri, Lukar, Mafote and Ibrahim to look after the horses, twenty boys and bearers. Some of them will come the whole way with us, others only for the first day, and we'll pick up fresh ones as we go along. They get paid (not much) but they have to come whether they like it or not.

Quite dark when we set off, and rather glorious, 'cos the boys had got a lot of twisted grass torches ready to light the way. So we rode along like that, the orangey light, and shadows jumping among the trees, the glisten off black shoulders, the last stars. Then the belt of thorn scrub creepy and mysterious, and out into the real bush. Plenty of dry grass here, so the boys tore it up by armfuls to make fresh torches till the sky went pale. Soon as it was light enough we kicked our heels in and took the horses cracking along, whooping like children having donkey-rides on the beach.

Funny about the bush. You feel you're right out in the open but actually you can't ever see all that far 'cos there's always a clump of flat-topped trees in the way, so soon as we were well ahead of the boys we left the track and found a way up a little hill—a bit of a wrestle, specially with Tan-Tan, but worth it 'cos of the view from the top, absolute miles, all the same. Clump after clump of trees mottling away. Most of them haven't any leaves in the dry season, and everything's yellow and brown and fawn and grey, specially dark grey, almost black, where the grass fires have been. (Almost all the grass gets burnt in the end, and 'cos of that the trees have corky, twisty trunks. The villagers start the fires 'cos they're tired of the grass, or it's honey hunters, or just an accident.) There were a few fires still burning, smoke drifting away across the sunrise. Everything else clean and new in the sideways light. Immense space and sky. Up on our hill—only a pimple really—I could *feel* how simply huge Africa is.

And all so empty! No one there! Us the first people ever! I know that's nonsense—bits of it are just as crowded as England and the people have been there for centuries, but it's how it *feels*. I could see what the explorers saw—all that, and not belonging to anyone, so finders keepers! I didn't have time, but one day I'll try and get that feeling into a picture. We waited to watch the bearers come by (my tin bath is the first thing you see!) and then down and on to Ofafe where we were going to meet Zarafio's lot.

Typically African, he was two hours late. The whole idea of starting so early was to get the business at Ofafe done and move on before it got too hot, so we could all have a bit of a rest at the next village. I didn't see any point in waiting for Z. I thought Ted might have got on with the assessment and so on at Ofafe, but Ted says no. There's an official rule that D.O.s don't conduct business with natives except through a representative of the Native Authority (that's KB in our case). The idea is that the N.A. is really in charge and the White Man is only advising—rubbish, of course, and a lot of D.O.s don't pay a blind bit of notice—but Ted says rules are rules and how are we ever going to teach the native to take responsibility if we keep going behind his back, so all we could do was wait. Our boys had brought a sort of folding roof which they put up to give us a bit of shade, but after a bit I thought I'd have a wander round Ofafe and see if I could find someone to practise my Kiti on. I took my medicine kit so as I could have an excuse.

Ofafe's quite a big village by Kiti standards, Ted says, but it's still only about thirty huts, round, thatched like ours but much smaller and with the main pole over to one side which gives the roof a tipsy look—and *very* ragged at the edges. The women do the thatching. Ted says they can build a hut in a day! All terribly poor-looking. Not a lot of people about. Dry season, so nothing much in the 'gardens' which have sort of woven mat fences round them to keep wild animals out. Some of them are quite a bit away from the huts 'cos there's only certain pockets where the soil's good to grow crops on. Seeing it all so dry and barren it's hard to see how even that few people stay alive. I went down to the water-hole, about two hundred yards from the village, where they've dug a hollow in a dry stream-bed and patiently scoop the water out with a bit of broken calabash, a saucer at a time. It took a woman ten minutes to fill her calabash. I sat on the bank beside one who'd finished and was waiting for her friend and wished her a strong spirit. She wished me back, a bit dubiously.

I felt terribly excited. I longed to reach out and touch her glossy brown skin—she wasn't wearing any clothes, of course, just a grass belt and a pretty grass collar woven to a pattern, like lace. She was so real, the first really real African I've met. Even dear Elongo isn't quite the same, wearing a housecoat and not being in his own proper place and so on. It was a bit sticky, at first—she didn't seem to want to talk to me, but then a horrid biting fly came and jabbed me and I slapped it dead and laughed and so did she and that was better. When her friend had filled her calabash I walked back with them and their three small children to the village. On the way I asked if there was anyone with cuts or sores I could help, and one of them went off and got an old woman who came hobbling along 'cos of a sort of boil on her ankle. I was terribly afraid it might be a guinea worm, but I don't think so. I lanced it (I am getting brave!) and squeezed the pus out and put some boracic ointment on and a sticking plaster. The old woman was rather jolly about it all and some others came to watch, and I felt I was just getting somewhere when there was a noise from the other side of the village, one of the squeaky Hausa trumpets, and they all shut up like clams. They really didn't want to talk to me at all. I know when I'm not wanted (Daddy taught me that, at least!) so I shut my box up and kept smiling and slipped away.

It was cracking hot by now and everyone was in a filthy temper, us for being kept waiting and the Hausa for having to come at all, but everyone determined not to lose face by showing it. Ted took Zarafio aside and gave him a terrific wigging and Z. tried to get his own back by pretending it was terribly offensive to him as a Mohammedan to have to travel around with a woman, which Ted says is complete nonsense as everyone knows white women don't count! And *anyway*, believe it or not, KB had sent a message out with his Bangwa Wangwa (who always comes on tours like this) saying he specially wanted me to come so I could make pictures of his kingdom! (Typically native, leaving it till too late, almost.) Even so Z. barely allowed himself to be introduced to me and turned his back on me soon as he could and was obviously determined to make the whole tour as difficult as possible, which is why Ted has gone off to sort things out with him now, so I could see it would be easier all round if I left them alone and went off and sat under the shade-roof to do a sketch of the village. Quite good, except that I was cross and that came out. Not a happy sketch, closed in, secret, frightened. I kept wondering what really happened among those funny roofs, what they think and talk about when we aren't there.

I asked Ted when he came back for lunch.

'Nobody knows what the African really thinks,' he said.

'Specially when you don't know the language,' I said.

'I hope you're not going to put on side about that, Rabbit. It's no use. When they tell you it'll still only be what they think you want to think they think. Anyway, a fair number of the men speak Hausa this close to the river. They're a contented lot, compared with the tribes up on Jos Plateau, for instance.'

'You just mean they don't make much trouble, but I don't think that's 'cos they're contented. I think it's 'cos they're frightened.'

'What do you mean?'

I explained what I'd been doing, and what had happened when we heard the trumpet.

'Peasants always detest being counted,' he said. 'They know it means taxes. That's all we're really up to, checking the census and the tax assessment. These ones probably still associate the whole process with Bestermann's Patrol.'

'I'll ask, next time I'm doctoring. I'll have to think how to say it.'

'Better not. Seriously, Rabbit. You don't want to go putting ideas into the African's head. You never know what shape they're going to come out.'

We talked a bit more, then just rested in the shade to let the worst of the heat go by. I got out my kit and did a good sketch of Zarafio's people lounging around under a group of knobbly trees. Five of them—Z., his Bangwa Wangwa, and three spearmen. I'm afraid there may not be a lot to paint . . .

Tues March 11
Had to stop there 'cos I heard Ted coming back. I'd got ready for him before I started writing. All a bit difficult in the tent to start with, but lovely in the end—rather thrilling, really, with mad Africa so close outside in the dark. Ted's my fetish, and I'm his. We can beat that lot between us.

What I'd been going to say was there won't be much of KB's kingdom to do pictures of, with it all so samey and no proper distances. Sometimes I feel a bit frightened about us getting lost when we go off alone for a canter. Even Ted says he'd have precious little idea where he is if he didn't have local guides. Sometimes if you can find a hill and get a view you can spot where there might be a village by the greener bush near the water-holes, but not always. This morning we went ten whole miles without seeing one hut! There's great empty patches on Ted's map, specially down south where the bush is thicker and the tsetse gets worse.

Glad to say Z. has become a bit less hostile. We'd done the first two hours in the dark again, and while we were having a stop for breakfast I did a quick sketch of his horse. You don't put horses into the shade, 'cos of tsetse, poor things, but they don't seem to mind provided they get plenty of water. So there it was, alone in the middle of empty Africa, with a rather splendid saddle and cloth, and the rising sun on them. I should've guessed it was Z.'s from the saddle, but when I found out I gave him the sketch and Ted says he was pleased, tho' *I* couldn't see any difference. It was a present, you see, and that's something the Hausa understand. So at the next village I went and sat with Ted while they were doing the tour-work, talking to the villagers and checking the census and assessment so as to work out how much tax the village ought to pay. (I'd kept out of the way for the two they did yesterday afternoon.) It's the Bangwa Wangwa who does most of the talking. He knows more words than I do but *I* don't think he's so good at the tones. Sometimes the Bakiti he was talking to looked decidedly puzzled—difficult to tell, 'cos they all look puzzled all the time with those scars. It's quite obvious all the Hausa think they're absolutely stupid. It's all only counting, over and over, getting it right, how many men, how much of the different crops. Lots of muddles, 'cos of the Kitawa thinking in twenties and us and the Hausa thinking in tens. I don't believe Lukar and the Bangwa Wangwa really understand this. I haven't told Ted yet. I'm learning to be careful, not saying things like that till I'm sure, or he'll decide I'm just saying it because I'm so against KB and his people. From his point of view women who meddle in the administration aren't much better than Africans in shiny blue suits coming up from Lagos.

Anyway, I'm really not sure, 'cos I didn't stay long enough. I slipped away and looked for the women so I could do a bit of doctoring and practise my Kiti. Same this afternoon. Much more fun. They're getting quite friendly. I can't help thinking someone must have run on from Ofafe and got here first to tell them we're coming and that the White Woman doesn't bite! They think I'm funny 'cos I talk men's language, which is what dear Elongo uses, so they're not quite sure I'm really a woman—specially wearing clothes so they can't see! If only we stop somewhere for more than a couple of hours I'll find a girl to teach me women's language. Two villages this morning. Long rest middle of the day. One this afternoon. Rest house now—not as nice as our tent but Ted says if we don't use it no one will look after it. Ted out trying to shoot something for supper. We'll have an evening together. No gramophone, tho'. Pity.

Wed March 12
Very unhappy. I've had a row with Ted and he's gone out with his gun, tho' it was far too late, to try and cool off. Really to let me cool off, 'cos he was terribly calm and patient, which only made it worse, of course! But it isn't my fault, really it's not. I haven't done anything wrong.

I'll write it down to see if that helps. Day started just as usual. Bit stiff from sleeping two in one bed, but comfy inside—T. swore he wasn't leaving me and I swore I wasn't getting out in the dark 'cos of the rats! Riding under the stars, good moon, slight dewy smells, then dawn. (Wonder if I could paint that, but we're always moving then to take advantage of the cool—I'm trying to write this like it felt before the row.) Breakfast. Move on, dusty and hot already. First village, quite a big one. I sat in on the counting, pretending to sketch. Z. didn't seem to mind. It's always the same. The headman comes up and grovels (I *hate* that) and Z. questions him in Hausa for a bit—just how-d'ye-dos really, and then the Bangwa Wangwa takes over 'cos now we're away from the river the headman's Hausa isn't v. good and Lukar tells Ted what they're saying and Ted and the Bangwa Wangwa write it down in their account books and when it's all over they check with each other and then they have to question the headman again to settle the differences. 'Cos I had a pencil in my hand I could make notes without anyone seeing, and I was right. Lukar and the Bangwa Wangwa are in a complete muddle about tens and twenties. They don't always get it wrong, but they did four times I made notes of. Lukar's too lazy to listen properly. He just agrees to anything the Bangwa Wangwa says, so we had twenty-three chickens when it should have been forty-three, and seventy baskets of beans when it should have been a hundred and thirty. Things like that.

I told Ted while we were riding on to the next village—quite close, so there wasn't much time—and I don't think he really believed me, so I said I'd stay and keep my ears open again, which I did and the same sort of thing happened, and luckily one of the times they got it wrong was where there was a disagreement between Ted's accounts and the Bangwa Wangwa's. I showed him my notes while we were having the long mid-day rest, and we worked out that one of the muddles in the first village had been the same thing. Then Ted sent for Lukar and questioned him. I pretended to be reading *Henry Esmond* and Ted made out that he'd worked out himself something was wrong. Of course Lukar said no, the counts were right, and all Ted could do in the circumstances was tell him to be more careful in future. But he made it quite obvious he didn't believe him, and showed him the places in the book where the accounts were wrong.

I spent the rest of the rest-time trying to teach Ted to count in Kiti—I can't imagine how he ever passed his Hausa exams, tho' he's pretty good now. I wrote the numbers down for him, best I could, with lines and dots to show the tones. I think he must have guessed already how Z. might react to all this 'cos he told me not to come to the accounting at the next village, which I didn't mind—it's much more fun doctoring the women and trying to chat to them.

That's just what I did. We were having a lovely gossip, just like a hen party at the vicarage only more interesting. The boss woman at that village—that's something we've got wrong, by the by, only dealing with the men. The women are just as important and their old women sit with the village elders, only there's usually one who speaks for them. That's who I mean by calling her the boss woman. Anyway she was telling me about her nephew having a pain in his stomach, but she saw I hadn't quite understood something so she explained he wasn't really her nephew. She said all Kitawa boys, before they can have their face-scars made, are sent to the hut of a young married woman and she tells them the things poor blushing Matron tried to explain to us, and shows them how and helps them do it the first few times. With her. She wasn't at all shy about it, and I wasn't shocked either. I just thought how terribly sensible. I mean, it's worked out all right in the end with me and Ted, but it easily mightn't have. Oh dear. I don't like to think about that. But this nice old woman was worried about one of her 'nephews', tho' he's got his own wives and children now, but they stay important to each other. While they're in her hut the lads have to do exactly what their 'aunt' says, and work like billy-oh in her garden, or they don't get their prize that night!

We were all giggling away about this when suddenly they stopped as if I'd just said something awful and I looked up from the dressing I was doing and there was one of the Hausa spearmen staring at us. I told him to go away, which he did, but the women didn't want to talk any more after that.

Naturally I felt a bit miffed but I came back out here to the rest house to wait for Ted and to see what Kimjiri was doing about supper and to try and make up my mind whether I could stand the bat-smell or would I insist on using the tent tonight and after a bit Ted showed up and I knew at once something was wrong. It's the way he scrapes his pipe, when he's just done it anyway, so I asked what was up.

'Nothing, really,' he said. 'Zarafio's got it into his head you

85

ought to have one of his spearmen with you while you're doing your doctoring.'

'Well, he can jolly well get it out again!'

'It's not an unreasonable suggestion, Rabbit.'

'Yes, it is. They won't utter a word if there's a spearman there.'

'He won't understand what you're saying.'

'That doesn't make any difference. One showed up just now while we were gossiping away and they closed up like clams. They wouldn't say a word even after he'd gone. And we'd been having such a jolly gossip.'

'What about?'

'Darling, I couldn't possibly tell you!'

'Not Bestermann's Patrol?'

'Course not. You said I wasn't to.'

'Good girl. I've had quite an encouraging time. Lukar's pulled his socks up and is keeping a proper check on the Bangwa Wangwa. Figures clean as a whistle, almost. They've had a very good season here, some crops up getting on fifty per cent.'

He wanted to change the subject and he's not very good at that sort of thing. There was something he hadn't quite told me. Not difficult to guess.

'You've told him alright, haven't you?'

'Eh?'

'You've said a spearman can come and spy on me while I'm doctoring.'

'I don't know what you mean, spy. It's most unlikely he'll know a word of Kiti.'

'Well, you can jolly well go and tell him it's off!'

Long pause. Awful feeling. I've never talked to him like that, and never imagined the day would come. And about something like that! Why's it so important? I don't know. But it is.

'I don't think I can, Rabbit.'

(Tender, patient voice, like when you've got to break a promise to a child. But not ashamed, not him in the wrong—*me*, and too silly to see!)

'Course you can. He's only a native. He's got to do what you tell him.'

'That's not what I meant. Of course I could tell him I'd

changed my mind, but I'm not going to. This is a man's world. Our authority here is based on respect.'

'Piffle! It's based on them knowing that if they don't do what you say you'll send for the soldiers!'

'That may be its origin, and it may still appear to be the case, but it is largely a bluff. We cannot afford any disrespect of our authority because that will lead to disobedience and eventually revolt, and no British government these days would countenance the large-scale use of force to suppress revolt. And even if they were prepared to, think of the misery, Rabbit. The shootings and hangings, the ruined harvests, the starving villages. Even in so trivial a matter as this I am not prepared to lose the natives' respect and diminish our authority by being seen to go back on my word to please my wife.'

'I'm your wife, Ted, but I'm not your dog or your horse. I'm a person. You aren't allowed to make promises for me!'

'Yes, I am. In fact I have absolute authority in my district to say what any European, other than my superiors in the Political Service, may or may not do.'

'Oh.'

'I'm sorry, Rabbit. I agreed to Zarafio's suggestion for what seemed to me the adequate reason that he is perfectly capable of complaining about your being a disruptive influence, and de Lancey and Kaduna are then equally capable of suggesting that you should not accompany me on tour. Is that what you want? Kaduna are extremely sensitive to anything affecting the relationship between the N.A. and pagan subjects, and de Lancey would be happy to put any kind of spoke in my wheel. If I had realized you were going to object so vehemently I would not, of course, have agreed. But since I have I must ask you to go through with it.'

'Alright,' I managed to say.

But he *did* know! He just didn't think it was important. He tried to start talking about something else but I snapped and sulked till in the end he couldn't stand it and got his gun and went out to try and shoot something. Now it's almost dark and he isn't home and I'm not even sure I want him. Kimjiri's boiled a guinea fowl, and we'll eat it, and then we'll read. Usually we'd chat, but I don't know. Too late to get the boys to put the tent up, so it's the rest house and the bats and snakes. And then . . .

I *think*—I'm not sure 'cos it's the sort of thing you can only find out by seeing what happens—I think I'm going to pretend to be sorry and forgiving and good. Inside me I'm still seething, but that's my secret. Perhaps things aren't going to be the same again, ever.

Fri March 14
Goodness, what a lot to write! Rather frightening, some of it. Come to that in a mo. And things happening inside me too—v. interesting. Kept thinking about that yesterday but didn't get a chance to write, and now what's happened this morning . . . Pull yourself together, Bets!

Well, going back to where I left off, I was *very* lovey-dovey with old Ted when he got back. I'd never realized how cold the nights were going to be out here (just think of the Kitawa—you have to be rather rich to own *one* blanket!) so it was extra nice to have someone to snuggle with, and we spent the whole night like that. My poor little bed! It creaked quite a bit, but it stood the strain. God bless the Army & Navy Stores. I did boot Ted out a couple of times to look for snakes, just to show him I hadn't totally forgiven him, and actually that seemed to stir him up so we didn't get an awful lot of sleep in the end! But I knew inside me all the time there's a different sort of not-forgiving, like a little dark ball, secret, waiting. I wonder if it'll ever come out!

Yesterday, riding along, I brooded quite a bit. Mainly after the first village, where I'd done some doctoring. A small boy with a terrible sore eye. I explained to the mother she must keep it clean, and tho' I knew I'd said it right 'cos it's something you have to keep saying to all the mothers, I really don't think she understood at all. She was so frightened, 'cos of the spearman watching. Frightened of me, too, tho'. Much more than anyone before. And none of them would say a word, only yes and no. V. upsetting. All since yesterday too! *I* think Zarafio's sent ahead, telling them they mustn't say anything to me. That way it doesn't matter the spearman not understanding Kiti. I didn't tell Ted, 'cos it wouldn't have done any good. He'd have thought I was making it up to get my own back on Z.

So I brooded, not just about that. About being me. So strange. My body so happy, with that nice slightly bruisy feeling all over, and prickly under the eyelids from not much sleep, and Ted riding beside me humming a bit to himself and thinking about the same things (I knew, he didn't!) and the sweat drying on the horses and the hard dusty heat bouncing back off the ground, and one of the spearmen riding on ahead, shimmering in the heat-haze like a dream. Lovely! Paradise, in a funny way. But then, riding on the same horse, wearing the same clothes—the same *skin*—there's another me, brooding about the spearmen and Zarafio and Ted and the women they've stopped me talking to . . . But not just about that, about the way it's all managed —the whole world—and what Daddy did to Mummy and nobody would help her 'cos he was her husband so he was allowed! And thinking *I know about this. I understand it. I've been shown.* I used to think it was just that Daddy is a horrible person. But Ted isn't—he's decent and loving and kind, but he's *still* part of all that. It's funny how people don't all understand this. It's so obvious, but it's so difficult to see because you're inside it, part of it. It's like your own smell, which you don't notice. But I understand now. I'm a sort of spy in their country, with my secret inside me. I don't know who I'm spying for, but perhaps I'll find out some day.

But the *really* interesting thing is that I was wrong saying there are two me's, 'cos there aren't. They're all the same. The spy and the secret are part of the happiness, and the happiness is part of the understanding. You've got to have that, or you won't understand how it happens. You've got to have it as much as you can, which I jolly well intend to! But you mustn't let it stop you understanding. That's what really matters. This is my Paradise, I said, and I suppose that means I must be Eve. But I'm the snake, too!

Well, apart from all that inside me, yesterday wasn't very interesting till the evening. Two more villages. Me doctoring. The women too frightened to talk. Bush, just bush. We got here, to Tefuga, about an hour before dark and then straight off we had to go out and watch a dance they put on to welcome Zarafio 'cos he's KB's representative. A bit like when the Governor General comes to a station, Ted says, and there's a parade for him and a guard of honour for him to inspect and everything, not just 'cos it's pretty to watch, but to show everyone he really is the big man. It's even more than that here, tho', or it would be if it was KB they were dancing for. This is what I find so hard to understand. Here are these lovely, simple, honest, open people and there is that horrible fat black brute, and yet to them he's a kind of god! He's holy. They're deadly afraid of him too, but not just 'cos of what he might do to them, but 'cos of what he *is*! Zarafio's not that yet, but he will be one day if Ted has his way!

Well, long as it was light the dancing was rather a disappointment. Three whole hours, on and on. Pattery little drums. All you could see of the dancers was their feet, 'cos the rest of them was hidden by the costumes, just tall tubes of grass about eight feet high with a painted round for a face at the top, swaying and stamping round and round. A bit boring, really, but soon as it got dark and the grass torches were lit, that was different. Tall thin shadows, shapes you couldn't quite see properly, moving not like people or animals. Spooky. I did rather a good picture, a sloppy dribbly one, not my usual style at all, but then I could hardly see to paint. When I showed it to Elongo this morning he put his hand over it to cover it up, so's he shouldn't look at it! Then he laughed (that lovely noise) and said the dancers were messengers from the ancestors sent to welcome us and when the dance was over they had to be sent back to the hill. I suppose he was afraid I might have trapped them in my picture. Interesting he could see—when I'd shown it to Ted he couldn't make out what it was supposed to be of!

Well, this morning I decided I'd go and do a picture of Tefuga Hill before it got too hot. I've forgotten to say about the hill —we'd ridden fairly close to it on our way to the village. It's about two miles out and not at all impressive, a pimple with a fuzz of trees on top. You'd hardly call it a hill except that the country round here is absolutely flat 'cos of the river which runs close by. Doesn't run, I mean, except in the rains and two or three weeks after. But I thought I ought to try and do a sketch for old KB, seeing the hill's the most important place in his kingdom. I didn't get off quite as soon as I'd have liked—we're staying two nights at Tefuga and there wasn't any hurry and you're always late when it's like that—and I started to ride out quite alone, but I'd hardly got half way when two of Zarafio's spearmen came cantering up after me and said they'd been sent to guard me. I wasn't terribly pleased but I didn't feel like arguing.

Just to make a bit more of my picture I put my easel up close against the bank of the dry river, which gave me a wiggly line running away past the hill. I told the spearmen to go and tether the horses about thirty yards off, and to stay there themselves. They propped their spears against a termites' nest and then, without me having to say anything, sat down in exactly the right pose—pure Africa!—and began to play that game of theirs with pebbles on a patch of earth, like noughts and crosses gone mad. They looked as tho' they'd been at it for days. I did a quick sketch in case they moved.

Suddenly I'd got a picture I really wanted to paint. The trick was to make people see that tho' the hill wasn't really anything, really it was everything. This was where KB and his forebears had come to be accepted as Kings of Kiti. This was where horrible things had been done, under that fuzz of trees at the top. This was where the Kitawa began. This was where the nine ancestors, the first real people, were buried—only they were still alive, inside the hill! Elongo'd told me that, back at The Warren. It was only one of his fairy-stories there, but you could see here it might be real! If I got my picture right, I mean. The spearmen might look more interesting, but tomorrow they'd be gone. The hill was always. I could paint that, I thought.

It began to get hot. Sweltering. Windless. Bleached. Very, very lonely and empty. After a bit, down in the river to my left, half a dozen women came creeping along, bent low, hunting for something. Little bubbles of their talk floated across to me. Soon as I'd done my picture, I thought, I'd go and ask them what they were up to. Only they'd be too frightened to tell me. I started thinking about that, and it made me sad. Sadder when I thought about how Ted had let me down over being watched while I'm doctoring. I began to wonder if he'd been absolutely straight with me. Of course he has in his own mind, but I wonder if there isn't part of him which actually rather resents me talking to the Kitawa in their own language, 'cos it means there's something I do which doesn't belong to him. He can't even share. And the same with why he didn't say no to Zarafio right at the start—I don't think Kaduna or Mr de Lancey would pay a blind bit of notice to a little rat like Z. They'd lose face dreadfully if they did. But then Ted's terribly jumpy about the idea I might be stopped coming on tour and being with him all the time. This business of s ⋆ ⋆. Oh, I like it too, much more than I'd ever expected. I sometimes even wonder if that isn't why my painting's picked up so terrifically. Africa *is* thrilling in its funny way, but my pictures aren't just that. There's something inside me, coming out, set free, making my eye and hand work the way they're doing. I honestly can't see any connection between that and me and Ted doing it in our little tent, but I know clever people are saying it's there, only you don't know. So perhaps it's a bit unfair of me to worry about Ted, but I do. You see, with him it's almost as tho' nothing else in the world mattered any more. I'm sure that's not right. Dangerous. All your eggs in one basket. Sorry now I'd played up so the night before . . .

Well, I was painting away and thinking about that sort of thing and the thinking was getting into the painting, the way it does, heavy and sad, spite of the light, but coming rather good, specially the feeling of sheer heat, when all of a sudden, close by my foot just below the lip of the bank a brown head popped into sight. It stared at me with big eyes, all the whites showing, put a finger to its lips and popped out of sight again. I almost dropped my brush but I don't suppose I really jumped much. When I glanced their way the spearmen weren't even looking.

Nothing happened. Soon I couldn't bear it so I twisted round and pretended to be looking for something in my satchel. She was just there, only a couple of feet below me. Two other women huddled against the bank behind her with their faces in the gravel but she was looking straight up. Naked of course, except for their grass collars and belts. I supposed they must have been inquisitive about the white woman and come sneaking along for a closer look, but 'cos of the spearmen I couldn't tell them to come up and be friendly. All I could do was smile. The woman put her fingers to her lips again.

'Do the horsemen listen?' she said.

Luckily those were easy words. 'Horsemen' is what the Kitawa call the Hausa, not just 'cos some of them ride horses but 'cos they all *are* horses really. I say luckily 'cos actually Kiti's a terrible language for whispering—the tones almost disappear —if you've been talking it since you were tiny perhaps it's not so bad, but for me it's v. near impossible. That's why I'm not honestly sure I really understood anything else the women tried to tell me. Besides, when I was doctoring the women in the villages they soon realized I was a bit stupid at their language

92

and spoke slowly and went back when I asked and so on. Now I couldn't even look at them. I had to pretend to go on painting almost at once.

'The horsemen are far off,' I said.

I looked at them as I twisted back to my easel. They still hadn't noticed. The women were muttering to each other below me. Suddenly I felt v. nervy, as tho' something important was going to happen and I wasn't sure I wanted it to.

'Femora Feng speaks,' one of them whispered. 'I am the aunt of Elongo Sisefonge. He sends words that you are a friend.'

'A strong spirit in Femora Feng,' I whispered. 'Betty Jackland speaks.'

This was all quite easy, of course. It's the usual form. I'd even got the right women's language for it, doing my doctoring. And the old woman the day before yesterday had told me about the business of 'aunts'. I absolutely longed to turn round and look at the woman who'd done that for dear Elongo. She'd be older than him, of course, but she could still be young and pretty. What Africans think is pretty, anyway. (I've sometimes wondered—if I had a black skin would Africans think I was pretty? White men don't, as I am.)

Another long pause. More mutterings. Then . . .

'The White Man is the friend of Kama Boi.'

'That is and is not,' I said—useful phrase—the Kitawa say it a lot. 'I am the friend of the Kitawa. I am strongly the friend of Elongo Sisefonge.'

(And I hadn't even known his whole name till then!)

She drew a deep breath and started. I'd sort of guessed what was coming, only I expected it to be all about KB stealing Elongo's sister, but it was a different story. I didn't understand it all, anything like. There were places and people she seemed to think I knew all about already, which of course I didn't, and lots of words I didn't know. I tried to make her slow down, but I couldn't keep interrupting or the spearmen would have been bound to notice, so all I could hope for was to try and pick up bits and bobs and piece something together. Anyway, I think it was a story about one of KB's other sons, not Zarafio, coming to the village and spearing the elders and burning the huts and taking everyone else away to sell for slaves. It all sounded perfectly ghastly, but it was the sort of horror that used to happen all the

93

time before the British came. The only surprising thing I thought was KB letting it happen to the Kitawa, after the agreement Ted had told me about. He was supposed to be protecting them from things like that. I didn't know quite what to say when she'd finished, but obviously I had to be sympathetic and try and explain it couldn't happen now.

'This is a bad story,' I said. 'But it is many rains ago.'

'It is two rains ago,' she said.

I thought I'd heard wrong.

'Two rains?'

'Two rains.'

She was absolutely certain about it.

You can paint a bit while you're listening, even when it's a difficult language you aren't v. good at. Sometimes your hand knows what it wants and does better if you aren't really thinking about it. Mine had been blobbing away at the fuzz of branches on top of the mound, dirty grey-brown, getting them spot on—you could almost feel something pretty unspeakable might have happened up there—but now I saw it had given a jump and made a great splodge just where I didn't want it, up in the sky. I started trying to soak it away tho' I knew I'd never get back to the plain smooth wash I'd put there—my system I have to get things right first time or it's no use. If I hadn't needed to pretend to the spearmen I'd probably have chucked the picture away then and there.

Of course I wanted to check I'd understood right, so soon as I'd mopped up the worst of the damage I twisted round to my satchel again to try and make sure, face to face, but the women were changing places and there was a new one waiting to tell me something. She was absolutely terrified, sort of purply-grey, and trembling. Probably it was 'cos of that, but she was almost impossible to follow. Even if I'd understood every word I'd have been muddled. Somebody had taken something from someone else, and someone had gone to someone to complain (I think) but no one would listen and instead he'd been beaten very hard and then on his way home he'd been attacked again and beaten till he was dead. And the horsemen wouldn't let his wives take his body away but made them leave it by the path so that everyone could see. Oh dear, I've made that sound much more sensible than it was. The only thing I'm at all sure of is that somebody was beaten till he was dead and the horsemen sent the wives away. I'm not honestly sure it was the dead person's wives. I've sort of guessed it together, the way you do with dreams. At least I didn't have to ask how long ago.

'This is new,' she said. 'This is done these rains.'

'No one has spoken to the white man about this,' I said. I knew that, 'cos it would have been still going on with memos to and fro when I'd been helping Ted with his papers. She didn't answer. More shufflings as the women changed places. It was Femora Feng again.

'Who can speak to the white man?' she said. 'He is the friend of Kama Boi. The sons of Kama Boi stand at his side. We must speak through the mouth of the horsemen. Will he say what we say? Where will the white man be when the horsemen come to punish those who have spoken? We speak to you, Betty Jackland.'

Oh, how I wanted to help, but I felt absolutely helpless. The trouble was she was sort of right. There's an absolute rule against political officers hearing complaints against the Native Authority without an N.A. representative there, and of course this doesn't just mean the N.A. knows who's making the complaint, the complainer knows they know. Suppose a chief's had your brother beaten for not giving him a present, what's he going to do to you for complaining about it? You've got to have an awful lot of trust in the White Man, and how can you if he doesn't understand your language and you have to speak to him using someone who's one of *them*? Besides, even if the White Man believes you he doesn't do anything, far as you can see. He doesn't get rid of the chief—Kaduna hate deposing chiefs. So the chief'll still be there when that White Man's gone and a new one's come. I'm not making this up. It's what Ted says too. But it's part of the system and the rest of the system won't work if you try and put it right so you have to lump it. Like these poor women. Terrified.

Best I could think of was somehow to persuade Ted to listen with me to interpret. Go out for our evening ride and meet someone, where Z. and his men couldn't see. It'd have to be an eye-witness, tho'.

'Did you see this spearing and burning?' I said. 'Or the beating? Who saw them?'

'It is far away. Three days and two days.'

That wasn't any use, not even on this tour area. Ted wouldn't be able to make enquiries on the spot.

'At this place, at Tefuga, the horsemen have done nothing like this?'

She sucked in her breath. She was going to speak but one of the other women must have stopped her. I could hear mutterings, angry and frightened. I couldn't look 'cos the spearmen were getting fidgety. I hummed and pretended to be busy with my painting. Quite spoilt now, so just to have something to do with the brush I scrubbed in a quick trick thunder-cloud to cover up the mess. One of the spearmen started to get up.

'Don't move,' I shouted in Hausa, but he pretended not to understand and came striding over. I was furious. I snatched up the study I'd done and went to meet him and bullied him back to where he'd been sitting and made a great fuss about posing him just how he'd been. (Me! Bullying two big men! Isn't that extraordinary? They didn't like it but they took it.)

When I got back to my easel the women had gone. Crept away under the bank, I suppose. I waited for them to come back but they didn't. I had to pretend to go on with my painting so I finished the cloud—all wrong with that heat and light below, so I messed around with the shadows a bit and then gave up. It wasn't quite as bad as it might have been—effective in a creepy kind of way. It'll do for KB, at least. He won't know.

I tickled up my study of the spearmen so I could give it to them and by then it was too hot for anything so we all came back to Tefuga. Ted's still at his census palaver. I'm supposed to be doctoring but I don't feel up to it. I'll have to tell him—get it over. Oh, if only I'd understood a bit better!

Awful. My fault. Perhaps I shouldn't really have tried. But I had to. I told him while we were having lunch under our little shade roof. Too hot to eat much, specially tinned tomato soup. Everything so still, drained, veiled with heat, nobody moving, nobody even talking or singing or pounding food among those funny sideways-tilted roofs. Lots of people somewhere, in for the dancing and the palaver, but where? Just our bearers under one lot of trees and Z. and his people under another lot, waiting. Waiting for the heat to go, so life could start again.

What was awful was that he didn't believe me!

I don't mean he really thought I was lying. Of course not. At least . . . Oh, how can two people trust each other absolutely and then suddenly not? I started it, wondering if he was being straight with me, and now it's the other way round.

Pull yourself together, Bets.

Of course he was terribly nice about it. He *is* a nice man, but that doesn't help. I explained how difficult it had been for me, 'cos of her whispering and me having to pretend to paint. I didn't want him to think I was making out I knew anything I didn't. I kept saying I couldn't be sure. He'd started filling his pipe but then he just sat teasing the baccy to and fro in his fingers. When I'd finished about them burning the village I waited for him to say something. He took a long time. He looked hard at me, then away.

'Oyalirri? Or something like that?' he said.

'I think so. She only said it once, at the start, before I knew it might be important. I never got a chance to ask.'

'Anyway, not Fadum.'

'No, I'm pretty certain. Longer than that.'

'You've never heard of Fadum?'

'No. Why?'

'That was in 'seventeen. It's up in the north. It was a Tuareg raid, but apart from that it was exactly as you describe. We had a diplomatic dust-up with the French, who were supposed to be keeping the Tuareg in order, but I doubt if much was done.'

'But this was only two rains ago, darling. I asked her specially.'

'Alright. Go on.'

I tried. I was doing my best about the beating and the murder, and what a muddle it was but I was sure it was something wicked and only just this rains, but in the middle of that I suddenly saw why he'd asked if *I'd* ever heard of Fadum. *I* might have been making it all up. Why, there mightn't have been any women at all!

I don't think that now. I mean if he did think something like that it was only for a mo. But when it happened it was perfectly awful for me. I stuck, with my mouth wide open. He stared at me and I stared at him. Then I managed to go stammering on.

When I'd finished he gave a great sigh.

'Do you want me to send for this woman, Rabbit? She could presumably be found.'

'I don't think it would do any good.'

'Oh?'

'She wouldn't tell you anything. She thinks you are on Kama Boi's side. I told her she ought to go to you, but . . .'

'Alright. But I have to make this clear, Rabbit. Officially I am not allowed to listen to complaints against the N.A. except in the presence of a representative of the N.A.'

'But then they'll never tell you anything! They're terrified as it is!'

'You are never going to educate the native to a concept of justice until he is persuaded that a complaint openly made against someone in authority will be fairly investigated and if found justified the culprit properly punished.'

'But what actually happens is that somebody starts trying to complain but before he gets anywhere near you he's beaten to death and his body's left lying by the path for everyone to see. That's the concept of justice they're being educated in!'

'Let's take that case, Rabbit. Suppose it came to my ears . . .'

'Which it has.'

'. . . that something like that had happened I would, of course, look into it. In order even to begin I would need something to go on, a location, the name of the victim. You understand that?'

'Would you tell Kama Boi what you were doing?'

'Unless I had reason to believe he was in some way personally involved I would not be prepared to go behind his back.'

'Then no one is going to tell you anything.'

'I can't accept that, Rabbit. They will come to me, or to my successors, in the end.'

He stuffed his baccy into his pipe at last as tho' he was shutting the argument off. But I didn't feel like giving up.

'I haven't quite finished telling you,' I said. 'Course I saw it would be harder for you if they only told me about things which had happened miles away, so I asked what about Tefuga, and the one called Femora Feng was going to tell me, I think, but the other two stopped her. Then they all ran away. They were absolutely terrified.'

'I can well believe it. For a peasant to bring an accusation against a powerful noble must be an alarming experience, all the more so if the accusation is false.'

'Darling! But why on earth . . .'

'I've warned you before about attempting to read the mind of the native, but I can suggest a number of possible reasons. For instance, in the peasant mind the N.A. is not merely an instrument of taxation, it *is* taxation. These women might well believe that if they can discredit the N.A. their husbands might no longer have to pay tax.'

'I don't believe it. In fact, I think that's why Zarafio's so set on stopping me talking to anyone, 'cos he thinks they might tell me things like this. I suppose you told him I was going painting.'

'As a matter of fact, yes. But I think you are doing him an injustice. The Hausa have a very strong sense of propriety, and it is simply not in his eyes proper that a person of importance, which you are, should roam about the bush unescorted.'

I felt utterly miserable, not just about Ted perhaps not believing me and then saying the women were lying, but about me letting them down when they'd been so brave (I'm sure it was a frightful risk for them) and been so sure I could do something. Usually I'm quite good at hiding my feelings (practice with Daddy) but it must have shown. I mean, even Ted noticed.

'Cheer up, Rabbit,' he said. 'It's not the end of the world. It's something you have to get used to. Africa's full of things we haven't a hope of understanding and which our system simply isn't geared to dealing with. I really think you'd best try and put all this out of your mind for the moment, and I promise you that I'll keep my eyes and ears open and if I come across the slightest hint of anything of the sort I'll be on to it like a terrier after a rat. I've got to be off, now. Don't brood on things, Rabbit. We'll go for a ride this evening, shall we?'

'Lovely,' I managed to say.

Well, I've not been brooding. I've been writing instead, to get it clear in my mind, and in a funny way I think Ted's right. Not his way, tho'! But I'm going to let him think I've done what he said and stopped worrying about it, 'cos I can't do anything about it till I can talk to some Kitawa all alone, and that's not going to happen *this* tour.

But am I? Going to stop worrying, I mean. Am I going to *do* anything? What *can* I do? She said, 'We speak to *you*, Betty

Jackland.' *She* thought I could, 'cos if she'd been me she'd have been able to.

You know, suppose it had been a man who'd come to Ted with what I told him—no more, same kind of muddle and not being certain. He'd have taken it a bit more seriously, wouldn't he? Even a man he barely knew, when he knows me so well. Or does he? At all? I wonder. What does it mean, knowing someone? But I think I *understand* Ted much, much better than he'll ever understand me. He doesn't have to, you see. It's his world, so it's the shape he makes it, and I have to fit into the bits left over, so I've got to understand where that is. It was the same with Daddy. I hated him, but I had to watch him and think about him a lot so I'd know how I could go on living my own secret life without him noticing. I hated Daddy and I love Ted, but in a funny way that doesn't make much difference.

Anyway, I *am* going to do something for those women. I haven't got much to work with, only Ted. For instance, I could stop being nice to him till he did something himself. Dangerous. He's got such a strong sense of honour. If he thought I was trying to blackmail him with that . . . Not much fun for me, anyway. And too soon. I do see there's precious little he can do at the mo, till we find out more. Better the other way. If he thinks he needs me so much he doesn't mind what else happens . . . he's half way there already . . .

You know, I ought to feel sneaky and horrid and disloyal thinking like this, but I don't. You have to have a life of your own, and the way things are that means it's got to be a secret life.

And anyway, it's more interesting.

SEVEN

The trucks boomed north along the great K.H.P. road for thirty miles, then took a spur westwards. The tarmac surface ended suddenly, not in any chosen geographical location but at the point where the money had run out. A rough track continued westward. Where the bush was open enough to allow it the trucks drove in wedge formation to avoid the heavy reddish dust-trail churned up by the leader. Occasionally the one carrying Pittapoulos would surge ahead so that he could film the other two coming past. They had no need for these sequences in the film, though possibly they might find a place later in Jackland's series, but it is apparently ordained that where two or three trucks are going through bush together one must stop to film the others. And conceivably the shots, with those taken at Tefuga itself, might mollify some accountant fretting over the cost of the unbudgeted expedition. It was early afternoon by the time they reached Tefuga, the heaviest heat of the day in this supposedly cool season, but that had to be endured if they were to make the round trip before nightfall.

The drivers were steering directly for the huts when Miss Tressider, who had been conducting her interview with Miss Boyaba in the back of the lead car, leaned forward and said, 'Don't let them go right in, Nigel.'

Jackland spoke to the driver, who pulled aside into the shade of a clump of flat-topped trees, their trunks gnarled with annual grass-burnings. The other cars followed. The technicians, so calloused by the long delays of their trade that no arrival on location could now excite them, certainly not another bunch of grass-roofed huts in flat bush, climbed down, lit cigarettes, picked desultorily over their equipment. The petrol feed on one truck had been playing up; the three drivers gathered round the open bonnet and discussed the mystery without enthusiasm. The others, nine in all, walked towards the village through the heavy, hazed sunlight. Black people wearing only grass belts, and in the case of the women plaited grass collars, had appeared in front of the huts to stare at the visitors.

'Hold it,' said Burn. 'We don't want a great gang crashing in on them. Jalo, you go ahead and sort it out. They'll know what we're up to—Trevor was out here last month. All we want is some long-distance shots of the hill. One or two of the village too, maybe.'

'Perhaps Miss Boyaba might go too,' said Jackland. 'She speaks Kiti.'

'Oh, no! I've forgotten it all, almost. But I'd love to go.'

The white group watched their two black emissaries cross the thirty-yard gap. The villagers, all elderly, had the look of genuine primitives. There was no hint that they had dressed up, or rather down, for their visitors, or that crumbs from the table of consumer civilization (a radio, an old bike, an aluminium cooking-pot) had been brushed out of sight into the huts. The gap between them and Miss Boyaba seemed vastly greater than that between Miss Boyaba and, say, Miss Tressider.

'Nice sexy walk, that,' said Pittapoulos.

The comment caused a faint alteration in the currents that existed between the members of the group, easing some because it gave voice to what most of the men were probably thinking, heightening others because Miss Boyaba had arrived as Jackland's protégé and Jackland already generated certain currents because of his relationship with Miss Tressider, inevitably the focus of the group's interest in matters sexual. Miss Tressider actually glanced at Jackland, but he seemed not to have heard. He was watching intently as Miss Boyaba said her first words to the villagers. They smiled and answered. She laughed. Miss Tressider pinched Jackland's forearm, using her nails to make it hurt. He looked down.

'I've got something else in common with your mum,' she said.

'Oh?'

'We've got the same ideas about harems.'

She made no show of keeping her voice down.

'I will endeavour to respect your prejudices,' said Jackland. 'Did Annie tell you what happened after my mother left Kama Boi's palace, that day she painted his wives?'

'No.'

'There's a level of irony I'd missed. Good thing, probably. You can't get it all in, ever. I've promised to show her the diary.'

'Haven't you got a typescript?'

Jackland didn't answer. He seemed absorbed by the encounter in front of the huts. The interpreter, Jalo, who despite his claims had turned out to speak no Kiti at all, was evidently trying to negotiate in Hausa. Three old men were listening; their tribal scars made it impossible to tell whether they were as bewildered as they looked. Miss Boyaba had moved slightly apart and was engaged with a mixed group, using as much body-language as speech. A sense of surprise and cheerfulness emerged strongly from around her. Suddenly she broke off and ran back—an absurd, incompetent, high-kneed gait dictated by the heels of her shoes. She snatched Jackland by the hand.

'Come and meet them,' she said. 'I think I've found a cousin. I told you I could still say hello.'

'A strong spirit in Annie Boyaba.'

'And a strong spirit in Nigel Jackland.'

She repeated the sentence in what was evidently Kiti, musical syllables that seemed to slur into each other, making the shape of each individual sound very hard to pick out. Her intense, unforced excitement at this twenty-five-per-cent home-coming—her other three-quarters belonging genetically elsewhere in Nigeria—was easy to share, seeming almost to colour the oppressive pale light around her. Prattling away she dragged Jackland off to be introduced to the villagers. Burn and Pittapoulos went to join Jalo—the three old men, it turned out, spoke perfectly adequate Hausa. The others followed Jackland, and Miss Tressider found herself included in the introductions in a marginal fashion. She showed no resentment, and may well have been pleased and amused to find herself in a community where her name, though repeated several times, meant nothing whatsoever.

After the first two or three introductions she made an attempt at the Kiti, but despite her gifts and training must have managed to say something else, happily inappropriate. The villagers laughed, and laughed again as she repeated or perhaps compounded the error. She mimed stupidity and shame, clowning precisely enough to let her audience realize that she was as amused as they were and they could continue to laugh without offence.

'I will teach you,' said Miss Boyaba.

'No. You stay and help Nigel make friends.'

Miss Tressider beckoned to two old women and drew them aside for a lesson. In the main group Miss Boyaba continued to unearth shards of her childhood vocabulary. Jackland, characteristically, moved outside the group to watch. Pittapoulos came up to him.

'We've got a problem,' he said.

'Oh?'

'Notice something? It's a geriatric community.'

'That's what tends to happen. The younger ones head off for the towns.'

'You don't have to tell me. Seen it again and again. Only you can usually find one or two who've not been bright enough to clear out. Can't see 'em here.'

'We'll do without. It'll be ten seconds' screen-time, if that.'

'Unless we can persuade yon dusky charmer to strip off.'

'Wrong colour. She's supposed to be dark brown.'

'I'll use a filter. Do you mind asking her, Nige?'

'Yes, as a matter of fact, I do.'

Pittapoulos raised a bushy eyebrow and glanced with deliberate lack of tact at Miss Tressider, intent on her Kiti lesson. Though he had worked successfully with Jackland before, they could not be said to have liked each other. It might have seemed that this was simply because Pittapoulos thought Jackland a snob, and Jackland thought Pittapoulos a vulgarian. Though this was probably true, other tensions arose in their attitude to their work, Pittapoulos being uninterested in ideas of any kind that could not find expression in a visual image, and also being prepared to fake that image to any extent he needed. To him the picture shown on the screen was in itself the truth, or at least a truth, whereas Jackland was invariably dissatisfied by its failures, distortions and omissions. To use one of his own favourite images, the world was a fish that invariably got away; all he could do was come home and stretch his arms across the screen to show the size of it.

This time there was a further mild cause of tension. Pittapoulos's hobby was the compilation of a tape, already several hours long, of naked women, filmed by himself, the subjects being unaware of the event. He was not interested in professional models, but was as it were a visual rapist, adept at manoeuvring events to suit his purpose, using both the patience and the ingenuity of the wildlife photographer. He did not only pursue his hobby in remote areas where nakedness was the norm. His tape was said to include a brief clip from a royal event in the English shires.

He had early expressed disappointment at the way Jackland's script respected the superficial reticence of the diaries, with its asterisks and circumlocutions. Not that Pittapoulos would have included in his tape anything shot for public viewing, but there would have been moments in the preparation for such scenes when a camera would somehow have been left running. Miss Tressider would hardly have minded, but Jackland probably would. Perhaps the fact that Jackland was currently enjoying an actuality to which even Pittapoulos would not have claimed the screen image was preferable added to the desire to needle.

Jackland followed his glance, apparently unruffled. Miss Tressider seemed by now to have mastered the sentence. Her tutors' giggles had changed to clucks of approval. They swapped greetings a couple of times more, and then Miss Tressider turned. Her face became her version of Betty Jackland. She spoke the brief phrase, experimentally, to empty air. The final syllables were the name 'Femora Feng'.

Instantly the two old women went rigid. Miss Tressider had been facing away from them, but with an actor's sense of audience she knew at once that something had gone wrong, and turned. She smiled. They backed away. Their eyes wavered between her and the space of air to which she seemed to have spoken. Jackland, standing nearest, could barely have heard the name, so most of the others could not have known what had happened, but still the infection spread fast. All the villagers broke off the attempt to communicate, leaving the visitors gesticulating and mouthing at emptiness. They too fell silent. Miss Boyaba was probably the most bewildered.

'God,' said Burn. 'Who's put their wee foot in it now? Jalo?'

'Hold it,' said Jackland. 'Better leave it to Mary.'

Without any obvious decision visitors and villagers had

separated, moving into a rough circle on the arena of bare earth in front of the huts. Miss Tressider stood near the middle of it, facing the two old women. There was nothing to prevent them stepping further back to join the circle and become, as it were, just two anonymous villagers, but they doubtfully stood their ground as her accusers.

'I'm sorry,' said Miss Tressider. 'That was pretty stupid of me.'

She half spread her arms, palms forward, the universal signal of openness and innocence. The women did not respond.

'I seem to have raised a ghost, you see,' she said. 'What can I do? Oh, yes. Look serious, everyone. Lend me your penknife, will you, Sally?'

She was wearing a yellow blouse, blue Bermuda shorts, track shoes, gamine-style short-peaked cap. Beneath the dust of the journey her bare smooth skin was golden with pricey lotions. She moved tentatively, as though feeling her way by faintly perceived electric discharges, towards the area to which she had addressed her greeting.

'About here, wasn't she?' she said.

She knelt and with a single wide sweep, three-fingered, outlined an invisible circle on the earth. She rubbed dust from the circle, pinching it up into her other palm until she had enough to dribble it over the back of her bowed head. She opened the knife, tested its point and slid it into the round of her thumb. She pressed a glistening bead of blood from the slit.

She spat into her palm, picked up the bead on her fingernail and mixed it in with the spittle. She added fresh dust from the circle, making a paste, which she rolled with her fingertips into a pellet.

All so far in silence. Now, as she held the pellet—about the size of a pea—between finger and thumb over the centre of the circle, she started a low humming noise, very like a cat's purr, deep in her throat. The hum seemed to have no centre, but to be located in the air around her. She took the pellet back into her palm to breathe on it, then, humming again, placed it in the centre of the circle. She took dust, from outside the circle this time, and dribbled it over the pellet till its shape was lost. With one hand spread wide she pressed the small mound flat, moving the hand in an outward spiral until it reached the edge of the circle. She stopped humming and rose to her feet.

'Show's over, folks,' she said.

The tone of release after the focused intensity of the improvised ritual was so obvious that one or two of the villagers laughed. When Miss Tressider turned towards the two old women with her previous spread-hand gesture they replied with only slightly troubled smiles. An old man came over and joined them.

'That was terrific,' said Miss Boyaba. 'How did you think of it? Gosh, it really did the trick, didn't it?'

Miss Tressider grinned at her, teasingly uncommunicative. Burn and Pittapoulos began to discuss possible shots. Jackland joined them.

'Don't want to waste much time here,' he said. 'The hill's the thing.'

'Won't be able to do anything with it this light,' said Pittapoulos. 'Much better wait and get the sun behind it.'

'That'll mean going home in the dark,' said Burn.

'Just leave me with one good truck. You lot can push off soon as we've done the village.'

'All right, Nigel?' said Burn.

'I suppose so. I'll take Mary out to look at the hill now, while you get on here. You won't need us. Stupid to come this far without seeing it.'

'Nothing to see, Trevor says,' said Burn.

'Still, it's where it happened. What'll you do here?'

They had hardly begun to discuss this when Miss Tressider came and touched his arm. He turned.

'They want an encore,' she said. 'Somewhere else. The old boy will show me. Jalo says he's her son.'

She nodded to where the interpreter was talking to the old man, while the two old women watched. All three of the villagers glanced frequently towards Miss Tressider.

'You want me to tag along?'

'If you can tear yourself away.'

'I'd like to. My sort of thing, this.'

It turned out that only the old man was to go with them. He led them along a barely perceptible path that wound between the tree-clumps. Small irregular patches of 'garden', fenced with mats of cane, lay on either side of the path wherever there were workable pockets of soil, but in places the fences sagged or gaped and the area inside had evidently not been worked this year. The old man seemed to have something wrong with his hip, but hobbled purposefully along in silence.

'Did you really make that up on the spur?' said Jackland. 'It was decidedly impressive.'

'Good. It was fun. I don't want to do it again, really, but I suppose I'll have to. Ages ago when I was in rep in Liverpool I went out to that beach. I was mooning round wondering whether to drown myself—not me, of course, just the girl I was playing next week—when I came across a grimy little kid all by herself, crying. She wouldn't tell me what the problem was but she let me watch her magic. I lent her a pin for the blood. She didn't hum. That's one of my exercises.'

'It gives a new meaning to the phrase "White Man's magic".'

'It doesn't need to be white. It wasn't man's.'

Jackland laughed, perhaps not so much at her remark as at the fizz of her company, the shared euphoria of a successful performance. At this moment their guide stopped and spoke, pointing down a long grassless glade to their left. Well over a mile away, and so little more than a hummock in the heat-haze, rose a small hill crowned with a fuzz of trees.

'That's where it happened,' said Jackland. 'I thought we might drive out there as soon as we've done whatever this chap wants. All right?'

'We could look at where she met Femora Feng first time, too. You'd have liked to shoot the whole thing here and on the river, wouldn't you?'

'If they'd have let me have the cash. Wouldn't you?'

'Not specially. You think that way you'd get nearer to letting people see what really happened?'

'If the words have any meaning.'

'It's no good. The only way you can know things like that is by imagining them. You can't ever know what Betty was like but you can imagine what it was like to be Betty. That's what I'm for, to help people imagine. If you keep packing in things because they're real—real places, real clothes—they start to clog the pipes up. All you need is scraps. A couple of things to get started. The diary was . . . I was going to say it was perfect, but I'm not sure I wouldn't rather have had only a few pages saved from a bonfire.'

'You must ask Annie about . . .'

'Did Betty know?'

'That's the point. If she had . . .'

'Then I don't want to. Not yet.'

'We're almost through. It can't make any difference.'

'It does.'

Tefuga Hill had vanished behind scrub but could be glimpsed once or twice as the path wound on and only came properly into view again when they reached their goal, a clear space too large for a garden, unfenced, randomly dotted with mounds that might have been ant-hills or termite nests, but were on inspection graves. Presumably so small a village as Tefuga did not supply more than one or two burials a year, so either the bodies of Kitawa were brought in from elsewhere or the graveyard was centuries old, judging by its hundreds of mounds, many of them no more than faint undulations, discernible only by the context of their more recent neighbours. Between the mounds, and sometimes on them, grew tussocks of spiky grass. Nowhere was there any sign of the graves being attended to or cared for, no small fetishes such as are usually found in the cemeteries of animists. It was not guessable whether the clearing was accidental or whether the trees were deliberately prevented from growing there, so that the long suns and brief rains could beat straight down on the graves.

The old man hobbled between the mounds. At a place no different from any other he stopped, pointed and spoke.

'Femora Feng?' said Miss Tressider.

He nodded, apparently unperturbed by the name.

'I really don't feel like it,' said Miss Tressider. 'And I gave Sally's knife back. Have you got anything?'

Jackland patted his pockets.

'Find you a thorn, I should think.'

'No. Anyway they say don't give blood more than once a week.'

She knelt in a space between two tussocks that grew by the flattened mound and drew her circle, visible in this looser earth. Her movements had no drama, no intensity. She dragged her hand along the back of her neck as if to remove a smear of the dust she had poured there at the earlier ceremony, and so link it with this later one. She spat, took earth from the grave and tried to roll a pellet, but the paste would not cohere. Her hum seemed no more than a hum in her throat. She scraped the messy crumbs from her hand into the centre of the circle, smothered them with more dust, erased them in an outward spiral. The old man made no sign that he thought the ritual inadequate. Miss Tressider rose and bent to brush the dust from her knees.

'God! Nigel!' she whispered. 'What's that?'

Half way up her right calf was a dark purple hemispherical growth, about the size of a hazelnut but visibly still swelling. She touched it with a fingertip, then shaped her nails into pincer-formation to pluck it away.

'Hold it,' said Jackland. 'Not like that.'

He had a cigarette out and was lighting it. He squatted beside her, puffing the cigarette to a bright glow. When he pressed the tip against the creature it loosed its hold and dropped. He scuffed the thing clear of Miss Tressider's foot and stamped on it, smearing it on to the grave-mound.

Miss Tressider gave a sighing shudder.

'We didn't need the knife,' she said. 'It's like that horrible bit in the Bible. God will provide the sacrifice. Oh, well.'

She bent, scooped up earth and dribbled it on to the smear. The old man spoke, not in Hausa but in Kiti. He looked pleased.

'Are you all right?'

'No. But it's not hurting. Yes, it is. Ow. What was it?'

'Tick of some kind. Extraordinary life-cycle. They can go dormant for years . . .'

'I don't want to know. Ow. Do you think there's anything left in?'

'Not supposed to be if you use a cigarette. Of course, they inject a bit of fluid . . . Stand still.'

Jackland put on his spectacles and squatted again to look. The place was clearly visible, a pale circle in the golden skin, with a small bright blotch at its centre. He squeezed at it with careful thumbs. A bead of watery blood emerged. Miss Tressider muttered with pain. Jackland wiped the blood away, put his lips to the place and sucked hard. He rose and spat.

'Best I can do for the moment. How does it feel?'

'Better, thanks.'

'Shall I go and get one of the cars?'

'No, I'll walk.'

She limped only slightly as they made their way back. Sounds of enjoyment could be heard from the village, and when they came out of the screening scrub they saw that all the small crowd visitors and villagers could muster was gathered round some spectacle, from which rose an erratically rhythmic thud. Craning over the shoulders of the spectators Jackland saw that Miss Boyaba was being given a lesson in the use of a pestle and mortar. She was wearing only a grass girdle and lace-like grass collar, as was the older woman who was teaching her. Despite their shared nakedness and shared laughter they could not have seemed more different. Miss Boyaba was still completely out of place, with her paler skin and her urban hair-style, her youth, her pointed up-turned breasts on the long and lissom torso which swayed like a dancer's as she tried to master the to-and-fro rhythm of the big pestle. She was a child dressing up in grandmother's ball-gown and tiara, which she herself would never wear as an adult because society no longer went in for that sort of party. That was the joke she and the spectators were so enjoying. Pittapoulos from behind his purring camera waved a V-sign at Jackland, who laughed in answer.

'Nigel, my leg is hurting.'

'I take it you don't feel like the trip out to the hill now?'

'If you don't mind. I'll wait.'

'The hill can wait. I'll have a word with Malcolm. We'll have to take at least two of the others. It'd better be the good car—they can come home in convoy when Fred's got his sunset. What about Annie? Do you think she's green enough not to grasp she's got a story? We can't have the insurers taking fright.'

'Get Malcolm to tell her I threw a tantrum seeing someone else in the limelight . . . Nigel, you know she asked me about my love-life—I'll make it true if you stand there goggling any longer.'

'What did you tell her?'

'I said I fancied Major Kadu.'

EIGHT

Monday March 24

Back home. Something really amazing! Must write about it. Didn't write any more during the tour—fact, after Tefuga I almost thought I'd give up doing this. It brings things out of me I'm a bit frightened of, you see. I mean like what I said while I was waiting at Tefuga for Ted to come and take me riding. When I looked at it next day I felt perfectly horrid. I wonder if I'd had a touch of the sun ('tho I *did* see the women and they did tell me those things, far as I could understand, and so on) but really I'm not like that. I know I'm not. I'm an ordinary loyal little wife. It's just something that sort of spills out of the pencil while I'm scribbling away, and it's none of my business how Ted runs his show. My job is to back him up.

Well, just to join the story up—we did ten days' more tour, and I was v. good and didn't complain any more about the women refusing to talk while I was doctoring, or even keep telling Ted how frightened I was sure they were. Or how disappointed I was not getting much chance to practise my Kiti. I painted quite a bit. At first Z. always made sure I had a spearman watching, but after a bit he gave that up, but even then the women wouldn't come near me. They didn't like me painting them, either. I could have insisted, but that's no fun. All a bit sad, but it couldn't be helped.

We did a wide circuit and got back yesterday, Sunday. We'd been held up an extra day 'cos of a muddle about bearers—the old lot had gone home and the new lot didn't show up. So it was almost evening when we reached the river, a bit south of here—just a barrier of trees running each way far as you could see. Surprising how green they looked after the fawny, ashy, strawy bush—real leaves, with proper sap in them, tho' when we've been back a couple of days they'll get that dark, stodgy look again. Z.'s men cheered up no end. They don't like tours —much rather leave it to their agents, pet slaves really, to squeeze the taxes out of the villagers. They forked off towards

Kiti Town and left us with only our bearers. We were just going into the trees when I saw a man, a Bakiti, standing by the track. It was only wide enough for one here and I was leading. I didn't recognize who it was till he held up his hand to stop me. He looked so different without his housecoat, grown-up, not a boy any more. (Of course we call all our servants boys, even when they're grandfathers!)

'A strong spirit in Elongo Sisefonge,' I said.

He didn't look at all surprised at me knowing his whole name, tho' he'd never told me.

'A strong spirit in Betty Jackland.' (Not cheek at all, absolutely right!) 'A white man has come. Dlanzi. He came two days ago.'

He turned and ran off down the path. I explained to Ted.

'Oh lor,' said Ted. 'De Lancey's not supposed to be here till Tuesday.'

'It's all right, darling,' I said. 'Old Kama Boi asked me to go at the last minute. There wasn't time to tell him.'

'We don't exactly see eye to eye over Kama Boi.'

'It'll be all right. I'll wheedle him.'

'You'll do no such thing. He's not that type.'

He was quite right about that, anyway. We found Mr de Lancey in the dining-room smoking a Turkish cigarette and reading Homer in Greek(!) He is a small, round-faced man with pale blue eyes. Rather bald, blotchy brown over the top. What's left is silvery blond. He wears a monocle to read with. He's always dressed, right in the middle of Africa, as tho' his clothes were fresh from the shop. He has a special boy to wash and iron them—Ted says he pays him more than his cook! And he's got enough boiled shirts to be able to post them home to London two dozen at a time to be washed and starched and posted back! He talks in a drawly, bored way and gives a little nod when he's finished to show it's your turn but you'd better not say too much. I thought, 'cos of the nod and the name, he might be half French but Ted (who can't *stand* him—I hadn't properly realized till I saw them together) says he isn't. He says Mr de Lancey likes people to know his family have lived in the same house in Derbyshire since the twelfth century and his mother is one of the Norfolk Dudleys. (That *means* something, I gather.)

So we got home fagged and dusty and wanting to flop in our

chairs with a b. & s.—and we found this horribly non-flop man waiting for us. Ted introduced me.

'I'm afraid your boy seems to have run off,' he said. 'He didn't like the look of me, no doubt. I hope you'll forgive my using your room, Mrs Jackland. You have made it very pleasantly inhabitable.'

That all looks perfectly polite, written down like that, but he's got a sneery way of saying things, as tho' it was terribly gracious of him to bother to apologize, and quite surprising our house wasn't a pig-sty! I couldn't help wanting to get my own back.

'That was Ted,' I said. I tinkled my little glass bell. Elongo came in at once, wearing his white housecoat and skull-cap. I was watching Mr de Lancey sideways to see how he took it, but he just stared contemptuously at Elongo.

'Pass tea-chop,' I said, as tho' everything was just ordinary. Elongo bowed in his dignified way and left. One up to the Jacklands!

'Didn't you get my message, sir?' said Ted. 'We weren't expecting you till Tuesday.'

'I rather fancied a couple of days' fishing. I expected to find Mrs Jackland here, but not wanting to force my company on her I set up camp in that clearing down river. I have simply been taking advantage of your admirable mosquito-defences in the evening. I haven't suffered one whit from your boy running off.'

'He's bush Kiti,' said Ted. 'We're still training him.'

'I stick to Ibibio. They've been in contact with the white man for long enough to have a reasonable idea of what they can get away with. In the words of the poet, they steal in measure.'

'I'm absolutely certain Elongo isn't a thief,' I said.

'My dear Mrs Jackland, of course he's not. Very few Africans are. To be a thief you need to have a clear notion of property, of a society in which everything has an owner with an absolute right to it. The African grasp of such ideas is, to put it mildly, erratic. The cattle Fulani has it, for instance, as applied to cattle. If you took one of his cows from him you would be a thief, but take almost anything else and you would merely be stealing. All Africans steal, from the emir in his palace to the fisherman in his canoe. If your boy does not, he is not merely an exception, he is a nonpareil.'

Oh, I wish I could . . . It's the *tone* you can't write down, even if you've got the exact words. The beastly man was amused, not just at the idea of stealing being different from thieving, which I suppose some people would think was clever—I mean amused at telling *me* 'cos he knew I was too stupid to think of something like that for myself.

'Ted told me . . .' I said, but then Elongo came in with the tea things. I was going to explain about Ted's Resident at Jos who used to drive his Morris out to the Plateau and just leave it in the open for days on end while he tried to talk to the savage tribes up there and no one ever touched it. Of course I didn't want to talk about stealing in front of E. Mr de Lancey didn't care.

'Wonder where he's been hiding,' he said, staring at him while he moved around. 'It's quite a good sign him showing up like that the moment you came back. Years ago, when I was fresh out, I was idiot enough to bring a bulldog bitch with me. Inevitably I spent half my time nursing her from one disease to the next, but I'd got her pretty well seasoned by my first leave. You remember Pop Allen, Jackland? Died in Bauchi in 'seventeen. He took her over. I got a letter from him before I'd been home a week. Apparently the moment I was out of the house Doris had vanished too. Allen had sent the boys out to hunt, offered a reward and so on. He realized I'd be cut up about losing her. I wrote back, of course, telling him it was all my fault bringing her out in the first place. Six months later, my first evening back on seat, I was sitting out on the veranda when Doris crawled up the path. She was skin and bone. Sores all over her body. One eye gone. She died in my arms.'

'How awful,' I managed to say. Goodness, he was lucky he didn't find himself with an eye gone! Really! Our boy, my Elongo, in our dining-room, drawling away about him as tho' he was no better than a dog! I said I'd just run and clean up but as soon as I'd got away I snatched up a bit of charcoal and drew a picture of Mr de Lancey on the wall of my little room. I made him a French poodle, all bobbed and clipped and pom-pommed, wearing a monocle. It was terribly like. I longed to fetch Ted and show him. And at least it made me feel better enough to go back and make tea-chat after I'd changed into a frock.

It was all horribly sticky at first. He must have known I absolutely *loathed* him. And there was absolutely nothing to talk *about*, not even small-talk. For instance he can't stand dance-music—*his* favourite records are by someone called Bartock—at least he hasn't brought them, thank heavens. *He thinks Rupert Brooke is a bad poet!* And I hardly know anyone in the service, part from the ones I met coming up. Or the people he knows back home. (His face when I said Daddy was an auctioneer!) Poor Ted's better than me at hiding his hates. He was just ghastlily embarrassed and scraped away at his pipe (which of course he couldn't light tho' if we'd been alone he'd have done it like a shot). And worst of all I could see Mr de Lancey was really rather enjoying it all inside him, finding out what a dreadful common little wife Ted had picked up. It was one of the worst half-hours I've ever had in my life, bad as when Daddy insisted on asking people to dinner.

I was just thinking at last I could ring for Elongo to come and clear away so Ted could take the man off to his office or somewhere to look at files or something when Mr de Lancey said, 'Jackland tells me you are an artist, Mrs Jackland.'

'I only try and paint a bit,' I said.

'May I see?'

Oh, how I longed to say no! Vulgar little daubs by Jackland's ugly common little wife. I glanced at Ted, begging him to get me out of it, but tho' I did catch his eye he looked away. He knew what Mr de Lancey would think, too. So there was nothing for it. I fetched the album I'd been putting together before the tour, mostly river paintings. I couldn't say anything—I'd have choked. I just gave it him.

He screwed in his monocle and slowly, slowly opened the album at the beginning. The first picture is a quick sketch I did of a fisherman throwing his net, the sort you get right straight off or tear up. He looked at it. I could hear Ted's pipe-scraping and the evening dove-calls and the tick-tick of things in the thatch. At last he turned the page. I could have screamed, waiting for the axe to fall. Then after five pages he looked up and opened his eye muscles so that the monocle dropped on to its string and stared at me with his horrid pale eyes. It was as tho' I'd been a cockroach on his breakfast tray.

'These are extraordinarily good, Mrs Jackland.'

IT ABSOLUTELY ISN'T FAIR!!! Why should darling, kind, decent Ted, whom I truly love, not be able to understand, when horrible, horrible Mr de Lancey could see at once? In fact I saw Ted's jaw drop and he picked up his cup and took a swig to hide it but it was all cold dregs and he almost choked. I didn't understand at first. Nobody's ever said anything like that before —only people who don't know being polite—I'm almost crying with a stupid sort of happiness now while I'm writing. The point is, you see, he meant it. And he *knew*. He wasn't being nice. He hadn't any reason at all to say anything nice—quite the opposite. Oh!! (Pull yourself together, Bets!)

Well, of course I couldn't do anything except stammer. I'm simply not used to people thinking anything I do is any good. I don't know how to behave. Mr de Lancey looked at me as tho' he still thought I was a perfect fool, then put his monocle in and went back to the album.

'Who taught you to do this wash?' he said.

He tilted the book towards me so I could see. It was the one of the rapids at Kiti. I'd got the sky just right, hazed but huge. All that emptiness, and Africa going on for ever underneath it.

'Fraid I just taught myself,' I said. 'I saw some Japanese pictures and thought I'd like to copy their kind of wash. It took me ages to learn, and it's still not quite the same.'

'Ordinary camel-hair brush?'

'Oh, yes.'

'No wonder it took a bit of learning. The Japs have a different trick.'

'I didn't know.'

'Ignorance has its rewards, and this is evidently one of them.'

He went through the whole album, looking at every picture as tho' he was reading the pages of a difficult book. I caught Ted's eye. He was still totally amazed, I could see, dear man, but he made a thumbs-up sign to me. I rang my bell and Elongo came and cleared away. I don't suppose Mr de Lancey even noticed him.

I hadn't finished doing the album and there were some loose pictures in the back. He took them out one by one to look at them. I'd forgotten, but I must have shoved in the sketches of KB's wives and the copies I'd made for the old brute. I'd been meaning to mount the copies to make them look a bit special, but what with Ted's guinea worm and then getting ready to go on tour I'd not got round to it. I only remembered when I saw Mr de Lancey comparing two, glancing from one to the other. He put three on one side before he closed the album. I knew what he was going to say before he opened his mouth, which is quite extraordinary 'cos it's never happened to me before.

'May I buy these three, since you have duplicates?'

I just shook my head. I couldn't say anything. I must have reached out without thinking, 'cos next thing he was handing me the three pictures. Oh, he knew all right. They were the real ones, the ones I'd done in the harem.

'The copies are for old Kama Boi,' said Ted. 'Betty did them because she wanted to stick to the originals.'

'I wouldn't have credited the brute with an eye for aesthetics,' said Mr de Lancey.

'He appears to have,' said Ted. 'He sent a runner asking me to take Betty on tour so that she could paint his domains.'

(So *that* was alright. Only I wasn't interested any longer. Nor was Mr de Lancey.)

'Seriously, Mrs Jackland,' he said. 'I would very much appreciate it if you would let me buy something. I am not asking for a gift. I prefer to buy. I like to think that I have built my collection out of my own resources. I grew up surrounded by paintings and sculptures, many of them first rate, and though as a younger son I had to start afresh and my finances limit me to water-colours, I have the nucleus of a satisfactory little collection waiting in England to comfort me in my retirement.'

'I don't know,' I said. 'I'll try and think of something.'

'Please do,' he said.

After that Ted took him off to the office to go through files for a bit so I could make arrangements for supper. We'd been meaning to have a picnic out of tins and then fall into bed, but of course with Mr de Lancey there we had to lay on something. Dinner was sticky in a different kind of way, tho' Mr de Lancey did most of the talking. At first it was about being sick. Ted's guinea worm. He wanted to know all the ugsome details and tell us much worse things which had happened to other people. Another of his little hobbies, like collecting water-colours! He's famous for his medicine chest, which he takes everywhere, full of his own special remedies. Hope he's never here when I go down with something!

After that we got on to the subject of schools. Quite a lot of the

Political Officers are a bit potty about which school they were at, and ride eighty miles to see someone who was there too so they can swap stories about when they were boys and what's happened to the other boys. It matters. Mr de Lancey was at Winchester, but Ted was at somewhere called Garsford where they wore sandals and called each other by their Christian names. (So stupid of them to choose that for him. He does mind being different.) Mr de Lancey isn't quite so sneery now when he talks to me, but he obviously still thinks I'm stupid and need things explained. Actually what he said was quite amusing. His idea was that the reason we are so keen on Indirect Rule is 'cos we think it works like a public school. At places like Eton and Winchester the masters use the big boys to govern the rest, and the big boys have special privileges and are very grand so they feel it's worth their while keeping order in the school. That's what we're doing here with the emirs. Course, there's one big difference—in the schools the big boys keep leaving and the little boys grow up and do the governing. Mr de Lancey thinks it's poppycock to suppose that's ever going to happen here.

'The analogy is not of Zarafio taking over from Kama Boi, which heaven forfend,' he said. 'It is of your boy there and his kind taking government into their hands. You won't see that in our lifetime, or our children's, eh, Jackland?'

Ted just grunted. He's often said the same to me, but he wasn't in a good mood. Mr de Lancey hadn't been talking about his idea just to amuse me—he'd been using it to get at Ted about having gone to a school where they didn't have prefects or fagging. No wonder Ted laughed so loud when I took him into my room at bed-time and showed him my poodle!

Tues March 25
Oh dear, I don't understand at all! Me, I mean. I thought I'd made up my mind to be good, and all along I must have been only pretending. It's difficult to explain, 'cos nothing's really happened, but it has, and now everything's different again.

I didn't realize then but I think it must have begun in the middle of last night. I was lying awake, thinking. It hadn't been as nice as usual—Ted rather rough and careless. I hadn't thought I'd minded. It was so easy to understand after a day like that. With Mr de Lancey all day long, first in the office going through files, and then riding down river with him to try and deal with the fishing-rights problem—it's all to do with some islands which are supposed to be in Kiti but a lot of Sokowa have moved in and our District Head down there has been quite spineless and KB hasn't done anything and Ted won't go over his head which Mr de Lancey thinks he ought to—all desperately complicated and frustrating, specially with our people letting Ted down the whole way when Mr de Lancey has got his lot toeing the line. And then to come back and listen all evening to me and Mr de Lancey jawing about pictures—terribly interesting for me, but I shouldn't have hogged the whole evening like that . . . well, no wonder he wanted to show whose wife I was.

As I say, I thought I was being very loyal and understanding while it was happening, but then I woke up in the middle of the night and I found I was lying there brooding about me and Ted and Kama Boi and his wives, and wondering what the difference really was, and remembering how I'd felt that time at Tefuga when I thought Ted had let me down so, and how I was somehow going to use s * * to get my own back, and then I'd been ashamed in the morning. But now here Ted was using it, his way, to get *his* own back . . . I lay awake quite a long time, thinking that sort of round-and-round night thoughts, and then I fell asleep. In the morning I just put it all aside, I thought. But I can't have.

I'd better explain that one of the things I'd been jawing about with Mr de Lancey was doing a picture specially for him. I felt v. nervous about it, in case it wasn't good enough, so I suggested I actually did one of him fishing, so if it didn't turn out quite right for his collection it'd still be a sort of keepsake. He agreed to that, so we settled he'd go down and start fishing soon as it was light and I'd come down a bit after and try and do a picture. I told him about a place I'd looked at once or twice, just below his camp, but hadn't tried 'cos it needed a bit more interest in the foreground.

So down I went with Elongo to carry my things. It wasn't too hot yet, and the river had bits of mist on it I didn't want to lose, and tho' I was still nervous I was excited too at having the chance to show what I could really do. But I got a terrible shock when I got there, 'cos I could hardly see Mr de Lancey at all! I knew where he was, I mean. That was obvious—only too obvious!—but I couldn't see *him*! It turned out he does his fishing from inside a special little mosquito-net tent with only his rod poking out. I was amazed. I mean somebody who understood so much not seeing how impossible that was going to be, a fuzzy shapeless blur, not interesting at all, just puzzling. I was terribly disheartened but I settled down under my brolly to make the best of it. I soon found out why he'd needed it, tho'. The place was swarming with flies. I'd been meaning to send Elongo back but I kept him to whisk them off me.

I didn't bother about the *thing* at first. I was in a hurry to catch the mist and the shadows along the far bank which would be gone in half an hour. I'd been expecting to put Mr de Lancey near the middle, but instead I left a blank at the side for the near bank and the *thing* and laid on one of my washes for the sky and another for the sheeny water with the mist just fading and dabbed in the far bank—all not bad—and then I had to decide what to do about the *thing*. It was terribly awkward. I was sure it was going to spoil what might have been quite a nice little picture. I did a few trial sketches on a spare sheet but it wouldn't come right, then in the middle of that I had an idea—one of my cartoony ones—so I dashed it down and showed it to Elongo. He saw the joke at once and laughed his lovely round African laugh.

'What's up?' called Mr de Lancey.

The rod went down, the *thing* shuddered and collapsed, and out he came.

'My arm was getting tired,' he said. 'I could do with a rest.'

I ought to explain he was tiger-fishing. You can't eat tiger-fish but they're terrifically game. You catch them by casting a 'spoon' out and trolling it back which makes it look like a silver fish in the water and the tiger-fish grab it. Only they hadn't so far.

He strolled across to look. I was embarrassed but I had to let him see what Elongo had been laughing at. I'd drawn him huddled into his *thing* and labelled it 'White Man Fishing' and next door I'd drawn one of our natives casting his net with that big open gesture and labelled it 'Black Man Fishing', tho' you could see the joke without reading the labels—at least Elongo had. Mr de Lancey didn't laugh, but he sounded a bit amused. Then he looked at the painting.

'Coming along admirably,' he said. 'Have you ever looked at anything by Bonington?'

'Only in books, I'm afraid. I can see they must be lovely.'

'I have a very decent specimen. I often wish I could have risked having it with me. I mention it because it catches the morning light on the Grand Canal in much the same way you have. I shall be very glad indeed to add this to my collection, Mrs Jackland —it will be adequate compensation for your refusal to let me buy the ones of Kama Boi's wives . . . I suppose you're still adamant about that?'

'Fraid so. They're rather special. I'll never do anything like them again.'

'Oh, I hope you will. You seem to me to have immense potential. It's very rare, the combination of freshness of eye with natural technical skill. I'd be interested to know why those three pictures mean so much to you.'

I didn't like telling him, but I managed to stammer a bit about how the harem upset me, and how I'd tried to paint those women as they ought to have been, only KB didn't let them.

'And what do you make of old Kama Boi himself?' he said.

'I think he's perfectly disgusting,' I said. 'If you've made him one of your prefects then I think you're running a very bad school and I'm not going to send *my* sons to it!'

'Fortunately a remote contingency,' he said with a snickering little laugh—thinking of Ted and Garsford perhaps! Then he asked if he might smoke and lit one of his sickly cigarettes (like an R.C. church) and looked at my sketches of the *thing*.

'I had not realized the problem,' he said. 'Of course I have never seen my tabernacle from the outside. It looks almost transparent when I am in it. I see I must endure the flies for a while, so that you can portray the man himself.'

'Well, it would make it easier,' I said.

He turned to Elongo and rattled away at him in Hausa about clearing the *thing* away up the bank. Never asked *me*, of course. Fussy little instructions which I was sure Elongo hadn't understood, but E. pretended he had (Africans always do) and started off. I *knew* Mr de Lancey wanted a reason for shouting at him for a fool in front of me, so I called after him in Kiti to undo the guy-ropes first.

'Is that Kiti, Mrs Jackland?'

'Yes, I've been learning it, for something to do. Elongo's Hausa isn't very good, nor's mine, so we talk in Kiti.'

'That's rather enterprising of you. I'm told it is far from straightforward, even by the standards of native languages.'

Suddenly, then, out of nowhere, I knew this was what I'd been waiting for! That's what I mean about pretending to be good. It wouldn't have been any use me nagging at Ted or . . . I don't know what else I could have done. I mean even when Mr de Lancey turned up I couldn't possibly have told him, straight out like that, and he couldn't have listened, either. So I just said to myself it was all none of my business and I was a loyal little wife and so on. Now, though, when the chance came, I *had* to take it. It was almost as tho' something outside me, something much stronger than me, was telling me what to do! I was still v. careful, tho'. I had to make it *seem* like an accident.

'Oh, it's a pig!' I said. 'All those tones! I'm getting quite good at household things and fairy-stories and so on, but . . . for instance, when we were at Tefuga some women came to me with an extraordinary story about someone burning a village and killing the men and selling the others as slaves because they couldn't pay their taxes, I think . . .'

'Really?'

'Well, it was something like that but the woman was talking in whispers because she was frightened of letting Zarafio's spearmen know she was there . . .'

'You told your husband about this, of course.'

'Oh, yes. He said it was all to do with a Tuareg raid in 1917.'

'That certainly occurred.'

'Well, you see, that's what I mean about Kiti being difficult to understand. I actually asked the woman when it happened and she said two rains ago. I'm almost sure. I couldn't ask her a lot, with the spearmen so close.'

'You imply that they were there to prevent you talking to the women.'

'Oh, yes. You see, Zarafio didn't want me coming on tour at all so he tried to make things as difficult as possible. He tried to pretend it was because he was a strict Mohammedan, and when I started doctoring the wives and children and practising my Kiti he kicked up a fuss.'

'What utter impertinence.'

'Yes, but you see . . . well, it was a bit tricky for Ted. Suppose Zarafio had complained to Kaduna, you never know what Kaduna will do, do you? They always take both sides. They might have said Zarafio was in the wrong but I'd better not go on tour next time, anyway. We didn't want that at all.'

'It was still utter impertinence.'

'Well . . .'

'You think it was more than that? That there was some motive in preventing you from communicating directly with this woman?'

'There were three of them, actually. One of the others tried to tell me about something that happened during last rains, a murder, as far as I could make out.'

'There are no murders in Kiti on the files for 1923.'

'That's what Ted said. It's so difficult to *know*, isn't it? Specially if they won't complain about what's happened to them. I tried to ask the women if anything bad had happened at Tefuga—both these other things were up in the north, I think —and they just slunk away.'

'That can be interpreted in two lights, Mrs Jackland. The motive you suggest is one, but if the stories are fabrications it would be well for the tale-bearers to set them at a distance where they cannot immediately be checked. Your boy's bush Kiti, though. Has he nothing to contribute?'

You know, I hadn't even asked Elongo since we got back about what Femora Feng had told me. That's what a loyal little wife I thought I'd been being! Elongo had got the *thing* down by now and was folding it neatly into a bundle. Mr de Lancey shouted at him to come over, which he did, carrying the *thing*. Mr de Lancey asked him in Hausa, speaking slowly and simply, if he knew of any wrong doings by Kama Boi. (Ted wouldn't dream of asking a native something like that. It's breaking all the rules.) Elongo looked at me. I nodded that he could tell, but he still looked desperately worried. He got down on his knees and grovelled in front of Mr de Lancey, Hausa-fashion. I hated that, but there was nothing I could do.

'I do not know,' he said.

'Elongo Sisefonge,' I said in Kiti, 'Femora Feng told me the story of men burning a village and killing the men and taking the others away. The men were servants of a son of Kama Boi. Is the story true?'

'I must not tell.'

'But if things of this kind are done the White Man must be told. How else can he punish those who do them? The White Man is the protector of the Kitawa.'

'Kama Boi is the protector of the Kitawa, because of what was done at Tefuga when his father died. It is the sons and servants of Kama Boi who do wrong, and Kama Boi does not punish them. How will the White Man do this when Kama Boi does not? How will the White Man protect those who bring such stories to him? When they go home to their villages, will the White Man be by their side, night and day, to shield them from vengeance?'

I explained this to Mr de Lancey, who nodded.

'That's the problem with the native,' he said. 'Their logic's different. I hadn't realized what a hold the old rogue's got on them. At least we shan't have that problem with his successor. It will only be a goat sacrifice at the ceremony, I imagine. That should weaken the juju. But the real problem's one of communication. We are not going to improve the situation until we have a bridge at Kiti, and proper roads so that the Kitawa begin to understand the real extent of our power. And we are not going to get the roads and bridges built while Kama Boi is Emir. Nor are we going to persuade the Kitawa to bring the necessary complaints to depose him until they understand that we can protect them. It is a vicious circle.'

'They don't even seem to blame it on Kama Boi. It's his sons and servants.'

'He is the root of the problem. We can't expect them to see that. Our only genuine hope is that we shall discover some serious financial peculation on his part.'

'Cheating over taxes, you mean?'

'We don't need natives to bring a complaint over that. It is an offence against ourselves. But to get Kaduna to act we would need to prove a major fraud over a period of years, and to judge by the files, though Kama Boi's accounts could hardly be said to be in order, your husband and his predecessors have kept too tight a rein on him to allow more than the odd casual attempt at peculation.'

'That's what Ted says, and he's terribly careful about that sort of thing. I don't know. I can't help feeling there's something going on. It's none of my business, though, is it, really?'

He looked at me with his funny pale eyes.

'I suppose we'd better get on or the light will have changed,' he said. 'It is typical that on the occasion when I am to have my angling prowess immortalized I should in fact catch nothing.'

He went back to his place and started to cast. My heart was hammering so I thought I wouldn't be able to keep my hand steady. I was terribly keyed up, tho' I'd made a bit of a mistake at the end, saying it was none of my business. Too obvious. But soon as I got painting I was alright—keyed up still, but somehow it went into the picture. Much more promising now. The tint of Mr de Lancey's shirt and trousers—pale, almost cream—was just right to set off the whole flat, empty, still river. I wasn't going to do him with any fuss, just blobs—a risk, but worth it. I actually had the colour mixed and on my brush when he hooked into something. The rod bent. It was all there in an instant and I whipped it in, his stance, his tension, the incredible curve of the rod, no line of course, but right at the focus of the picture one white fleck where the fish threshed, fighting to live. I got it in one (you have to!) and then I messed around for twenty minutes touching the details up while he landed his fish. It was a big one. He came over, carrying it, smiling like a cat. It jerked a bit in his hand, with its white needle fangs yawning.

'Well done,' I said. 'It's a whopper. Just the right moment, too. Look.'

He took a long time, sometimes standing back and sometimes using his monocle to peer up close. I wasn't at all nervous. I knew it was alright and I knew he'd understand.

'Well, well,' he said at last. 'Just the right moment, as you say. It's almost a pity in a way, because that's all most people are going to be able to see. They'll think the rest is mere background. That's a lovely passage along by the far bank. I shall be extremely pleased to own that. Would you like me to suggest a price?'

'Oh, no, I couldn't!'

'I see I shall have to do your haggling for you. You will ask me ten guineas, I shall offer two and we will settle for five. Later on, Mrs Jackland, if you decide to start selling, will you get in touch with me, because I know the ropes?'

I just stammered. I didn't know what to say. I felt I was blushing as tho' he'd tried to kiss me (as tho' I'd said yes! Nightmares!) I began to shuffle my sketches together and the Black Man/White Man cartoon fell out on the ground.

'Oh!' I squeaked. 'Would you like this? As a present, I mean? Just to remember by? You could hang it in your . . . er . . .'

(I was sure he didn't say W.C. but I didn't know what.)

He made his snickery laugh and took it. We looked at each other. *That* was the moment, handing over that piece of paper, like a treaty. A secret treaty. We didn't say anything. Mr de Lancey shouted for his boy to come and collect his gear, and Elongo helped me pack up and I trudged up through the heat, back to our own dear house, to have breakfast with Ted. I showed him the picture but he was much more interested to hear about the fish, and a bit jealous.

After breakfast Mr de Lancey came up to say good-bye. He's going down river by boat to call on Mr Skarrett, the D.O. at Magundi. I walked down with him through the broiling heat towards the landing-stage, where Ted was making arrangements with the canoe men.

'You'll be sure to let me know if there's anything I can do for you, won't you, Mrs Jackland?' he said.

He was only pretending to be talking about painting. We both knew.

'All I want in the world is for Ted to be happy,' I said.

'That is in your gift, not mine, Mrs Jackland.'

The thatchers were still at work on the Old Palace porch, a simple but, as Betty Jackland had remarked, incongruous veranda-like structure spreading along a standard Hausa mud-wall frontage. Its function was obscure. Perhaps indeed it had none, other than to symbolize, consciously or unconsciously, the ancient symbiosis between the pagan Kitawa and the Muslim ancestors of Kama Boi. At any rate Jackland, with Miss Boyaba's help and a cash inducement, had persuaded the thatchers to revert for the day to the dress and methods of sixty years ago. Not many adjustments had been needed. The ladders and scaffolding were already stone-age lash-ups, with only the odd bit of nylon cording to be concealed or replaced. The dump truck —the letters KHP still blatant on its side—had been driven away. Piles of unused thatch concealed other modern intrusions. The old thatcher seemed delighted to renew lost authority by showing his sons how to manipulate primitive tools in the manner his father had taught him. The young men had been more reluctant to abandon trousers and T-shirts for loin-cloths (full nakedness being implausible in a supposedly Muslim citadel), and it may have been because of some such obscure resentment that one of them had chosen, between takes, to fetch his large digital wristwatch from his trouser pocket and strap it back on. The intrusion was not noticed until the procession— Miss Tressider, the actor playing Kama Boi, and half a dozen of Sarkin Elongo's own officials in ceremonial robes—was poised to pass in front of the now picturesquely primitive thatchers on their way to the palace door. Burn was the first to spot it.

Not given to tact at the best of times, and more than usually fretful so near the completion of his first big project, he yelled at the young man for a stupid bastard. The young man turned and began to descend his ladder. Then he must have realized that he would lose some of his advantage if he went out of camera shot, so he stopped half way down and yelled back in the vigorous local English. The line he took showed considerable political awareness, demonstrating that beneath the apparently stagnant conservatism of the Kitawa there moved, at least among the urbanized, strong radical currents. Burn—at home a proponent of a very British form of leftist insularism—found himself being described as a colonialist dog at the heels of Reagan.

It was by now well beyond mid-morning, the air heavy with steamy heat. Everybody was anxious to get on, to be done with hanging around and get into somewhere air-conditioned and have a drink. But despite the heat the filming had attracted a fairish audience, including the Sarkin, dressed slightly less formally than at The Warren in a light-coloured robe and turban and accompanied by his brolly-man who carried a modern light-weight parasol and an aluminium folding chair. The young man, now seeing the strength of his position and the size and quality of his audience, embarked on a full-flown political harangue. His theme, emphasized by gestures towards the new palace, was that in this supposed democracy the old power-wielders were still in office and still cheating the people in order to increase their own wealth. The accusation was of course a commonplace of Nigerian politics, but here there appeared to be a local term for it, namely 'Elongism', whose particular offence seemed to be failure to complete the bridge at Kiti rapids.

The Sarkin's reaction was unreadable behind his large sun-glasses, but when his brolley-man began to shout in protest against this outrage to decency he stilled him with a gesture and led the way down towards the Old Palace and in under the shadow of the porch, thus moving out of the young thatcher's line of fire. In any case the harangue was cut short. The old thatcher had hitherto shown no understanding of English, but his son's gestures were unmistakable, and he had no doubt heard the same speech in Kiti or Hausa many times over the local equivalent of the breakfast table. Now, moving with the slow assurance of the craftsman, he swung himself across the scaf-folding, and almost as if nudging a bundle of thatch into pos-ition, placed his foot in the middle of his son's back, and shoved. The young man fell sprawling. Someone helped him to his feet and led him away, too winded for oratory.

'Right!' shouted Burn. 'We'll carry on without him. Ready, Fred? Trevor? God! Nigel, the Sarkin! Can you . . .

The Sarkin's move under the porch had brought him to the

doorway through which the procession was due to pass. He seemed for the moment oblivious, apparently still trying to calm his brolley-man's outrage. Jackland strode down.

'Excuse me, Sarkin,' he said. 'We're in the way. Do you mind? Quickest if we go inside.'

For a moment the Sarkin seemed about to refuse, but then he let himself be shepherded through the big doorway into what might once have been a fine ante-chamber, tall and cool, whitewashed walls lightly patterned with geometric designs. But the paint had peeled and the domed ceiling fallen away in one corner; the floor-space was used for the storage of various kinds of junk, much of it near-rubbish; and to judge by the smell something had laired or nested, and perhaps died here. The Sarkin led the way on through a similar room, less cluttered but just as derelict, and out into a courtyard. A single large-leaved tree spread its branches over one end; at the other the stump of what had been its twin stood bleached in the glare. All round the courtyard doorways led into the rooms where the lesser members of Kama Boi's household had lived or worked, but the roofs had mainly collapsed, their beams weakened by Africa's voracious chewers and borers. Unprotected from the yearly rains the walls had begun to lose definition, like chocolate left in the sun.

Now that he was out of sight of his people the Sarkin seemed to admit to weariness. His spine drooped slightly. His head went forward on his neck and he walked with an old man's half-shuffle to the shade of the big tree, where the brolly-man opened his chair for him. He sat slowly down and closed his eyes. It was a good minute before he seemed to remember Jackland's existence, and opened them again. Jackland, in fact, was out of sight, having given way to the European instinct to poke around among ruins. By the time he emerged and came strolling across the Sarkin had regathered his energies and was sitting bolt upright.

'I have been advised to turn all this into a tourist attraction,' he said. 'What do you think, Mr Jackland?'

His tone, though calm, made it apparent that he was not specially interested in the question, but was carrying out the royal duty of getting a conversation going on minor matters, whatever else might be on his mind.

'As a romantic ruin, or a practical demonstration?' said Jackland.

'My consultants suggest complete restoration, with life-size models of the inhabitants. I have estimates in my office of the numbers of black tourists who possess the means and urge to investigate their own African-ness.'

'Plenty of money in it for the consultants, anyway.'

'Oh, yes. But also substantial grants from Central Government for capital projects likely to earn hard currency. Furthermore there is a high level of unemployment in Kiti.'

'But you're not going to do it.'

The Sarkin smiled.

'I am still considering. But what do you think? You have, after all, come to Kiti yourself in an effort to re-create your own past.'

'Only marginally mine, old boy. But I'd have thought, supposing you can get the tourists out this far in the first place, a reconstruction might be a success. Nostalgia seems to be an almost universal urge.'

'It is becoming so, but it is strange to me. Where I was born . . . It seems to me, Mr Jackland, that there are two kinds of peoples. The difference does not lie in colour or wealth or climate, but in what is expected of life. There are people who expect tomorrow to be the same as today. To them, all the past is the same. They have a myth of their own origin, but no history. Only when times are bad they have another myth, of a golden age.'

'Before the White Man came it seems to be, these days.'

'Not only these days. It was so when I was a child. I was born among just such a people, but I left them when I was a young man and found a different kind, people who expect tomorrow to be better than today, themselves richer, their lives easier, their power more. They expect to know things their fathers never knew, and to their own children they will soon seem fools. All over the world now, not only in Africa, these people are eating up the other sort. And all over the world at the same time they are searching for something they have lost in their own past. The richer and freer they are, the more the future holds for them, the more they search. This is what I find strange.'

There being no chair for Jackland he had settled unself-consciously on to the ground, sitting cross-legged and looking up at the Sarkin with his habitual mask of interest, inquisitive

131

but tolerant. Despite the good shade the Sarkin had not removed his sun-glasses, and his real feelings were equally unreadable.

'Where do you stand, Sarkin?' said Jackland. 'After all, you were kind enough to help me get this film off the ground. I doubt if we'd have got the various permissions without you.'

'You would certainly not.'

'I'm very grateful. Much in your debt, in fact. But why did you bother if you don't share in the general nostalgia?'

'Because you are your mother's son.'

'Ah. There's something I've been wanting to ask you about her, Sarkin . . .'

Jackland paused, but there was no nod or grunt of permission from the Sarkin, who sat very still, apparently brooding at the leaning silvery pillar of the dead tree-stump.

'My mother kept a diary,' said Jackland. 'Now . . .'

'I am an Elongist, it seems,' said the Sarkin.

'Rather a compliment in some ways,' said Jackland, not apparently put out by the deliberate rebuff. For several seconds it seemed as though the Sarkin did not wish to expand on this topic either. Voices rose from beyond the outer wall. Burn's squeak, exaggerated by tiredness, was the dominant note. Clearly there had been yet another interruption in the apparently simple process of filming six people walking across a patch of bare earth and disappearing through a door.

'I will tell you the history of this so-called Elongism . . . Tefuga . . . The Incident . . . The British understood some things, but not others. After the Incident they saw that our agreement with the family of Kama Boi was ended, but not why. They abolished the Emirate of Kiti, which meant nothing to us. They chose a young man, Yakali, from the family of Kama Boi to be District Head of Kiti Town, but so that the disgrace should not be too apparent they let him call himself Sarkin Kiti, as Kama Boi had called himself before the British made him Emir. Both town and province of Kiti they placed under the Emirate of Soko. All the Kitawa would now pay taxes, but because they were very poor the amounts would be nominal, and the British gave assurances that no extra taxes would be levied by the Native Administration, and no seizing of people in lieu of taxes would take place. It was, in British eyes, a tidy compromise. It did not seem to them to matter that the Emir of Soko was a Fulani, and an hereditary enemy of the family of Kama Boi, nor that his ancestors had been those who used to raid the Kitawa for slaves.

'In the eyes of the Kitawa the arrangement was also a compromise, but a different one. They had unmade the agreement with the family of Kama Boi and had made a new one with the White Man, but the agreement itself was almost identical. There was even, under this new agreement, an official who spoke for the Kitawa to the White Man. Indeed they continued to refer to him as the Bangwa Wangwa, though the White Man called him his Messenger. All this was ratified in their eyes not by the conference of elders which was called by your father after the Incident, but by the Incident itself, at which both the White Man and the new Bangwa Wangwa had been present. The payment of taxes was a disagreeable necessity.

'There was, however, one major difference, unforeseen by the Kitawa and of no obvious importance to the White Man. Kama Boi had ruled for over thirty years. Each White Man seldom stayed for as much as thirteen months. After your father died there was Mr O'Farrell, then Captain Roth, then Mr Smith Hampson, then Captain Roth again—I will not tell you all the names. In 1931 there were three different D.Os at Kiti. The Messenger, however, remained. I was the Messenger.'

'You didn't go for promotion? I'd have thought . . .'

'I could not then read or write. I had no wish to leave Kiti. Elders listened when I spoke. So, soon, did my masters. New D.O.s would come with instructions from Kaduna to respect the Messenger's views on matters affecting the Kitawa. Moreover I had been on the hill at Tefuga that day. I was, in my own eyes, bound to the task.'

'You still are?'

'Yes.'

'Things have changed a lot since then.'

'In those days change seemed far off. The world was one where today was the same as yesterday. If your mother had come back to Kiti in 1945 she would have found very little difference. None at all out in the villages, apart from a few dirt roads and travelling health clinics.'

'De Lancey didn't get his bridge?'

The Sarkin shook his head, smiling with what seemed like nostalgic half-regret at this forgotten foible.

'Mr de Lancey and his bridge. I saw the plans. He contracted hepatitis and was invalided home. Soon with the world recession there was no money for such things. No bridge then, no bridge now.'

'How did that happen? I take it that your young admirer outside . . .'

'Oh no, Mr Jackland. He is, in a sense, right. It is part of the history of Elongism. Would you like me to go on? I was speaking of the war. Now, though nothing had changed, I could smell change in the air. White Man and Black Man might talk as though the British would still be here for a hundred years—the emirs especially talked like that—but in their hearts they did not believe it. Then in 1951 there was a new constitution. Political parties now permitted. Suddenly it became apparent to all thinking people that in a few years the British would be gone. They talked of limited self-rule, but we all knew this was nonsense. A ruler has authority over the ruled. It is not divisible. As soon as they take the smallest part of it back they have effectively taken it all.

'Now, there was a rush to form parties. Those who already had power and authority formed parties to protect themselves. The rest formed parties to take it from them. Here in the north the emirs and chiefs formed the N.P.C. Yakali, who was Sarkin Kiti, was among them. I will tell you about him.'

'I met his son in Lagos, as a matter of fact. One Umani Ban.'

The Sarkin closed his lips tight, sucking them inward, as if to seal off the pressures of speech. The check was a physical effort, a measure of the vehemence of those pressures. The old man had hitherto shown himself affable but in no way self-revealing. Now, though, circumstances—the young thatcher's public attack on him, the mention of his obligation to Jackland's mother, perhaps even the place where he was sitting—seemed to have compelled him to rebut that attack for the benefit of Betty Jackland's son. Whatever the causes, the reference to Umani Ban pulled him up short. His head tilted back. His unseen eyes could only be looking half-sideways down at Jackland with querying suspicion. Jackland as a very experienced interviewer may simply have recognized the nature of reassurance now required. On the other hand his response may have been perfectly genuine—despite his pose of tolerance he was given to sudden vehement dislikes.

'I thought he was a total and unmitigated shit, if you want to know,' he said.

'Umani Ban is my brother-in-law.'

'Ah well. We can't choose our relations. Or our wife's.'

The Sarkin laughed aloud, not an old man's cackle but a hardly enfeebled version of the open, generous laughter Betty Jackland had remarked on.

'I chose my father-in-law, at least,' he said. 'Umani Ban is as you describe him. We Kitawa would say that he has a small spirit in him. Small and mean. He intrigues continually against me. Yakali was a vain, lustful, greedy man, but with a big spirit in him, such as Kama Boi had too. Yakali's great wish was to be Emir of all Kiti, and we knew when he joined the N.P.C. and became a politician this was his chief aim. I resigned my post as Messenger and went out among the villages. The Kitawa wanted to form their own party, but I persuaded them that the emirs would then eat us up. I was right. This is how it has been in Nigeria. So I told the Kitawa to collect money, and I went to the Emir of Soko and paid him two hundred pounds for nomination on his list of candidates. Politicians, radicals and men from the south, came and pleaded with me to tell the Kitawa to vote against the N.P.C. but I refused. I had worked almost thirty years with the British and I knew they would not let the emirs be unseated.

'There were then five constituencies among the Kitawa, and at the next elections I agreed that two should choose members of Yakali's household. One of those thus elected was the then Bangwa Wangwa, an office that had become purely ceremonial since the Incident. This man was too stupid to understand the new situation, and within a year complaints were brought against him for extortion and corruption . . .'

'By his constituents?'

'Who else?'

'But with your help?'

'They came to me for advice, of course. Since I had stood on the hill that day it was my task to prevent such oppression, both in their eyes and in mine. Let me go on. The Bangwa Wangwa was sent to prison and I then asked Yakali to give me his office. I gave Yakali presents. It was the custom. No doubt he saw other advantages. He believed that I would become, as it were, his Messenger and he would thus control all five constituencies. Later I married his daughter. Yakali was already working to bring about the K.H.P.—the Kiti Highway Project, you know? —and he wanted to feel secure on his own power base. By this time the British had left. Instead of a white Resident at Birnin Soko we had a black Provincial Commissioner to represent the Government at Kaduna. The emirs still ruled. They chose the candidates for the N.P.C. lists. They treated the candidatures much as they used to treat the offices in their Native Administrations, things to be given away in return for presents. Among the Fulani and Hausa there is still great competition for the prestige of office. It is part of their culture.

'The emirs despised the black men from Kaduna. Many of them thought that now the British had gone they could begin to do just what they liked. Our Emir of Soko was such a one, a pious scoundrel of the old sort, learned in the Koran, very dignified in public, always making speeches about his duty to lead and protect his people while stealing by double handfuls from his own treasury. Yakali went to him with presents and unfolded his scheme for the K.H.P. It was very grand—a bridge at Kiti, great highways into the interior, communal farming schemes, the fish-factory, and so on. Of course the Emir was eager for the Project. He saw that immense sums of money could be milked from it in one way and another. He did not foresee there was any need to take precautions against being found out, because now that the British were gone Kaduna would never dare depose an emir. Yakali thought otherwise. He too, of course, intended to milk the Project, but more carefully. At the same time he intended to collect evidence of the Emir's depredations and then inform against him. The Emir would then be deposed and Yakali, by giving presents to the right people, would get the old Emirate of Kiti revived in his favour.'

'I don't suppose the Kitawa were even consulted. How did they take it?'

'No peasant will refuse a road to his door, provided it goes through his neighbour's garden and not his own. Motorway protests are a phenomenon of rich countries. The proposal for farming co-operatives was always nonsense. The land is mostly useless. Everybody knew that. My concern was to see that Yakali was not made Emir, so I collected evidence to prove his frauds—it was not difficult, he was a man who talked to women and I was married to his daughter.

'Then in 1963 the Emir of Kano, one of our great emirs, was forced to resign on a charge of corruption. Now our little Emir was frightened. He had already begun to milk the Project, though the actual construction had barely started. I went to Birnin Soko and had audience with him and laid bare for him Yakali's scheme. I told him that while there was a Sarkin of Kiti who was of the lineage of Kama Boi there would always be intrigues for the revival of the emirate. The solution was not far to seek, for one versed in Fulani and Hausa politics of the traditional kind. Yakali must be deposed and the lineage of Kama Boi replaced by another. Therefore on my advice the Emir disburdened himself of such sums as Yakali might have evidence of his taking, and let Yakali learn that he had done so.

'Now, I knew through my wife that Yakali had long held schemes for the construction of a grand new palace when he became Emir. Seeing that time postponed he was likely—he was not a patient man—to begin building at once. Furthermore, now that he was not going to be able to bring evidence of fraud against the Emir, his need to protect himself against counter-accusations . . .

During the ten minutes or so it had taken the Sarkin to tell his story Jackland had listened with apparently total attention, not even stirring when another outburst of frustrated cries told of further breakdowns in the process of filming six people walking from A to B. The interruption to the story came from the other direction. Miss Boyaba appeared at an opening in the inner wall so small and dark that it might have been taken for the entrance to a dog-kennel. Blinded by glare, despite her sun-glasses, she craned towards the sound of the Sarkin's voice, then evidently made out who was there and stilted over, laughing with delight. She prostrated herself in front of her great-uncle then rose and kissed him on the cheek. He seemed equally pleased by both gestures, though a bystander might well have thought they were performed as much for Jackland's benefit as for his.

'Look what I found,' she said.

She unclenched her left hand, holding it low enough for

Jackland to see. In the pale palm glinted what looked like a fluffy piece of seed-head. She smoothed it with a gentle fingertip and it became a few criss-crossing threads, gold, with crumbling faint millimetres of green silk caught here and there.

'In the diary,' she explained. 'Don't you remember—when the wives got out the best dresses so that Betty could paint them? I found it in a tiny room beside the harem courtyard. I wonder if it's all that's left.'

'Of course not,' said the Sarkin. 'They are stored in the new palace. I have offered some to museums, but they are not interested in the traditional dress of women.'

'Typical,' said Miss Boyaba. 'So they just sit there. What a waste.'

'Nonsense, Annie. You have seen some with your own eyes. When you last came to the anniversary celebrations of my inauguration as Sarkin, your great-aunts wore them. And I will give you one for yourself on the day you marry.'

'It almost makes it worth the awfulness.'

There is a curiosity about conversation with royalty, in that the faces of courtiers may express reactions at variance with the superficial politeness of their prince but expressive of his inward feelings. To judge by the brolly-man, though the Sarkin smiled at Miss Boyaba's unthinking liveliness, he was not amused. He turned to Jackland.

'Many are of Damascus weave,' he said. 'The ancestors of Kama Boi were nobles in Katsina long before the jihad.'

'Eighteenth century then.'

'At least.'

'Astonishing in this climate.'

'The jars are sealed and we use the bark of local trees to prevent fungal and insect damage. It is safer than air-conditioning, because the power may fail.'

'I wonder if there's any of the ones your mother painted,' said Miss Boyaba. 'Wouldn't that be thrilling!'

'The Sarkin let us copy some for when we shot that sequence,' said Jackland.

'Oh, what a pity. There's nothing like the real thing.'

'The real thing tends to produce real worries, insurance in this case. If we'd been able to shoot those scenes here I'd have risked it. As it was the Sarkin sent us photographs.'

'Would you like this to keep?'

Jackland shook his head.

'Give it to Mary,' he said. 'She likes scraps of things.'

Miss Boyaba's fingers twitched as if restrained from an impulse to close round her find. Jackland seemed not to notice.

'God!' he said. 'What's holding them up? There's nothing to this shot. I do apologize for keeping you bottled up in here, Sarkin.'

The sounds of breakdown and exasperation were once more rising from beyond the outer rooms. Somebody was trying to shout to someone else a considerable distance away. The call, its words inaudible, was repeated and repeated, growing fainter each time as the caller moved towards whoever he was shouting at. The Sarkin smiled at Jackland and spoke to the brolly-man, who unfolded from the side of the chair an aluminium shelf, on which he placed a miniature board for the ludo game, drawn from a pocket. He and the Sarkin started to set up the pieces.

'I know,' said Miss Boyaba. 'Let's go and see if we can't find some more. It was pretty dark in there, but you've got a lighter, haven't you?'

Jackland let her help him to his feet and followed her across the glaring space beyond the tree-shade into the dark burrow of the harem entrance. They returned in about ten minutes to find that the filming had at last been finished. The Sarkin had been joined by the borrowed members of his entourage, who stood and watched the ludo game, silent and dignified in their grand robes, while the film people milled and chattered. Burn was arguing with the actor playing Kama Boi. Miss Tressider stood just beyond them, looking as drained as if she had just completed some huge role. If the sequence showing Betty Jackland being helped into the saddle by Elongo had been part of the script she would not have needed to mould her features to exhaustion. Miss Boyaba pranced up to her, proffering the scrap of fabric, and explained what it might be. Miss Tressider picked it up and listlessly let it fall back into Miss Boyaba's palm.

'I'm feeling perfectly foul,' she said.

Jackland must have understood her to be referring to her mood rather than her physical sensations.

'Almost through now,' he said. 'What held you up?'

Miss Tressider sighed, glanced at him, then at Miss Boyaba and then away. But Burn, in earshot, swung round.

'The bloody Army. Deliberately getting in shot. That pan to the outer battlements, up there with their berets and guns against the skyline. Each time we got rid of them up they popped again soon as we started shooting. They seemed to think it was some kind of joke.'

TEN

Mon April 7

Just to tidy up the tour—this morning was Ted's weekly official visit to K B, and I rode over with him to give my present to the old brute. I'd made it really rather nice—I didn't think any of the pictures were much good so I felt I'd better make the wrapping a bit special, and I'd mounted them and bound them into a sort of album with a nice stripy cover (made from a pair of Ted's pyjamas, actually, which I won't let him wear!). The best pictures were things like Zarafio's people and their horses lounging around during the mid-day rest. I put in two or three of the villages, tho' I'd never managed to get any of those *going*, somehow. I couldn't get hold of them, the way you have to. Looking at them now I can see I wasn't sure of myself the way I like to feel when I've got a brush between my fingers—as tho' my hand hadn't quite believed what my eyes thought they were seeing. Difficult to explain. I don't usually mind so much —you've got to expect to do some duds—but I long to do a good one of the Kitawa. I feel so drawn to them. In a silly sort of way I can't help feeling I'm meant to be their protectress, and that's why I came to Africa at all! Childish.

Anyway, tho' Ted had sent a message I was coming K B didn't seem at all pleased to see me. 'Cos it was the official visit it took place in the outer courtyard of his palace. All his entourage were there, more than twenty, including horrid little Zarafio and two other sons. I had to go and sit and wait under the other tree, the dying one, while the palaver went on. And on. They made a lovely group and I'd have had masses of time, but I hadn't got anything with me except a pencil and my little notebook. I did sketches, with notes about colours and effects, the way you're supposed to, but it's never the same thing for me 'cos of having to think about it. Mine only really work when I suck the scene in with my eyes and send it straight down to my hand without my tiresome brain getting a chance to interfere.

Ted told me after that K B was in a whiny mood, his salary too small and Sokowa crossing the river and settling on his land but still paying their taxes to Soko (which is true, but it's KB's own fault) and why is his Native Court still only a 'D' court ('cos if it were made 'C' he'd try bigger cases and get better presents from both sides). Things like that. KB knows he's not going to get anything out of Ted but whining is his way of keeping his end up in front of his entourage. It went on for ages. I began to feel—the way you do when you're kept waiting—he was trying to punish me for something *I'd* done.

At last he got up from his stool and came waddling across to talk to me. V. royal and grand. I gave him the album. He leafed quickly through (Ted says he was hoping I'd put a pound note or two between the pages 'cos that's the sort of present chiefs expect!). He didn't seem at all interested, specially remembering how excited he'd been about my paintings of his wives—I forgot to say, I'd put them in too and tho' they were only copies they still weren't bad. He hardly glanced at them. Then, all of a sudden, he stopped. His eyes popped. Really. They bulged as tho' someone had come up behind and started to strangle him. His hands shook. He'd have dropped the album in a mo, so I grabbed it and he stepped away from me. Everyone was staring, tho' only a couple of the others had come over with him and even they couldn't have seen what was bothering him.

It was the picture of Tefuga Hill. I should have known. I'd put it in 'cos it was a picture of somewhere a bit different from everywhere else. Besides, tho' it was still wrong, it had sort of got interesting. There was *something* in it, nothing to do with it being a good picture, which it wasn't, but . . . I don't know how to explain . . .

'Why do you bring that place into my house?' he said.

'It is a place in your kingdom. You asked me to make pictures and bring them to you.'

'I did not tell you to make a picture of that place.'

'You did not ask me not to make one. But I will take it out of the book if you wish.'

'Take it out.'

So I took my little penknife and slit down the edge of the page and removed the sheet. When I gave KB the album his hands were still trembling and he only pretended to look through it, but really it was more as tho' he thought there might be a snake in it now! He still seemed frightfully bothered, so I borrowed a match from Ted and set light to the sheet at one corner. Tho' we were in the shade the light was so strong you couldn't see the flame, but KB watched the black fringe creeping across the paper with his eyes still absolutely popping. I held on long as I could and dropped it. It burnt right to the last tiny piece. KB rolled his eyes, looking at the wisps of ash and then at me and then at Ted. Suddenly he seemed to make up his mind that I hadn't been working some frightful juju against him after all and he turned quite pleased and jolly in his leering way and took us all back to the other tree and shouted at Zarafio and the others about I don't know what. He watched me all the time. I could see he wanted to make sure I understood he was the big man here. He was, too. They are all afraid of him, not just the Kitawa, the Hausa too, including his own sons. He's a terrible old man but I'm beginning to understand why Ted secretly admires him. He'd never admit it, but deep inside himself Ted would quite like to be the KB sort. I keep telling myself how decent Ted is (and he is—it's true) but sometimes I can't help wondering if it isn't really because he's afraid not to be. If he *dared* he'd be more like KB. I wonder? Anyway, we made uncomfortable talk (good for my Hausa, tho') till it was time to go.

We rode home, Ted rather jolly, me a bit flat. You can't help minding when people don't like what you've done, even tho' you tell yourself you don't give a snap for what they think. Besides, if I wasn't KB's blue-eyed girl any longer he wasn't going to let me into his harem again, to try and talk to Elongo's sister, which would have been much easier now that my Kiti's come on so. I started to explain this at our language lesson this afternoon.

I said (we were talking Kiti), 'Kama Boi is now not friendly with me. I will not be able to see your sister again, perhaps.'

'My sister is very well,' he said. He sounded surprised, as tho' he'd expected I'd forgotten her.

'Did she send messages?'

'Kama Boi sent good presents to my uncles.'

I didn't understand. I just stared.

'So now everything's absolutely hunky-dory,' I said. That was in English, of course, and I haven't been teaching him slang 'cos I like to think of him talking grave, old-fashioned English, like the Bible, almost. He must have realized I was miffed—and I was! Bitterly disappointed, honestly. My fault for imagining he'd be thinking about things like a European, when he's so totally African. I can't have it both ways. I want him to be African, so I can't expect him to be upset about losing his sister 'cos he was fond of her and that was why he'd come to us in the first place, when really what he'd been minding about was KB not coughing up a proper bride-price! And why should KB take it into his head to pay up now, months after he'd stolen the child? I'll never know, tho' if I was African I daresay I wouldn't even bother to ask 'cos it would be so obvious!

Anyway we got on with our lessons. I love to hear him talking English in that deep, careful voice—careful 'cos he wants to get it right but it makes him sound so wise. My Kiti's really coming along. My tongue does the tones without me having to think and my ear can hear how different words are that used to sound practically the same. Now I'd be shocked as a Bakiti if Elongo said he'd fetch me intestines when he meant a drink. I boasted about this, and Elongo looked at me, grave as ever.

'You must learn the women's words,' he said.

(We were talking English now. I make him call me 'you' as tho' he was an equal so he learns how the language really works, but he knows he's got to be careful with anyone else.)

'Are they very different?'

'Some are different. You say words that cannot come out of the mouth of a woman. You must talk with Kitawa women.'

'That's going to be a bit difficult,' I said.

'You will go out to the bush to paint more pictures. I will take you to a place.'

'Oh dear. Ofafe's much too far—we'd have to start back soon as we got there.'

I couldn't say, but I was pretty sure no one in Ofafe would risk talking to me.

'It is not Ofafe.'

'There isn't anywhere nearer.'

'I will show you a place. It is far, but there will be time. In eight days, when Master goes across the river to make arrangements about the settlers from Soko.'

I absolutely stared. How did he know about that? Ted's going to make a dash Tuesday week half way to Soko to palaver with

Mr de Lancey and the Emir. KB ought to be going too, except that he refuses to cross the river 'cos of the juju. But it wasn't just Elongo knowing that, it was the way he said it, as tho' it'd be a good idea me making the expedish while Ted was away so he didn't find out what I was up to! I mean there's absolutely no reason why I shouldn't just say, 'I'm going out into the bush, darling, and Elongo's going to find me some women to teach me women's talk.' I'd have to tell him something in any case, 'cos otherwise he'll want to take Salaki for his trip and I don't think I can manage Tan-Tan. I suppose Elongo might have heard something about what happened on tour and got it into his head Ted's laid down I'm not allowed to talk to any Kitawa without a spearman watching, but the funny thing is now he's put the idea into my head I'm terribly tempted just to tell Ted I want to go on a painting expedish while he's away and can I have Salaki for that? You see, if I am let alone with them for a bit and if I can get them to talk I'm sure I can worm something out of them, but I don't want Ted thinking before I go that's what I'm up to. He thinks the whole thing's blown over. I'm pretty sure Mr de Lancey never asked him about it—Ted would have told me, and even if he didn't I'd have known. I'm getting to understand my dear man better and better. I usually know how he'll react to anything. For instance, now, if I told him I wanted to go and learn to talk women's talk he wouldn't say I mustn't. But he might make me promise not to talk politics—or he just might say he didn't want to ride Tan-Tan all that way and insist on taking Salaki. So . . .

And besides all that, it's my secret. If I'm going to go on being a good, happy, loving little wife for him, I really must have bits of my own he doesn't know about. Otherwise all I'll become is a boring sort of human pet.

It's in his interest, really. It's part of my job of keeping him happy, like Mr de Lancey said.

So I said alright to Elongo and we went on with the lesson. And I'm not going to tell Ted.

Wed April 30
I've hooked my tiger-fish! I think. The fish doesn't know yet, but I'm almost sure I've done it! Me!

Don't get too uppity, Bets, it was a complete fluke really, but another way I can't help feeling it was really somehow *meant*. I certainly wasn't expecting anything like it, tho' I was a bit excited about getting a chance to talk to real Kitawa again.

I got up with Ted at 3 a.m. and kissed him good-bye and waved him off on his way to the ferry, but I didn't go back to bed again. I told Mafote, who'd brought Tan-Tan round, to get Salaki ready straight off, and I'd got my own kit together the night before, so quite soon, before dear Ted had even reached Kiti Town I should think, I was riding off through the dark the opposite way with Elongo striding ahead. There was a good moon, so I could follow his white housecoat—a bit spooky when we went in under the trees. Then out into the thorn scrub. Millions of insects creaking away. Fireflies. The dawn seeping up. Doves beginning to call. By this time we were out beyond the thorns. If I'd really been on a painting expedish I'd have stopped then and there and tried to get that special moment, only about half an hour before the sun comes up, it's so quick, when the sky goes indigo and suddenly the whole world is there, all round you, flat bush stretching away for ever, empty, waiting . . . I'd always had Ted with me when we were on tour. Now it happened for me alone. My Africa.

Well, we went on and on. I asked Elongo if he wanted a rest but he didn't seem to get tired. There wasn't a road, not even a path some of the way, or only just, but he seemed quite sure where he was going through all that sameyness. The sun got up and soon it was pretty hot. I was in a sort of dream after that dawn. Every few minutes something would cry out to me, call to my eyes, I mean, a tree or a termite's nest or a clump of spiky grass, as tho' they were saying, 'Look at me. Understand me. Understand how I am what I am, the only one of me in all the world!' It was a very strange feeling. Of course, that's what I try to get when I paint things, but I've never felt it so strong and clear before. There are things I saw on that journey, ordinary, ordinary things, that'll still be bright and new in my mind's eye when I'm an old, old woman.

Well, I suppose we must have been going nearly three hours —8 miles? Anyway, a long way to go for a Kiti lesson!—and it was getting quite hot when Elongo turned left. I wasn't at all sure but I'd got a sort of idea from where the sun was that we'd been going sort of parallel to the river tho quite a long way out.

I'd better explain that the thorn belt isn't smooth on that side. It goes in and out, like a coast, with bays and capes, and it moves, too. Some places it's spreading and others it's dying back, nobody's sure why. Something to do with underground water, Ted thinks. After a bit I saw that now we were going into one of the bays, more of an inlet, really, like a river mouth, with thorn on either side. The sides got closer, and there, right down at the end of it, was a village! Tiny and terribly poor, I could see at once. Only half a dozen huts, and some of the roofs very shabby, but others nice and new, and one actually being mended when we arrived. Only two 'gardens' I could see but sometimes they have them a long way from the villages.

I didn't really have time to look 'cos the villagers all stopped what they were doing and came to meet us. Such smiles! Quite different from when we were on tour. A bit nervous still, tho', I could see. 'Strong spirits' all round. It must have been a tiny village if this was everyone, just two old dodderers, five splendid women, two of them with babies, and some boys. No grown men apart from the dodderers, in fact the 'headman'—tho' the Kitawa don't really have headmen—seemed to be a woman called Atafa Guni, which is a good old Kiti name. It comes in one of Elongo's stories about the Woman who Tricked the Lion. She was perfectly lovely, absolutely typical Kiti, only more so, with the wide, honest face and the proud walk and the glossy skin. The others all respected her, waited to see what she would say, and so on.

After a bit the women shooed the lads off to work in the gardens. They looked sulky, but went. I guessed the women must be their 'aunts', like Femora Feng and Elongo, so the lads had to do what they were told. The old men sat down in front of one of the huts, three of the women went back to the hut they'd been mending, and I stayed with the other two. Atafa Guni wanted to take me into her hut but I decided the women building would make an interesting subject, so I set up my parasol and easel in the open and told her to come with me. Elongo tethered Salaki, then went and joined the old men.

Soon as I really looked at the village I saw it must have been much larger once. There were only four or five good huts, the mended ones. The others were more or less completely ram-shackle, and I could see where more huts must have once been, only they'd fallen right down. Anyway, there were just about enough people for the good huts, so that made sense. Still, it was something to talk about. I wanted to put the two women at their ease, 'cos I could feel how nervous they still were.

'Why are the huts empty?' I said. 'Where are all the men?'

'The thorn trees have eaten up the gardens,' said Atafa Guni. 'Not many people can live here now. The men must go a long way to find food.'

'It is sad,' I said.

'Elongo Sisefonge says we must teach you women's talk,' said Atafa Guni. She obviously didn't want to talk about the village. It was silly of me to have asked—if our house started rotting round us I know I'd be snappy with nice kind visitors who came and told me what a pity it was. So we started straight into the lesson. It wasn't as difficult as I'd expected, apart from some special tones, things like when a woman asks a man a question, or when an 'aunt' is giving orders to the lad in her hut about what he's got to do—that was a tricky one to get right. I had to stop painting while I practised, and I don't suppose I shall ever need to use it! Otherwise it was just words, most of them about the things that happen to us 'cos of being a woman which I can't imagine myself ever wanting to have a conversation about—in fact, I don't even know the English for some of them! That's the other side of being open and easy about s * *. I'm not sure I'd like it to go that far.

Soon I was thoroughly enjoying myself, practising words and chatting a bit and painting away. One nice thing, there weren't nearly as many flies as there usually are round a village. I was wondering whether this was anything to do with women being cleaner than men when suddenly my eye was hooked by one of the women building the hut. She was on a ladder—just a pole with cross-pieces lashed to it—with a loose bundle of thatch on her shoulder. Something special about her pose. I shouted to her not to move. She stopped, exactly right, and soon as I started to sketch her in I saw what it was—there's a painting, Italian I should think, of dead Jesus being carried down from the cross, a man on a ladder, the body drooping over his shoulder just like that. That sort of eye-echo is rather exciting, and I was so busy concentrating on getting it down that I didn't realize for several minutes at least that it wasn't just the woman on the ladder staying beautifully still—it was everybody! Dead silence, not even the work-chant of the lads in the gardens. Creepy.

I thought for a mo it was 'cos they didn't know who I'd been talking to when I called out, so they'd all frozen. (I'd called pretty loud.) Then, I don't know how, I understood it wasn't that at all. I looked at Atafa Guni.

'Why are you afraid?' I said.

She looked at the other woman—her name was Manonka —and back at me. She made up her mind and drew a deep breath.

'We do not cry with loud voices,' she said. 'We walk on small paths. We make no smoke. The toes are hidden.'

Yes, that's what she said, the exact words. I didn't understand at all. I thought it must be one of the funny Kiti riddles Elongo's sometimes told me, where the riddler talks about something like an egg in a roundabout way and the guesser has to try and work out what it is. But I wanted to get the last few bits of the woman on the ladder right before my eye forgot them, so I dabbed away. All of a sudden it came to me. Toes. Counting. Just like the mistake Lukar and the Bangwa Wangwa kept making about counting the men in the villages when we were on tour. If it was a mistake. 'Cos Atafa Guni seemed to be telling me that this village (its name is Jabu, which just means 'Near river') wasn't counted *on purpose*. They were frightened because I'd shouted and they were supposed to keep quiet all the time.

I looked at Atafa Guni. She was watching me with huge eyes. The other woman was absolutely terrified. The ones in the village had started moving again, but now they'd stopped and were watching, not straight but out of the corners of their eyes.

'Who must not hear your voices?' I said. 'Who must not find your paths or see your smoke?'

'It is the White Man.'

Of course. It had to be. First sight you think you could hide hundreds—thousands—of natives in that bush, but it would only work for a few days 'cos of them having to get water, *and* there'd have to be only one or two people looking for them, *and* the hiders would have to know when the seekers were coming. *Well, that's just what happens!* The D.O. says he's coming to do a tour, where and when and how long, and he tells them all to get ready. Which they do! But the Hausa absolutely *must* know. Not just 'cos there's more of them, but the important ones have their own districts which they're supposed to look after under the N.A., with their own servants there all the time. Perhaps you could hide one or two natives from them, but not whole villages. Goodness! (I'd stopped painting by now. Ideas were coming at me in a rush, not making nearly as much sense as what I've just written.)

'Who orders you to hide?' I said.

'It is the horsemen.'

'Kama Boi?'

She didn't answer at once. She looked at the other woman, then at the ground, then back at me.

'The servants of Kama Boi came to us. They carried his word in their mouths.'

Manonka made a little whimpering noise. I thought she was going to get up and run away, but Atafa Guni put out a hand and touched her wrist and she was quiet again. It gave me time to clear my wits a bit.

'There are finger villages and there are toe villages, then?' I said.

'Yes.'

'And the White Man must see only the finger villages?'

'Yes.'

'And the finger villages pay the White Man's tax?'

'They pay two taxes. The White Man comes and counts some men and says what must be paid as his tax, and when he has gone the servants of Kama Boi come again and count all the men and take more tax. If we cannot pay they take our children to work on their gardens.'

(I'm writing all this down much less muddled than it was. I had to ask lots more questions. She didn't like it. She kept almost making up her mind to stop answering and then deciding now she'd got so far she might as well go on.)

'The men hide when the White Man comes? Why do they not hide also when the servants of Kama Boi come?'

'Who can hide from Kama Boi?'

Manonka actually looked over her shoulder when Atafa Guni said that, as tho' she expected to see KB there, huge and scowling, like a thunder-cloud.

'What about the toe villages?' I said. They pay tax to the servants of Kama Boi but no tax to the White Man?'

'Yes.'

'When I was at Tefuga I spoke with a woman called Femora Feng,' I said.

I saw Manonka jump at the name and try and look away, but Atafa Guni didn't seem surprised.

'I have heard her name,' she said.

'She told me of a village in the north to which the servants of Kama Boi came, and burnt the huts and killed the men and took the others away. Is the story true?'

'It is spoken of.'

'What was the name of the place?'

'I do not know. It is far away.'

'Did the servants of Kama Boi do this because the village refused to pay the tax?'

'It is spoken of.'

'Was it a toe village?'

'It is spoken of.'

'Why did no one come to the White Man and say that this was done?'

I expected her to tell me what Elongo had said to Mr de Lancey when I was painting him fishing, about it being too much of a risk for any of the Kitawa to complain. But she looked at me with her brown clear eyes and said, 'It is forbidden.'

(That's not strong enough—it's a special word, magical, as tho' there's a terrible curse on doing whatever you mustn't, which is really going to happen only you don't know what it is.)

'But you have told me.'

'You are not a White Man.'

I almost laughed at the childishness of it. I'm glad I managed to keep a straight face, 'cos suddenly I thought, No, I am not a White Man. I am not. How extraordinary. I share more with this black savage who I'll probably never meet again than I do with dear Ted, who I'm going to spend the rest of my life with. She was sitting on the ground beside me, half in and half out of the shade of my parasol. I reached out with my left hand and took hers where it lay across her glossy naked thigh. She understood at once and gripped it with her strong clean fingers. She looked straight into my eyes.

'Yes,' I said. 'I am your friend. I will help you.'

151

'I will tell you my dream, she said. 'I have seen this dream seven times. It comes from the ancestors. I see a black horse. It stands among the huts. Its legs are the trunks of trees. The breath of its nostrils is the thunder-cloud. It tramples to and fro. Its hooves break the cooking-pots. Its hooves trample the huts. It sucks the spirits out of the men so that their strength is gone. Their spears fall from their fingers. They are afraid. Then I see a white thing. It rides the horse and maddens it. The white thing is a great termite. But now I see a second white thing which rides beside the first. It is a termite also, but it has the face of a woman. And now it arches itself up and is great and wise, and it leans forward and bites the terrible horse in the neck, so that the horse falls down and dies. This is my dream, which the ancestors send me.'

Oh, lor, I thought. Me? I mean, it was obvious what her dream meant, soon as you remember the Kitawa say the Hausa are really horses and the white people are really termites. The Kitawa pay a lot of attention to dreams—Elongo's stories are full of them, and I suppose if you take your dreams seriously you start dreaming things that matter. Anyway she was still holding my hand and still looking into my eyes, eager and searching, but before I could think what to say she spoke again.

'So now you will kill Kama Boi,' she said.

I'm afraid she felt my hand go limp, and understood. It was awful. It simply didn't seem fair to pretend.

'I cannot kill Kama Boi,' I said.

She and Manonka looked at each other. They were appalled. They started to get up.

'Wait,' I said. 'Perhaps I can do something. I will try. I cannot kill Kama Boi, but perhaps I can cause him to be sent away, far away, across the river, and he will never come back.'

'He cannot cross the river,' said Atafa Guni. 'It is forbidden.' (Same word.)

'I will do it if I can,' I said. 'I promise.'

They didn't believe me. Everything had gone wrong—I could see that—and they wanted me to go. No point in finishing the painting. Elongo must have been watching 'cos soon as I started cleaning my brushes he came over to help me pack up. No real smiles this time when we said good-bye, and when I took a last look over my shoulder I saw that the women had come down from their thatching and the boys were running back from the gardens to gather round Atafa Guni and hear what I'd said.

I was pretty dumpish at first. It was roasting hot. Salaki didn't like it at all, so after a bit I called a halt and we rested under some trees and had something to eat. I tried to get more out of Elongo about what Atafa Guni had told me, but he kept saying he didn't know, and he was obviously terribly unhappy about being asked, so I gave up. Then I started thinking what I should do. The obvious thing was tell Ted, but I knew it wouldn't work. He would tackle KB about it, and then he would insist on taking KB, or one of his courtiers, out to Jabu to check what Atafa Guni had told me and she'd be much too frightened to say anything. Really I wanted to tell Mr de Lancey without telling Ted, but I couldn't think how.

It was still too hot to move on and it struck me I ought to have something to show Ted as the results of my expedish so I set up the easel and did Elongo, with Salaki out beyond in the pale flat dusty glare. Out of darkness, into light. Only a few flecks and mottles through the leaves. It was difficult, so I couldn't think about much else, which was good, 'cos all of a sudden I saw an answer. I suppose I'd been half-thinking about the other picture, the women thatching, and not being able to show it to Ted 'cos he'd want to know where it was, and then thinking I'd really like to show it to Mr de Lancey so I could ask about the Crucifixion picture the woman had reminded me of, and *then*, out of nowhere, that was the answer. I'd send the picture to Mr de Lancey to ask about that, and put in a chatty bit about the village, and it being not on the census. I'd have to be careful not to say too much, so it was just chat. Of course, he'd know and I'd know but we'd have to pretend—that's v. important. The picture of Salaki and Elongo went really well, one of my best, so I thought that was a good sign.

Ted didn't get back last night. I still haven't made up my mind. I know I ought to tell him, but . . . you see, I also know what he'll say. He simply won't believe in lots of hidden villages all over Kiti. Perhaps there are one or two we've never found so they aren't paying taxes, but *lots*? It *is* a difficulty. I do see that, but . . . oh, the way her fingers loosened from mine when she thought I'd let her down! I don't know.

Thurs April 17

Well, I've done it now. I mean I haven't. I suppose I could still go back, but I don't think I shall. I'm talking about not telling Ted. It just happened. He got back tired and a bit sore 'cos of having to ride Tan-Tan all that way, and we had a nice snuggle and then I brought him a big b. and s. and he lit his pipe and he asked if I'd kept out of mischief while he was away and I showed him the picture of Salaki. He was terribly pleased. It's the first of my pictures he's ever really liked, and he just likes it 'cos he can see it's her and not any old mare. In fact, I caught him trying what it might have been like without Elongo by putting a corner of paper across that bit. Dear man, he can't possibly see that you need that sort of wedge-shaped blob of weight that side. I'm going to mount it for him to hang in his office.

After that we just chatted. That was when I could have told him about Jabu, and Atafa Guni, and shown him the picture. I could have done it so it seemed I didn't understand it was important. But I didn't. And I didn't this morning at breakfast, either. And each chance I miss, the more I see that I'm really not going to at all, and I *shall* send the sketch to Mr de Lancey, and then see what happens. I promised her, didn't I? I've got to do something.

I know it's a terrible risk. I *think* I can rely on Mr de Lancey not to let on to Ted that it's got anything to do with me, but you can't be absolutely sure with someone as tricky as that. Suppose he lets me down, or it comes out some other how, what'll I do? Make out I was just too silly to understand? No go—we've talked about this sort of thing too much, Ted and me. No, I'll have to own up. Floods of tears. Terrific wheedlings. You see . . . you see, in a funny way I'm not sure Ted wouldn't rather enjoy all that, having me crawling about on the floor and clinging to his knees and sobbing like billy-oh, and him being ever so honourable and upright and forgiving. It'd all be part of the big K Bish bullying Ted he's always been too frightened to let out. (Mustn't blame him too much. After all, there's a side of me too that rather longs to sob and cling and be trampled on, so in a funny way I might rather enjoy it too—tho' we'd both be just acting, really. I'm much stronger than he is in some ways.)

Anyway, one thing's obvious. I've got to go on making absolutely certain he really really needs me, so much he couldn't bear to give me up, whatever I've done. I do love him, I truly do, so I won't be pretending something that isn't true. That's all that matters.

Fri April 25
Not quite so hot last night, and a shade cooler now too, I think. Ted says it's too soon for the hot weather to really break, but you can't help looking for signs. Oh, how I sometimes long for England, deep winter, lying close, close all night, sharing our warmth, with the bedroom air icy round us! That's something I've never had. I keep thinking what a funny business all that is. Before I got married, when I didn't suppose anyone would ever ask me anyway, I used to wonder about it. I'd finish a soppy novel and then try and dream myself into the heroine's nightie, but it was all misty and stupid. It never even struck me that it was going to be great fun when you got it right, like tennis when your eye's in. I do rather long for someone to talk to about this sort of thing. Some woman (Atafa Guni?). Poor Ted's no use. If I say 'That was nice' when we've finished he just grunts (supposing he's still awake!).

The only thing they do tell you is about mystical union (is that right, or am I thinking of the Prayer Book?). I wonder. I *am* truly fond of Ted, not just grateful to him for getting me away from Daddy, as well as admiring him for being so decent, and doing it is a way of saying that sort of thing, as well as making us feel happy with each other and belonging together, but it isn't at all mystical and holy, especially with our tummies going suck and smack like rubber cups because we're so hot.

It's surprising you don't get bored of it, considering how samey it always is. There doesn't seem to be much you *can* do different, or if there is we don't know (and Ted probably wouldn't approve, just like breakfast isn't breakfast if he doesn't have porridge). Actually, I wonder whether I'm quite telling the truth about that. I believe I might have been getting a wee bit bored, without noticing it, 'cos I do think it's got much more new and interesting again since I sent my letter to Mr de Lancey. Ted sent it for me, actually. I showed him the sketch I'd drawn of the woman on the ladder so he could see it was only about art, and he popped it in with his reports.

Funny how you don't understand things till you write them

down. They're just feelings, till then. But yes, there is something extra. The secret. The game. Ted not knowing. He spends most of his day-times trying to stop Africans cheating and bribing. He doesn't really believe he'll do any good, but I think he gets a special sort of pleasure out of being so honest and decent when everyone round him's so absolutely rotten and corrupt. And then he comes home to me and we chat and have supper and put on the gramophone and dance till we both feel ready and then we go to bed . . . and he doesn't know but I'm bribing *him*! It's exciting. I don't know why. It sends a kind of tingling shiver through me. It's like the sprinkle of salt on your food which makes all the difference.

Of course it's a risk. That's part of the excitement. If he found out! Oh, idea! Is that why I so badly want to write this all down, 'cos it gives him a chance? Not much of one—I can't imagine dear Ted reading anything I'd written without my permish.

But aren't I extraordinary? I'd no idea!

Wed April 30
A horrible two days. I honestly believed I'd spoiled everything and we'd never be happy again, but I think it's going to be all right after all. Just. If dear Ted had an ounce of suspicion in his nature—if I hadn't worked so hard keeping him happy . . .

Well, day before yesterday, quite early . . . Ted was gone over to Kiti for his weekly confab with KB. I'd got a bit of an upset tummy—you get them all the time in Africa, however careful you try to be—and I'd just got back from the B.G. thinking I'd have a lie-down 'cos I was feeling a bit washy, the way you do, and there in our dining-room was Mr de Lancey! I just stared. Of course I see now he must have known it was confab day and he'd come up the river by canoe and camped just down stream so he'd catch me alone.

He didn't apologize for barging in. Just 'Good morning,' and then, 'Mrs Jackland, will you please take me to this village you say you found.'

He had my letter in his hand. I tried to start talking about who the Italian painter was, but I could see it was no use.

'Shouldn't we wait for Ted?' I said. 'I mean it's his district.'

He stared at me with absolute contempt.

'Have you told your husband, Mrs Jackland?'

I should have said yes, and pretended, and hoped, but I was sort of hypnotized. I just shook my head.

'Let me make one thing clear, Mrs Jackland,' he said. 'You came to Kiti against my wishes and recommendation. I would now be sorry to see you leave, but if I thought it necessary I would not hesitate to report to Kaduna that you had been interfering with the work of your husband's district and intriguing with tribesmen behind the back of the Native Authority. If I were to do that they would have you out like a shot.'

'Please,' I said. 'I'm not feeling very well.'

'You had better sit down. I can see that you are not well and I apologize for choosing such a time. Perhaps I had better wait for Jackland after all.'

'No. Let me think.'

'Very well. Perhaps you will tell me how you stumbled on this village.'

'Elongo took me.'

'Why should he do that?'

'I wanted to learn women's talk. In Kiti, you know.'

'I see. In that case Elongo can take me, and I need not trouble you to make the trip. Would you please send for him.'

I rang my little bell and he was there at once. I told him (in Hausa, I don't know why) I wanted him to take Mr de Lancey to Jabu. He just looked bewildered, but then he always does, a bit.

'I do not know this place,' he said.

We both tried. I pleaded, Mr de Lancey bullied. It was no use. He totally refused to admit he'd shown me anything anywhere. I didn't know what to do—I was desperate to get Mr de Lancey out of my house. In the end I switched to Kiti.

'Elongo Sisefonge,' I said. 'You will take Mr Dlanzi to the place where I talked to Atafa Guni.'

I don't know why—I think 'cos it was the strongest way of putting it I knew—I used the tones Atafa Guni had taught me for when the 'aunts' give orders to the lads in their huts. Elongo stared at me as tho' I'd hit him. Then he said, 'I will do it.' I almost collapsed from relief, in fact I don't really remember much after that for a bit, except that Mr de Lancey went away and came back with some medicine from his famous chest, his own special gippy-tum brew. He wasn't being kind. His eyes absolutely glittered while he stood over me and explained how much I ought to take, how often (I hardly understood a word!). Then he watched while I gulped some down and off he went, and I tottered to my bed and lay down.

Actually it was v. good stuff, 'cos soon I started feeling quite a bit better. Terribly weak still, and terribly worried, but suddenly seeing everything absolutely clear, specially, just as if I'd been there, what was going to happen. Elongo would take Mr de Lancey out into the bush and get a good way away and then he'd 'forget' how to find Jabu after all, and that would be the worst thing that could happen 'cos Mr de Lancey would come back furious and tackle Ted. I'm saying what I thought *then*. It seemed totally obvious what I'd got to do was go after them and make sure Elongo did what I told him. (Actually now I can see I was being stupid. Much the best thing I could have done was stayed where I was and waited for Ted to get back from Kiti and then told him how bad I'd been—stopped playing my silly game—asked him to forgive me—let him take over. It would have been alright. I know it would. He's just too decent for anything else.)

So I got up and scribbled a note for Ted and took another good swig of Mr de Lancey's magic potion to be on the safe side, and then went and found Mafote and told him to water and saddle Tan-Tan for me—Ted had taken Salaki to Kiti. I'd never ridden him before. I just knew I could, because I had to. Then off I rode. I felt wonderful, light as air, strong as steel. Tan-Tan tried to have his own way and fought with the bit but I showed him who was master and he gave in. Almost before I'd noticed we were right out through the thorn-belt. I don't remember any of that part at all, but suddenly there was the big, empty, flat bush, Africa for ever. I felt like riding right across it, but I knew I had to find the others so I set off the way Elongo had taken me. It wasn't difficult. I knew the way. I could remember everything, tree and ant-hill and tussock, clear as crystal. I said I would, didn't I? They sang to my eyes. I don't remember having any trouble with Tan-Tan at all. I felt as tho' I was floating through a kind of dream Africa, looking for my Elongo, knowing I was sure to find him. And I did.

Actually they found me. I was floating along when I heard a shout, miles over on my left. I looked, and there they were, quite the wrong place. Lucky they'd seen me at all—it was just while I was crossing one of the opener bits of bush. Soon as I got near I saw there'd been a row. Mr de Lancey was furious and Elongo was frightened but stubborn. It turned out he'd taken Mr de Lancey down one of the inlets into the thorn-belt, and of course they hadn't found anything there, and Mr de Lancey knew he'd taken him to the wrong place, and Elongo knew he knew and Mr de Lancey had tried to bully him and he'd stuck it out. (Secretly I was rather pleased!)

'But you haven't gone nearly far enough,' I said. 'It's miles on!'

Mr de Lancey looked at me v. oddly.

'Are you sure, Mrs Jackland?'

'Course I am. Come on!'

So off we went. I had to slow down a lot 'cos the others were only walking tho' Mr de Lancey made a v. good pace, spite of being a fat little man. He's a lot less pansy than he looks. He kept worrying about whether I was sure I knew my way and I kept showing him my landmarks and telling him what we'd see next and there it was! So we couldn't argue. Tan-Tan started playing up and I had to fight him most of the way so I was too busy to talk a lot and Mr de Lancey hadn't much puff to spare, but spite of that he got interested in my illness again and I told him how terrific his medicine was and I'd had some more and I was quite all right now. He looked at me again and then looked at his watch and warned me it would wear off quite soon.

And then, at last, we were there. I rode down the inlet feeling absolutely triumphant, waiting for the moment when we'd come out from between two tree-clumps and see the tilted pale roofs.

But the roofs weren't there!

I couldn't believe it. Everything had been so right till that moment, my eye-memory so exact, it absolutely couldn't be true. I rode on, with my heart hammering. It was just like that moment when you're having a delicious dream and something goes wrong and you know, before anything else happens, that it's going to turn into a nightmare now.

It did.

The huts weren't there, but they had been. Where they'd stood, where those lovely women had thatched so cleverly, there were just eight black circles on the ground. Ash. My heart stood still. How had Kama Boi known? I mean, he'd have known the village was there, but how had he known they'd talked to me? Had someone heard my shout, after all? Was it all my fault? I could see it so dreadfully in my mind's eye, the flames roaring up (it would have been night, wouldn't it?) the women running out of the huts, the firelight glinting off the spear-points, the smoke streaming away. At least I couldn't see any bodies —perhaps they hadn't actually *killed* anyone.

Mr de Lancey walked to the edge of one of the black circles and poked the ashes with his toe. He found a stick and poked around. Just ashes. No pots, no ornaments, nothing. The Kitawa don't have much, but the spearmen must have taken everything. In a few months, after the rains, you wouldn't be able to tell anyone had ever lived here. They'd even taken the mats from round the gardens and thrown them onto the bonfire. They didn't want to leave any trace.

I started to feel awful again—the shock, and the medicine wearing off. Then I had one of those terrible warning spasms and had to rush off behind some trees and cope with things. Too beastly. I really felt I couldn't face any more. I longed to get hold of Tan-Tan and slip on his back and sneak off home, only I knew I wouldn't be able to ride him now. I was so weak. And sore—not just the sickness, it was the ride out. I must have had to fight him much more than I'd realized. All the time I felt I was just floating, my poor silly body had been wrestling away!

Anyway, after a bit I managed to drag myself back to the burnt huts. Mr de Lancey had gone off to look at the nearest garden. You could see where the lads had been working at the poor, thin soil, getting rid of a frightful crop of weeds. After a bit he came back and stared at Elongo.

'Come here you,' he said in Hausa. 'Get down.'

Elongo knelt and grovelled, the way natives are supposed to in front of chiefs. Ted says it's just the custom, no different from me curtseying if I met the King, but I think it's disgusting. Mr de Lancey kept him grovelling there while he barked at him in Hausa. Who had lived here? What were their names? Who had burnt the huts? Why? Were there other villages like this? Did they pay taxes to the Hausa? And so on.

Actually Elongo didn't tell him anything. He just kept mumbling that he didn't know. I knew it wasn't true for some of the questions, but I was so much on his side I didn't care. Then Mr de Lancey started real bullying, calling him a thief and a liar and saying he was going to prison for twenty years and suddenly I couldn't stand it any longer. Tho' I was feeling awful inside and scared out of my wits at what had happened, something snapped. I saw Mr de Lancey swing round and stare before I realized I'd been yelling at him to stop. I burst out before he could say anything.

'You're doing this all wrong,' I said. 'All quite wrong. You won't get anywhere with the Kitawa by shouting and bullying. They won't tell you anything. It's useless. They've kept quiet for years and years because they're afraid, so it's no good trying to make them more afraid than ever. It's not just that they think Kama Boi's going to send his spearmen to burn their villages —it's much more than that. They're afraid because they think he's a kind of god. They really believe that. When I told Atafa Guni we weren't going to kill him at once, she suddenly stopped trusting me any longer. She was terrified. Absolutely terrified. Of him. Much worse than anything you can ever do.'

'What course of action would you propose, Mrs Jackland?'

He said it in his usual sneery way but I hardly noticed. I was so dizzy I almost fell over. Elongo was muttering with his face in the dust, Kiti, something about Kama Boi. He was terrified too. All of a sudden, for a moment, I understood what it's like to be a Bakiti. Here we were in this utterly lonely place, miles from anywhere, but we weren't hidden. If Kama Boi looked this way he would see us, he would smell us, he would send his spearmen, we would never escape. He was here too, all round us, above us. You couldn't see him, you could feel him tho', everywhere, like the dull weighing-down heat of the sun, pressing everything into the dust. You carried him on your shoulders wherever you went. He was your never-ending sickness, fever, buzzing, aches, a huge pressure on you making you feeble and helpless.

I waved my arm at the jigging black circles.

'Isn't this enough?' I said. 'Isn't this evidence?'

'Mrs Jackland, this is not the work of Kama Boi. This village is a fraud, and the people you saw here left it as soon as you were out of sight, taking their possessions and setting fire to the huts. I have not the papers with me, of course, but I seem to remember earlier censuses reported a village in roughly this area, which was abandoned because of the failure of its water-hole. You can see for yourself. No crops have been grown in that garden for at least three rains. Where are the food husks and the animal bones? Where is the excrement?'

I didn't understand. I still don't, properly.

'There weren't any flies,' I said.

That's the last thing I remember.

Now I'm lying in bed, feeling weak and stupid. I *think* everything's going to be all right, when it could have been dreadful. Yesterday *was* dreadful, lying here, feeling ghastly, worrying about what Ted would say and do, not knowing what Mr de Lancey had told him, not daring to ask. In fact I just pretended to be worse than I was so's not to have to answer questions, only I didn't want to get him so worried he'd send for the doctor, so this morning I thought I'd better perk up a bit, only be drowsy—I *was* feeling better inside, too—and when Ted came to see me he was very loving and gentle and not even hurt or angry, and he said Elongo had done very well and I must say thank you when I saw him. So it does look as tho' Ted doesn't know yet what really happened, and that means Mr de Lancey is going to do his best for me.

Now I'm tired after writing all that. It was terribly strange. I've never felt so odd. I think there must have been something in the medicine, 'cos when I asked if Mr de Lancey had left some for me (he's gone now) Ted just laughed and said, 'You're not having any more of that!'

Thurs May 1

It *is* all right! So extraordinary. Ted's been in and made everything easy by calling me a silly girl and asking how much I remembered and all I had to say was I didn't remember anything and he just told me. Mr de Lancey came up the river 'cos he wasn't far and he wanted to talk to me about the picture I'd asked him about and he found me with my gippy tum and gave me some of his special medicine and then went off to fish till Ted came back 'cos there were things he wanted to talk to him about. But he'd left the bottle behind, and I must have had another swig at it when you're only supposed to take it in tea-spoons, four hours apart. The point is it's full of opium! (That *does* rather explain things!) So I'd got up and gone and found Mafote and told him to saddle Tan-Tan and just ridden off, but Elongo had seen me going and so he'd run and fetched Mr de Lancey and they'd tracked me right out into the bush and found me wandering about, drugged silly, looking for Ted. Tan-Tan had got his reins tangled into a tree so they caught him and strapped me into the saddle and led me home.

So that's three of us lying like troopers! Elongo's only a native, and you expect them to lie, and what I say to my husband's my look-out, but de L.! Mind you, I don't suppose he told Ted all that, straight out—he'd just have said enough to let Ted work it out. And I bet he'll say, if it ever comes out what really happened, he had to tell Ted something different in order to protect *me*! (As if he gave a hoot!)

Ted called Mr de Lancey all sorts of names for leaving such dangerous medicine where I could get it but secretly he's rather pleased 'cos de Lancey was very apologetic and anxious, when normally, Ted says, he's not famous for his civility to anyone below the rank of Lieutenant Governor. He left me a note.

> Dear Mrs Jackland,
>
> I must apologize profusely for not having realized that you were in no state to understand my instructions about my 'brew'. I do hope that you now make a speedy recovery.
>
> I believe I can discover the painter of the Deposition about which you wrote to me, but shall have to do further research. If I were you I should not trouble my mind with this particular problem for the moment. You will only confuse the design of the picture. Leave it in my hands, and I will do my best.
>
> Yours very sincerely,
> B.V.X. de Lancey

Isn't he sly? I showed Ted the letter. He didn't spot a thing. Then, very shy, as tho' he was ashamed about it, he pulled another scrap of paper out of his pocket. It was the note I'd left for him before I rode off. I thought I'd just been telling him I was all right and I'd be coming back, or something, but all it said was 'I love you. I love you. I love you.' We had a laugh at me being so silly with the opium, and then a bit of a snuggle, but actually it did make me feel rather dreadful.

ELEVEN

'Would you prefer me to move out?' said Jackland.

Miss Tressider was lying on the bed in black Bermuda shorts and a white, wide-collared blouse. On the side of her calf, where the tick had sucked, was a white circular patch with a dark spot at the centre. Jackland had just straightened from examining this. He had his reading spectacles on and a small square book in his hand. Miss Tressider did not remove her stare from the ceiling of the cabin.

'Not specially,' she said. 'Your not being here won't stop me from feeling perfectly ghastly. Being an actor I feel the need of an audience to be ghastly at. Do you want to go?'

'It isn't . . .'

'You give that impression.'

'I don't want to leave you. I want to go and ring Ilorin and make arrangements for you to go into hospital for treatment. I also want to get Sally to set up an immediate flight home, with medical attendance.'

'No.'

'My darling, I'm ninety per cent certain you have tick-fever.'

'It can wait another day.'

Jackland consulted the book in his hand.

'. . . no longer a serious matter,' he read, 'provided modern antibiotic treatment is supplied without delay.'

'One more day.'

'One more day and it'll be Sunday. New Year's Day. Monday's a holiday too, like as not. I know the W.H.O. project has closed down already. I tried them.'

'So'll your hospital be, too.'

'They'll have emergency staff. If I ring them now, tell them who it is . . .'

'I am going to finish the film.'

'You have, darling. All that matters. We can do the landing-stage close-ups in the studio, and Janine can stand in . . .'

'It is going to be me in every fucking frame. Me. That's final.'

'I wish I could say I found your courage . . .'

'For god's sake, Nigel! I don't even know if I'm ill. I'm so shit-scared I can't tell. I knew something like this was going to hit me one day. I've spent the last ten years conning my body into reactions it had no reason to produce—weeping, feeling randy about men who were complete turn-offs, hysterics, breakdowns—how'm I to tell if it's not doing that to me now? It knows I'm shit-scared, so it does the trick I've trained it to and gives me something to be scared of.'

'You have the classic symptoms of tick-fever.'

'It could run those at the drop of a hat.'

'You might at least . . .'

'I am going to do the departure scene, Nigel.'

'Let me advance another argument. It is a condition of your insurance that we take all reasonable care of your well-being. Not getting you immediately to a modern hospital . . .'

'I'll sign something.'

'I don't know that that would be adequate. You are not, so to speak, entirely your own property.'

'I am. I am. I am.'

'You are under contracts . . .'

'I refuse to talk about it any more. Anyway, you can't do anything tonight. They're still working on the trucks, aren't they? And the ferry won't be running.'

'Annie's car is parked on the bridge. I thought I'd borrow that.'

Miss Tressider sighed, shivered, flicked a blanket over herself. She seemed to reduce her physical volume as the fever-chill took her. Jackland straightened the blanket and spread another over her but she didn't thank him. He stood looking down, presumably choosing words for a fresh appeal. She spoke before he did.

'Did you screw her while you were in the harem?'

'No. Too hot, for one thing.'

'Not even tempted?'

'She was moderately attentive.'

'I could see that. A fresh experience missed, Nigel.'

'More in the savour than the act, probably. At my age . . .'

'You're not going to get many more chances like that.'

'You'd have advised me to take it?'

'It would have given me an excuse to be bloody to you, which is what I feel like.'

'I want to take you to Ilorin. Tonight.'

'There won't be anyone there.'

'Leave around four and we'll be there by eight a.m. But if we wait till after the shooting we won't be there till six in the evening. Sunday and Monday, both holidays, to come. Same applies about getting to London, only more so. Leave now, or as soon as we've got some flights booked, and you'll be there Sunday. Leave tomorrow afternoon and it'll be Tuesday, if not Wednesday.'

'Betty would have stuck it out.'

'You're not her.'

'Yes I am.'

'Balls. It's over, darling. It's in the can, bar one last sequence we can do in the studio and with a stand-in. You've given absolutely everything possible, and much more than anyone else conceivably could have given. I thought I was an unimpressionable old sod, but watching you playing my mother I've been deeply moved. I feel extraordinarily lucky that you should have taken it on.'

'It happens. I get offered juicy parts with stupid great wads of money attached and I do them if I'm interested, and usually I get as much as I give, and that's worth it. Then, suddenly—I don't suppose it's happened more than four or five times so far—I find myself playing someone who really matters. You can never give as much as you get. All you can give is all you've got. Betty. I owe it to her. No one knows about her, or if they did they've forgotten. I didn't know it was going to be like this when I took her on. Alphonse was becoming a bore and I was mildly interested in you and there was a gap in my schedule, so I thought why not. Then you gave me the diary to read . . . There's a ghost to be laid, Nigel. No one else can do it.'

'Unfortunately that is an argument I am not intellectually equipped to grasp, let alone to rebut.'

'Thank God for small mercies.'

The effort of her previous speech, though it was only a slurred mutter, seemed to have heated her up again. She twitched the blankets aside, drew a sighing yawn, reached for the diary, put on her spectacles and, opening as usual at random, started to read. The air conditioner chewed at its indraught. Insects blipped against the skin of the cabin, enhancing its sense of being a sealed environment, a space capsule protecting its occupants from the void outside but continually bombarded by flecks of star-stuff. The impression was wrong. Just as the moths and beetles were not batting into the cabin by chance but had chosen their path towards some chink of light, so outside lay not emptiness but the excess of Africa.

Jackland, naturally, was fidgety. It was clear that Miss Tressider did not want to talk, but it was impossible for him to settle to work of his own. He spent a few minutes organizing his bed on the floor—years of experience ensured that he would sleep tolerably well under such conditions—then sat down with an air-line timetable (also a sign of those years) and began to make a list of flight-connections. There was evidently some gap in the chain. He leafed to and fro, looking for alternatives.

Suddenly he took off his spectacles, thought a few moments, and rose.

'Where are you going?' said Miss Tressider.

'Had an idea. I want to see if we can't get you to London by mid-day Sunday, leaving here after the shooting. The flights don't fit. I'm going to see if I can lay on a helicopter.'

'No.'

'Be sensible.'

'You're going to drive me to Ilorin, Nigel.'

'All right. I am prepared to regard that as a probable course of action. I am not prepared to have other courses of action closed to you. Then Sally can get on with booking the seats. You don't have to use them.'

'But you're going to drive me to Ilorin. You and no one else.'

'I will also arrange either to borrow Annie's car or to have a hired one waiting and ready.'

'A hired one means a driver. I just want you.'

'I will ring Annie at the palace.'

'Promise.'

'A conditional promise.'

'Don't be long, Nigel. I'm frightened.'

She looked at him over the top of the diary, brilliant-eyed, flushed. Her obsession with his driving her to Ilorin might well be the beginnings of delirium. As he opened and closed the door the torrid, odour-thick air seemed to jostle in the slot of dark like an invisible crowd. Miss Tressider continued to make a pretence of reading the diary, flipping to and fro, reading little more than a line at a time, as if searching for the one talismanic sentence that would relieve her fever. She tugged her blankets over her when another fit of shivers shook her, but had tossed them off again by the time Jackland returned.

'How are you feeling?' he said.

'No bloodier than before.'

'Something's up.'

She did not respond.

'Your friend Major Kadu is up to something.'

'That's news?'

'At least it helps explain his general bloody-mindedness. He wanted an excuse to hang around Kiti. Pretending to be mainly interested in us, holding us up so we didn't clear out too soon . . .'

'You had a lovely chat with him, Nigel? You asked him to come and lay a healing hand on me?'

'I asked him for a helicopter—pretty slim chance, I thought, but as far as I can make out there's not one civilian helicopter to be had anywhere in Northern Nigeria. All grounded. Flight control decided to take the holiday off, or something. So I thought I'd try Kadu as a last chance. The first odd thing was that the switchboard was manned by someone who put me straight through to him. He was extremely brusque, just about to cut me off when I managed to slip in that it would be good publicity for the Nigerian Army. Silence. I thought I'd lost him. Then "A helicopter will be at your camp at twelve noon tomorrow, Mr Jackland. The Army will see to it. Good night." Click. Very rum.'

'What about Annie's car? I don't want a helicopter.'

'No answer from the palace. Sally's still trying. But listen, I want you to understand that if we go to Ilorin by car there's absolutely no way I can get you to London before Tuesday. I'll come with you in the helicopter if there's room.'

'You can't talk in one of those things. Tomorrow I'm going to finish being Betty, and then you're going to drive me to Ilorin and on the way you're going to tell me what happened to her after. That's her life, not mine, you see. It's a way of letting her go. It's important, Nigel. You remember how I called up Femora

Feng by mistake and had to find a way of sending her back? It's the same thing.'

'All right. I take your word for it.'

'Promise? Unconditional?'

Jackland hesitated, unusually disturbed. She pushed up her spectacles and stared at him, forcing her will through the shimmer and haze of fever.

'Yes,' he said.

Miss Tressider sighed and relaxed. Her eyes closed. The blotched patches on her cheeks lost their sharp edges. Small changes of posture signalled a slackening in the tension of the muscles, a tension no doubt stimulated by the earnestness of her argument, though that in turn might have been mainly the product of a fever-ridden brain. Jackland watched her for a while, then moved round the bed to slip the spectacles off her forehead and pull a blanket over her. He watched her again, and was just reaching for another blanket when there was a gentle double-tap at the door, barely louder than might have been produced by two of the battering insects, but somehow different. He finished spreading the blanket and then turned and opened the door. Annie Boyaba stood on the step of the cabin. She put a finger to her lips and moved immediately down into the shadow of the cabin wall.

Jackland glanced back. Miss Tressider lay still, not apparently noticing the warm draught of unfiltrated night. He moved out on to the step and closed the door.

'I've been trying to ring you,' he muttered.

'Where can we talk?'

Jackland stepped down beside her. The night was moonless, with only a few stars, faint and fuzzy, overhead, and over on the horizon the hazy aura from the few lights of Kiti Town. The embers of a fire glimmered at the end of the horseshoe of tents and cabins, whose windows provided a few bright squares of electric light. The loudest noise was the pulse of the generator that powered these and the air-conditioners. From one of the cabins came the sound of a radio playing Afro-Rock.

'I can't go far,' said Jackland. 'Mary's not at all well. I have to keep an eye on her.'

'Oh.'

'That's what I was trying to ring you about. I may have to drive her to Ilorin tomorrow, for tests and treatment. I don't trust the local hire-cars to make the distance, nor our trucks, for that matter. I would be extremely grateful if you would lend me yours. More than grateful.'

No doubt Jackland had chosen to sail straight in in order to avoid misunderstandings about his motives and to emphasize the nature of his duty towards Miss Tressider. After more than twenty-four hours with the film unit Miss Boyaba could not be unaware of the relationship. Both faces were invisible to each other, apart from slight glints where an eyeball reflected one of the faint lights. She felt for his forearm and gripped it.

'My uncle sent me,' she whispered.

'The Sarkin?' Not, from his tone, what Jackland had expected.

'He needs your help. There's going to be a coup. The Army are arresting all the chiefs. That's what Major Kadu's here for. They cut off our telephone.'

'Are you sure?'

'Aunt Isai—that's his daughter—she's married to a colonel. She rang him up to tell him, in Kiti, of course. The telephone went dead. His waziri was turned back when he tried to leave the Old Town gate.'

'But they let you out?'

'No. There's a door at the back of the Old Palace, half way up the wall, where they used to throw the rubbish out. Some of his people let us down from there.'

'He's here?'

'Just out in the trees. We thought there might be soldiers . . .'

The noise of the night changed as the pop from Lagos broke off in the middle of a phrase. There was a short fanfare of brass, the classic tones of an announcer, and then a heavier voice speaking in slow sentences, the words inaudible at this distance but definitely English. Whoever was in control of the radio untuned the frequency and started to search the wavebands for more pop, only to find the same voice speaking from every station.

'What does he want me to do?' said Jackland.

'Take him to Tefuga.'

Jackland drew a breath but did not speak. As a journalist he must have been deeply intrigued to find himself involved in such an event. There were also calculations of interest—by no means all military coups are successful, and the brief broadcast announcing the take-over might well prove to be the high-water mark of this particular revolt. To have refused to help a senior politician in such circumstances could turn out awkward not only for Jackland but for the whole unit. But if the coup succeeded, to have helped might be even more dangerous.

'Please, Nigel.'

'I don't think I can. I am absolutely committed to driving Mary to Ilorin tomorrow morning.'

'In my car?'

'If possible.'

'There won't be any hire-cars. Not with a coup on. You could take him to Tefuga first.'

'Even if we started at first light . . .'

'He wants to go now. Major Kadu'll find he's got away . . .'

'He'll have road-blocks up already.'

'Uncle doesn't want to use the Highway. He wants to go out along the old track.'

'In the dark?'

'He says he can find it. He got us here without going on the road. I was utterly lost. That's why it's got to be one of your trucks. And there's no one else. Please, Nigel. I'll *give* you my car if you'll take him.'

'If it weren't for Mary I would. But . . .'

'Please. He's so sure you will. I warned him. He kept saying, "For the sake of his father he will do it." And then you can have my car.'

Jackland sighed.

'I'll see what I can manage,' he said. 'I can't promise. The trucks aren't mine to take, not like that. I'll have to talk Malcolm round. He might be glad of a chance to dish Major Kadu. No. Second thoughts, I can't tell him. I can't tell anyone, in case things go wrong. I'll just have to take one. Bugger. I don't like this at all.'

'But you're going to . . .'

'God. Yes, I suppose so. About twenty minutes. You'll hear the engine start. Wait for me where the track runs off the road.'

It was in fact slightly more than that before Jackland was ready to go. Last of all he returned to Miss Tressider's cabin. She was deep asleep. He tidied her blankets, then sat down and wrote a short note which he left propped up on the diary by her bedside.

TWELVE

Wed August 6
Marvellous news! For me, I mean. Bit sad for Ted, tho', cos it means Mr de Lancey's winning. Not the whole game yet, but a set anyway. Thing is, we're going on tour, specially ordered from Kaduna, and I've got to go too *so as I can talk to the villagers!* That's in the actual memo. Ted brought it over and showed me. Terribly decent of him. It's going to be a big show—the Resident (de L.), Ted, a detail of soldiers, our policeman *and* 'a speaker of the Kiti language not allied to the family of the Bangwa Wangwa or any other dependant of the Emir'. *There absolutely isn't anyone else.* So there.

It's all a terrific secret. That's in the memo too. 'E. Kiti is only to be informed in general terms that a tour will take place towards the end of the rains. Location and purpose of tour (detailed survey of Binja area to verify accuracy of 1917 census and assessment) are not to be revealed until the last practicable moment.' Oho, and likewise aha! Even little me can see what *that* means.

You see, after I took Mr de Lancey to the burnt village he must have gone home and thought about it. First off, he must have wondered if it meant anything at all. That's bothered me too. I mean, it does seem a perfectly extraordinary thing for natives to do, *inventing* a village just to show me. But I don't think it was quite like that. It sort of grew as they went along. First off, they'd tried just *telling* me at Tefuga, and that hadn't been any use, so they thought now they'd *show* me. It had to be somewhere near enough for me to get to, and they remembered this old village and decided that would do, only when they got there they saw they'd have to patch it up a bit or I'd see at once something was wrong. That must have been how it happened, and I think Mr de Lancey must have worked it out too.

The trouble is, *that* means it wasn't an accident me going there. The women must have told Elongo to bring me, and he thought of teaching me women's talk as an excuse. I've tried to

173

ask him, but it makes him so unhappy I haven't the heart. But it's obvious from what Atafa Guni said that she'd worked out that telling me about the 'toe' villages—actually showing me one—might be a way of getting rid of Kama Boi, which I'm absolutely certain is what they want to do if only they dared. And tho' she felt at the time I'd let her down dreadfully saying I wasn't going to kill Kama Boi (me!) I think it's going to turn out all right in the long run.

Anyway, Mr de Lancey must have decided that if something like that had been going on the best place to look was in the old assessment returns. There's always something wrong with them, of course—you can't expect illiterate natives to count right—but if the Hausa had been cheating on purpose there ought to be a pattern. So he got a crony of his at Kaduna to start looking back through old files and he came up with all sorts of things, mostly just counting mistakes, but almost always the same thing, ten or twenty or thirty too few—that's what you get by leaving out the 'toes'. But the most exciting thing was a whole missing village! Mr Mooreshed found it. He was D.O. in 1919, only about four months, but he was a mad keen bug-hunter and he was out near Binja, which is a wild part in the south, after butterflies one evening when he walked right into a village which wasn't on the census. He just popped it in at the bottom of a page as tho' it was the most ordinary thing in the world (much more interested in his butterflies, I suppose) so no one ever thought to ask whether there mightn't be more like it. Mr de Lancey thinks there are, and so do I (in fact, I'm absolutely certain) and Ted thinks there aren't. So that's why we're going to Binja!

Reason I know about all this is rather interesting. I mean Ted would have told me anyway—we have to talk a lot of shop 'cos of there not being much else to chat about and of course Ted's had to spend hours and hours writing reports to Kaduna saying Mr de Lancey's got it wrong—but it didn't quite happen like that. Sometimes I think what happens inside us is really just as interesting and peculiar as anything that happens outside—and goodness knows you couldn't ask for anywhere more interesting or peculiar than Africa—peculiar, anyway . . . I'm in a muddle.

You see, *I think Ted knew!* Isn't that extraordinary! I don't mean he knew I'd let him down with Mr de Lancey—he absolutely couldn't bear that. He's still fighting de L. tooth and nail to save KB, and that's real. That's war—very polite and stiff-upperlip, but war all the same. Fighting me's different—that's just a sort of game to keep us amused—it doesn't matter 'cos I can't actually *do* anything—but the rules of the game were that we had to pretend it wasn't happening.

I've only just worked it out properly 'cos of what happened after Ted showed me the memo (come to that in a mo), but really I've sort of half-known for ages, and so's Ted, I'm almost sure. I don't know since when. I've rather lost track. You see, after I had my gippy tummy (that horrible time I went out and found Mr de Lancey and took him to the burnt village) I didn't actually get better for quite a long time, and slap after that I had another go of malaria, and by then it was the rains.

You long for the rains. You can feel the electricity building up. You hear grumbly little bits of thunder and nothing happens. Everything, and everybody, gets horribly tense. Even dear Ted. Then, several days running, there's proper thunder and lightning, terrific! Boom, boom boom, and jigging stilts of lightning across the river, hardly stopping at all. For a few days you feel rather well (tho' I was still v. weak with my malaria) but after that it's rather miserable. Damp, muggy, hot, drizzly, everything streaming with wet, the mud floors slimy to walk on, shoes you put away clean yesterday green with mildew next morning, and the horrible reek of rot in your nose all day and all night. And almost worst of all, specially for Ted, no horses to ride. He sent them north with the grooms soon as the first drops fell and we aren't going to get them back for another month, except that now we are, 'cos of needing them for this tour, probably. Another worry for Ted. The rains are almost over now, but one way and another the last couple of months have been a pretty mouldy time. (Excuse the pun!)

So quite likely I mightn't have felt much like scribbling even if I'd been properly well, and on top of the malaria there was the ghastly fright I'd had after I'd shown Mr de Lancey the burnt village and found how wrong I'd been about that and how nearly I'd spoilt everything for ever between Ted and me. 'Cos of that I made up my mind I'd do just what Mr de Lancey had told me (well, he didn't, but that's what he meant) and stop worrying about KB and the Kitawa. Not just stop trying to do something about them, stop even thinking about them. Put my secret away in the back of a cupboard and lock it up and forget about it. Go back to where we were before we went to Tefuga.

But you can't. It's never the same—that's impossible. It was new, then. Even tho' we do and say exactly the same things it can't ever be new again. That's the difference. That's why you *have* to keep changing. If you don't it's like stagnant water. It's funny how much it can matter. You wouldn't have thought it would actually make my painting go flat, would you? But it did. I'd do everything right, but when I'd finished it wasn't any good. Nothing wrong with the picture, except that it was empty. Dead. And in the evenings, we'd chat and have supper and dance a bit, working ourselves up, and go to bed and . . . no salt!

The funny thing is it was Ted who worked out what had gone wrong, and what to do. I know I keep suggesting he isn't the most sensitive type, dear man—in fact, I wasn't sure he'd even noticed how samey and usual things were getting till about a fortnight ago. We were dancing after supper. Rather a nice night, not so muggy and sticky as it's been . . . dancing's funny when you're in that sort of mood, rather like taking a dog out on a walk and meeting somebody you're not sure you feel like talking to only they've got a dog too, and there you are saying 'Good morning' outside and 'Oh lor' inside and trying to smile while your two dogs (our bodies, I'm talking about) are hoicking at their leads and quivering all over and sniffing at each other! I don't mean I was really saying 'Oh lor' about Ted—I don't think I was thinking about anything really, just feeling a bit dismal when I didn't want to—and then he slid his pipe sideways in his mouth and muttered in my ear, 'Odd thing. Kaduna've dug up a report by a chap called Mooreshed . . .' and he started telling me about the missing village near Binja. He'd been saving it up, too. He could easily have told me at supper. That's what I mean about Ted knowing. You see, all of a sudden, deep in its cupboard, my secret gave a little squirm and reminded me it was there, and I was still thinking about it and wondering when we went to bed, and everything was all right. Much better. Lovely.

That's all wrong. I've made it sound as tho' I understood straight off what he'd done, and so did he. *I* certainly didn't, in fact I've only just really worked it out 'cos of what happened after Ted showed me the Kaduna memo. And I don't think he had it all plotted and planned either. People aren't like that. And anyway if he did it was different for him. My guess is he thought he was playing a sort of game, cat-and-mouse, telling me little secret tit-bits in the evening just as tho' he was the fat old general and I was the beautiful spy. (You think 'How *could* they! They *must* have known!' Of course they did—that was part of the excitement. Bit of that with Ted, too, I think.) Of course, dear man, if he dared think with the top of his mind about any of this he'd shut up like a clam. He's got to keep it in the shadows underneath. Even there he thinks it's still only a game for him, 'cos he knows I can't do anything about it. There's nobody for me to spy for. That's what I mean about cat-and-mouse. He's teasing me, he thinks.

And I thought the same, I suppose—it was just fun, being teased like that. There wasn't anything I could do, and after my fright I didn't want there to be. Much better keep it just a game. Only now the memo's come and I *am* going to do something, I can see I was just pretending all along, waiting for my chance to come when I could break the rules of the game. Now it's going to happen. Hooray!

Oh dear, that does sound heartless. I oughtn't to feel like that when poor dear Ted *minds* so much. I simply didn't realize till just now, after he'd shown me the Kaduna memo. I was so cock-a-hoop it took me a while to see Ted wasn't. Usually he'd look forward no end to a tour. Of course he was grumbling away about Kaduna desk-drivers thinking they understood what went on in the bush, and how were we going to get bearers when every fit man would be wanting to work his land after the rains, and did they think we'd be able to make a surprise tour without horses—it'll still be the tsetse season, specially down south, and hammocking's far too slow. And that'd give the Hausa a reason for digging their heels in, too, as well as the business about working their land—oh, the usual Teddish things, and I was saying, 'Yes, darling,' and chortling inside myself when all of a sudden I saw how absolutely miserable he was. He absolutely hates Mr de Lancey, and he's got to be a good loser in public . . .

So I jumped up and ran to give him a comforting little hug but he absolutely snatched at me and started to kiss me so hard it hurt (my mouth's still puffy) so I guessed what he wanted, tho' we've never done it before in the middle of the day but I thought why not . . .

But afterwards, oh, poor man! Honestly, it was almost as tho' I *had* been the beautiful spy and he'd come and said, 'Look. This is what you asked for. I sold my honour to give it to you. Now you must pay me.' So I'd paid him, and he'd found it wasn't enough. Usually I think I understand my dear man rather well, but I'm not sure I do about this. I mean, if he *knew* it was me who'd started Mr de Lancey off on the right track, but he can't. That's nonsense, except that it feels as tho' deep inside him, without him understanding at all either, *something* knew.

Anyway, I'm going to be specially nice to him now. My side of the bargain. (Women have honour too!)

Fri August 8th
Terrific dramas! Kimjiri has run away! First we knew was me coming back from a painting expedish yesterday and sending Elongo to fetch K. so we could talk about meals and stores and E. coming back and saying the huts were empty. Gone, with all his wives and children! Ted was over at Kiti making arrangements for the tour (only three days to go!) and telling KB he'd have to see that enough of his people come, so I sent for Mafote, who said one of the big trading canoes had come to the landing-stage —K. must have arranged that while he was at the market yesterday—and K. and his wives and children had been ready and had all run down and gone away. M. called K. all sorts of names. He's not a good witness 'cos of being jealous of K. and wanting one of his wives for himself, Ted says, but I looked everywhere and I really don't think he's taken much. All I could do was hash up some tinned beef and carrots for Ted's lunch and try and break it to him gently. I knew he'd be cut up, and he was. K.'s been with him for years. Complete mystery. Couldn't have happened at a worse time. We absolutely have to have a cook to take on tour. Mr de Lancey's not bringing his.

Sat August 9
More drama (both kinds, inside and outside I mean). I remember Mummy when I was a little girl saying nobody who employed a cook ever need go to the theatre, 'cos of having quite enough comedy and tragedy at home, thank you! Of course I'd no idea

what she meant then, but I see now. First thing, Ted came over for lunch saying it was going to be all right about not starving on tour 'cos Lukar said he could find someone. So that was all right. Great relief. But then, soon as he'd gone back to the office (loads of extra work 'cos of being off for the next fortnight) Elongo came to see me. He stood in front of me where I was sitting and looked at me like a schoolmaster. He didn't put his hands together and do his usual stiff little bow, but stood up straight as a soldier and said, in English, 'You must not hire this man to be your cook.'

I knew at once why he used English. We only talk it at lessons so he doesn't get in the habit and irritate Ted, but he'd been waiting on us at lunch and heard us talking about the new man and he wanted to make sure I realized.

'Why not?' I said. 'Do you know him?'

'I do not know the man. Lukar is your enemy.'

'Oh, it's not as bad as that. We've got to have a cook to take on tour.'

'I will be your cook. You must not hire this man.'

'But you don't know how to.'

'You will show me. I tell you, do not hire this man.'

He was so earnest I couldn't laugh. I know it sounds funny, being given orders like that by your servant, but he was so impressive, like a young black Moses—we were only talking about hiring a new cook, but really it was like that—I felt I had to try and take him seriously.

'I'll talk to Master about it,' I said.

'Do not tell him it is my advice. But you must not hire this man. Remember, Lukar is your enemy.'

Terribly difficult. All I could say was, 'Well, I'll see.'

After he'd gone I felt rather strange. It sort of preyed on my mind, and the more I thought about it the more I felt I really didn't want a cook Lukar had found. It wasn't just what Elongo had said, it was the way he'd said it, like a messenger from a different world, a black world, speaking my white-world language to make sure I understood. I don't think I'm superstitious but suppose I was and I'd been on my way to something important and a great black cat had crossed my path, that's how I'd have felt. After a bit I just felt I had to talk to Ted. The rains are meant to be over but there was a grumbly little thunderstorm coming up the river and just starting its first sprinklings, so I scuttled across to the office before it really got going.

I smiled at Mr Yo who was adding up an account book (all wrong, pretty certainly) and tip-toed through into Ted's part. I don't go there much. It's the side of him where I don't fit. Even when he had his guinea worm and I was doing all his writing for him I felt uncomfy there so we did most of it in the dining-room. That's why he was surprised to see me. He was sitting in his usual fog of baccy smoke writing another great boring report on the Sokowa settlers. The office is tiny, just room for his files, desk and two chairs, but he keeps one of them folded to make a bit more space so when he swivelled round to say hello I plonked myself on his lap and put my arm round his neck.

'What have I done to deserve this?' he said.

'I've come to wheedle you.'

'The machinery of Empire can wait, in that case.'

'I don't think I want a new cook.'

'Why on earth not? We've got to take one on tour.'

'That's just it. Suppose we wait till we get back, Kimjiri might change his mind.'

'I'll have something to say to him if he does.'

'Elongo can cook on tour. I'll show him what to do. We'll manage between us.'

'I'm sure you would, in an emergency, but it will take up a lot of your time, Rabbit. I don't want to be stuck alone with de Lancey all evening. I'd much rather have you jawing away to each other about art, and I'm sure he would too. There's no reason this chap Lukar's found shouldn't turn out perfectly adequate.'

'I don't want anyone Lukar's found.'

'My dear girl . . .'

'Please, Ted. I don't want to owe him anything. I don't want one of his friends in our house.'

I felt Ted change. Sitting on his knee stopped being comfy. He jerked his head towards the door to remind me Mr Yo was just the other side of the partition, tho' he couldn't have heard anything 'cos it was raining properly now, booming on the pan roof. The two doorways made a sort of tunnel, v. dramatic, with a lightning blink down onto the river, dark sky and dark trees beyond. Just the weather for cosying up, but he wouldn't let me.

'I'd have thought you'd have learnt by now, Rabbit,' he said. 'You really mustn't take any notice of what natives say about each other. Lukar and Elongo appear to have had some kind of dust-up about a fortnight ago. I deduce that from the fact that Lukar has been taking every opportunity to insinuate that Elongo is a thief and I ought to get rid of him.'

'Nonsense. And why didn't you tell me?'

'Because what one native says about another has no meaning. Or rather, it does not mean what it appears to. In this case some petty feud has arisen which I intend to have nothing to do with. That applies to you too, Rabbit.'

'But they don't have anything to do with each other.'

'My darling Rabbit, that's something you don't know. You see about a tenth—a twentieth—of Elongo's existence. What goes on in the remaining ninety-five per cent is a closed book. All you can be sure of is that it contains a great web of feuds and alliances and obligations and distrusts, and the one thing you must not do is go blundering in, taking sides, trying to alter the web for the better. Only disaster can result.'

'Then what are we doing in Nigeria at all?'

'That, if de Lancey has his way. I take it you told Elongo that Lukar has found a new cook and was sending him out to interview us this evening?'

'Please, darling. I don't want him.'

The rain was really roaring down now. You couldn't hear the thunder 'cos of the noise from the roof, but you knew from the lightning-blinks it must be there. If we hadn't been sitting so close we'd have needed to shout. The rain made it colder. I tried to snuggle into Ted but his body didn't answer.

'What I propose to do,' he said, 'is interview this fellow. You can be present, of course, but unless he is clearly useless we will hire him.'

'Please, darling.'

'I have already told Lukar to send the man out.'

'And Lukar's gone to collect a present from him.'

'Very likely. So it is not in Lukar's interest to send us someone unsuitable. It follows that if we refuse to hire this fellow Lukar will be perfectly well aware of the reason. In effect you will have forced me to take sides publicly against him in his feud with Elongo. Is that what you want?'

I started to cry.

It really wasn't fair. It was breaking the rules of the game. But you see, all of a sudden it wasn't just a game. The whole point about the game was that it didn't make any difference in the real world. Ted wasn't being beaten by Mr de Lancey 'cos of anything *I'd* done (that's what he thought and it's sort of true 'cos I hadn't actually done anything since long before we'd started playing). Now I was trying to make something real happen. I know it was a silly little thing, hiring a cook, but it was part of everything else and that's why it mattered.

I didn't care. I still don't. I'm not at all ashamed of myself. I don't usually cry when there's anyone there—Daddy cured me of that—but once I'd got going it was easy to keep it up so I sobbed away and wheedled at Ted's shirt with my fingers and watched the rain slithering over the mud outside the door—he couldn't even send me away while it was sheeting down like that—and said to myself, Come on, Bets—you're winning. Ted was terribly embarrassed and kept telling me to pull myself together and then I'd sob a bit more and say, 'Please, Ted!' until at last he gave a great sigh and said, 'Oh, all right. Have it your own way. Mind you, I shall expect *haute cuisine* all the way to Binja and back.' Then I kissed him like a puppy until the rain stopped and he pushed me off and told me to run away and I sploshed my way home. Extraordinary how *well* all that's made me feel—like a swim before breakfast!

Mon August 11

I absolutely must scribble this down, spite of the rush and bother of getting ready for the tour—Mr de Lancey here this evening and then off first light tomorrow—cooler than last tour, so no more torch-light treks. I don't think I'll take the diary with me, not with de L. there, too public. But something v. strange has happened I've simply got to get down before it goes fuzzy.

It started with a letter from Kimjiri. First off I just thought it was a complete hoot. K. must have got hold of some sort of mission-educated clerk in Birnin Soko and together they'd cooked up their letter. It started off 'Dear Mr Edward Jackland Esquire Sir, with reference to the absence of the undersigned from his duty as cook to your goodself . . .' and on it went like that, apologizing over and over to Ted, and boasting how well he always boiled everything and kept all the lids tight on the boxes and scorned those who begged him to steal food from our stores so *a fortiori* (yes, really—Kimjiri!) he scorned one who came to him with improper gifts, and then a really funny bit about Madam being the jewel of Mr Edward Jackland Esquire's soul and his heart's treasure, and then straight back from that to boiling the water and not letting improper substances get into the food lest he should be hanged by the neck till he was dead (really, I don't think Ted's ever gone quite *that* far) but he was a simple man and afraid of damnable pagan practices and his heartiest wish was to cook for Mr E.J. Esq. again as soon as he left Kiti, and he would pray every day that Mr E.J. Esq. and Madam stayed alive and perceived the wiles of their enemies. And then a lot of flowery farewells.

I wanted to shriek with laughter when Ted showed me the letter. Dear old Kimjiri talking like that! *Not* a poetical soul.

'What on earth does it all mean?' I said.

'Somebody offered him a bribe and when he wouldn't take it they threatened him with some kind of juju and he decided to clear out.'

Ted wasn't anything like as amused as I was. He's minded about Kimjiri running off when they've been together so long, and natives using jujus on each other can be a serious nuisance, but it wasn't that made me suddenly stop chortling. I read the letter again. The bit about the wiles of our enemies. Elongo standing in front of my chair, so serious, warning me about enemies.

'Lukar,' I said.

'Oh, come, darling. I must say I'm getting a bit tired of your obsession with Lukar.'

'I've often wondered, in the old days, when our people were dying like flies anyway, how was anyone sure what they actually died of?'

'What on earth are you talking about?'

'Improper substances in our food.'

I was feeling very cold and shivery and frightened. Elongo'd warned me, hadn't he? That's why it had mattered so much.

'This is perfectly ridiculous,' said Ted. 'Old Kimjiri's only talking about kitchen hygiene.'

'He wouldn't know the difference.'

'Are you feeling all right, Rabbit?'

He tried to put his big warm hand on my forehead to feel if I had a fever, but I pushed it away.

'I'm feeling a lot better than I might've if you'd let that friend of Lukar's come and cook for us,' I said.

'What earthly motive would Lukar have? He's a shrewd chap. He's been Messenger nine years. He knows how the world works. He's got a well-paid job with a pension coming in the end.'

'Not if we go on tour and find that Kama Boi's people have been cheating us out of a lot of tax and Lukar's been in it up to his neck.'

'Now that *is* nonsense. Lukar doesn't read English. I didn't say a word to him about going on tour till three days ago when I went over to see old Kama Boi. That was the morning Kimjiri cleared out, so whatever he was frightened of must have happened before that—several days before.'

It's funny how people will go on arguing after they've changed their mind. I could hear it in Ted's voice. He didn't agree with me—I mean what he said about Lukar not knowing was quite true—but all of a sudden he wasn't sure. He picked up Kimjiri's letter and started to read it again. I got out of my chair and put my arm round him so I could read it too. It wasn't really that. I was still rather trembly, thinking about what might have happened. I needed to hold him. I wasn't wheedling—it was real. He put his spare arm round my shoulder and went on reading. We felt very one.

'I suppose it's just possible,' he said. 'Something might have got out the Kaduna end. First thing is to get hold of Kimjiri. He'll have headed for his home village, pretty certainly. I'll drop a line to Burroughs at Jos and have him arrested as a material witness.'

'Poor Kimjiri.'

'Just shows you can never read the African mind, any more than you can expect an African to read ours. By all European lights the sensible thing would have been for him to come to me with the whole story. Surely he must know I'd stick by him after all these years. But no. I'm still as much of a mystery to him as a juju in a jungle pool.'

'What are you going to say to Lukar?'

'I suppose I shall have to tackle him. It's only fair. We may be barking up completely the wrong tree. Chances are old Kimjiri had some quite different bee in his bonnet.'

'But you do think there's a chance . . .'

'I honestly don't know, and nor do you, Rabbit. I'm still completely at sea. All I know is this. You are—what's the fellow say?—the jewel of my heart and my soul's treasure.'

Aren't men peculiar? I could feel it all through him, not just in his words and his voice, a terrific sense of relief. He was quite right about K.'s letter being useless to go on, it could've meant dozens of different things, but it was just enough. It gave Ted the excuse he'd been waiting for, without knowing it. Now, 'cos of what might've happened to me, *he could change sides*! He's known for weeks it was no use going on trying to protect KB, but he had to, or he'd lose face. He thought he was honour bound, but he's even more honour bound to look after me, so Kimjiri's letter saying one of KB's people had tried to have me poisoned (if that's what it meant) let him off. I think he's still very bitter inside about being beaten by Mr de Lancey, but it's not so bad as it would have been otherwise. At least it'll make the tour a bit less sticky.

Tues August 26

Long sigh. Flop into chair. B. & s. The river. The gramophone. Home . . . And we've done it! We've won! I've won. Yes. It was really me. If I hadn't been there it wouldn't have been any good. Oh, some day, in five years, or ten, someone would've found out. But I did it, this year. It was my private war, and I won. Now I'm going to write it all down, before the men start telling it their way.

Well, now, starting at the beginning, the tour began very badly indeed. Off we went with Bevis (which is what we're supposed to call Mr de Lancey now!) and our six soldiers and our bearers (you never saw such a job lot!) to Ofafe where we were going to meet KB's people, same as last time. Not a sign of them. And not a sign of Lukar, either! Ted was perfectly furious—I've never seen him really angry before—and in the end he took the soldiers off to Kiti to find out what had happened and when the ones who were supposed to be coming with us—the Bangwa Wangwa and KB's waziri and one of his sons called Alafambo —said they'd changed their minds and tried to make excuses like being ill he arrested them on the spot and gave them the choice of coming on tour as tho' they liked it or coming in handcuffs! I wish I'd been there to see their jaws drop, tho' I don't suppose they did—Hausa nobs try not to show their feelings, ever. It's one of the things that makes them so tricky to deal with. And Lukar still missing. Not in his house, nowhere. Ted got back to Ofafe middle of the afternoon, still raging, then we plugged on till long after dark and set up camp in the middle of nowhere, everyone in a filthy temper except Bevis. He was v. gracious and smarmy to Ted and didn't complain about anything, even supper, which was only just eatable though poor Elongo'd done his best! I do wish I could find a way of liking him. He's so much cleverer and more amusing and well-read than Ted, as well as understanding about painting, but as a *person* he isn't a patch on him. Oh, yes, I was in a foul mood too, 'cos when we were waiting at Ofafe I went off and tried to chat to the villagers. Nobody stopped me, but it wasn't any good. They were terrified—some of them absolutely grey with fear. They tried to pretend I was talking a foreign language. Only one or two children, till their mothers called them away. Such a let-down!

Then, in the middle of the night, all our bearers tried to run away. Mercifully Corporal Igg, who was in command of the soldiers, is an absolutely splendid type, straight as a ramrod, black as a squashball, a real advertisement for what army training can do for the African. If only there were a few more like him we wouldn't need to be here at all! Anyway, he'd got wind of what the bearers were planning and told his men to be ready and when it happened he rounded them up—just like a first-rate sheepdog—and came and reported. Ted and Bevis questioned the bearers, but course they only said they wanted to get back to their gardens. But it was clear as crystal somebody'd put the wind up them. Even Ted agreed. He was a changed man, by the by. In a funny way he was rather enjoying himself, breaking rule after rule, losing his temper and so on. It started after he'd read Kimjiri's letter and now everything that happened gave him a fresh excuse, but I don't think it was just that. There's a lot of frustration and rebelliousness been bottled up inside him for years. He's been longing to throw his weight about and bully people a bit, spite of what he's always said about being patient with the native and doing things the African way. That was only what he thought he thought—what he thought he *ought* to think—but he didn't really, not deep inside. Aren't people funny, living whole lives pretending to themselves, until something happens? I'm not going to let that happen to me. Well, I hope I'm not—don't get cocky, Bets.

Well, next day we did a huge march, v. exhausting for everyone. I've forgotten to say how *different* the bush is after the rains—you almost wouldn't know you were in the same country! The grass has shot up, some places high as a man or more, and then it's got heavy with the wet and its own seeds, and sort of tired so it flops across the track and whoever's going first has to shove their way through—we used the horses for that, and they hated it—and all the loose seeds fall off and get inside your shirt. And the insects! Ouch! And top of that you can't really see more than a few yards most of the time, even from a horse. It was an absolutely *rotten* time to go and look for hidden villages. Ted had known all along, of course, and so'd Bevis, but Bevis had got the bit between his teeth and was absolutely determined to get on with it. Really we'd have done much better to wait till the grass-burning starts, tho' that doesn't always mean there's a village near—it's mostly the honey-hunters who start the fires.

Anyway we started before dawn and hardly stopped at all till noon, when we reached a place called Gokwo. Our poor bearers were practically dropping by then, so the soldiers rounded up every able-bodied man in Gokwo and Ted paid the old bearers off and on we went and got to Binja utterly exhausted just before dark. The horses were in a dreadful state and all us riders were saddle-sore, and the Hausa were groaning and clutching their stomachs and swearing they'd been poisoned and the bearers —usually bearers sing on the march to help them keep going, but these ones just made a sort of moaning chant up and down the line as tho' they were going to a funeral! Even the soldiers were limping a bit. Only Corporal Igg looked as tho' he'd have liked to do the whole march over again. But at least we'd got to the part we'd been aiming for.

Next day Ted and me stayed in Binja to check the census with Alafambo and the Bangwa Wangwa. Actually Alafambo is rather a nice-looking man, about forty, I'd think. He's been to Mecca and he's supposed to be a good Arab scholar—if he was white he'd look just right pottering round Oxford in a gown and mortar-board—but he was just as determined to be difficult about everything as any of the others. While we were doing that Bevis and the soldiers went out to explore. We didn't find anything, and nor did they. Censusing is terribly difficult with people like that. You can count huts but you don't know how many men are using one 'cos brothers often share, tho' the huts belong to the women. We only count men, of course. You can look at the gardens and try and work out how many men from that, but the ground's so poor that the Kitawa have to get a lot of their food from the bush, hunting game and finding wild plants. The idea of trying right after the rains was to catch as many at home as possible, working their gardens, but there didn't seem to be even as many as there were supposed to be. It was terribly slow. They did their absolute best not to tell us anything. Even the simplest question they'd think ages about before answering. At least they stopped pretending they couldn't understand my Kiti after I'd got Elongo along to help. (Alafambo tried to object to that, by the by.) But the awful thing was E. was obviously almost as frightened and nervous as they were. I asked him why when I got him alone to make arrangements about supper, but he wouldn't tell me. And then Bevis and the soldiers trailed in. They'd split up into three parties and between them they must have gone miles. No good.

We had to leave the horses at Binja, 'cos from then on it's much thicker bush and swarming with tsetse. You don't get them nearly so much out in the grassland, provided you're careful about not watering the horses in the shade and so on. So we had to plug on on foot. I could've hammocked but I was d——d if I was going to 'cos that would've given the Hausa an excuse to say they wanted to hammock too and there weren't enough bearers. Funny, broken country, much more interesting to paint if there'd been time—not actual hills but all crumbled and wrinkled into crooked little valleys. Much more water about, and sudden terrific strong smells after the rains, specially from a bush covered with tiny green flowers the size of pinheads. Mr Mooreshed's butterflies. Bags of game, Ted thinks, but v. difficult to hunt.

Got to Sollum early afternoon. I was thoroughly fagged after my tramp, so Ted and Bevis took the soldiers out for a first explore (no luck) and after that we decided we'd have a change of tactic so Ted and me went down to the village (the rest house is on a ridge outside—come to that in a mo) and got the elders together and told them that tomorrow we were going to count them and they absolutely must make certain that all the men were in the village. I actually asked them if there were any people hiding. It wasn't terribly promising 'cos they clammed up, like at Binja, and they wouldn't look me in the face, tho' I noticed that usually one of the ones I wasn't talking to kept glancing over to where the Hausa had set up camp. We purposely hadn't brought any of them with us. Another rule broken, but it didn't do much good!

We went back to the rest house feeling thoroughly dumpish. It still wasn't dark so Ted and Bevis decided to go and see if they could shoot anything and I went round to the back of the rest house to see how Elongo was getting on with supper. Sollum is in the bottom of the valley, but the rest house is up on a ridge, terribly tumbledown, stinking of bats and crawling with huge spiders. That's what happens in Africa the moment your back's turned. Nobody'd used it for four years, Ted said, and we'd all three taken one look at it and said we'd sleep in our tents, but we had to pretend to use it for supper so Ted could make a fuss with the elders about getting it cleaned and tidied.

I tried to put Elongo at his ease by talking to him about supper, and telling him tactfully as I could what he'd done wrong the time before. It was almost dusk, something like a proper sunset for once, orange in the west, and the bush beneath beginning to turn dark and strange. You could feel it watching you. I'd heard one or two shots, and now there was another one. Everything seemed stiller after it, listening, waiting before it dare breathe again.

'There is a lot of game round here,' I said.

'It is good bush.'

'There are men hiding.'

I hadn't planned to say that. It was the stillness after the shot that had made me feel them. Elongo looked at me but didn't say anything.

'Why do they hide? Why are they afraid?'

'I do not know.'

This was all Kiti so far. I decided to switch to English.

'You're afraid, Elongo,' I said.

189

'Yes.'

'You needn't be afraid. We'll look after you.'

'I am not afraid for me, myself, Elongo Sisefonge. There is a big fear and I am part of it. All the men are afraid. I cannot speak to you more.'

'What about the women, then? Femora Feng spoke to me, and Atafa Guni.'

'They have seen a dream.'

'Yes, I know. But . . .'

'I cannot speak more.'

He was so unhappy I couldn't bear it. I could see how torn he was. Part of him—the part that had lived with us and done lessons with me and wore our housecoat—that part longed to help, only all his old Kiti side was locked up in fright, and that was too strong for the new bits. I mean, that new Elongo was so young, just a baby really, only six months old, terribly helpless. I suppose I might have bullied and wheedled him into telling me more but it didn't seem fair, so I went round to the front of the rest house to wait for the men to come back. Sun almost down now, with the bats flooding out, hundreds, so quiet and quick, ugh. I sat in my folding chair and tried to think. It was obvious the men weren't any good. I mean if dear Elongo, who's really quite brave and sensible, could be so afraid . . . it was interesting what he'd said about one big fear and being part of it. They really think like that, as tho' they weren't separate people but part of one big creature like an ant's nest or a bee-hive. That's one of the reasons KB's got such a hold on them. The only hope was for me to get hold of a woman, get her alone or with one or two others. No men . . .

Next thing I knew I was walking down towards the village.

I should have waited. It was a rotten time really, but I did it without thinking, 'cos it was *my* time, inside me. I had to. Kiti women spend all day getting food ready, pounding beans and roots and so on, but they don't put it to cook till the men come home, and then they sit outside the huts together drinking a specially foul kind of beer they make from roots and talk about this and that till the food's cooked. So I didn't actually have much chance of finding one of the women alone, far enough from the others to talk to. Still, I thought I'd at least have an explore.

I didn't want to go straight in 'cos I was sure people would be watching our way, so I snuck off down a little side path. There's always a lot of little paths close to a village and it was still light enough to pick my way. I worked my way round to the far side and then stole up towards the huts. There was a good deal of noise, voices, men and women, arguing. It meant I could get right up close behind one of the huts without them noticing. The argument was only just the other side. I stood there in the dusk and tried to hear what they were saying.

First off it was v. difficult, so many voices, and interruptions, and me not being able to see any of the faces. It was practically all men, doing the talking. Luckily they said the same things over and over (natives do) so I picked up quite a bit in the end. First it was about us. Why were we there? Why was there no word from the mouth of Kama Boi, saying men must go in the bush and hide? Why had the White Woman asked about men hiding? She was a witch. Did she see the men hiding in the huts? Why had the horsemen not come to the palaver with the White People? The horsemen were very angry. Then someone started on a story about people who were more dangerous than the horsemen, the servants of the White Man who had come with guns and burnt Binja and Dolo and shot men at Dolo who tried to stop them (Bestermann's Patrol, I think) and now they had come again with the White Man. They were terrible. If they found the men hiding in the huts they would shoot them and burn the village. The men must go to Kailungi and hide there, go in the night. No! Who would go out in the dark with the white woman so near? She was a dangerous witch. She made magical pictures. Nobody must talk to her. That was the word from the mouth of Kama Boi. She had seen the men hiding in the huts. That was why she had asked questions. They must go to Kailungi while it was dark. No, no—they were afraid! (That's a funny thing about natives and the dark—till you know them you think that 'cos they don't have electric lights and so on they'll be used to the dark, but really they're just as afraid of it as I was when I was small. There's so much might be out there, not just leopards and snakes and so on, but witches and demons and the ghosts of dead neighbours. They're real. Soon as you're afraid enough, things become real.)

Well, they hadn't settled that argument when one of the

women broke in, telling them about a dream she'd had, a great black horse, but she'd hardly started when a man shouted, 'The women are always telling us this dream!' Other men joined in, shouting her down. The women screeched back. Horrible racket, like animals. They were all so frightened, you couldn't guess what they mightn't do.

I don't know how long I'd been standing there, but it was really quite dark now. Suddenly, I was absolutely terrified too. I mean till then I'd been jumpy, a bit scared, didn't want to be spotted tho' I knew I'd be alright really. Nothing could happen to me. I was a White Woman. They wouldn't dare. But all of a sudden it was as tho' a great cold black pool of fear had oozed up round me, up to my neck, rising, rising, I couldn't move! It wasn't just fright about what the villagers might do if they found me, tho' that's where it started, but soon it was horrible pure nightmare when you don't even know what you're afraid of. I didn't think I could move, but next thing (just like in nightmares) I found I was away from the huts, stumbling off in the dark, waving my arms in front of me. I couldn't see the paths, too dark. If my fingers didn't touch something I went forward. Bushes everywhere. Quite lost. Things in the dark round me, waiting, watching, following. My own voice, sobbing with fright, calling for Ted. I don't know how long.

Then I heard a shout, up in the sky, it seemed—only the top of the ridge, really. Ted's voice calling my name. A greeny light, our Primus lamp. I called and he came down and got me. Oh, it was marvellous! Those dear strong arms!

Bevis had a blissful time patching up my scratches with his special ointment. Supper, then I told them. Not everything. About the men hiding, and Kailungi and so on, and orders from KB not to talk to me. Not about the dream or me being a witch. Even without that I'm not sure they completely believed me. Ted got out the census forms and looked up Kailungi but there wasn't anywhere with a name anything like that and I was pretty sure about it 'cos I'd heard it several times. We put out the lamp to stop the moths and beetles whapping against it and sat with only the firelight flickering against the outside of the rest house and the huge dark night all round. Incredibly silent. You wouldn't have known there was a village (quite a big one) just down in the valley. Nothing like our river villages—there there always seems to be some kind of a party going on, with drums and singing and shouts all night. Ted and Bevis argued what to do. I was completely done up and hardly said anything. We'd been meaning to do the same as at Binja, with Bevis and the soldiers looking for hidden villages and Ted and me checking the census with the Bangwa Wangwa and Alafambo, but now with me so tired and a place we actually knew about (Kailungi —if I was telling the truth!) seeming close enough for the Sollum men to go and hide in, they thought they'd try a big push to find it, with Ted exploring too. Then I could have a rest and we'd do the census next day.

Well, I was absolutely fagged and all I wanted to do was crawl into our tent and fall asleep, which I did soon as I decently could, while Ted sat up with Bevis for a bit, but that wasn't good enough for Ted and he woke me up again soon as he came. Of course I knew he might, so I'd got ready, but really I was so sleepy I hardly knew what was happening till he grunted and fell asleep. Then I lay awake for a bit, thinking about him. He's been funny—really since he got Kimjiri's letter, I think—and then there's having Bevis's tent so close and needing to be quiet and secret (quite amusing in a giggly way, nice change) but sometimes it's almost as tho' he'd forgotten who I was and he wouldn't have noticed if it had been someone else! Perhaps it was only 'cos of me being so sleepy, so I didn't feel real, almost. Not his fault, then. I don't know. But it was bothering and I took a bit to get to sleep again and when I did I had a nightmare.

I was small again. Holidays at Littlestone, just with Mummy. Usually I like dreaming about that—only times I was properly happy, far as I remember. It started all right, me and Mummy making a sand-house. Tide right out, seaweed smells (you *do* smell things in dreams, sometimes) lots of other children, and the donkey man going to and fro. Then a big fat boy coming and laughing at our sand-house 'cos it wasn't a castle and Mummy telling him to go away and him slouching off towards the donkey man. And then me looking at the lovely dolls' house Mummy had made for me, with a real opening door and a front that came off so you could see into the rooms, and then Mummy not there and people streaming across the sand looking back over their shoulders, back and up, and me running into the house to hide 'cos I knew I'd be safe there and then going to the window (upstairs, I think) and looking out and seeing the donkey tramping towards me with the fat boy's red face grinning above and then me noticing how useless the wall was, only thin dolls' house wood . . . Then I woke up stiff with fright. Usually when that happens I wake poor Ted and make him cuddle me but this time I didn't want to. I lay quite still till my body went soft again and then I thought about it and remembered the dream Atafa Guni had told me, and what Elongo had said last night, and the woman the men had shouted down, and I understood I'd dreamed the dream too because I was supposed to. I mean, so I could share what they felt, and it was extraordinary. From being so frightened I felt terrifically glad and joyful, as tho' it was the best thing that had ever happened to me. Then I went to sleep again.

While we were having our morning cuddle I whispered in Ted's ear that I'd had an idea.

'Hope it's a good one. I'm beginning to think this isn't going to come off.'

'Take the Hausa with you when you go exploring.'

'They won't fancy that.'

'Please, darling. Yesterday afternoon, you know how the villagers kept looking towards where the Hausa were whenever we asked them anything. I want to try and get a few of the women quite alone, with no one around to frighten them.'

'Oh. Alright. Depends on Bevis, of course.'

Well, Bevis thought it was worth a try and then Ted actually enjoyed bullying the Hausa into doing what he told them, so soon I was pretty well alone. I had another mug of horrible Camp coffee to give the men time to go out to their gardens and off into the bush, and then I got some painting kit together and made Elongo help me carry it down to the village, but soon as I'd set up I sent him away.

I'd chosen a place where two of the women were pounding the root they use for making the beer—there's a special rhythm, almost like drums, yumpa-boo-bump, yumpa-boo-bump—they can keep it up for hours, with the pestle jumping from side to side as tho' it were live. I chose them 'cos I knew they couldn't get away. They were quite frightened, but not as bad as I'd thought. It was a bit like getting a bird to trust you till it'll take a crumb from your fingers. Very slow, very careful. I talked about ordinary things, not too many questions, just a little at a time, while I drew. Crayons, brown and yellow and orange. The huts. I showed them as I went along. Of course they were interested. I'd been worried they might be too scared of my magical pictures, but it was day-time now. So I did one of them pounding their root, and they liked that and called to two of their friends to come and look. Feeding from my fingers, you see. Then I started another one of the huts, rather tricky, 'cos I had to put my viewpoint further away than I really was 'cos of needing the huts small to leave the top of the paper free. Six of them round me now, chattering away.

When I'd finished that I took a charcoal stick—too long, so I broke it. I was frightened now. I didn't think I could do it. They'd stopped talking, waiting to see what I was going to do. I felt they knew it was important, too. I got that feeling of us all seven being almost one, holding our breath waiting to see what my hand would do. Ready. Now.

I scrubbled the horse in—the side of the charcoal, my storm-cloud trick. It took about thirty secs, terribly crude, but a horse all right, a huge thunder-horse trampling among the huts.

I could feel their gulp of fright. Excitement too, tho'. I know, because I was part of it. It was difficult to keep my voice ordinary.

'I saw this in a dream,' I said.

Murmurs, agreeing.

'I did not finish the dream. I woke. Who has had this dream? Who can tell me what comes next?'

Murmurs. Fright, doubt, thrill.

'Something was coming. I did not see it before I woke. What was it?'

I didn't dare look at them. No, that's not right. Really, I was sort of hypnotized by my picture, my thunder-horse filling the sky. Not the beach donkey I'd seen in my dream—the horse *they'd* seen. *Their* nightmare. I knew. I could feel I'd got it right. A bit like the feeling I'd had at the burnt village, K B filling their sky, pressing them down, their fever they wouldn't ever get well from.

'A white termite comes,' said someone. Just a whisper, but enough. They all broke out together in a jabber, telling me the same thing, the termite with the woman's face biting the horse and the horse falling down dead. It was like the first rain—tension, heaviness, waiting, waiting, and then the lightning shooting down and the thunder rumbling about and sheets of rain washing the dreadful tension away. They were almost hopping about, waiting to see me draw the termite biting the horse, 'cos then it would happen, like that, magic coming out of my fingers.

I turned the paper over. Silence. Now I wasn't part of them any more, only a White Woman, trying to help them from the outside, trying to talk in ideas they'd understand.

'Elongo Sisefonge is my friend,' I said. 'He tells me this. In the first time the Kitawa were the only people. Then the animals grew jealous of them, so they made themselves the bodies of people to live in. The Fulani were cattle before that, and the Hausa horses and the Yoruba foxes, and all the other tribes were other animals.'

'This is the story,' said someone.

'And the White People—what were they?'

'They were termites.'

'A termite with the face of a woman, the termite in your dream—who is that?'

They didn't say anything.

'I think it is me. So, if the dream is true, I must bite the black horse. I must bite it in the right place. I do not know where that place is. Who will show me? It is a place called Kailungi. Who will show me this place?'

Long, long silence. Nobody moved. I stood up and turned to look at them—more than a dozen, I hadn't realized. I felt, oh, if only I could go back to being part of them, feeling their fright and excitement and worry, I'm sure they'd tell me at once. They stood looking at me, each waiting for the other.

'Soon I will go away,' I said. 'I will not come back. I will never bite the black horse. It will never fall down.'

Still no good. I chose one woman, 'cos she looked most like Atafa Guni, older, more wrinkled, hair going grey, but the same wide, decent gaze. I held out my hand and put my fingers on her wrist. She didn't shrink back.

'You will show me Kailungi,' I said.

She looked straight in my eyes. She squared her shoulders.

'I will show you,' she said.

Terrific jabber, all the women agreeing, on her side, but then two men bursting out of the hut nearest, trying to argue. The women screeching them down. Several more men, but women too. More argument. The men must have been hiding in the huts, but there weren't enough of them and the women won easily, so after a bit off we went, all of us, a great gang trooping along through the bush, the women leading and the men trailing behind to see what would happen. It was a long way, twisty paths, crooked little valleys, terribly easy to get lost. Getting hot, too, but the women were singing and chatting. The old woman—her name was Manamu—told me they'd been arguing with the men for a long time because of their dream—they'd practically all dreamed it—isn't that odd? But you know I felt I had too, almost—and now they'd won.

A couple of miles out we met Corporal Igg and one of his men. Everyone fell very silent. They were terrified of the soldiers. I felt I had to show them I could look after them, so I was pretty bossy with Corporal Igg. I told him to find Bevis or Ted and send them after me and get his men together and take everyone else back to Sollum. He reacted beautifully, saluting as tho' I'd been a general, so *that* was all right.

On we went talking and singing, tho' I was beginning to get pretty fagged by now. I tried to get people to stay behind to show Ted or Bevis the way at the tricky bits, but they wouldn't. I know just how they felt. They had to stay with the others. Soon as they were left alone they'd have got terrified of what they'd done.

And then we got there. No wonder nobody'd found Kailungi. There was a perfectly good path if you knew where to look, but it was blocked by what looked like the worst possible kind of thorn tree, only it didn't have any roots. I'd have walked straight past, but Manamu and two of the women took hold of branches and pulled it out and there was the path winding up the side of the valley, only just wide enough for one person. Manamu went first and me second, and the others behind, Indian file. They'd stopped singing now—you don't make a noise near 'toe' villages. Up we went, over the ridge, down the other side, and there was Kailungi! A perfectly good village, twenty huts, gardens, chickens, goats, everything. *And*—this was an absolutely incredible bit of luck—a man who wasn't a Bakiti at all. I spotted him at once 'cos he was wearing clothes, and he turned out to be a slave from Alafambo's household who 'looked after' all the villages round there and had got trapped at Kailungi by us turning up. A nice, gentle little man, v. polite. Of course *he* couldn't see he was doing anything wrong! It was just what had always been done.

Well, that's really all. No, it isn't, tho' it's all that matters. I had to wait hours for someone to show up so I sat under a tree and talked about ordinary things, the way I've always wanted to, and that was quite nice, but not as good as I'd have liked. My fault for drawing the horse. It wasn't exactly that they were afraid of me 'cos I was going to do something nasty to them —more as tho' I was like a bit of wire which sometimes had live electricity in it. You just don't take risks, that's all. A bit sad for me.

Then at last Ted and Bevis came, together. Corporal Igg had taken them to where he'd seen me and there'd been enough of us to leave a good trail and we hadn't pulled the thorn bush back so it wasn't difficult. They got hold of the poor slave and he told them everything about the secret taxes and so on—I didn't listen. That's their side. And then we all trooped home to Sollum. There'd been ructions, 'cos the Hausa had been trying to frighten the villagers but the villagers had stood up to them. They'd burnt their boats, you see. There might have been fighting, but Corporal Igg had done the right thing and arrested all the Hausa. He *is* a good man. He could have got into fearful trouble but he did it 'cos he thought it was best. Marvellous to come trailing out of the bush and see that calm black face and that snappy salute and hear him report as tho' he'd been talking about a missing bucket in his barracks. That's what Africa needs (except it wouldn't be Africa then!).

Then we had some food and a rest and in the evening we went back into Sollum and had a palaver with the villagers. I made sure it wasn't only the men. They were pretty worried by now, but they saw they'd have to stick by us and they told us as much as they could. Thing is, we'd been extraordinarily lucky. Ted was quite right. There aren't lots and lots of 'toe' villages—if there had been they'd have been found years ago. Apart from Kailungi and the one Mr Mooreshed stumbled into there are only three others! They're all down in this rather unexplored bit.

It's the 'toe' *men* who matter. Ever since Bestermann's Patrol, when a lot of the men ran away and hid in any case, KB's people have been sending messengers round ahead of our touring D.O.s warning the villages to keep some of their men out of sight, and then coming around again after the tour to collect the extra taxes. The men who hide are called 'toe' men, so naturally they called the hidden villages 'toe' villages, tho' there aren't nearly as many of them as there are 'finger' villages. Ted thinks it might all have started right back in the old slave-raiding days when a lot of villages did their best to keep themselves secret, and then times like Bestermann's Patrol, when they wanted to again, they knew how. We found the other three 'toe' villages later in the tour. We just asked and people took us. They'd heard what had happened at Sollum, you see. I don't feel like writing about any of that—it wasn't special.

Supper that night the men talked on and on about what to do next. Same old argument, except that now Ted agrees KB is going to have to go, spite of it not being really him who's been doing all the cheating. We could punish Zarafio and some of the others, but no one will believe things are really different while KB's still there. The problem is, who is to take over. Bevis wants a clean sweep—well, clean as you can get 'cos it has to be one of the ruling family or all the other emirs will kick up no end of a fuss; their whole system depends on that, not just the emirs but all down the line, the same sort of hereditary offices and perks. So Bevis's idea is to get hold of a boy, about twelve, and pack him off to the chiefs' school at Katsina and drill some decent ideas into him. Ted says it won't work 'cos the other Hausa will never respect him.

'Take our pal Alafambo,' he said. 'He is genuinely outraged by what we have been up to. I have no doubt he thinks of himself as a thoroughly moral and upright Muslim gentleman, and of us as the cads and scoundrels. At least Zarafio's got brains. He's a slippery little wretch, I'll give you, but he knows which side his bread's buttered. He will be able to see that it's not in his interest to push things too far. That's as much as we can hope for. You are never going to be able to see inside the African mind.'

'It would do you precious little good if you could,' said Bevis. 'There's nothing in there worth study. Our only way forward is to prise open the African skull, remove its present contents and replace them. Until the African comes round to our way of thinking, in the literal sense of the word, the European method of organizing one's thought-processes, he will remain intransigently unreliable and backward. The key, the surgical instrument for this operation, is communication. In the first place, roads.'

I was still thinking about what Ted had said. I'm usually about one behind in conversations like that.

'I think you can sometimes see inside,' I said. 'I mean a lot of it's just ordinary, about food and babies and things, but even the funny parts . . . I didn't tell you how I got them to tell me where Kailungi was.'

Ted hadn't asked me, nor Bevis. I suppose they thought I'd done it their way, reasons and orders. I'd still got the picture in my shirt pocket. I showed them and told them about the dream. They just laughed, but when I got the picture back there was something about the way the firelight wavered across it which made it really rather creepy. No, worse than that. I got a proper shock for a mo, pure fright. Quickly I scrunched it up and threw it in the fire. Better.

Ted was chortling away about the dream. He said if he'd known there was a termite behind all that white gauze at the altar he'd have thought twice about saying yes. Mr de Lancey was quite interested in his brainy kind of way.

'It's an ethnological curiosity,' he said. 'Presumably an individual started it and told others, who then dreamed the same thing. A mass dream hysteria. I wonder if there are any similar events in the literature. But, my dear Betty, you cannot rule a country by means of such insights. They may be marginally useful, but you cannot systematize them. All good government is system. That was Rome's great invention, and now it is our European heritage, which we hold in trust for the world until the world comes of age.'

Spite of calling me 'my dear Betty' he was much less sneery than he used to be talking to me—still talking *to* me, tho', not *with* me—him the teacher, but me not a complete idiot any more. I might have been chuffed about that, only soon as I'd finished telling about the dream—while I was watching the picture burn—I'd started to feel rather odd. Ashamed, not 'cos of what I'd done—I'm sure that was right—but having to do it that way. Here we were, chortling over how cunning I'd been, tricking the ignorant Kitawa into thinking I was a terrible witch who knew everything, so they'd do what I wanted. Like that horrid place in *King Solomon's Mines* when they used the eclipse to trick the natives into thinking they're great white magicians from the stars. I suppose there *was* something a bit magic—only a teeny bit—about the way that terrible horse flowed out of my fingertips as tho' it was really there all along, waiting to be made visible. And at least once or twice—just now too—I'd felt inside me what it was like to believe in the magic, to be really afraid of it, so it wasn't pure hocus pocus, not quite. But still, I do wish there'd been some other way.

And my dream. I was so sure when it happened, so glad I'd been allowed to be part of them and have it too. But now I keep thinking it didn't come from outside, after all. Perhaps I only dreamed it 'cos I'd heard the women talking about it. In that case it didn't mean anything, really, did it?

Better stop writing now. I've worked myself into a dump again. It's been like that ever since Sollum—terrifically up one moment like I was when I started writing this, and then soon after right down again. Stupid things. I keep worrying about the 'toe' villages. Why were there only four? It isn't nearly enough. I mean it's enough for Ted and Bevis 'cos they've made up their minds to get rid of KB anyway, and Kaduna can't go back now without losing awful face, but it isn't enough for *me*. After what Atafa Guni told me at Jabu. I've read what I wrote about that again and again, and I know she didn't actually *say* how many, but . . . I mean, I think I understand why she and the other women sort of invented Jabu so's to have something to *show* me, but what was the point if really there were only four real 'toe' villages, miles away in the south? It bothers me. Trouble is, I can't talk to Ted about it either, 'cos that would mean telling him lots of other things I really daren't.

Another dumpish thing is that he's decided as part of his clean sweep that he's going to take Elongo on as his Messenger. It's a marvellous chance for the boy and I mustn't stand in his way. If only I'd had time to teach him to read and write, he really might have gone far. Oh dear! Nothing will ever be the same again.

And then, even worse than that, such a blow for poor Ted, who'd been perfectly marvellous not showing how much he minded losing to Bevis, and keeping cheerful, and getting the work done—two days ago, on our way home, riding ahead through the long swishing grass, suddenly Salaki didn't seem to know where she was going. The track was so narrow she couldn't go wrong, but she weaved around and stumbled and I couldn't keep her straight and after a bit I had to get down and lead her. She looked so sorry for herself it was dreadful. We got her home all right, leading her most of the way, but she isn't any better, and three of the Hausa horses are just as bad. We're almost certain she's been bitten by tsetse and got *nagana*, which is usually fatal for horses. We've had to separate her from Tan-Tan, tho' it may be too late.

Ted feels it dreadfully, but he's ashamed of letting himself show it and that makes it worse. He makes his usual awful jokes, but they sound different, bitter. Last camp of the tour we finished up the brandy and pretended to be jolly.

'Joke is,' he said, 'all those fellows we found, they're not going to get off anything. Now they're going to have to start paying taxes to us termites, and doing road-gang work on top. I bet you in ten years' time they'll be talking about the good old days when the horse was their master!'

I laughed and Bevis snickered, but it didn't sound like a joke at all.

THIRTEEN

Without warning the engine died. Jackland tried the starter a couple of times, then switched off lights and ignition. The reek of unburnt petrol joined the soft night smells.

'Flooded it, I should think,' he said. 'I'll give it a couple of minutes' rest. It may have over-heated—all the low-gear work.'

'It does not smell very hot,' said the Sarkin. 'Is there a gauge?'

'Not registering. All three trucks have been playing up in different ways. I'm not sure which one this is—fuel-pump, I think. I had to take the nearest.'

'Are you mechanically minded, Mr Jackland?'

'No.'

'Nor am I.'

'Cigarette?'

'Thank you. My last for some time, I should think.'

'What are your plans?'

There had been very little chance to talk so far, what with the noise of the engine and the constant tension of trying to pick their way by headlights through virgin bush. Despite Miss Boyaba's confidence in her uncle's skill they had managed to miss the remains of the old track almost as soon as it had emerged from the thorn-belt. Even as a young man the Sarkin could seldom have been used to night journeys—as Betty Jackland had guessed, few primitive people like to be out in the dark—and in such country the narrow beam of headlights has the effect of seeming to make a path almost wherever it points. It had been possible to stick to a rough general direction using the moon and the few hazed stars, but that apart they were wholly lost.

'I think both you and your colleagues would be in a better position if I did not tell you,' said the Sarkin.

'OK.'

The Sarkin seemed slightly taken aback by this ready response. It was as though he had wished to be pressed a little.

'Let us say I would rather live in the bush than die in prison.'

'Oh, I'm with you there. But . . .'

'In fact I would rather die in the bush than live in prison.'

'That's more arguable. It depends how long.'

'You cannot forecast the course of a military regime. They have taken on insoluble problems. Soldiers do not have the patience of politicians. They are trained for action, and action implies results. Assuming this coup succeeds, and there is nothing to stop it, there will be frustration and dissension among its leaders by this time next year. I suspect that in any case the coup is pre-emptive, to prevent a more radical revolution by young military hotheads. One way of maintaining the popularity of a regime is to find scapegoats to try for its failures. They will need confessions. I am too old to stand much pain.'

'Do you think it'd come to that? Last time round they shot a few people, didn't they, but then Gowon took over and they settled down into comparative stability, at least by the standards of military regimes.'

'The problems are more intractable this time. No, I do not think they would resort to torture. This is Nigeria. But I will not take the risk.'

'Presumably they'll come and look for you.'

'I am a modest catch. My arrest is of importance mainly to Major Kadu's career. He will certainly try and find me. But remember this same bush hid several thousand Kitawa from the British for many years, and one old black man in a grass belt looks much like another. Should you try the engine again?'

'A bit soon. It's about sixty miles to the border, isn't it?'

Presumably it was professional pride that forced Jackland to hint that he did not immediately accept the Sarkin's account of his plans. Perhaps the old man had never really intended to reach Tefuga, but had been leaving a false trail for Miss Boyaba, and now Jackland, to pass on. If so, he did not seem put out by the question.

'Less than that from here. How far do you think we've come?'

'Hard to say. Ninety minutes, plus. Ten miles an hour average, would you think? Fifteen miles?'

'Another fifteen to Tefuga, then.'

'Something like that. Do you think you can make it on foot?'

'If I must.'

The Sarkin appeared entirely calm. He dragged deeply at his cigarette, but this did not seem to be a sign of suppressed anxiety, more a deliberate enjoyment of the moment.

'You think there'll be show trials?' said Jackland.

'Where they can produce the evidence.'

'There should be plenty of that around, from what I've seen.'

The Sarkin checked his response. He had not perhaps known Jackland long enough to be aware of his normal tactlessness, in this case compounded by the journalist's tendency to believe that news events operate in a different sphere from individual lives, so that it is reasonable to discuss the problem of corruption with a man fleeing from a purifying coup. The Sarkin took a slow pull on his cigarette, then chuckled.

'There was an Emir of Gwandu in the 'Thirties,' he said.

'Yahaya?'

'Yes, his name is in all the textbooks, of course, because he was, in British eyes, the perfect example of Indirect Rule. His accounts were a model of accuracy and probity. He built schools and hospitals. He rode about Gwandu on a motor-bike. He had only one wife. In fact his first act on achieving the emirate was to dismiss the court procurer. He made Gwandu the showpiece of British rule.'

'I've often wondered what the other emirs thought of him.'

'They thought variously. Many despised him. Some tried to copy him but lacked his intelligence and discipline. But that is not the really interesting question. *I* have wondered how he would have fared had he needed to maintain his authority in post-independence Nigeria. What did the people think of him? How would they have voted had they been given the chance? There are some votes in schools and hospitals, there are very few in financial probity, none in monogamy. But there are many, many votes in being a great man, giving public displays of one's greatness, in being able to advance the careers of one's protégés and petitioners, so that they in turn can help a further circle of their own dependants, and so on. It seems to me that even the saintly Yahaya would have found he needed to make certain compromises. This is something that very few of the British understood. Anyone who is not a fool can perceive the pragmatic benefits of honest government, but that does not necessarily mean he feels them in his heart. Your father and his kind actually felt deep admiration for probity, and determination to show it themselves, but they did not manage to instil that feeling in the peoples they ruled. All they have left us with is the rhetoric of probity. The virtues we genuinely feel are different —generosity, spontaneity, boldness, bravura, personal authority. You will tell me you can't run a country on those. I tell you you can't run even a small province of Nigeria without them.'

'And somebody has to do the running, so why not you?'

This time the Sarkin seemed genuinely affronted.

'I did not choose, Mr Jackland. I was chosen.'

'Yes, you told me, old man. I accept that. But I wonder whether you're right about the voters. I saw the start of that little market riot you had—was it only yesterday?—and it struck me rather forcibly . . .'

'I read the reports. And I tell you, Mr Jackland, that there was not one man or woman in that mob who would have hesitated to accept dash, or to take whatever small pickings came their way. You have talked to my niece Annie, I think. I have heard her very indignant over corruption in high places, but she thinks nothing of driving a car paid for, ultimately, in bribes from the manufacturers of foreign dental equipment supplied by her father to Nigerian state hospitals. One of the reasons this coup will achieve so little is that many of its leaders—I do not yet know who they are, but I can assure you of this as a fact—are as deeply imbued with this so-called corruption as any of the politicians they are trying to replace. But suppose they were not. Suppose they were each and every one of them untainted and untaintable. How long can they rule a people without our consent? How long can they retain that consent—they will have it for a while because of the unpopularity of the present leaders, which has as much to do with the decline of world oil prices as with the excessive depredations of a few individual politicians and businessmen—how long can they retain consent without display of the virtues which Nigerians truly feel and understand? What have they to offer instead? Discipline? Is that a virtue that springs to mind when you think of Nigeria? I tell you, Mr Jackland, I have given my life to my people. I have consistently done what seemed to me necessary in view of the circumstances that arose. I refuse to be presented in a military court as a scapegoat for the failings of others.'

'I'm sorry . . .'

'I am not blaming you. All I am saying is that you may perceive certain facts about Nigeria, but unless you can also feel certain other facts you do not know the truth and have no right to pronounce. This is as true now as it was in your parents' day, for all your modern open-mindedness. Should you try the engine again?'

Jackland pinched out his cigarette, switched on and tried the starter for several long bursts. There was no sign of a spark, only the smell of petrol as before.

'Not the fuel-pump, anyway,' he said. 'Come and hold the torch for me, while I waggle the odd wire.'

The Sarkin made no more fuss about acting as Jackland's garage-hand than he would have sixty years before about carrying Betty Jackland's easel. They craned in under the raised bonnet while Jackland tested the leads to the sparking plugs, unclipped the distributor and peered at its points, and with visibly pessimistic fingers tugged at cables to see whether there might not be a loose connection. Having done that he climbed back into the driving seat and tried the engine again, without result. After a few more tries he gave up and lit fresh cigarettes for the pair of them.

'May I ask you a few questions?' he said.

'Of course. But I would advise you for your own sake not to broach subjects that might be of interest to my accusers.'

'It wasn't that, actually. I still feel I haven't got to the bottom of my parents' story. I'd be interested to know what you made of them. When I've asked you before you weren't very forthcoming. I thought perhaps now . . .'

'Now that we are half way to Tefuga? What do you want to know?'

'Anything you care to tell me.'

The Sarkin sat for a while in silence, perhaps first making up his mind and then collecting his thoughts. But when he spoke it was as though he had been doing something more than these, undergoing an almost spiritual transformation as he willed his own time-tangled perceptions back to an earlier phase. He spoke in the same deep voice with the same purity of diction, but now with a faint lilt, and in shorter sentences, with longer pauses between them.

'All times are the same to a child,' he said. 'Then something happens, and they are no longer the same. He becomes aware of other times before and after. I remember that very day. We were called from our hut by our chief uncle, and all the people from other huts were called too, except for the men who were out in the bush. We stood in an arc before the huts. Before us stood a great black man on a horse. There were other men on horses besides—two were white—as well as strange black men in clothes like the white man's but with red hats and guns. But the big man on the horse was the one at whom I stared. There was gabble in strange words, and then another black man spoke to us in Kiti, but though I knew the words they had no meaning for a child. One of our elders answered very humbly. I knew he was very afraid of the black man on the horse, and so were all the others, and I too. When we went back to our huts I knew that what had been said and done was very bad. I did not know how or why.

'That was Bestermann's Patrol. They came to us after they had burnt Blini and shot three men who tried to stop them, but they did no harm at Tefuga. I understood then that the world had changed, and new times had come. I had bad dreams in which the big man pursued me on his horse. The people were still afraid and spoke in small voices. They feared the white gabblers, and the men with red hats, but those were, so to speak, day-time fears. They were fears such as one might have of a leopard when one is alone in the bush and finds his fresh track. Their fear of the big black man was different. That was a night-time fear. It was one fear, filling all the people. They did not speak of it.

'I grew older. My age-set moved to the houses of the women who would teach us to be men. My teacher was Femora Feng. She was a woman in whom the spirit was very strong. Often she would speak before the uncles and they would listen. In her hut I learnt that all times are not the same, and that there had been another and a better time when Kama Boi had been our protector, but then certain white men had come and worked a magic which tricked the spirit in him so that it sought to punish us. In the hut of Femora Feng I learnt to long for the days before the white man came. This was the great longing of our people when I was becoming a man, and that is the time, Mr Jackland, that makes you what you are. That is when the clay of the pot hardens.

'Next my age-set moved again and left Femora Feng, but before I had finished making my first garden she sent for me, which she had the right to do. She told me she had seen a dream. She had seen it three times, so she knew it came from the ancestors. She had seen a terrible black horse trampling among the huts, smashing them down, stamping on the cooking-pots. A termite rode this horse, driving it mad. But then the termite arched itself up and bit the horse on the neck and it fell down and died. Then she saw me, Elongo Sisefonge, come out of the hut with my mattock and smite the termite so that it broke into little pieces and crawled away.'

'A termite with a woman's face?'

'No. Later, after she had spoken with your mother at Tefuga, she began to say that she had seen that the termite had a woman's face. I think she told your mother when they met again . . .'

'That was somebody called Atafa Guni.'

Surprised by this apparently lost fragment from the past the Sarkin chuckled.

'I had forgotten.'

'I don't think she met Femora Feng again until just before the Incident.'

'It does not matter. All the women dreamed this dream in the end. It caused great dissension between them and the men, and by then certainly the dream showed the termite so, and the women agreed that it signified your mother. But when Femora Feng told me to go and find the white man and ask for work on the house he was building she did not know that your mother was coming. The termite was simply a termite.'

'Wasn't there something about your sister being stolen?'

'How do you know that?'

'It's in my mother's diary. You told her.'

'I cannot have told her in those words, but yes, one of the nephews of Kama Boi who was overlord of Tefuga had taken my sister to work for him for a year because my uncles could not pay their full taxes. This was common. We did not like it, but since Bestermann's Patrol we did not dare fight against it, so the custom had grown up.'

'I'd have thought it broke the agreement you'd made with Kama Boi and his predecessors.'

'It was not done by Kama Boi himself, but by his nobles and family. He benefited because of the presents they were thus able to send him.'

'He must have known.'

'He knew and he did not know. But to us Kitawa the case was that his spirit had been tricked by the white men. We did not want to harm him. We wanted to release him from the magical power of the white men, so that he could protect us again, and we could go back to our golden age. It was Femora Feng and then the other women who first saw that this could not be done, and that therefore Kama Boi himself must somehow be destroyed. The oppression, you see, was not static. As the Hausa discovered they could get away with one thing, they then went on to another. The case of my sister was only a minor example. Her overlord, seeking a favour from Kama Boi, had included her in his gift. This was against custom but my uncles did not dare complain. Only that rains a man who had caused offence by trying to bring a complaint had been beaten to death and his body left by the track for all to see.'

'So you went to the river. How did you manage to get taken on?'

'I do not know. Perhaps because of what Femora Feng had seen me do in her dream I did not feel afraid of the White Man. I stood up straight in front of him. I spoke very little Hausa, but one of the river Kitawa had taught me what to say. At least your father gave me work. Then, without my doing anything more, your father asked me to stay and be his houseboy when his new wife came.'

'She didn't know much about Africa. He thought experienced servants would take advantage of her and cheat her.'

'Probably. I thought the White Man a very strange creature. He was old and rich. He had two horses and many huts, but only one wife and she neither old nor young, but ugly. I thought perhaps he had eaten his other wives. He certainly ate much boiled chicken in order to keep himself white, and kept a smoking-stick in his mouth for the same reason.'

'It must have been pretty confusing.'

'That is not the reason I tell you. I want you to understand what sort of boy it was who saw these things, how he thought, what was the shape of his mind. For then, you see, your mother caused me to change again, in a new way, the first of my people. Just as Femora Feng had taken me into her hut to show me how to be a man, so your mother took me into hers to show me how to be a White Man. Indeed she spoke to me once in words such as Femora Feng might have used, telling me to do something in a manner I could not refuse. This was very important to me. I owe those two women an equal debt.'

'What did you make of her as a person?'

'She had a strong spirit in her, much more than your father. In some ways I did not find her so strange. She was like any young bride. Of course there were many things I did not understand. She drew and painted everything she saw. At first I was a little afraid to see how she could take a big river and trap it on a small piece of paper, but then . . . I remember a day when she painted Kama Boi and some of his people in front of Kiti Gate. I kept the flies off her while she did so, so I saw how she took that great and dreadful man and made him small on the paper. I saw him with her eyes, and for a little while I was not afraid of him. I learned by her painting to see our world in the way the white man saw it. And she taught me English also.

'But I was always wary of her. You do not change in one week from being a simple savage into being a westernized politician. Despite her kindness to me I continued to think of her as having dangerous powers, but I decided that these were mostly devoted to preventing her husband from marrying a second wife. She had a magic for this which she would wear inside her before they copulated, which they did often and with vigour. At night I would hear her crying out aloud to encourage him. But yet she had no children. Among our people when a wife has no children she must find another woman to bear her children for her, so all this was very hard to understand. I could not ask her about it. It is women's talk. But I watched all her movements, and your father's, because of what Femora Feng had told me about my part in her dream.'

'You still took that seriously?'

'Of course. Why not? I take it seriously to this day. Femora Feng was a great spirit. Such people are close to the ancestors. She had foreknowledge of what would happen. Dreams do not speak clearly, but that one spoke clearly enough. There is as much evidence for its truth as there is for many of the scientific propositions which you accept without question. Because of what your mother did and said Kama Boi was destroyed and the rule of the Hausa over the Kitawa ended.'

'And then you smote the White Man with your ballot-box and he fell to bits and crawled away.'

The Sarkin laughed.

'You hadn't thought of it like that?' said Jackland.

'Not that interpretation.'

'Oh?'

But the Sarkin was apparently more interested in the details of this new reading of the dream.

'Certainly the White Man fell to pieces,' he said. 'How can you rule when you doubt both your own right to do so and the means by which you do it? In the 'Fifties you could hardly find one British administrator who would not tell you openly that in his opinion the whole system of Indirect Rule had been mistaken from the start.'

'Some of them must have felt that all along. Judging by my mother's diary, my father had a fairly pessimistic view of the sytem.'

'Ah, yes, the diary.'

'Did you know she was keeping it?'

'I knew she wrote often in a book. I thought there was a magic in it which renewed her spirit, because when she had finished writing she put it away in the box where she kept her other magic and the spirit was bright in her eyes.'

'Yes.'

A slight pause, a definite tension, as though both men knew what was coming.

'I've tried to ask you about this before, Sarkin,' said Jackland. 'You've always shied off, but it is something I seriously would like to know. For my own spiritual peace, if that's not too grandiloquent a phrase. My mother says in the diary that she is going to finish by writing her version of the Incident and then give the book to you and ask you to bury it in a termites' nest in the bush. Evidently that did not happen. I would be grateful for any light you can throw on the question.'

'I do not remember,' said the Sarkin.

'The mystery is that I found the diary among my father's gear. I would like to know how it got into his hands. You see why?'

'I tell you, I do not remember.'

'I'm sorry about that.'

They sat in silence, stiff and still.

'I can tell you this, Mr Jackland,' said the Sarkin at last, speaking with evident care. 'The boy I then was would have been reluctant to do what your mother asked. She would have seemed to him, especially after the Incident, to possess truly dangerous magical powers, of which she herself was largely unaware. Some of these powers would have been connected with her pictures, but those would have been as it were the outward manifestation of a central magic. That magic lived in the book in which she wrote. Now, what would it mean to such a boy that he should be told to bury such a thing in the land of his people? In a termites' nest? Remember that we had only recently, after much tribulation and danger, contrived to rid ourselves of another magical presence. To the European mind these arguments may seem fanciful, but I can assure you that to such a boy they would seem as solid and practical as the arguments, say, for fiscal responsibility.'

'Yes, I see. Thank you. You can't tell me what you think the boy would have done, then?'

'He would have done the best he could, no doubt. Now, Mr Jackland, I think the time has come to do as the White Man did and crawl away.'

'Hadn't you better wait till it's light?'

'It is possible Major Kadu will follow your tracks. I would like to be well clear of the truck by then. I am not afraid. I belong to this land, but I have lived long enough in contact with the outside not to believe in bugbears any more.'

'I was thinking about leopards.'

'I will take my chance with them. Perhaps Major Kadu can be persuaded to think I was unlucky.'

The Sarkin climbed slowly from his seat and stood by the car, a tall pale pillar like an i, with the dot of his white cap separated from the column of his white robe by the invisible patch of blackness which was his face. The pillar swayed and the dot disappeared as he tossed the cap on to the passenger seat. After a rustle and slither the robe joined it, followed by a string vest and linen underpants. He knelt to unlace his shoes. When he stood up his blackness, lacking the contrast of linen, seemed less, and his figure was clear in the moonlight.

'Will you be warm enough like that?' said Jackland. 'The harmattan's about due, isn't it?'

'Overdue, if anything. I have a blanket. To that extent I go back to the bush richer than when I came out of it. Goodnight, Mr Jackland. My only fear is that the breakdown may result in your part in my flight being discovered.'

'Can't be helped. I wish I could have got you the whole way.'

'I do not think you need anticipate too much trouble. The military will be anxious to ingratiate themselves with foreign powers.'

'I'm more worried about getting Mary out, and then the last cans of film. I come third.'

'Do you think you will be able to make your rendezvous?'

'With a bit to spare, starting at first light. I've done this sort of trek before. No point in trying before then if I'm going to follow our tracks.'

'Well, I wish you good luck, and give you my sincere thanks for your help. Perhaps we will meet again.'

'Hope so. There's quite a bit more I'd like to ask you. Good luck, old man.'

The Sarkin turned and walked away. Despite the moonlight he became invisible after the first few paces. Jackland lit a last cigarette and smoked it before trying the starter motor once more. There was still no sign of a spark, so he huddled down on to the bench seat, spreading the Sarkin's robe over himself as a coverlet, and tried to sleep.

FOURTEEN

Thurs Oct 9

To Kiti this morning, to watch KB going into exile. I thought I'd do a picture for my album 'cos it's an historic occasion (*and* I did it!) but it didn't come out at all well. Not just 'cos there was nothing special to paint, no brolly-men or trumpeters—they haven't got a ceremony for that sort of thing—but I felt v. low. I've got a funny sort of tummy-bug I can't shake off—not too dire, but sick every morning and queasy most of the day. It does drag you down. I expect that's why I keep wondering if I've made any difference at all to my dear Kitawa, or if I have whether it's a good idea after all—when Bevis gets his bridge and his roads, what'll that do to them? Clothes and tinned peaches and the clever ones going to Lagos and wearing suits and ties and pretending to be just like us! Oh, dear.

Anyway, we wanted everyone to see KB going in disgrace, so that the Kitawa would know he'd really crossed the river and the new Emir (whoever he's going to be—terrible ructions about that) saw what'd happened to *him* if he didn't behave. We thought everyone in the town would turn out and Elongo might persuade the Kitawa to send a few elders, but it was quite the other way round! When we passed the market it was clattering away just like an ordinary day and there were only a few traders up by the ferry, and no Hausa at all far as I could see, but over on the other side of the track hundreds and hundreds of naked bush Kitawa, women and men and children, one silent dark mass, waiting.

'Good for Elongo,' said Ted. 'He's going to be a decided asset. Last thing I want is rumours going round the bush that old Kama Boi's still in Kiti. Wish I had some of those Kaduna desk-drivers here to see that the Emir crossing the river actually means something to the Kitawa.'

'If Bevis gets his way the next Emir's going to start off crossing, to go to school.'

'If Bevis has his way there'll be a railway siding at Tefuga by 1940.'

'Oh, I hope not!'

'Bit late to change your mind now, Rabbit.'

He's been quite snappy with me these last few weeks, sometimes. He's still dreadfully cut up about losing Salaki, and he can't help wanting to blame someone and I can't help feeling guilty. After all, it *was* my fault, sort of. I'm quite sure Ted doesn't know, but there's been a sort of awkward feeling between us. The new horse, Beano, isn't bad, only a bit dull. *And* a bit expensive—we couldn't really afford him. On top of all that there's still the strain of being a good loser with Bevis, or pretending to be. Bevis is *not* a good winner!

Well, I had a bit of a problem with my picture. I'd like to have painted it with KB going past my Kitawa, but there was nothing to give it a shape, so thought I'd do it from the other side with Kiti wall and the rapids in the distance, and the islands. Besides, that meant I could set up close to them and have a chat. But they didn't want to talk, even among themselves. There was a bit of a rustle when I walked over and started to get ready. Perhaps they thought I was going to do another magic picture. No more of that for me. Not if I can help it.

KB was late, of course, but he came in the end. Bevis had sent a couple of lorries from Birnin Soko to take KB's party to Ibadan. They were standing on the far side of the ferry crossing. I dabbed them in at the edge of my picture while I waited. I knew already it wasn't any good. Then he came. Quite a lot of Hausa, and him in the middle. We'd said he mustn't wear his turban or have a brolly-man, so he was wearing a white cap and a pale robe (clean, far as I could see!), but all the Hausa who weren't going with him were in their party best. We're only letting him take a few servants and half a dozen wives. (He couldn't afford more on his pension.) The wives were bundled up like accident patients, but I don't suppose my little girl was one of them.

I must say KB behaved with terrific dignity. Ted says he still doesn't believe he's the slightest bit in the wrong. It wasn't him, you see, who'd been burning villages and murdering people, or even taking taxes and not telling us. It was his sons and nephews and hangers-on, using his name and his juju power to terrify the

Kitawa. Of course, it meant they could afford to give him much better presents, but if you're an African that's something quite separate! Anyway he still walked past like a king, so in spite of all the crowd round him you knew it was all about *him*. If I'd been on form that's what I'd have got in my picture. (Spilt milk, Bets.) The town people had shouted a few times as he went past—just good-byes and wishing him luck—but it was too solemn for that. We all watched him walk down to the ferry. Ted was waiting there. They shook hands. KB walked onto the ferry and gave a present to the ferry-master, who'd fallen flat on his face to greet him. The wives and servants followed, the baggage was on the lorries already. The tail-board was slotted in and the ferry-master shouted to go. The men sang out and heaved at the cables, all together, like dancers. Slowly, heaving and chanting, they hauled the ferry away. As the gap of water showed between it and the bank I heard a long deep *hoo-o-o-o* like wind in a chimney, all round me. The Kitawa, watching the juju broken. They didn't say anything else till we'd seen KB and his people pulled up into the back of the lorries, and then the lorries driving away along Bevis's road.

Then the muttering began. I turned, trying to catch eyes, and smiling, but they wouldn't let it happen. I'd hoped they'd look a bit joyful (a bit grateful, even!), but no. I couldn't even tell if they were worried or unhappy. Perhaps Bevis is right, and we'll never know what's going on inside their heads. It isn't enough to speak the tones. You have to belong to understand.

Then Ted came up to take me away.

Thurs Oct 30
Well, I was right about that last bit, anyway! To think we've been here twenty years and there's still something quite important nobody'd told us! We found out almost soon as KB had gone, and Ted and Bevis tried to get on with their battle about the next Emir. It's been a pretty dire time for Ted, but at least he'd got Kimjiri back, and that's something! The poor fellow got here good as under arrest 'cos the D.O. at Jos had sent a policeman along to see he didn't run away again, so at first he was too scared to talk sense, but soon as he found KB had gone and Lukar was under arrest already (they'd found him hiding in the Bangwa Wangwa's house) he spilled the beans about Lukar

trying to bribe him to put poison in our food and then threatening him with KB's juju powers. All so's we shouldn't go on our surprise tour. Not such a surprise as we thought! Kimjiri even knew how Lukar'd found out. Elongo'd told him! Lukar'd tried to frighten Elongo away too, before any of that, but Elongo'd stood up for himself but he'd got to have something to fight with so he'd threatened Lukar back with *my* juju powers(!) and said I was going to find everything out with my magic pictures. (Doesn't all this seem absolutely mad when I write it down? But it was real for them, and true, and Lukar already sort of half-believed in my juju 'cos of the Tefuga picture I'd given KB. And isn't it totally extraordinary them knowing all this and us not having any idea—except that Ted *had* guessed Lukar and Elongo had had some sort of a row?!! And spite of what he tried to do, I do think it's rather awful Lukar will probably be hanged now.) So *that* was all right.

But about the next Emir? Even Ted saw he'd have to give up Zarafio, who it turned out had been the ringleader in the whole business—no wonder he'd been so keen on having me watched on my first tour in case the Kitawa told me anything! Quite likely he'll go to prison now! So who? Before we British came all the emirs got chosen by special electors, and the only rules were that the new man had to come from the right family and the electors weren't allowed to choose one of themselves. (*They* didn't mind, 'cos they'd been getting masses of presents from all the hopefuls for years!) We still pretend it's like that, but usually we make it pretty clear who we want, tho' it's no use us picking a man they won't respect. This time Ted thought Alafambo was the best bet and the Hausa would have been happy with that, but Bevis persuaded Kaduna to insist on a young prince called Azikofio—KB's great-nephew, far too young to have given anyone any presents!—and there was a terrible fuss. In the end Kaduna told Ted to say that if they didn't choose Azikofio we'd abolish the emirate completely and lump it in under Soko, and Alafambo could be just District Head, which would have been a frightful comedown. So they gave in and we thought that was that.

But *then*, believe it or not, the meek, peaceful, downtrodden Kitawa dug their heels in! Elongo brought a deputation to Ted. They wanted me there too. And they explained to us *they* had a choice too. *They* have special electors. You see, they are the real owners of the land, and KB was only there because they'd allowed him to be and given him his juju-powers to protect them. And now he'd broken the juju and crossed the river they weren't going to choose anyone else. They were going back to the old days when they didn't have an emir at all, not even chiefs.

This was a real poser. Ted told them that was impossible. You can't work Indirect Rule without chiefs—besides, we'd already good as promised the Hausa. (Typical of the Hausa they hadn't told us, tho' it turned out they knew perfectly well, in spite of nobody having had to do any of this for thirty years!) Anyway Ted sent the Kitawa away and told them to consult their people while he whizzed off messages to Bevis and Kaduna, and yesterday we had another palaver with them out in the bush. The choosers came this time, five old men, very scrawny and used up and unimpressive to look at, but solemn and dignified too. We gave them ginger-nuts and lemonade. They thought the fizz was some kind of trick and were v. suspicious, but Elongo calmed them down. He was marvellous. They treated him as an equal, which was nice to watch. Kaduna had said we'd got to offer them the same choice as the Hausa—Azikofio, or come in under Soko. They thought that was a terrible idea. They said Soko people would come and take them away for slaves again (they talked just as if that had been happening yesterday, when it's almost a hundred years!) We tried to explain we'd never let it happen but they said how did they know we weren't going away again as suddenly as we'd come?

But they didn't want Azikofio either. How could a child protect them? He wasn't even a young man—he hadn't reached that age-change. How could he take part in the Tefuga ceremony? That was v. important. They kept coming back to how young he was. I explained we'd chosen him exactly 'cos of being young, so we could send him off to Katsina to the chiefs' school where he would learn to be a good chief. It wasn't much of an argument, seeing they didn't really want a chief at all.

But then Elongo, without Ted or me telling him, said, 'The White Man will bring this boy to Tefuga for a ceremony. It will be a new ceremony. No man's blood will water the graves. And then immediately the White Man will send the boy across the river for many years.'

That did it really. They asked me about it, and I explained to Ted, who said yes, they could have a sacrifice at Tefuga but it would have to be a goat or something, and yes, Azikofio would have to cross the river to go to school, and I explained back to them, very slow and clear, and they got up and walked away into the bush. Elongo told us to wait. I didn't hear any voices and it was more than an hour before they came back. They asked us about the sacrifice and the river again, just to make sure, and then they said all right and finished off the lemonade. (They quite liked it by now and were disappointed there wasn't any more!)

We were riding back—I was thinking how well it had all gone—when Ted gave a funny yapping laugh, angry and sad, not like him at all.

'What's funny, darling?' I said.

'It's a complete farce,' he said. 'We've got to go through with it, but it'll never wash.'

'I thought it had all come out rather nicely.'

'Total waste of time. Just now we've good as told your pals that Azikofio's never going to be more than our puppet. The ceremony at Tefuga won't mean much without a human sacrifice, and then our very next act will be to send the new Emir across the river. They'll know, and he'll know, so he'll never have any respect from them, which at least old Kama Boi had. That'll mean in turn he'll never have any incentive to rule properly, and—you and I'll be gone by then, thank God—my successors are going to find themselves having to run Kiti direct. I hope old Bevis is here to see it, driving his motor along his roads!'

Of course we'd been terribly careful not to say anything to the Kitawa about having to work on roads as well as paying proper taxes. I don't think they'd have understood, so what's the point? But it's going to be a horrid shock for the poor dears.

Now I must stop—we've got a dinner party! Bevis and the engineer he's brought to survey for the bridge. I'm v. nervous. Eleven months married and my first dinner party! Bet that's a record.

The direst thing possible. I've found out why I'm being sick. I haven't told Ted yet, but I'll have to, soon as we're back from Tefuga. It's not just me who knows, you see.

I found out in rather an awful way, too. What happened was Kaduna made up its mind we'd have a proper show for installing the new Emir, spite of Kiti being such a potty little place. Idea was to let everyone see it had been all KB's fault things got so bad, and none of us British were blaming each other, and now there was a lovely fresh start and everything was going to be hunky-dory from now on. So we had quite a party at Kiti, Bevis, and the Soko D.O.s, and Bevis's Emir, and two other neighbouring Residents and their Emirs, and several bigwigs from Kaduna. Wives, too. The Lieutenant Governor's on leave, but his Deputy came to read the main speech and take the salutes.

Ted had the stalls cleared away to make a space in front of the Old Town gates, and there were soldiers marching past with a brass band, and bangy native music and brolly-twirling and horse-charges, all jolly exciting tho' I couldn't do any pictures and had to watch between two huge floppy hats belonging to Kaduna wives sitting in front of me. The Deputy has the most beautiful voice, like an actor's, and was v. inspiring about the responsibility of the rulers to the ruled, except that it didn't really seem to have anything to do with what happens when you come to a village and try to work out how much tax it ought to be paying and persuade mothers to wash their babies' eyes when they get sore. Or even explain to an emir that the money in his tank isn't his to do what he likes with. The new Emir is tiny and thin, with big eyes. Looks quite bright but a bit shifty already. (Sad, after all that. Katsina *might* drill it out of him.) He behaved jolly well, v. solemn, and made the speech Ted had written for him in a nice clear voice.

Then I had to hurry home and get ready for another dinner party. Two in two months—what a whirl! I don't really enjoy them, actually (even without what happened this time, I mean). Ted and I aren't much good at shining, except for each other. We both go dim when anyone else comes. Not that this lot were all that brilliant, Soko people, Johnstone and Cadbury who're D.O.s and Cadbury's sister who's staying with him. She'd dim *anyone*! Like a buffalo with huge black eyebrows and a booming voice. Terrifically strong opinions about the way we treat the natives—Ted says it's astonishing Lagos ever let her into Nigeria! *And* she's writing a book about it all, which'll be the end of Cadbury's career if she ever gets it published, Ted says. But he was obviously scared stiff of her. Me too.

Well, it was quite a nice dinner. River fish and then francolin which is a sort of small guinea-fowl Ted had managed to bag three of, and the reason I'd had to rush home was to stand over Kimjiri and see he didn't roast them black, and see our new boy (Sixpence) laid the table right, etc. It was nice in the end so I was greedy, besides being twitchy with strangers and Miss Cadbury so rude to the men, and half way through I got one of my queases and had to rush out and be sick. And then (imagine!) she came after to see I was alright. Ted swore later he'd tried to stop her but you might as well've tried to stop a hippo! Then to get her to go away I said I was quite alright and I'd been having little sick goes for a bit but they weren't anything to worry about. But instead of taking the hint she started asking *the* most intimate questions, which I'd be shy of talking about even to a lady doctor, and she isn't even married! I sort of said yes or no and she told me to sit on the bed and then she said, sort of triumphantly, 'I have to tell you, Mrs Jackland, that in my opinion you are pregnant.'

And *then*, believe it or not, before I'd even had time to understand let alone get my breath back, she started off about men and what thoughtless brutes they were insisting on doing it just to gratify their animal impulses without a thought of the woman who'd have to bear the consequences!

Something snapped. I'm not like that, really I'm not. But I jumped up and started to screech at her, saying *exactly* what I thought of her behaviour, coming and accepting our hospitality and being unspeakably rude without even noticing that the men she was criticizing were doing their level utmost—literally killing themselves quite often with disease and overwork—while people like her went gallivanting round the country in the cool season putting themselves up at other people's expense and then going back to safe comfy England to pass judgement on the very men who'd looked after them.

'And what's more,' I said, 'I don't believe you care a brass farthing about the poor native. It's just your way of getting at men because you haven't got one of your own!'

All this at the absolute top of my voice, like our natives in the compound, tho' I was standing with my nose only a few inches from hers. The men positively *must* have heard, but I didn't care. She tried to interrupt, but I wouldn't stop. When I'd said my say I stalked back to the dining-room, leaving her to come along or not as she pleased. It was too funny—or it would have been if it hadn't been us in it—the men sitting there pretending they hadn't heard anything and me and Miss Cadbury—she must have a hide like a rhinoceros—absolutely despising each other and nobody daring to talk about anything except fishing. *And* I'd arranged with Ted that after the sweet course I'd take her out for a bit and leave the men alone to smoke their cigars! Well, that was off, for one thing.

But actually me winning the fight made me feel so well and uppity that I didn't really start thinking about what she'd said for quite a long time. I suppose I thought she was so awful she couldn't be right about *anything*. But when Ted had taken them all off to catch the last ferry (Bevis has organized a sort of White Man's camp across the river) and I was sitting alone I began to understand and realized that actually that might be it. I did know you got sick like that—I just hadn't put two and two together. Not as stupid as it sounds, 'cos you're sick half the time in Africa anyway. So feeling very scared I snuck off to look at my thingy. They did tell me it was important and I used to, always, when we started but I must have got out of the habit. Of course I've sort of looked, but not properly. It's horrible, horrible Africa that's done it. Everything here rots. Everything goes wrong. Just two tiny splits, but they must have been enough. Isn't it strange how you live in a sort of dream world where you feel safe and nothing's going to go wrong, and then the worst thing of all happens right inside you! I don't know what to think. I don't know how to feel. I know there are ways of not having babies after you've started, but I don't know how to find out. Or who to ask. It's only last night I realized, but I seem to have been swooping up and down for days! Even had moments when I felt rather excited, just knowing I can. And then right down again, like knowing I've started a disease which isn't ever going to get well—I mean, even after it's born somebody's got to take care of it—and now there's this wriggler inside me swelling and swelling, a little more every day, till I burst. Ted's guinea worm. Ugh! I know it's different, but that doesn't help, just knowing.

Ted got back last night in absolutely tearing spirits about me giving Miss Cadbury such a wigging. I'd been in bed for an hour and was longing for him. Terribly down and frightened. I hadn't the heart to tell him, and now I think I'll put it off a bit longer. I don't feel guilty not telling him—in fact sometimes, in my downs, I feel almost as tho' it wasn't his baby at all. It's Africa did this to me, so really it's Africa's baby.

Pull yourself together, Bets! Mustn't start thinking like that. Anyway, I'll jolly well have to tell him before someone else does! Miss Cadbury knows, for a start, and she'll tell *everyone*. Luckily we won't be seeing them before Tefuga, and anyway men don't talk about this sort of thing. Tefuga'll be the end of the story, all that old rubbish cleared away. Time for a new start. It'll be lots easier for the poor man then.

FIFTEEN

Jackland came sweating through the bush. There had been several minor delays where the tyre-tracks had disappeared on hard ground and he had needed to cast about, but there had also been places where the headlights had failed last night to show him a possible way through and he had now been able to take a short cut. By all outward signs, then, he was roughly on schedule, but there was an inward miscalculation of which he only gradually became aware, not his estimate of distances, but of his own ability to cover them, and of the effect that two or three years may have on the physical endurance of a man in later middle age. Jackland was by no means soft. Though he smoked too much and drank quite a bit at times, he also enjoyed using his body to the point of self-punishment, and assumed that he would be able to cope better than most with journalistic treks to hard places. It had so happened that his last few assignments had not involved that kind of test, so he had had no warning of the mild but definite slippage that had taken place. What should have been a five-hour tramp was going to take him six, the last three under the full heat of Africa.

At first and for some time he assumed he was making the progress he expected; the sameness of the bush landscape gave him no clues. It was the condition of his own body as the heat increased that slowly made it clear to him that it was not the miles that had stretched but his pace that had shortened. He had imagined he had an hour to spare. Now it was doubtful whether he would reach the camp by noon.

Various options presented themselves. He could give up the attempt to be on time, slow down, rest in patches of shade; he could stop completely and sit out the noon heat—perhaps Burn would send out a rescue mission, following the tyre-tracks; or he could increase his speed and try to make the rendezvous. The risk in the last course was that he might so exhaust himself that he would collapse, possibly having wandered in the last delirium away from the tracks. In that case he would nearly certainly die. Jackland had always been a cautious campaigner—had twice in the past saved his own life and those of his companions by this trait—but this time he chose the risk. He revised his calculations and deliberately forced another two inches on to his stride.

He very nearly made it. Coming over a slight undulation he saw ahead the same phenomenon his mother had recorded—above the grey mass of the thorn-belt a line of darker vegetation, genuinely green, running into the distance to left and right. He held his watch at arm's length and peered through sweat at the blurred digits, then drove his legs into a shambling lope. Sweat streamed all down him, mixing with dust and encrusting into the folds and seams of his face. When his head tried to loll he jerked it upright, a furious-looking gesture, implying perhaps that he himself could not understand his dangerous obstinacy, and whether it was a mere sense of honour or something else—though he had told her flatly that he had never in his life loved anyone—that made it matter that he should keep his promise to Miss Tressider.

He was well into the old track through the thorn-belt when a loud rattle arose, penetrating the rasp of his breath and the thudding of his blood. He halted, gasping, and tried again to make out the time on his watch, but his eyes refused now to focus. The slamming rotor rose, out of sight behind the trees. Quickly the noise dwindled southward, leaving only the faint ticks and whirrings of the unnoticed creatures that made their small livings among the thorns.

Jackland shook his head. There was no shade under the noon sun so he sat down where he was, too exhausted, and perhaps dispirited, to brush away the insects that at once buzzed round him. He did not move till the noise of a large truck's engine reached him from the direction of the river. He found a niche in the bank of thorns at the trackside and stood in it to let the thing pass. The truck braked just beyond him. Three or four soldiers climbed down and a sergeant squeezed round from the front. The sergeant asked him where he'd been and whether he had seen the Sarkin. Jackland shook his head. The sergeant cuffed him, tentatively, as if experimenting with the sensation of treating a white man in this fashion, but then with more vigour and enjoyment. Jackland continued to shake his head. Perhaps he was genuinely refusing to answer, or perhaps he had driven himself so far that he now did not understand what was happening to him. When he collapsed the soldiers picked him up and lifted him into the back of the truck, which then drove on.

SIXTEEN

Sat Dec 11

I am going to write this as tho' nothing was different, nothing had changed. It's the only way I can think of. Perhaps it's a providence I started keeping this stupid diary in the first place, as tho' I'd known at the start I'd need it for this in the end. Then I'll give it to Elongo (not Sixpence—he was never part of things) and tell him to take it out into the bush and find a termites' nest and bury it inside, and the termites will chew it up and it will be gone. A sort of juju, I suppose, making Africa take it all back, so's I can go home and pretend none of it happened. Not to me, anyway. To someone else with my name, far away in a hot country where I've never been. It might work.

Oh, I'm so glad I've got an *excuse!* To go, I mean. I'm not interested in the baby—perhaps that will come. (Or perhaps it will be born with MADE IN AFRICA written invisibly somewhere on it, so's only I can see.) But I've got to have it now, so I don't have to come back, ever. I haven't told Ted yet. It doesn't seem fair, while he's got all this terrible mess to deal with. I know what he'll say, tho'. He'll want to put in for a job in one of the other colonies, where you're allowed babies, so we can go and live there. No. That won't do. I don't want Africa at all. Or India. Or anywhere except England. But first I must try and work my juju.

Well, after the jollifications and parades the nobs went back to Kaduna and left Ted and Bevis to tidy up. At least they'd seen enough of the problem to understand there's got to be a proper Resident and two D.O.s, or just censusing and assessing is going to take five years. Loads of work for Ted anyway. But first off, before any of that we had to get everything hunky-dory between the Kitawa and the new little Emir before he went away to school, which meant having a ceremony at Tefuga, with us there, part of it, so the Kitawa could really see we were both sides' friends and everyone was going to be nice to everyone from now on. Then, at the last minute, a D.O. called McCrum went mad and shot himself on the other side of Soko which meant Bevis had to dash off. So it was just Ted and me.

The tsetse season is over so we rode out, without any horrid Hausa either. They'd got to come separately so the Kitawa could *see* we weren't part of the same old gang—a bit of seeing is far better with natives than any amount of telling. So the trip out was lovely, like a tour with no work. We paid calls at the villages, of course, to pick up fresh bearers, and they almost fought for the honour of carrying our stuff. Lots of them were going our way anyway, you see, to be at the ceremony, so it was a good thing for them if they got paid for going. And such smiles! Still very shy of me, tho'. I was full of electricity still, and they might get a shock, you see. Sad, I thought. I kept thinking of that time when Atafa Guni held my hand at the burnt village, and how I felt the easy friendship flowing between us, until she asked me to kill Kama Boi. It would have been nice if I could have gone back to that with one of them, somehow. There was something else I kept wondering about. Those scrawny old electors we'd talked to out in the bush, Ted and me, why weren't any of them women? Elongo'd told me you get women elders in the villages quite often, so there ought to have been. Probably it was because the Hausa didn't like it, and the electors were really there to choose a Hausa. But I kept remembering how really everything I'd done I'd brought off 'cos of the women, and 'cos of being a woman myself, and now they were being left out. It didn't seem fair.

Anyway, we had a jolly ride out, camped once, and got to Tefuga next day late in the morning. It was rather exciting 'cos the nearer we got the more people we saw, and by the time we were almost there the bush was absolutely streaming with them, all coming to the ceremony, whole families together —whole villages, happy but not nearly as noisy as Africans sometimes are. They're a secret people, the Kitawa. Very.

We set up camp in the old place and Ted went off to have a palaver with the new Emir (with his advisers, really, but we had to pretend). He didn't need me. I didn't mind 'cos I truly wanted to go off on my own and find Femora Feng and talk to her. It would have been so awful if the only time we'd met had been with her crouching in the river bed, grey with fright, and me pretending to paint Tefuga Hill so I couldn't even look at her properly. There was plenty of time. Nothing was due to happen till after the worst heat was over, then some Kiti dancing, then the ceremony on the hill at sunset.

I wandered about the village looking for someone to ask. It wasn't as easy as I'd thought. Lots of them didn't belong, just going through on their way. Such masses, too, floods, streaming towards the hill. All across the river bed, like ants. It was funny how they managed not to come near me. They sort of flowed apart, leaving a space round me, my white island. In the end I saw a girl going into a hut and I waited outside and trapped her and asked her to take me to Femora Feng. She looked v. dubious. She'd got a little pot of something in her hand. I could've ordered her to do what I said but I didn't want to start off on that foot so I just asked, as tho' I'd been a Bakiti too. She told me to wait and ran off. After about ten minutes she came back and beckoned and I followed her out, sort of sideways through the bush, quite a long way, till we came to a place which I thought was one of their gardens 'cos there were mats all round only bigger and newer than sometimes. The girl pulled a mat aside, just enough to make a slit, but she covered her eyes with her hand before she poked her head through. Then she stepped away and someone the other side opened the mat a bit further to let me in. I said thank you to the girl but she had her head turned right away.

Inside was full of women. I don't know how many, more than a hundred, but too crowded to count and—this is difficult to explain—sort of not separate from each other. You see, they'd gone there to get painted up for the dancing, all those lovely, naked, graceful bodies covered in great streaks, white and ochre and a super rich raw siena which I wished I'd had in my box and little round circles of almost ultramarine—all over their bodies, like bright lizards. Dazzling and confusing, so till you looked hard you couldn't be sure whose bits belonged to who. But marvellous too. I don't think I've ever seen people looking so beautiful, so dressed to kill, tho' I saw Queen Mary and her court at Bournemouth on a special visit before the war, all with osprey feathers and yards of lace and dripping with jet and pearls. *They* weren't as grand. In fact they were vulgar, compared.

The woman who'd let me in passed two empty pots to the girl outside (paint-pots—*I* should have known) before she shut the mat and faced me. She was painted already, her face a complete mask, but she had the right wide clear open gaze. I thought for a mo it might be Atafa Guni till she spoke.

'Femora Feng speaks,' she said. 'A strong spirit in Betty Jackland.'

And she wasn't afraid of me at all. She was triumphant.

I wished her a strong spirit back and wondered what to say. This wasn't what I'd really wanted. I mean, rather like expecting to have a long easy chat with the vicar's wife on the morning of the church fête when she's trying to get everything organized. Then, worse still, I realized that all the others had stopped doing anything and were listening.

'You are all very beautiful,' I managed to say.

'It is for the ancestors,' she said.

'How do you make this blue?' I asked.

I'd reached out my hand to touch one of the light spots on her upper arm, but she pushed it away, polite but firm.

'It is not spoken of,' she said.

I'd got it all wrong. Everything much too still, like being in church. And them all listening, as tho' they were just one person, one woman.

'Why do you come to Tefuga again?' she said.

'I come because my huband comes. He must watch the ceremony so that everyone can see that all is right between the Kitawa and the new Emir.'

That wasn't what they wanted. I could feel their disappointment.

'But I also come to talk with you, Femora Feng,' I said.

Better. Much better.

'What do you say to me?'

Oh dear. What I meant was I'd come to chat about ordinary things, children and husbands, and dear Elongo, of course, and how much I admired him. That wasn't what *she* meant. She was expecting a *message*. They all were. A message from the magical white termite which had bitten the great black horse in the neck and made it fall down and die. Best I could think of was to try and remember bits of the speech Ted had written for little Azikofio and turn them into Kiti. They were nice and simple, 'cos of A. being only a child. Even so there were lots of ideas the Kitawa just don't have words for.

'Today a time ends,' I said. 'A new time begins. The old

stubble is dug out and thrown away and the ground made clean for new seed. Good rain . . .' (Ted had made Azikofio talk about the rain of justice and honesty, which you can do in Hausa but you can't in Kiti.) 'Good rain will water that seed so that all the people may have food.'

Then I got stuck. I managed not to um and er, but this wasn't my sort of thing at all. Femora Feng waited for a bit, in case I wanted to say more.

'Kama Boi has crossed the river,' she said. 'We saw him go.'

'Were *you* there?'

I wished I'd known.

'We saw him go. We saw him cross the river. But the spirit that was in him, where is that? Where is the spirit which the ancestors gave him? Can that too cross the river? Tell us, Betty Jackland.'

Suddenly I understood something which had been sort of puzzling me without me really thinking about it. When the Kitawa wish you a strong spirit they aren't just saying hello. They're actually doing something, giving you something. You see, the word doesn't mean what we mean, quite. With us your spirit is what makes you *you*. It's *your* soul, and when you die it'll still be *you* and *you'll* go to heaven, etc. But with the Kitawa what's *you* is only a sort of pot and then some spirit's poured into it which comes from the ancestors and when people wish you a strong spirit they're telling the ancestors to put a bit more in, and then when you die it goes back and joins up with all the rest till next time. That's why they sometimes talk as tho' there was only one big Kiti creature which they're all part of. I don't imagine they think like this all the time, any more than we really think all the time that somehow we're going to go on living after our funeral. But suddenly I saw—at least I thought I saw—why KB had such a strong juju. It was 'cos he'd come to Tefuga and stood on the tombs of the ancestors and had a huge spirit poured into his pot, 'cos of the sacrifice. It makes a sort of mad sense, doesn't it? Killing someone else, giving that spirit to the ancestors, as a sort of present, so they'd give a huge present back?

Anyway, that's what I thought I understood, then. I saw it quite clear, as tho' part of me belonged to the Kiti creature. But with another bit of me—the white bit—I had one of my ideas.

232

'The spirit is in Azikofio,' I said.

It seemed so obvious. I knew Ted was bothered about the Kitawa not respecting the new Emir 'cos of the ceremony not being good enough, but if they thought he'd already got as much spirit as KB had had there shouldn't be any trouble, should there?

One of the women started to mutter to Femora Feng, but she pushed her away. She was in charge. Everyone else was listening, holding their breaths, it felt like. So still.

'And now the White Man sends this child with the spirit of Kama Boi back to the place of the ancestors,' said Femora Feng.

'Yes. The White Man is your friend,' I said.

'Good.'

And that was all right. They started breathing again.

'I would like to make a picture of you in your beautiful paint,' I said—just for something to say, really. 'May I do that?'

Silence again. Femora Feng stared at me. Her eyes were very round.

'You made a picture at Sollum,' she said. 'A picture of the dream.'

'Yes. I dreamed the dream too, so I made a picture. This time is not like that time. We are women. We must do what we do with one mind. I will not make my picture if you do not want it.'

Murmurs and whispers. I stood there smiling. I realized I absolutely longed for them to say yes. It mattered dreadfully, I didn't know why.

Femora Feng drew herself up.

'Make your picture for us,' she said.

So I trotted off to the rest house and left a message for Ted and got my pad and my small paint-box and went back to the mat place and settled down in a corner. It became rather a special morning, a bit like the time I did KB's wives in his harem. Bodies are terribly tricky—naked ones I mean—and of course there was nothing like *that* at school. But they're much the most interesting, look how all the best painters have wanted to do them. I'd tried a few fishermen, but most of the river people wear clothes and this was my first real chance to have a go at complicated poses. I didn't feel I was ready for a whole picture so I just did studies, but even so it *was* like the time in the harem 'cos I had the same feeling of something, some power, flooding

233

through me, in at my eyes and out down through my fingers and brush, something to do with it being that stifling crowded place, and full of us women. They were lovely to paint, standing poised or moving so gracefully spite of the crush, caressing each other with long flowing movements to make the stripes—they did all their painting with their fingers. It was almost like a dream —you know for instance when you've been blackberrying all afternoon and at bed-time the berries and brambles come back and make patterns over and over inside your closed eyelids. Same now, hands floating across bodies, leaving their trails of paint. I caught them and dashed them down, a hand and wrist on a shoulder-blade, a neck and face craned sideways to squint at an effect, a leg and foot up on someone else's knee to have the ankle ringed, the bright-blotched swoop of a bosom, and hundreds of hands, black, thin-fingered, pink-palmed, making their paint-magic. I felt I was being let in on something very special, their gift to me, allowing me to see at all. And tho' they were only snatches, my little studies were good, real. They had that something, that power, it was there, in spite of sometimes being a bit clumsy 'cos of me not having had much practice at the nude, but that doesn't matter when the power is in you. I'd filled four whole pages, crammed them with legs and arms and hands and heads, before I looked at my watch and saw I was late for lunch already.

Soon as they saw me packing up everything stopped again. They wanted to see what I'd done. I passed my pictures round. They were amazed. I was pleased about that for a mo, till I realized that actually they were terribly worried. I asked Femora Feng what was the matter, but I knew before she spoke. I should have thought.

'Why all these pieces?' she said. 'What does this mean?'

She was so serious I didn't laugh.

'When I go to my hut,' I said. 'I will take a big paper . . .' (no word for paper of course—had to use the English) 'and I will put these pieces together and make a picture of beautiful whole women. I cannot do it now. I am not ready. I must wait.'

Femora Feng looked at the sheet she was holding for a long time.

'Good,' she said, and handed it back. I collected the others and slipped away.

I was a bit late for lunch but I found Ted feeling rather pleased with life. He said the palaver had gone well and Elongo was being very sensible and he thought everything was going to turn out better than he'd expected. I didn't show him my studies—he would have been embarrassed. Then we lay in hammocks in the shade for a bit and watched the last Kitawa coming past. Ted said even he hadn't realized there were so many, practically everyone in the whole tribe must be there. We rode off towards the hill in the middle of the afternoon. We wanted to be there before the Emir and his lot, still so's everyone could see we weren't part of that gang.

At first the bush was empty, just as usual—that feeling of Africa stretching for miles and no one else in it—but soon as we were about half a mile from the hill it changed. Every little clearing, anywhere you could see the top of the hill from, had a little camp of people in it. The scrub thins out as you get nearer the hill, tho' never quite completely, still a few bushes dotted about, and then we began to see how many there were. And the river bed when we reached it—just about where I'd painted my picture and listened to Femora Feng—stretching away to the far dry bank and right along for more than a mile, separate clumps and huddles of people, dotting the whole brown level with black blobs, like the spots on a leopard. We had to wind our way through to our place near the bottom of the hill where the main dancing-floor was. Ted had sent Mafote out in advance with our folding chairs and parasols, and he took the horses away and tied them by some bushes and we settled down.

First we knew the Emir's lot was coming was a drum, far away. Then another from somewhere else, and another and another answering, all over the plain. There seemed to be drummers all over the plain beating the message to and fro, just a mess of noise at first, deep thuds like heartbeats with plinks and rattlings on top, but then the heartbeats got together and *then*—this was really exciting—somehow they made a kind of wave of thudding so that the heartbeat seemed to start at one edge of the plain, right out in the distance, and come rolling towards you like a huge soft wave and on out across the river bed and then start rolling back. When it was right out there it was drowned by the plinks and rattles going on round you but somehow you could still feel it and then you began to hear it and your nape prickled and your hair tried to stand up as it came nearer and nearer and your own heart joined the thudding and your skin went cold as it rolled over—no, *through* you and out the far side and on, and you knew every single person in all that mass was feeling the same thing.

Then the Emir's procession came picking their way through. You couldn't hear their squeaky trumpets but they looked magnificent. Whatever else is wrong about them the Hausa really know how to put on a parade. Brilliant robes and turbans and tasselled spears and the Emir's lovely leaf-shaped sunshade and gaudy brollies twirling either side and everybody getting a chance to show off their horsemanship 'cos of the horses being half-crazed with the drums—thrilling. And little Azikofio at the middle of it, with his sad big eyes.

Before the procession reached the open space the first dancers came out to meet them, men (I think—you couldn't see) in grass spirit-suits ten feet high, pale swaying pillars with ogre-masks at the top. That did it for two of the horses, which bolted, but the rest moved on with the dancers swaying and twirling round them, with the dust rising 'cos of the way they stamped. And they went on twirling and stamping while the Hausa dismounted and set up under their awnings to watch. The wave of drumming had stopped—I hadn't noticed—and the dancers made their own 'music' with rattling calabashes and a waily thing, until they danced off in and out among the crowd further and further away so's everyone got a chance to see them in the end.

That's how it went on. Everything happened terribly slowly, with long gaps while the Hausa chewed kola and Ted and me had tea from my thermos. It must have been utterly exhausting for the dancers. Long after the first ones, the grass giants, had left us, I noted them right out across the river bed, still at it. Ted said a kind of dancing madness gets into natives which keeps them going, so that they collapse completely when they stop, and often go into a coma or even die of exhaustion. I'm afraid some of it seemed rather boring tho' I realized it would have been more interesting if I'd understood what the dances meant. I could see the dancers were all supposed to *be* different things, spirits or animals or ancestors, but I didn't know what.

My women were much the best. Lizards. I'd been right about

that. Or snakes. Their music was just a few old women sitting and clapping (v. cleverly, tho'). They came on in little lines, three in each line, holding the hips of the woman in front and bending flat. The lines wriggled about among each other in wavy patterns. Then they started to 'eat' each other by joining up, fewer but longer, and soon as the lines were long enough they very cunningly made the 'body' of the lizard ripple up and down as they moved. Then there were only two lines left and they did a sort of dance-fight (or mating?) which finished with them coiling inward side by side in a tight clump in front of the Emir. I thought they'd have to unwind backwards but then a head came through under the arms of the outside ring and a whole line of women slithered through and wriggled its way round the arena and off. Like a conjuring trick with people instead of rabbits. I kept trying to see which was Femora Feng but I couldn't under the paint.

I'd have loved to laugh and clap but it would have been like clapping in church. It was all deadly serious. Even the boring bits—there was one dance which was just men jumping up and down in the same place holding sticks with black feathers in the ends—but the Kitawa concentrated like mad on that too. Sometimes the ones nearby did join in by shouting or clapping, but that was all part of the dance—they were meant to. The Hausa looked bored by the whole thing. The little Emir kept picking his ear till I longed to go over and slap his wrist away. I could see how utterly they despised my Kitawa.

Well, we got through that bit in the end. The sun was quite low by the time all the dancers came back from doing their turns among the crowd and danced their way up the hill. The Emir climbed into a special chair with poles, which four of his people started to carry up the hill. Ted got up.

'Well, here goes,' he said. 'You're well out of it, Rabbit.'

'Shut your eyes, darling. Nobody'll be watching you.'

'I might, at that.'

He walked off up the hill with Elongo close behind him. I set up my easel but I didn't feel like painting. I kept having imaginary chats in my head, trying to break it to him about me being pregnant, making it easy for him. Funny thing—I know him so well that usually I'm pretty certain which way he'll jump over anything, but I wasn't this time. He'd hate the idea of me going—it matters so much to him. Part of me tried to persuade the rest of me I wouldn't mind if he got himself a native woman, specially if I'd told him he could, but actually I would mind, dreadfully. The thought of him coming back to me, after somebody else . . . But he'd be pleased about the baby, I knew. He'd be sure it was going to be a boy. Not so interested in a daughter —silly, he'd adore a daughter soon as she'd stopped being a baby. I didn't think I minded. Anyway, once you've started there's not much point in stopping at one, supposing you could afford more. Really, I didn't want either. My life had been pretty mouldy from the time Mummy died till I met Ted, and then there'd been a few exciting months, but now I was going to get myself trapped again. Babies, lodgings, my man thousands of miles away, no one to shield and cosy me. Horrible.

When you're in that sort of selfish mope you don't notice anything outside you. I really don't remember anything between watching Ted starting to climb the hill, with Kitawa going up all round him, and then me sort of waking up feeling something was wrong. Everything far, far too still. No one anywhere near me, when before there'd been thousands. And getting dark, just the glitter of the last rays of sun on the tree-tops up the hill. Pricks of yellowy orange under the trees, where they'd lit the torches. I couldn't think for a mo where everyone had gone. Then I saw the hill was different. Black, and soft, and smooth all over, almost as tho' there'd been a black snow-storm in just that one place. It was packed solid with Kitawa from the trees almost to the bottom, pressed tight against each other, tight as a swarm of bees, all one mass, those tens of thousands of people. You couldn't see heads or shoulders or anything in the almost-dark, only a tassely fringe of legs along the very bottom. I've said once or twice about the Kitawa sometimes talking as tho' they weren't separate people but all just parts of one big animal, it was like that.

And so still. They're a quiet people, anyway, but you didn't feel any of them was even breathing. They were alive, tho', snapping tense, waiting. Still. I felt my own heart thud, and thud. I got up—not on purpose but I was sort of drawn. I had to go forward to join them, to press myself against the lowest row, to be part of the animal.

Then there was a yell. I heard it before I'd moved a step.

Women, lots of them, shrieking together at the tops of their voices. Men shouting, almost drowned by the shrieking, not as tho' it was part of a ceremony, which the shrieking might have been. More like yelling orders. Then shots—two, or three. They only made the screaming get louder. I'd no idea what the screaming meant. I just stood there, with my hair prickling. I knew the best thing was to go over to the horses so I could get away if I had to, but it was no use. I sort of stuck.

Something had happened to the crowd on the hill. I couldn't see but I could feel. It had stopped being one thing. People were shouting to and fro with ordinary voices, questions, answers. I didn't see the crowd starting to break up but it must have 'cos suddenly a big Bakiti came rushing at me and banged into me as tho' he hadn't seen me, knocking me clean over. Before I could get right up it happened again, and while I was lying flat another one came and tripped right over me and took a terrific tumble but got straight up and rushed on. I started to crawl sideways towards a tree so's I could shelter behind it, watching in case another one came so's I could try and dodge. Had to do that several times before I got there. Extraordinary thing—the one who'd tripped over me had kicked me pretty hard just under my arm. It hurt, but that didn't bother. What I was chiefly worrying about was the baby, and getting kicked *there*. I didn't want the baby, I thought it was almost the most dreadful thing that had ever happened to me, but I couldn't help trying to keep it safe.

Anyway I got to my tree and crouched behind it and tried to see what was happening. It was almost dark now—I still couldn't make much out, just people coming down off the hill and going away. They weren't all running. I saw three women go past with several small children. They were hurrying the children and looking back over their shoulders as tho' something might be chasing them, but they weren't panicking like the men. I called out to them to ask what had happened but they didn't answer, tho' I knew they'd heard 'cos of the way they looked at me.

Mafote came up with the horses. He'd had a struggle to reach me, coming across the streams of Kitawa rushing away. I took Beano off him so he could try and quiet Tan-Tan who was wild with fright. Having a horse to hold and gentle and calm was a help. I kept looking towards the hill. I could just see something different happening. What had made it so difficult till now was all the people being so black you couldn't make anything out they were doing, but now they'd mostly moved away from the top, tho' there were quite a few sitting or lying on the slope under the trees. Shot, or trampled, I thought. Straight towards us some not so black were coming, all in a mass together, shouting in a different kind of voice. The screaming hadn't stopped but it had sort of split up, going different ways, which meant I could actually hear some of what these other people were shouting —mostly 'Out of the way' in Hausa. They barged their way down. The Kitawa didn't seem to be fighting back. I couldn't see Ted but I thought he must be there so I said, 'Come on' to Mafote and started to lead Beano that way.

He came running out of the dusk, gasping for breath.

'You all right, Rabbit?'

'Yes. Are you? What happened?'

'They went mad. The women.'

'What happened?'

'Tell you later. Hang on here. Get ready to make a dash for it. Don't wait for me.'

'What *happened*?'

'Later. Got to try and cool the Hausa off. They might . . .'

And he'd swung himself up onto Tan-Tan and dashed away. The Hausa had almost reached their own horses. They were shouting, furious. I've never heard them like that. Usually they're rather calm. Ted rode himself between them and the horses and started shouting back. Nobody else paid the slightest attention. Kitawa were moving past me in the almost-dark, arguing in low voices, frightened but excited. A flaming torch came towards me, a white pillar below, Elongo.

'What has happened?' I said in Kiti.

'The ancestors have drunk blood.'

'What do you mean?'

'All is well,' he said in English.

'Yes, but . . .'

Suddenly, there, under the flare of the torch (I couldn't see anything beyond it now) stood a woman. One of my women, streaked and blobbed with her dance-paint, her arms spread wide, wriggling to and fro, laughing with the dancing madness that was still in her. Her teeth and the whites of her eyes glistened in the torch-light. She was shocking, terrifying, the African nightmare I used to brood about, lying in our little tent waiting for Ted.

'Femora Feng?' I whispered.

She laughed and rushed at me. I put out my arms to push her away but the madness was much too strong, strong as a man. She came with her arms still spread and flung them round me, grappling me to her. I could feel her breasts against mine with only my blouse and bra between, the hard muscled tum below, and the shudder of dancing jerking through her. She nuzzled her face against mine, nose and nose, mouth and mouth. Then she let go. When I opened my eyes she wasn't there at all, only Elongo, holding the torch high and looking perfectly dignified and calm. I think seeing him like that stopped me from fainting. I grabbed hold of Beano's bridle—I'd had to let go—and patted his side and felt his bristly hide for its comfort and ordinariness, but he didn't really like it. Something about me seemed to make him nervous.

Ted came back and swung himself down into our island of yellow light.

'I think that's going to be . . .' he began.

He stared at me.

'Good God! Are you hurt, Rabbit? Elongo, who . . . ?'

He had to stop to wrestle with Tan-Tan, who was almost wild by now.

'Madam is not hurt,' said Elongo in English.

'But look at you,' said Ted. 'You weren't . . .'

I looked down. The whole of the front of my blouse was smeared, and the top of my jodhpurs, as though I'd been rolling in something. My face too, I guessed. I thought it was the dance-paint, but only for a mo. Then I noticed the smell and understood why Beano was so jittery. Horses hate blood.

They tore him apart, Ted told me. Little Azikofio, I mean. My women did it. Ted didn't see, 'cos he had his eyes shut for the goat sacrifice. By the time he opened them—only a couple of secs—all he could see was a scrum of women where the Emir's stool had been and some of the Hausa trying to wrestle them off. He fired his own revolver into the air but no one paid any attention. The spearmen were stabbing into the scrum and Ted was rushing to stop them when the women broke up and went dancing off into the crowd. There were bits Ted wouldn't tell me. He was too shocked. I can't help imagining. The Hausa speared quite a few more Kitawa on their way down the hill, but Ted managed to stop them getting on their horses and having a complete massacre. That part can probably be hushed up 'cos of the Kitawa having killed some of each other, trampling on them in the rush to get away from the hill. They didn't know it was going to happen either, you see. They were shocked and frightened too. It must have been something my women decided, just among themselves. I haven't told Ted anything about what I said to them, and I'm not going to. I don't think it matters. They were going to do it anyway.

I'm not being disloyal, not telling him. Kaduna are going to want someone to blame, and if they can make anything my fault they can blame Ted. They probably will anyway, tho' he's warned them all along there might be trouble and he did v. well keeping the Hausa under control when it happened. Well, I don't suppose it really matters. All I know is that I'm going away to have my baby and I'm not coming back to Africa again, ever.

I shall tell Ted about the baby tonight.

SEVENTEEN

Jackland had been reading but not, evidently, for pleasure. Narrow strips of paper rose in a methodical cockscomb above the spine of his book, marking pages he might need to return to. When the door-bell rang he inserted another before closing the book and adding it to a small pile, similarly ornamented. He opened the door to Miss Tressider and followed her into his living-room.

'Coffee?'

'Lovely.'

He had the makings ready and came back in a couple of minutes with a tray, spinsterly laid with doileys, the biscuits in a pattern on their plate. Miss Tressider snatched one and began to nibble it, tiny mouthfuls, like a rodent barking a sapling. She had curled herself into a corner of the big old sofa, and though the room was warm enough for Jackland to have been working in shirtsleeves she had not removed her grey fox fur coat, only opening it to show a chocolate-brown trouser-suit. She looked decidedly frailer than she had in Kiti, though this, as always with her, might simply have been because she had chosen to do so.

'How are you?' said Jackland. 'I've seen your Miss Julie . . .'

'You didn't come round?'

'Well . . .'

They had kissed in the hallway, but only in the off-hand actorly fashion. Jackland's imprisonment in Nigeria had combined with Miss Tressider's acting commitments to prevent their meeting since Kiti. Now he spoke with uncharacteristic hesitancy, though she seemed perfectly at ease.

'What did you think of it?' she said.

'If you're not bored of people telling you it was marvellous . . .'

'Never. It's a bit worrying when I think they mean it, but I'll forgive you.'

'You pour yourself out till there seems there can't be anything left.'

'There isn't.'

'Night after night. Don't you sometimes feel that night there's not going to be enough to pour?'

'Every time. I still haven't got rid of the bloody bug, you know.'

'Oh, God.'

'It strikes every five days. That helps the effect. Today's one. I'm drugged to the tonsils.'

'Ought you to be out at all? I mean . . .'

'I wanted to see you, darling.'

Jackland mimed surprise. He too had changed. The folds and wrinkles of his face seemed to have hardened, to have lost some thin inner layer, with the effect that the skin had, as it were, got nearer the bone. His movements too had a touch of caution, as though beginning to practise for the brittleness of age.

'I thought you might be going to suggest we should start again where we left off,' said Miss Tressider. 'I wouldn't mind. I've got no one on at the moment.'

'Ah,' said Jackland.

He tilted the coffee to and fro in his cup, staring at the ever-level surface.

'No ashtrays, I notice,' said Miss Tressider.

'Jail is a good cure if you're prepared to take it. The answer, my dear, is, I suppose, that I will do what you want.'

'Left to yourself, Nigel?'

'One must stop some time, I suppose. Make one's peace, if not with the world, at least with the flesh.'

'Poor old St Antony. Comfy in your desert with just the vultures to chat to, and I come wriggling out from under a rock with my lascivious suggestions. Actually I prefer my lovers to be a bit excited by me. You don't owe me anything, darling. The other way round, if anything. I just held myself together for that last scene and then I collapsed completely. The helicopter was a godsend. Major Kadu had laid on an army nurse, even. If you'd driven me I wouldn't have understood a word, and like as not I'd have died on the road. So I'll leave you with the vultures.'

'Only one of them.'

'You look a bit as though there might have been more.'

'No doubt they'll come. Have you seen a tape of *The Deposition*?'

'Yes.'

'What do you think?'

'Oh, it works, Nigel. It really does. I'm not saying that just because it's one of my best, but it is. I'm glad to have been in it, even at the cost of picking up this bloody bug.'

'You're taking that seriously, aren't you? I mean you aren't just relying on macrobiotics and mantras and that sort of crap?'

'I am a prize exhibit at the Hospital for Tropical Diseases. It makes a change being asked to autograph slides of my blood samples, but not a nice change. Do you want me to watch *The Deposition* again? Now?'

'If you can stand it.'

'Of course I can.'

Jackland got up and adjusted the Venetian blind to cut out the thin April sunlight. He settled into his arm-chair with the TV control on the table beside him. As with the coffee-tray he had everything ready. Miss Tressider snuggled herself round to watch as the screen cleared and the long curve of the river glimmered into view. The fisherman flung his net. The picture froze with the net floating in air while the titles went by.

'Is this your vulture, Nigel?'

'In a sense.'

'You really needn't worry. It's good—very original—different. Not mass-audience, but it ought to walk off with a lot of prizes. Don't you think?'

'That's not what I'm interested in.'

'The flesh *and* the devil!'

'I want you to tell me if you think it's true.'

'Darling, I'm the last person. Everything's true for me while I'm in it. After, it's just a story.'

Jackland said nothing. The net fell and the camera swung to take in the image of Jackland, standing in the foreground.

'This, literally, is where I began,' said the image.

Jackland pressed the fast-forward button, making the image gibber in silence. The camera whipped to the ramshackle remains of the hut with Sarkin Elongo in the doorway, streaky with the rush of the tape.

'Too sad about the old goat,' said Miss Tressider. 'I rather went for him.'

245

'Oh? He's not done too badly,' said Jackland, stopping the tape.

'What do you mean? I thought he was killed by a lion or something.'

'Kadu's men tracked him to the dry river where they found a bloodstained blanket. The river bed is mostly boulders. You could walk for miles along it without leaving tracks, until you reached a regular crossing-place with plenty of other foot-prints.'

'Isn't that a bit devious?'

'Yes, but not to my mind out of character. My latest information is that he's in Switzerland—Annie implied there was a family home there.'

'And living the life of Riley?'

'Comfortable, I should think, but not excessive. He'll have put a bit away.'

'You sound let down, Nigel.'

'Can't help it. I tell myself that he regarded himself as under an obligation to achieve and retain power in order to protect the Kitawa from a return of the successors of Kama Boi, and that he couldn't do that within the Northern Nigerian system without using the system. I tell myself that the Kiti Highway Project was a symbolic national scandal, and the Sarkin a safe scapegoat for arrest, because the younger Kitawa had become urbanized and the older ones no longer seemed likely to cause trouble. I tell myself that the inherent contradictions of our policy of indirect rule led to a backwardness in Northern Nigerian political sophistication. I tell myself that his behaviour was moderate compared to many of the big boys, some of whom are probably still operating under the present government. I tell myself that it would in any case have been understood and condoned by the vast majority of his constituents. But yes, I do feel let down. And he might perhaps have sent me a postcard of the Jungfrau.'

He started the tape again. The camera flipped to the river with the canoes whizzing into sight and Jackland's image fading in quick jerks from solid to ghost to nothing. He kept the tape speeding until the first canoe slid alongside the landing-stage, then took his finger off the button. The sound came up, river-ripple and insect creak and the vague mutter of voices.

The thwart tap-tapped against the staging as Piers Smith

climbed stiffly out, then bent to help Miss Tressider. The canoe lurched as she rose. She balanced for a second, then stepped up and stood beside him, clutching his hand as though the landing-stage were as uncertain to her footing as the canoe had been. As she raised her eyes towards the mound her face came into close-up. Jackland froze the picture. Under the big brim of her helmet her cheek was faintly barred with the waver of ripple-reflected light. Even in the stilled picture the slight quiver of her lower lip was somehow perceptible, the outward vulnerability, but also the inner will, the determination that as she had made her bed so she must now lie on it.

'I hoped you might be able to tell me whether it is true for her,' said Jackland. 'Whatever that may mean.'

They watched for the most part in silence. Jackland didn't interfere with the flow again until they came to a shot of the actor who played the young Elongo crossing the red sandy space that supposedly lay between the Jacklands' hut and the boys' compound. Jackland stopped him in mid-stride. Pittapoulos had used filters that largely eliminated the normal slight vague haze of Nigerian sunlight, and had produced instead a sharp-edged glare, a generalized idea of tropic light, an Africa clearly perceptible to northern eyes. In this light the actor stood in his housecoat, a study in black and white, wearing the permanent puzzled frown of Kiti facial scars—grease-paint in his case.

'About being devious,' said Jackland, 'he was, of course, a spy.'

'What do you mean?'

'Femora Feng sent him to find out about the White Man. My mother taught him English. Of course, she knew he could understand what my parents were saying to each other, and so did I when I wrote the script, but I assumed they didn't think about it. The diary's full of bits about how quietly he moves. They talked shop over their meals, but from something he told me I think he used to go and listen outside their bedroom at night. He must have had peep-holes, too. You notice how as soon as she needed to know anything somebody told her? De Lancey says in Elongo's hearing that the only way the British will depose Kama Boi is catching him out in a major peculation over taxes. Next thing my mother is taken to a fake village where a woman blurts out that exactly such a scheme is in operation.'

'It's not the sort of thing I think about.'

'It was Femora Feng, by the way.'

'Who?'

'The woman who called herself Atafa Guni. That's a name she took from a folk-tale. The Sarkin spoke as if it had been Femora Feng and when I put him right he laughed and said he'd forgotten. I misread him at the time. I thought he meant he had forgotten who had told me, but that can't be true. Femora Feng must have been a very remarkable woman, a Luther, a Lenin. She contrived the revolt almost single-handed, using any tool she chanced on, including my mother. The improvisation of a fictitious village seems to me in the context of a primitive African people an astonishing concept. You don't forget what a woman like that does and says—the Sarkin had merely forgotten that she had used an assumed name, partly to protect herself and her own village, but mainly to avoid the question what she was doing so far from home. What's the matter? Are you all right?'

Miss Tressider's face had changed, become alien, mask-like, the cheek muscles rigid, the eyes round and wide. She shook her head, at the same time shaking her features back to their norm, and smiled.

'I think I could do her,' she said. 'When I was delirious, in the helicopter, I was convinced she was there too. Then I went through a stage of thinking she sent the tick and she was inside me now. Don't worry, darling, I've got over that. Only bad days, just when I'm waking up . . . Anyway it's not what you want to know, is it? Shall we go on?'

They watched in silence almost to the end.

The canoe jiggled at the landing-stage as Miss Tressider stepped down, still clinging to Piers Smith's hand. Without letting go he crouched to allow her to sit. Her mouth was smiling and her eyes wide and dry, but a muscle in her left cheek twitched and twitched.

'Four months,' he said. 'Not too bad, Rabbit. Snowdrops will be out now. I'll be home before the roses are.'

'Home,' she said.

Her eyes left his and looked past him up the mound. Somehow their hands parted. The paddles stirred stiffly at the slack water and the canoe curled into the stream to join the two waiting there, loaded with baggage. Miss Tressider waved, twisting her body to a gawky tension. She maintained the pose, cross-cut once with Smith filling his pipe with a fumbling thumb, until the river-bend took her out of sight.

Jackland sighed and stopped the film.

'All that's phooey, I'm afraid,' he said. 'A hundred to one he'd have gone down river with her, at least as far as Fajujo.'

'It doesn't matter if he did. You have to show people the inside by showing them the outside, and leaving The Warren was saying good-bye. What happened to her after? You were going to tell me.'

'Nothing. She went to my father's sister in Sheen. They didn't get on. By the time I was born she had his pension, not enough to live on. She moved to Eastbourne, scraped in lodgings, got a job in a local prep school, pretty low-grade. They gave her a pittance but said they'd pay my fees eventually. Her father died before the need arose, and she could have afforded to leave, but she stayed on—for the rest of her life in fact. More than thirty years.'

'No other men, of course.'

'I don't think so. Doubt if I'd have noticed. But she was so obviously spinster material that people used to assume I was her nephew. Me too. I mean I felt that sort of distance between us. She had a knack for teaching. The boys liked her.'

'But no more painting?'

'She used to copy out of books for practice. Drawings for the School Play programme. That sort of thing.'

'Nothing real, though. That was Africa for her. And Ted. When did she die, Nigel?'

'1960. I was in Chile. Cancer of the liver. She used to write when I was away, but she didn't mention it.'

'No. The Africa paintings were good—they must have been. She knew and de Lancey knew. You haven't got any of them?'

'I think when the news came about my father she deliberately destroyed everything. When I was at Cambridge I found a book about tribal masks on a second-hand bookstall and gave it her for a birthday present. I thought they were stunning, in their own right, and she'd be interested for other reasons, but she barely glanced at it. "All those old horrors," she said.'

'But she didn't burn Ted's stuff? You said that's where you found the diary.'

'When I got back from Chile I went through her papers. There wasn't much, and all in order. She didn't want any fuss for people to remember her by. Almost the only unexplained item was a banker's order for a firm in Liverpool. I queried it. They turned out to be a warehouse firm who were storing three trunks. I went up to look. They were my father's possessions, with a note from de Lancey saying he had checked them. My mother had begun to pay the storage fees the moment the boxes had come, though she hadn't even got a job then and must have been desperate for money. There were my father's guns she could have sold.'

'She couldn't face it.'

'I suppose so. The diary was among my father's clothes, wrapped in a silk petticoat she must have left behind.'

'He might have nicked the petticoat while she was packing. To remind him.'

'Possibly.'

'And the diary?'

'No. I think I've worked out what may have happened about that. One or two things the Sarkin said. I'd tried to ask him several times before but he'd ducked the question. In fact one of the reasons I agreed to take him to Tefuga was that I thought he might tell me now.'

'It matters, doesn't it?'

'It matters to me whether my mother deliberately left the diary for my father to find. The Sarkin's attitude was curious. The truck broke down and we talked for a while. He seemed positively anxious to explain himself to me. Second time that had happened—it was about his political career before. He had very strong feelings about my mother, gratitude but also cau- tion. As a young man he had regarded her as a powerful witch, and had thought of the diary as a fetish object. When I asked him whether she'd given it to him to bury he said he didn't remem- ber, but then he thought for a bit and explained in hypothetical terms that he would not have done what she wanted. Then he decided to leave.'

'What had he got against burying it?'

'Too dangerous. They'd only just got rid of one magical presence, remember. She may even have told him what she says in the diary, that she thought of it as a sort of juju and wanted it to be absorbed back into Kiti. And a termites' nest, remember. I think that might have bothered him more than somewhat. In my parents' minds the notion that white people were really termites was no more than an amusing fairy-tale, but especially in the light of Femora Feng's dream it meant much more than that to the Kitawa. What happens if you feed a nest of termites on a fetish object prepared by a white witch? Hordes of white men coming and taking your country from you? He probably didn't formulate the danger in terms like that, he'd just decided it was dangerous. But he had to put it somewhere. Somewhere it would be under control. Somewhere which was as far as possible not part of Kiti. He was Messenger by now, in and out of the office. What's more, the office was supposed to be termite proof. My guess is he hid it in there.'

'And Ted found it.'

'There's one more thing to go on. The Sarkin told me some-thing new about Femora Feng's dream. That seems to have modified itself quite a bit as time went on, but in its earliest form the termite hadn't got a woman's face, and then after it had killed the horse Elongo hit the termite with a mattock so that it broke into pieces and crawled away. The Sarkin told me with some emphasis that he still regarded the dream as significant, but not to have been referring to his eventual political triumph and Nigerian independence. It was the Incident which remained the significant event in his eyes. This explains something which has been puzzling me all along, which was his general helpful-ness to us—it's not usual in Third World countries for public figures to welcome reminders of the colonial past and their own more primitive behaviour. But in the Sarkin's case it was the Incident which had originally invested him with his authority among the Kitawa, and with Nigeria so clearly on the edge of political breakdown he was glad of a chance to emphasize the non-political basis of that authority.'

'Go back to the dream.'

'Sorry. In his reading of the dream the death of the black horse symbolized not simply the deposition of Kama Boi but the total loss of authority on the part of the Hausa. This was immediately followed in the dream by Elongo hacking the termite to pieces which then crawled away. Now, when he'd told me about his political career in our earlier talk he'd laid great emphasis on the short tenure of British Political Officers at Kiti. This was another source of his power. You can think of each brief ineffective tenure as a piece of termite. But how conceivably could Elongo have been said to have caused this to happen? Suppose my father had lived, he might have stayed at Kiti for some time. From Kaduna's point of view that would neatly solve the joint problem of a post which nobody wanted to go to and an officer whom it might be embarrassing to post elsewhere. But in what conceivable way could Elongo be said to have caused my father's death? The only interpretation I have arrived at was that it was his failure to do what my mother asked him with the diary which was the crucial act. He put it in the office.'

'He couldn't read, Nigel. He couldn't have understood.'

'He wouldn't need to. He would simply link the effect back to the cause, in exactly the same way that I am doing, only he would see a magical mechanism whereas I believe I see a psychological one. Shall we go on?'

'Wait. I've just thought of something. The picture she did of Salaki. On their way back from the village. He was going to hang that in his office. That would have been with *his* stuff, wouldn't it?'

'It wasn't.'

'Perhaps Bevis nicked it when he was packing up.'

'Possibly. I think more likely my father destroyed it after he'd read the diary. I don't see how he could bear to look at it.'

'Poor Ted.'

'You have to think of him slogging the days away with no one to talk to. His career, such as it was, was in ruins. Though nobody in fairness could have blamed him for the Incident—in fact he'd consistently warned that the consequences of deposing Kama Boi were unpredictable—he was still the man on the spot, the natural scapegoat. Though he would probably not have lost his job there was little likelihood of promotion, and very little chance of transfer to another colony where my mother could bring the child. From now on he would only see her on leave. Added to that his enemy, de Lancey, had beaten him. It's clear from the diary that he resented that very deeply. Then the process of clearing up and reorganization after the Incident would have imposed an appalling load of work. In the middle of all this he stumbles on the diary. I imagine him starting to read it, coming to one of the intimate passages, not being able to face it, but then not being able to leave it alone either. Constant little dips. Soon searching for the stimulus of erotic recall. And then the ambush of finding out my mother's collusion with de Lancey, her deliberate deceit and betrayal.'

'It wasn't like that, Nigel.'

'Not in our eyes, perhaps. In his, though . . . and then the Incident. I must have read her account of talking to Femora Feng and then painting the women at least a hundred times. I still can't tell, but my impression of Femora Feng as a Lenin-like figure has hardened. A very remarkable woman, using her own will and drive to convert and control a small group, who in turn subvert a larger group and thus tip the balance of a poised moment of crisis. I think when my mother came to the painting-ground Femora Feng had been trying to persuade the women that now was the moment for the revolutionary act. My mother's appearance was an epiphany. First by her words she seemed to tell them that the White Man had sent Azikofio to Tefuga to be a sacrifice, so that the juju-power of Kama Boi could be restored to the ancestors, and then by her paintings she showed them how the sacrifice was to be carried out. And after that the women would be, in my mother's words, beautiful and whole.'

'Not Betty's fault.'

'Certainly not at the rational level. My father could hardly blame her for that any more than he could for the death of Salaki, which she could also be said to have caused and must have been another serious blow. In any case some kind of revolt by the Kitawa was clearly due to happen. The depredations of the Hausa had increased dramatically over the past few years as Kama Boi lost his control of his followers. In the end, from a pragmatic viewpoint, it could hardly have worked out better—less than a dozen dead, and the event itself shocking enough to force the British to impose and the Hausa to accept a more reasonable system. A full-scale rising would have been a disaster for all sides.'

'I think things have a pattern, Nigel. She didn't mean it, but still it was meant.'

Jackland shrugged, not prepared to argue the point, but

perhaps also not so ready since his African experience to dismiss such ideas as meaningless.

'Let's go on to the other question,' he said. 'This is what really interests me. One of the things I tried to put over in my script was the parallel between the relationship of the Kitawa to Kama Boi and that of my mother to my father.'

'Oh, yes. She says so, doesn't she?'

'And she was beginning to mind, I think. It's difficult for us to grasp what a male-dominated world that was, how absolutely she was supposed to exist for him. How little what she thought or felt mattered. Her exploration of her own sexuality, for instance . . . he just grunted and fell asleep.'

'She was getting tired of that.'

'Yes, I think so. It had been too much—too good to last, to coin a phrase. The question is, though, was there not merely a parallel relationship? Was there also a parallel Incident? Did my mother take her cue from the dancers? Did she, subconsciously at least, revolt too?'

'How?'

'She finished the diary. I am struck by the deliberate decision to try to write that final sequence as though without fore-knowledge of the event. She didn't quite manage it. There are no exclamation marks, for instance—as though she didn't dare risk letting go as she used to. It's a symptom of the effort needed, at a time of great stress and bewilderment, too. She then gave the diary to Elongo and asked him to bury it in a termites' nest. I find it hard to believe that that was all the effort was for. In any case I now think that Elongo didn't do what she asked. He hid it in the office instead. As you say, he couldn't have known what might happen if my father found it and read it, but my mother would. She had an unusual empathy with the Kitawa—a feeling for how their minds worked. So the question is, was she at any level aware of what Elongo would in fact do?'

He kept his tone dry, perhaps trying to persuade himself that the answer was now of no more than academic interest. Miss Tressider hunched her shoulders as though about to retract her head between them. Her face changed, the archaic smile becoming more pronounced and her other features assuming the unparticularized look of early statues, pure female nature as yet unprinted by the single soul. Jackland waited, watching her, no doubt aware that her knack of assuming the surface appearance of the part she was asked to play might be deceptive. It gave no guarantee that what issued between the smiling lips was truth.

He started the tape but turned the sound low. There was in any case no more dialogue, only the noises of bush and river, the rustle of papers as Piers Smith worked in the littered office or a two-step from the gramophone as he sat in the darkening dining-room with the brandy bottle at his elbow and dusk fading quickly from the river beyond the mosquito-wire.

'All this is guesswork on my part, of course,' said Jackland.

'It's the same as the other thing,' said Miss Tressider. 'She didn't mean it, but it was meant.'

'Subconsciously? I don't believe in a power out there, making things happen in an aesthetically satisfactory manner. God, the great script-writer. I can just about take the idea of people feeling compelled at an irrational level to conform to a subconsciously perceived pattern.'

'It doesn't matter. Africa was over, you see.'

'Did she know? Then? Did she actually want to finish things off?'

'No. Yes. I suppose when she said good-bye she thought he'd be coming home on leave and then she'd persuade him to look for a job in England. What d'you think it would have been like, Nigel? The evenings, for instance, with the kids in bed upstairs —a coke fire, those browny hearth-tiles—Ted on one side sucking at his pipe and reading his *National Geographic*, her on the other, looking across at him. Up in the attic his trunks, full of Africa—albums, papers, knick-knacks, old uniform. Or lying awake at night, him snoring beside her. If she moved her hand she could touch his side—just under the pyjamas and the skin, still there—Africa.'

Miss Tressider gazed at the screen, which showed the D.O.'s office, corrugated iron, gracelessly inappropriate to the lush and twining riverine trees beyond. Africans, three men and a woman, sat listlessly by the door. Piers Smith marched into view, his shoulders squared but his step uneven. He had not shaved for two or three days. He spoke briefly and with an irritated gesture to the natives, who rose, picked up their belongings and moved away. He went into the office. A moment later the clerk came hurrying out. The door closed.

'We're on firm ground again,' said Jackland. 'All that is in the inquiry papers.'

'There's a doctor at my hospital,' said Miss Tressider. 'He's nuts on my tick—he adores it. He says it gets born and mates and climbs a bit of grass and then goes into a sort of coma. It can wait for years like that, till a warm-blooded animal comes by. Then it jumps and clings and sucks its meal of blood and falls off and lays its eggs and dies. That's all it's there for.'

She looked flushed, as if back in her fever, and spoke of the mystic moment in a dreamy whisper. On the screen the office stood dead centre. With the sound still low they could not hear the shot, but could tell the instant from the flurry of green doves (supposedly feeding among the trees beyond but in fact trapped by local bird-catchers and then released by Trevor Fish crouching out of sight with the cage) as they rose all together and whirred away across the river.